The

The Cross,

and the

Burning Desert

Other Books in the Smoke Tree Series

The Carnival,

The Cross,

and the

Burning Desert

A Smoke Tree Series Novel

Gary J. George

Dedicated to the memory of my wonderful, wise, kind, elegant, beautiful and graceful Ginny. You are forever in my heart.

CHAPTER 1

Opelika, Alabama
August, 1954

The pastor returned home from visiting his wife's grave to find his driveway full of cars and the parsonage door ajar. Inside, he heard voices from the back of the house. Women's voices.

When he walked into the bedroom, the closet door was open and the dresser drawers had been pulled out. Elisabet's dresses and coats covered two-thirds of the bedspread. Her 'lady things' covered the other third. Her shoes were on the hardwood floor next to the bed.

"What's going on here?"

The pastor was so angry he stumbled on the "g", and his voice came out in a higher-than-normal register. With the slight stutter and the higher voice, it flashed through his mind that he probably sounded like Porky Pig.

If the women had been pointers, each would have lifted a paw as they turned in unison and froze into position at the sound of his voice. Mrs. Simmons stepped forward, hands on her hips, and stared at him with neither shame nor commiseration over her pink-framed half-glasses.

"The church board has decided this has gone on long enough. They have approved this action."

The pastor's voice returned to its normal register.

"What has gone on long enough."

"This mooning over Elisabet."

1

"It's not mooning, Mrs. Simmons. It's mourning."

Her face got red as her voice rose.

"It is unseemly in a man of God. Elisabet passed two years ago. Your continuous and conspicuous grief gives the impression you have forgotten your duty of Christian resignation."

"She didn't 'pass'. She was murdered."

"She was killed by a drunk driver."

"And the difference is?"

Mrs. Simmons sighed theatrically.

"Pastor, you have become an embarrassment to your congregation. You are seen walking around town and out on country roads, disheveled and unshaven, wearing an old t-shirt full of holes."

"That's the shirt I was wearing when the phone rang, and the state patrolman told me Elise and our unborn child were dead. The shirt I wore when I went down to identify her body. That shirt is a link from the time when she was alive to when she was not."

Mrs. Simmons continued as if he hadn't spoken.

"Not only that. You are neglecting your flock. There are other people with problems and grief, not just you. And that last sermon Full of questions instead of God's holy words."

"What's that got to do with you women being in my house?"

"Ladies, Pastor. Ladies, not 'women'. And let me remind you this is not your house. It belongs to the church. It is on loan to you from God. We are here to remove Elisabet's clothing and personal items. The board believes that if we remove the objects of your obsession, you will return to normal."

"And what do you intend to do with the items?"

"The dresses and coats and shoes will be disposed of at the rummage sale on Saturday, as will her combs and brushes and any unopened make-up. Her unmentionables will be dealt with in another manner."

"And I have nothing to say about this?"

"Not if you wish to retain your position as our pastor."

"I see. In that case, may I access my closet for a moment, or is my clothing also no longer mine?"

The women parted into what looked like two lines in an initiation rite. The pastor walked through the gantlet and dug around in the closet. He retrieved a worn t-shirt, an old pair of army fatigue pants and dusty paratrooper boots. He carried them into the bathroom, closing the door behind him.

The ladies shifted uncertainly for a few moments before returning to their task.

A short while later, the bathroom door opened and the parson's black suit, white shirt and black tie flew out the door, followed by a pair of wing-tipped shoes. The pastor stepped out, dressed in the items he had removed from the closet.

"It's all yours."

"You're giving us your suit? We came only for Elisabet's things."

"I'm giving you back your house. The keys are in my pants pocket, as are the keys to the car the church provided. You're welcome to the house, the car, and most especially to your capricious God."

There was a collective gasp as he walked toward the women. They parted again, this time much more quickly.

"Where are you going," asked the self-appointed spokeswoman, exasperation and perhaps even hint of panic in her voice?

"For a walk."

A moment later, the sound of the front door slamming interrupted their 'tut-tuts' and 'well-I-nevers'.

The parson went to the bank and emptied his checking and savings accounts. When he counted the money and realized how much of it had been set aside for their unborn child, he began to weep. Embarrassed, people in the bank looked away from him.

He walked out and turned north. He was soon out of town. As he walked, he understood that the death of his dear wife had been a metanoia. Albeit one that did not come with the subsequent healing. One that had caused him to abandon his faith and now his position and his parishioners.

He knew with a sudden, intense certainty he would never return to Opelika, the town of his birth and upbringing.

CHAPTER 2

Presque Isle County, Michigan
March, 1957

A typically awful, late-winter day on the lower peninsula. This one pretending to be early spring. In mid-morning, the sun put in a sudden appearance, coming out from beneath the lead-colored curtain of winter sky. By noon, things begin to melt. Tiny freshets snake from beneath the snow on suddenly mud-streaked hillsides, hillsides frozen since December. By three in the afternoon, streets are clotted with comingled mud and water.

The tiny, wood-frame house where the boy lives with his father and sister is overflowing. The mudroom floor is covered with galoshes. Overcoats piled in corners. Casseroles, salad bowls and desserts for the wedding reception jam the dining room table. Some of the food has spilled onto a lace tablecloth the boy has not seen since the death of his mother, and some of it has found its way onto the scarred yellow-pine floor. Heavy people with over-laden paper plates prowl the periphery of the off-kilter table, seeking one last morsel to pile atop the mass of food already mounded there. Attacking plates with cheap plastic utensils, others sit or stand in the dining room and kitchen. Paper cups filled with punch sit on countertops and on the floor beside the guests. Several have already been kicked over by increasingly inebriated celebrants, rendering the rooms sticky underfoot.

Cigarette and cigar smoke mingle in a noxious, blue-gray cloud just below the plaster ceiling, but no one opens a window. Outside, the sun is tilting to the west, casting elongated shadows

5

from the pines lining the street. The temperature drops rapidly. The mud on the hillsides is beginning to freeze, as is water on the roadways. There is a high likelihood of a minor accident or two when the crowd, full of cheap booze, makes its way to the cars parked haphazardly up and down the street in this neighborhood of dilapidated houses just outside Rogers City, Michigan.

From his throne, the straight-backed chair nearest the bottles of hard liquor, the boy's father is regaling all who come near. He talks and waves his cigar, the ash falling unnoticed on the coat and trousers of his only suit as he steadily refills the drinking glass in his hand with straight bourbon, rye, vodka or gin, whichever is closest to hand. No wine or beer for him. Nor any mixer: he takes it like a man.

Keep drinking dad, thinks the boy. Slam it down. Hurry before it's all gone.

The boy is happy for his sister, Helen, married at last. Her husband of less than three hours, Tommy Forrester, is also staying close to the booze, along with a number of his crewmates from one of the limestone freighters that ply Lake Michigan. Helen can now add her name to the list of women who spend dark winter days staring into stormy skies wondering whether their husbands will make it home. But at least, she will finally be safe from her father.

The boy had tried to convince Helen to leave home when she turned eighteen, but she was afraid. Said she had nowhere to go. Said she had no money and no prospects and would starve or freeze to death. Anywhere would be better than here, he told her. Better than having that vile man doing unspeakable things to you whenever he comes home with a snoot full. But Helen had always been a timid girl with no self-confidence. How could it have been otherwise, he thought, with their disgusting father after her from the time their mother had died? Indeed, beginning the very night of their mother's funeral when Helen was but fourteen and the boy nine.

But now, Helen will be safe and warm and fed and clothed in her own place with her own husband, although the boy is still amazed that Helen managed to meet and attract the handsome, noisy and boisterous Tommy.

After you're married, he whispers to her early in the morning, if that sonofabitch ever comes after you when Tommy is out on a ship, tell him as soon as he gets home. He'll bust that bastard up good. He's bigger and stronger and a fearsome fighter with fists like stones. Nobody in Presque Isle County gives Tommy Forrester any crap. Nobody.

As the boy watches, his father continues to hold court, pretending to be an actual human being. But the mean little eyes give him away. He's not human, thinks the boy. He's a weasel. Sneaky. Underhanded. A coward who bullies the weak. His hateful eyes are beginning to get that familiar, glassy look. In another half hour, he will be drunk enough to fall out of his chair.

When that happens, the boy will leave. His ragged coat is in the mudroom. His few clothes in a canvas bag under the porch. This will be his best chance. By the time the weasel wakes up with a hangover and begins to demand a cup of coffee spiked with something stronger, the boy will be far away. Headed for Indiana. He is determined to get at least that far, even if he has to walk all the way. Through the hardwood forests of red maple and black cherry and paper birch. Through the stands of red pine and white pine that provide the only color in an otherwise denuded and brown landscape. Beyond the forests and into fields where the black-capped chickadees flit from unleafed bush to unleafed bush; then onward yet across meadows that will not bloom with violets and fleabane until late April; through marshy lowlands where bloodroot and marsh marigold will not run riot until May.

He will walk down the railroad tracks if the tracks aren't too close to the road. Perhaps catch a slow-moving freight. But never walk on the roads themselves. The weasel will be driving the roads. Seething with anger as he seeks his thirteen-year-old son. Because now, all his wrath will be reserved for the boy. The boy the father will expect to fetch and carry and clean and cook now that Helen will no longer be in the house. But the boy will be gone.

Not forever. Someday, when he is fully grown, he will return and seek out the disgusting, vile creature who has tormented him and violated his sister ever since their mother was no longer there to protect them. No longer there to take the first blow. And the second. And the third.

CHAPTER 3

Friedberg, West Germany
November, 1958
3rd Brigade, 3rd Armored Division

Sergeant Major Yannity Scanlon, one of the highest-ranking NCOs on post, loved his NCO club. Alcohol was cheap there, and for him and the other sergeant majors, often free. He spent a lot of his off-duty time there. A whole lot. His wife, Hazel, said he drank too much. Hell, he said, show me an NCO that doesn't. What else is there to do? She suggested they travel around Germany. See the sights. Maybe even go to Austria and France and Italy. Everything in Europe was so close together. And so inexpensive as Europe struggled to recover from the lingering effects of World War II.

Sergeant Major Scanlon didn't like that idea. He didn't even like to take Hazel out to dinner "on the economy," as American soldiers referred to areas off-post. As far as the sergeant was concerned, those places were full of people who spoke the wrong language. 'Rads,' the soldiers called them. Short for *kamerad*, the kraut word for comrade. Didn't feel like comrades to him. Felt like a bunch of ex-Nazis.

As the holidays approached, always a dead time between fall and winter maneuvers, the unit was stuck on post for a long stretch. It got boring. Very boring. Not only that, but at the end of October that hip-swiveling Presley kid had been assigned to the brigade, and Sergeant Major Scanlon had to watch everybody from the brass on down make a fuss over the rock and roll star every day.

As boredom and envy combined, Sergeant Major Scanlon ramped up his daily quota of alcohol. Hazel got tired of it. She nagged him. Telling her to knock it off no longer worked, so he began to lay one upside her head now and then. Not hard enough to leave a lasting mark and give the other wives something to talk about at the PX; just hard enough to get her to shut up.

The Tuesday night before Thanksgiving, Hazel lost it. The minute he staggered in the door of their NCO dependent-housing apartment, she started in at the top of her lungs. Wouldn't let up even when he told her he had command reveille in the morning and had to get some sleep. Even when he fetched her one. Or two. Okay more than two. And very hard. She was going to have two black eyes to go with a broken nose. One side of her face was already ballooning. But at least she stopped screaming, and the neighbors stopped pounding on the walls.

Sergeant Major Yannity Scanlon took himself to bed. Hazel Scanlon didn't come along. Instead, she busied herself in the kitchen. She filled the biggest pot she could find with water and put it on the stove. When it boiled, she brought it into the room where Sergeant Scanlon lay passed out atop the sheets. She dumped it on him. Then he was the one doing the screaming.

The MPs came. They took Sergeant Major Scanlon to the infirmary with deep partial-thickness burns on the left side of his face, neck and rib cage. Mrs. Scanlon was bundled up and air-mailed back to the states. Once there, she filed for divorce on the grounds of extreme mental and physical cruelty.

When he healed, Sergeant Major Scanlon was court-martialed. After his trial, he was no longer a sergeant major. He had been busted back to E-6, a lowly platoon sergeant in a line rifle company where men of lesser rank referred to him as "Sergeant Scars" behind his back. Soon after that humiliation, the final divorce decree came down. Hazel had been awarded half of his Army paycheck while he was on active duty and half his pension when he retired.

CHAPTER 4

June 1964

Captain Carlos Caballo and Corporal Andy Chesney were headed for Piute Creek in the Sheriff's Department search and rescue pickup. The Captain was responding to a request from his long-time friend, Burke Henry, to come to his home in a place so far off the beaten path it lacked electricity, phone service and indoor plumbing. Two miles beyond the Smoke Tree city limits, the traffic ahead of them suddenly slowed but did not stop. In a few moments, they saw the problem.

In one hundred-and-twelve-degree heat, under a fierce, white-hot sun, a bearded man was dragging a huge cross down the shoulder of eastbound 66. He was wearing a white robe. Both the cross and his sandaled feet were kicking up dust as he struggled forward beneath his burden.

"There's something you don't see every day," said Andy.

"Yeah, and something tells me we're going to see more of that guy. That will give us three things to contend with. Operation Desert Strike, the carnival coming to Smoke Tree, and a crazy man dragging a cross.

CHAPTER 5

The Long Walk

Jedidiah Shanks continued to shuffle slowly forward as a sand-colored pickup truck with a Sheriff's Department emblem on the door slowed in the westbound lane of the highway. There was a light bar on the roof. Jedidiah was hopeful the driver would hit the lights and siren, make a U-turn, and come up behind him. It would suit Jedidiah's purposes if law enforcement stopped to question him. Extra attention meant free publicity. Publicity even better than he was getting in the Smoke Tree Weekly for the check mailed a week ago to pay for the ad.

As the truck drew abreast, Jedidiah ducked his head below the transom so he could see beneath the cross. The driver of the truck was also leaning forward and turning his head to give Jedidiah a long look. The deputy's dark face was rendered darker by the contrast with his snow-white Stetson. Then, perhaps something his passenger said amused him. Either that or he saw the irony in both men tilting their heads forward, each turning simultaneously at the same angle to see the other. The briefest of smiles, marked by a flash of very white teeth, flared across his face. He touched two fingers to the brim of his hat and nodded slightly to Jedidiah before accelerating and moving on. With the possibility of a confrontation and more publicity gone, Jedidiah continued his slow progress along the shoulder. He hoped at least some of the eastbound traffic was local and the drivers would fire up the small-town wireless when they got home.

Cars and trucks moving both directions continued to slow to get a better look at him. That was not surprising, given that he was wearing a long white robe and sandals and carrying a huge cross made of two-by-tens. Part of the six-foot horizontal piece of the nine-foot-tall cross was hooked over his left shoulder, the trailing bottom of the cross dragging in the sand, gravel and rock of the shoulder. Whenever the cross struck a large rock, it banged painfully against his neck and trapezius muscle.

I am a cross myself, he thought: my legs and torso the stipes, my outstretched arms the patibulum.

His face was obscured from passing motorists by the cross and by his arm looped over the horizontal piece to keep it from twisting away from him. Now, if I could just get a good, midday Mojave Desert mirage, he thought, I would look as if I were walking on water.

If passersby could have seen his face, they might have noticed his lips were moving. Perhaps they would have thought he was deep in prayer. Actually, he was talking to his wife, dead twelve years now. To her and to their unborn and unnamed child. It was a one-way conversation, but it fulfilled his constant need to reach out to her for comfort, wherever she might be, whether or not she could hear him.

"You should see this place, Elise. It is barren and sun-blasted and hostile. And hot. Fiendishly hot. Way over a hundred, the angry sun made more unbearable by heat from the engines of passing cars and trucks and the heat rising from blacktop itself. To top it off, I have no water. It would ruin the effect produced by these sandaled feet and this long, flowing robe. At least the robe is white and protects me from sunburn. But I have a terrible headache. Feels like someone wrapped a rawhide thong around my head and is twisting it tighter with every step. A crown of thorns could hardly be more painful."

His cracked lips stopped moving for a few moments as he walked on. Then he began to mumble again.

"But sweetheart, the pain is not as bad as this constant sadness. When you died, my love, you left a hole in my heart. You were such a big part of me, it was a huge hole. Sadness rushed in to fill it. It never left. Nor will it, ever."

Jedidiah fell silent as he forged ahead. He had told Elise thousands of times of his sadness. Would doubtless tell her yet more thousands of times. But for now, it was too hot to talk. Took too much energy, and he needed every bit he could muster to keep putting one foot in front of the other beneath his load. Making things even more unpleasant was the trash he was shuffling through. Trash thousands and thousands of passing motorists had carelessly tossed out windows. Mostly beer cans. It looked like Coors was

14

winning the beverage war in this waterless part of the country, followed by Olympia and then Lucky Lager.

And there were cigarette butts, thousands of them, as well as empty packs. Marlboro was leading by a large margin in the tobacco race. Must be that guy in the cowboy hat on billboards all over the country, he thought. The recently released Surgeon General's Advisory Committee report on smoking and cancer be damned. Cowboys are fearless. And there were candy wrappers, potato chip bags, and even a soiled baby diaper complete with pink-plastic-headed safety pins.

Stands of some sort of tall, green shrub stretched away from the highway. Some of them had small yellow flowers; some did not. They were numerous, but very evenly spaced. As if they had been planted by a master gardener or had all reached some agreement about proximity. As if each bush had demanded and received its own privacy. They were interspersed with smaller, grayish bushes. They too kept their distance from the green shrubs but were perfectly willing to crowd in on one other. At first, he thought nothing at all grew close to the big bushes, but when he altered his path to walk to the very edge of the shoulder for a closer look, he noticed there were small, purple plants, two to five inches high and full of thorns, taking advantage of the sparse shade afforded. If his sockless toes were to come in contact with those, he would regret it.

Careful not to get too close to the prickly things, he reached out his free hand and stripped a few of the small, green leaves from one of the bushes. They did not come off easily. He put them in his mouth. The waxy leaves had a foul, bitter taste. He quickly spat them out and regretted again not having any water.

Beyond a truck stop where he had to cross a broad driveway and dodge an eighteen-wheeler, the highway turned south. As he stumbled along, Jedidiah occasionally glimpsed the blue Colorado River through the tamarisk bushes bordering the water. He longed to put down his cross and walk across the highway, through the bushes and sand and gravel, and all the way to the distant river. Flop face-down in the water. Drink it. Let it soak into his pores. But he kept on.

As he trudged, he thought, as he had many times each day for the last twelve years, of the day Elise had died. It was as if his life had stopped when hers had. All the rest of the world, however, had hurtled callously onward. For the first two years, real life blurred at the edges as it moved. There was no way he could make it snap into focus. People told him he had to get on with his life, but therein lay the problem. Everything he could think of that he might

15

want to do, he wanted to do only in the company of his beloved. Every place he could think of he might want to go, he wanted to go with her.

Get on with his life? Elise was his life. Part and parcel. Body and soul. Heart and intellect. He was irrevocably and unequivocally tied to her. Her death was bad enough, but even worse was the fact that he was still alive. Her death was the event that ultimately set him on the road, northward out of Alabama, and eventually, many years later, to this barren and dangerous desert.

His connection to Elise was the only thing allowing him to continue his life, and he had no intention of ever severing the bond between them. He would carry her in his heart and talk with her until the day death found him. And as far as he was concerned, that day could not come soon enough.

The trash on the shoulder thinned out but did not disappear completely when Jedidiah reached the outskirts of Smoke Tree. The speed limit on 66 dropped to thirty-five miles an hour. He was grateful for that. Gave people longer to see him and his heavy cross and wonder who he was and why he was doing what he was doing. He wondered himself, sometimes.

Jedidiah tramped past a string of single-story, white-rock roofed motels lining both sides of the highway. Their signs advertised air conditioning and swimming pools. The water in the pools was probably warm, he thought. Still and all, he would like to prop his cross against one of the fences and jump in.

There were no sidewalks, and barely enough room for him to walk without being knocked down by trucks, especially when the shoulder narrowed and nearly disappeared as he rounded the curve where the highway turned west. He teetered atop the curb past the West End Shell and Diner, the bottom of his cross threatening to drop into the roadway.

Gethsemane without the garden, he thought. *And being more in agony, he prayed more earnestly; and his sweat was as it were great drops of blood falling down to the ground.* Luke 22:34.

"All right, my love," he said aloud, finding his voice again. "Maybe that's laying it on thick in my case. Not sweating blood here. Still, I hope any overly-aggressive drivers will settle for betraying me instead of running me down."

Beyond the corner, the shoulder widened again, and he felt less vulnerable to passing traffic. Forging onward with the cross rubbing his trapezius and neck, he passed a Foster's Freeze. Set well back from the highway inside a copse of salt cedars that made

16

precious shade, the swirled cone on its sign beckoned him. Tempted him. He resisted the call. It wouldn't do, he thought, for people to see Jesus having a root beer float. Get thee behind me, soft-serve.

When the highway crossed the Santa Fe tracks, a sidewalk appeared. Civilization!

The cruel, relentless sun was riding high in the white-hot sky. It burned with an intensity Jedidiah had not thought possible. Sweat ran down his back and chest and from beneath his arms. But as quickly as it reached his robe, it dried, leaving a salt-encrusted rime that stiffened the cloth. Sweat matted his long, blonde hair, flecked of late with traces of gray, and dripped off his straight nose, evaporating the instant it touched the ground. His throat was bone-dry.

This walk had been a very bad idea, even though such walks had been successful in other towns. At the very least, he should have had the big truck hauling the revival show drop him a little closer to town, publicity or no publicity.

Certainly nothing he had ever experienced in the low hills, green ridges and sandy-soiled valleys of the piedmont of central Alabama had prepared him for this blast furnace. A stand of the dogwood, persimmon or black tupelo common to that part of the country would have been most welcome. Eastern red cedar or loblolly pine would do, even smothered in kudzu. But there was nothing that offered him the least surcease from his travail, and he still had to walk all the way to the other side of this town strung out along the highway.

As Jesus had said to his disciples at the Gethsemane that had a garden, "the spirit is willing, but the flesh is weak." Jedidiah was beginning to doubt the part about the spirit.

The street, which had been continuing westward, turned south again. As it did, a convoy of army vehicles rumbled past. Jeeps with officers, jeeps with 105 mm recoilless rifles, jeeps with .50 caliber machine guns and jeeps pulling trailers. After the jeeps came deuce-and-a-half after deuce-and-a-half filled with soldiers, rifles between their knees, steel pots on their heads, and sweat running down their faces.

As the last truck in the long line rolled past, a soldier yelled, "Pick 'em up, and lay 'em down, Jesus." Jedidiah crooked his neck to look at the young faces. The peacetime army. Not around when the 101st jumped behind enemy lines at Normandy. He hoped it stayed that way. Hoped these boys would never see combat.

He continued south on the sidewalk. At the corner where Antioch Street dumped into 66, a heavy woman in a flowered Mumu,

17

who had been watching his labored progress down the street, levered herself off her porch swing and came down the steps, flip-flops popping. She planted herself directly in his path.

"Blasphemy," she shrieked in a high, tight, reedy voice that seemed incongruous coming from such a broad chest fronted by pendulous breasts quivering in indignation. She gave off an odor redolent of cinnamon and vanilla. Surely this woman is not doing her baking in this heat, he thought.

She was not done berating him yet.

"You should be ashamed of yourself, impersonating our Lord and Savior. I hope God strikes you dead!"

Forced to halt, Jedidiah lifted his pale blue eyes to her face and stared at her with raised eyebrows, his twisting neck still forced downward by the heavy cross. He tried to recite Luke 10:33. *But a certain Samaritan, as he journeyed, came where he was: and when he saw him, he had compassion on him.* But all that that came out of his parched throat was an unintelligible croak. The woman soon found his unblinking, haunted eyes disconcerting. She drew back and stepped aside.

Later, when the revival reached its startling conclusion, she would tell her neighbors the blonde-haired, blue-eyed, bearded pilgrim with the cross had spoken to her in tongues.

Jedidiah continued his relentless slouch southward.

He dragged himself down Highway 66, now called Front Street, until it turned west and became Civic Center Drive, and then to the point where it became Broadway and turned south again. When he crossed the street that separated the Hotel California from a movie theater, he saw a motorist at the Chevron Station on the east side of 66 drinking from a refrigerated fountain next to the repair bays. Jedidiah stopped and stared and licked his dry lips. He had a nearly overwhelming desire to lean his burden against the empty ticket booth, between the posters for *Bye-Bye Birdie*, and strike out for the fountain. But he knew he could not do that without spoiling the spectacle he had suffered to create.

He staggered on, overheated and dehydrated, his legs threatening to fail him. As he walked, music from *Bye-Bye Birdie* came into his head. He tried to sing *Kids!* as he walked. Had anyone heard him, they would not have known by the monotone he was croaking out that he was singing. He had once had a good voice: had loved to sing. Often sang along with the choir during services at his church. But within two months of his wife's death, he found he could sing no longer. Perhaps he had cried so hard and so often and

18

screamed at God in such uncontrollable rage he had damaged his vocal chords.

In all the twelve years that had passed since her death, he had never gone for more than few minutes without thinking of Elise. The center of his life before she died, she was that center still. And while the terrible events of the day she died sometimes faded when he was distracted, they returned immediately, re-emerging like a water stain painted over on a white ceiling, when the distraction ceased.

As he mumbled the words to more songs from the musical, he passed Milner's Market. Then came Me and Me Son's Butcher Shop, a five-for-a-dollar burger stand, the Methodist Church, the Ford Dealership, and then a replica of a Conestoga wagon with "Welcome to Smoke Tree" painted on the side. Beyond the wagon, both the highway and the Santa Fe tracks paralleling it angled southwest. He was nearing his destination. He began to think he might make it.

After another agonizing quarter of a mile, he reached the point where Palestine Street emptied into 66. It was a huge vacant lot where a number of cement slab foundations were all that remained of the large buildings that had once stood there. He saw the blackened, forlorn and skeletal remains of three big fan palms that had somehow survived the fire that had destroyed the buildings only to lose any chance of recovery due to lack of water.

I see the fire department saved the real estate, he thought. He would have giggled at his own joke if his vocal cards had cooperated.

The semi-tractor and trailer that had driven him through Smoke Tree and deposited him west of town to begin his ordeal was parked next to the largest slab. His crew was erecting the revival tent there, taking advantage of the concrete to create a solid floor. Other crew members were unloading hundreds of folding chairs. The generator that powered the carbon-arc searchlight to draw the nightly crowds was in place. A thick cable snaked along the ground.

His crew supervisor spotted Jedidiah and called for two workers to relieve him of the cross. The supervisor filled a tall glass with ice from a cooler and added tea, mint, and spoons of sugar. He hurried across the street and handed it to a grateful Jedidiah.

"How are you, boss?"

Jedidiah weakly waved the question aside with one hand. With the other, he lifted the glass and drained it in two long draughts.

"Easy, boss, you'll get yourself an ice-cream headache."

Jedidiah took a deep breath.

"It's all right, Tyson. I was so dry my voice wouldn't work. Some big woman came off her porch a mile or so back and yelled at me, and I think the noise I made scared her. I'm pretty sure I sounded like a raven. If we do this again in Parker, drop me closer to town."

The two men who had retrieved the cross had hauled it across the street and were planting it in a freshly-dug hole. It would be strung with lights and remain there until the revival ended.

Jedidiah stood rubbing his neck and shoulder. He handed his empty glass to Tyson and started across the street. Tyson followed.

"Hey, boys! Put one a them chairs in the shade for the boss."

When Jedidiah reached the other side, the chair was in place. He gratefully lowered himself. He kicked off his sandals and then quickly put them back on when his feet registered the heat of the ground.

Tyson handed him another glass of iced tea.

"Tell you, Tyson, these old bones are a-creakin'. Don't know how much longer I'll be able to keep doing this Via Dolorosa gig."

"It's this damnable heat, boss."

"The carnival in town yet?"

"No, but I saw their advance man marking out positions on a vacant lot over on Front Street. The show probably won't be here until sundown.

"Okay. Where we staying?"

"Place just up the street. It's called the Swank Motor Court. Ain't very swank, but it's clean. The air conditioner in your unit is already on. Shouldn't be much over ninety-five in there by now."

Jedidiah croaked out a laugh.

"Absolutely arctic! Where's everybody else staying?"

"As usual, the choir will stay at the motel with you. The crew and I will sleep on cots in the tent.

"Too hot for that. No one will get any sleep. Put everyone up in a motel."

"Boss, that's going to cost a whole slop jar full of money."

"We've got enough. The take from the gathering has been way up the last three places. Tyson, you know what I been dreaming about this last mile?"

"What's that boss?"

"A whole big tub of chocolate ice cream."

"Let me get you to the motel, and I'll go get you some."

"You're a good man."

"Mrs. Tyson always said that. Right up until the day she ran off."

20

CHAPTER 6

Danny and the Carnival

Danny Dubois stepped off the Greyhound bus from Kingman, Arizona, with a canvas bag containing his equipment. He walked to the phone booth in front of the gas station. It didn't look like anyone had cleaned the booth since his visit to Smoke Tree two years before. The plexiglass was so badly smeared it blurred his view of the steady stream of traffic on 66 and the market across the street. And it still smelled like vomit.

Somebody must come here a couple of times a week just to throw up, he thought as he stepped inside.

Danny piled the change from his pocket on the metal tray, just in case the call ran long, and dialed a number he had called long-distance many times over the past two years. Calls that sometimes produced the result he wanted and sometimes didn't. Depended on who picked up. When he first started calling, if Mitzi's mother or father answered, they told him to quit calling because they didn't want their daughter talking to him. After a while, they just hung up as soon as they recognized his voice.

He waited until the last moment before he pulled the door of the booth closed, trapping himself inside with the reek of vomit.

"Hello?"

Because today's call was very important, Danny had been practicing disguising his voice, pitching it higher and using the southern drawl so common with many of his fellow carnies to replace his lower peninsula accent with its hammered 'a's.

"Hi," he said, which came out 'ha'. "Is Miss Mitzi there, which came out 'theah?"

"No."

There was a momentary silence.

"Who is this?"

"A friend."

"This is Danny, isn't it?"

Busted!

"Yes, ma'am."

"That's not very nice, trying to fool me. You know very well both Mr. Sodermeyer and I have asked you repeatedly to stop calling here."

Well, at least she hadn't hung up yet.

"I know that, Mrs. Sodermeyer, but I'm not giving up. I'm calling from Smoke Tree."

There was another silence, but Mitzi's mom was still on the line.

"So, the carnival's in town. I'm assuming you're still with that carnival."

"I am. And Mitzi's eighteen now, Mrs. Sodermeyer."

"She wasn't eighteen when you were here two years ago, but that didn't stop you."

"That's why we just talked, but I do have to admit I held her hand on the Ferris wheel."

"I'd like to believe that Danny, I really would, but I don't."

"Mrs. Sodermeyer, we never even kissed. I know your daughter has told you the same thing many times. I don't mind you not believing me because you don't know me. But it's a shame you won't believe your own daughter. I don't want to argue with you ma'am. But like I said, she's eighteen, so it's really not up to you and Mr. Sodermeyer who she sees."

"She's still living in our house, Danny. Our house, our rules."

Danny noticed she said 'house,' not 'home'. Sometimes people reveal things without knowing it.

"If I was a local guy, you wouldn't object to me dating your daughter, would you?"

"But you're not, and we do object. Carnies are not the kind of people we want our Mitzi associating with."

"What can I do to change your mind?"

"Not a thing."

"Please..."

But Mrs. Sodermeyer had heard enough. The line went dead.

Danny stepped out of the phone booth, disappointed his effort had failed. He picked up his bag and walked to the corner where he watched the only traffic light in Smoke Tree change before crossing the street and entering a market. In the air conditioning, the sweat that had soaked his shirt in the phone booth made him clammy. He bought a Dr. Pepper and went back outside. Sipping his soda, he headed for city hall.

He liked the Smoke Tree City Hall, a grand old structure with Moroccan accents. It was the right kind of architecture for a hot desert town. Arches and verandas surrounded the building, and there were enormous shade trees, palms, and a manicured lawn. He sat down beneath an ancient, leafy cottonwood, its brilliantly green leaves sparkling in the sunlight, and leaned back against the rough trunk.

As he finished his drink, he realized he never should have called Mitzi's house. It had been unnecessary. She was graduating tomorrow evening. She would be having graduation practice close to sundown. If Carlyle let him slip away for a while during setup, he could see Mitzi there

Smiling, he got up and walked toward the tiled steps leading up to the city clerk's office. He hid his empty bottle in some oleander bushes, intending to return the bottle to the market for his five-cent deposit. He ran his fingers through his curly brown hair and tucked his poplin shirt into his faded Levi's as he climbed the steps.

When he came back down, he had the temporary use permit allowing the carnival to set up on the vacant lots Carlyle had rented. He walked around the building to the steps leading down to the basement. As he turned the corner, he realized there were no police cars in the parking lot. Puzzled, he walked down the steps to the police department office and jail. The door at the bottom read, "Smoke Tree Police Department," but it was locked. There was dust and debris on the landing. The place had the melancholy, deserted feeling of a once-busy place no longer visited.

He returned to the city clerk's office where he was told the Smoke Tree Police Department had been disbanded.

"County sheriff polices the city now," the receptionist said.

Danny thanked her for the information and went outside. He wondered what Carlyle would do now that the amenable-for-a-price police chief was no longer in town. He retrieved his empty, got back his deposit, and walked north.

Twenty minutes later, Danny was at Smoke Tree Hardware and Building Supply. He bought three sacks of lime and paid an extra two dollars to have both the sacks and himself delivered to the vacant lots. Danny climbed out with his bag. He set it on the sidewalk and off-loaded the lime.

He walked the site. One of the lots had once been occupied by a livery stable, a big hay barn and a blacksmith shop in the previous century. The blacksmith had also been a farrier who shod horses and a wheelwright who could repair the steel rims of wagon wheels, skills necessary for a blacksmith in a crossroads town. On a hot day like today, it was still possible to catch a hint of horse manure and flux over a half century later. The other lot had been the home of the first service station and auto repair garage in Smoke Tree, and the smell of oil and grease from the saturated ground competed with odors next door for dominance.

Danny picked up the canvas bag and took it to the back corner of the lot. Taking off his good shirt, he folded it neatly. He reached into his bag and pulled out an old pair of black PF Flyers, an extra-large, long-sleeved sweat shirt, a pair of bib overalls, protective goggles, a half-mask respirator, heavy gloves and two red bandanas, one for around his neck and one to cover his hair.

He put on the sweat shirt, which immediately began to live up to its name. Then he took off his engineer boots. Looking around to make sure nobody was coming down the street, he quickly shucked off his Levi's and stepped into the overalls. Balancing on one foot and then the other, he pulled on the PF Flyers. Wrapping one bandana around his neck, he covered his hair with the other and knotted it under his chin. He put on the respirator and the protective goggles. When he was finished, he looked like an oversized, bug-eyed, Eastern-European peasant woman in a babushka, but his skin, lungs and eyes would be protected from the caustic lime.

Danny knew the exact dimensions of every game, ride, trailer, side-show tent and ticket booth. Armed with his tape measure, he began to mark and number the location of each element of the carnival. When he was done, he trudged over and picked up one of the sacks of lime. He cut a hole in the corner of the bag and went to work outlining and numbering everything, so all would be in readiness when the carnival pulled into town.

The first position marked was for the arch: the place where customers would enter the midway. After that, he lined out the row of game booths, called 'joints' in carny parlance: the duck pond, milk bottle, pitch-a-dime-and-win-carnival glass, Pepsi-bottle-ring-toss, land-a-nickel-inside-the-bullseye and balloon/dart games. Some games were rigged ('gaffed' in carny speak) in one way or another although, unlike many carnivals, the show Danny worked for gave the marks a pretty good chance of winning a decent prize. Not so good that the carnival lost money, though.

For example, the ducky game was a hanky-pank: a game where everyone wins a prize. But the prizes the marks won when they picked up a duck and turned it over cost the carnival boss less than the price of the ticket they had purchased. The dart game required a dead-center hit with a lot of force to pop one of the underinflated balloons. Of course, if interest flagged because no one was winning any plush, a few fully-inflateds could be pinned to the board. The milk bottles required an arm like Sudden Sam McDowell of the Cleveland Indians to knock over. Far more dimes were collected than carnival glass given away in the game that rewarded patrons for pitching a dime that managed to stay on a dish. As for the nickel-a-pitch bullseye game, if someone was getting too many nickels inside the circle, the mark would be distracted for an instant while an assistant flipped the board to the smaller-bullseye side.

On the other side of the games, he established the line of food booths. Hot dogs, hamburgers, bratwurst, corn-dogs, cotton candy, candy apples, salted peanuts, popcorn and other junk food. He left space between the food booths and the rides for the long lines that would form. Because patrons could get impatient waiting in those lines, one of the talkers would work the row with an endless spiel to keep people entertained while they waited. 'If you're light, it's all right, as long as your stash is heavy with cash,' and, 'stop squeezing your boyfriend's muscles, honey, and tell him to turn loose of some money,' and on and on. Billy, with his straw boater, cane and peppermint-striped shirt, could go for hours without repeating a couplet.

Beyond the food booth were the rides. The Ferris Wheel, far and away the most popular, Danny marked dead center. To the left of the big wheel went the adult rides: The Octopus, the Tilt-a-Whirl, and the favorite of the boys with dates, the Rock-o-Plane, whose caged enclosures could be flipped upside down, eliciting shrieks from young ladies who suddenly had their charms revealed by topsy-turvy dresses.

To the right of the Ferris Wheel would be the kiddie rides: first the carousel with its endless loop of mind-numbing calliope music, followed by the flat rides, (so named because they moved slowly over a level surface): the tea cups, little metal cars, metal airplanes, metal animals and others. On the far end would be the pony ride, the corral giving a nod to the former stable history of the lot.

Beyond the rides were the side-show tents. A spook trailer with a pitch-black interior, eerie music and fierce-looking creatures looming out of the darkness. A fun house with distorting mirrors. A sword-swallowing flame-eater, a woman who would guess your weight or your birthday or tell your fortune, a high striker where boys who wanted to impress their dates tried to ring the bell and win a prize, and the ever-popular ape-woman: actually, a very pretty young blonde from Indiana who would be transformed by distorting glass, strobe lights and a penchant for high drama into a hairy aggressive and frightening orangutan.

In the very back corner, wedged behind two trailers parked in a "V" that would leave only a narrow opening, Danny marked out the spot for the hoochie-coochie show, the hardest attraction to reach. But men would reach it. They always did, as unerringly as hound dogs picking up a scent. The biggest money-maker on the midway, it would be fronted by an ever-present, never-silent show-talker who would hint, with many winks, nods, nudges and 'we're-all-men-of-the-world-here' looks, of the unbelievably sensuous and possibly even nude beauties inside the tent whose charms could be seen for just three dollars.

Danny then marked out the spots around the perimeter where the trucks and trailers would be lined up to cover three sides of the site completely and a good part of the fourth. This left just the opening for the arch where the customers would enter. Every trailer would be snugged tightly against its neighbor. There would be no way for trouble to sneak in, sight unseen: a very important consideration.

The big generator truck would be in the northeast corner, the huge carbon-arc searchlight in front of it. The beam would be focused on the top of the Ferris wheel so it could be seen by traffic on Highway 66, two blocks to the west. Heavy cables would snake off in every direction from the genny to also power the lights of the midway, as well as the rides that didn't have individual motors.

In three hours, Danny was done. He was also drenched with sweat and covered in dust and lime. He pulled the respirator off and picked up his good clothes and boots and canvas sack and headed for Broadway. At the first service station he came to, he went in the men's room and locked the door. The restroom had an odor common to desert service station bathrooms on hot days: baking metal, dried soap powder, and the sweat of previous visitors.

Danny stripped off the gear and washed his face, hair and torso with Boraxo. It was so hot in the metal-walled room, the aridity so acute, that the water dried on his face and body almost as soon as he splashed it on. He had to re-rinse several times to get the Boraxo off. The big puddles he had made on the floor were already drying as he left.

Wearing his clean shirt and Levi's, he carried his bag outside and headed across the street to the five-burgers-for-a-dollar place he remembered from his last visit to Smoke Tree. His hair was dry before he got there.

He ordered ten burgers and two frosted mugs of root beer. He bought a copy of the Smoke Tree Weekly from the rack next to the sidewalk. When his food came, he folded the paper under his arm and headed for a redwood table beneath a huge chinaberry tree at the rear of the lot. Drinking an entire mug of root bear in a long swallow that made his eyes water and his nose burn, he ate his first burger in three huge bites and began to read about the latest happenings in Smoke Tree.

CHAPTER 7

Joint Operation Desert Strike
Mojave Desert, June, 1964

Master Sergeant Yannity Scanlon sat in the sweltering 22nd Armored Brigade command tent in the foothills of the western slope of the Providence Mountains. He was sweating heavily as he thought hard about the gift that had just been handed him. It didn't look like a gift. It looked like a message from division headquarters. It wasn't even addressed to him. It was addressed to Major Ricks, his boss at Brigade S-4, but Major Ricks had handed off the job of complying with the order contained in the message to his sergeant. It was the old story: Officers consider, sergeants deliver.

But in this case, Master Sergeant Scanlon felt no resentment. Major Ricks may have handed him just what he needed to supplement the retirement for which he had long been eligible but had not yet applied for. He had been waiting. Waiting for just such an opportunity. An opportunity for one big score. An opportunity like the message he now held in his hands.

His ex-wife received half his pay each month. It was infuriating because she was the reason he had been busted from E-9 to E-6 years before. Busted from battalion sergeant major to platoon sergeant in a line infantry company. A platoon sergeant who was called Sergeant Scanlon to his face, but Sergeant Scars behind his back courtesy of the gift from Mrs. Scanlon that had covered half his face, one side of his neck, and all of his chest with the red badge of burns. Never the handsomest of men, Sergeant Scanlon now looked like Lon Chaney in full makeup to play some creature in a horror movie.

It had taken the sergeant four years and a lot of sucking up to work his way up to E-8. He knew he would never get back to E-9. Not with his personnel jacket. Plus, that ugly thing in Vietnam was heating up. Secretary of Defense McNamara was not going to let the Commies take Southeast Asia on his watch. The United States was stepping in to replace the Frenchies who had rabbited after Dien Bien Phu. LBJ was campaigning as the man less likely to get the U.S. into the land war in Asia President Eisenhower had warned about, but the Texan now had twenty thousand troops in Vietnam. Didn't feel like de-escalation to Sergeant Scanlon. It would be a full-blown, out-and-out war before long.

It was time to go. He had been through two wars and had no interest in being part of a third. He had been through the transition from the brown-shoe Army to the black-shoe army, to the gold-U.S.-Army-on-black-with-white-name-tag Army, and he was done with the Army. But he had to come up with something to make up for the half of his pension his old lady would get unless she remarried. And who was going to marry that old battleax?

So, the sergeant sat on his field camp chair and thought. And sweated. He gave a few moments of that thought to the new rifle that was part of the message in his hand and the problems that were going to come with that rifle. Like many division and brigade level supply sergeants, Sergeant Scanlon knew the M-16 was a weapon full of bugs. Bugs that were apparently not going to be fixed before it was deployed. The primary problem was the lack of a chrome-plated chamber. Absent chrome plating, chambers become pitted. Pitted chambers lead to extraction problems: a bad enough problem in a semi-automatic weapon; an absolute disaster in a full-automatic. But the rifles had been rushed into production, and now according to the message in his hands, were about to be delivered.

Too much money at stake. Too many big contracts. Too bad for the grunts. But not Sergeant Scanlon's problem. He stopped thinking about it.

Instead, he turned his attention to the gift hidden in the message. All three of the mechanized infantry battalions in the brigade were to be re-supplied in the field with the M-16. The re-supply would be done via a touch-and-go drop on Wednesday, the seventeenth, on the primitive airstrip that had been gouged out of the desert eight miles from where he sat. Those new weapons would be scrupulously accounted for. By assignment by serial number to individual soldiers. Because they were the Army's new weapon.

When new guns are supplied, what do you do with the old ones? Soldiers couldn't very well carry both. Probably McNamara and his Whiz Kids had never thought about that. They were the big thinkers. Thinking big thoughts. Not troubled with details. They left the mundane problem of how things actually worked to the multitude of planners walking the seventeen miles of corridors and filling the 3,700,000 square feet of office space at the Pentagon.

The planners in the corridors and at the desks inside the offices along the corridors had devised a plan. A plan handed down the chain of command to Field Army, to Corps, to Division, and on to Brigade, which is how it ended up on Major Rick's desk (M1952 field, wooden) in a command tent in the middle of the Mojave Desert. And where Major Ricks had passed off the responsibility for complying with that part of the message to Master Sergeant Scanlon.

Because that part was *Not Interesting!* Not anywhere nearly as interesting as a touch-and-go drop by a C-123 Provider in which pallets of M-16s would be pulled from the back of the plane and down the ramp by rapidly deploying parachutes. A plane that would never even stop rolling. A plane flown by an Air Force crew that included a loadmaster hoping the pallets had been packed and balanced well enough that they wouldn't do an endo when the chutes deployed and scatter three battalion's worth of the new black rifles across a temporary airstrip next to the Hayden siding of the Union Pacific Railroad.

But the old rifles? The M14s? Yesterday's box score. Not closely watched. Leaving room for maneuver by a clever master sergeant. The man who really ran supply for the 22nd Armored Brigade. The man Major Ricks relied on after the brigade commander, a full-bird colonel, relied on Major Ricks.

Officers considered. Sergeants delivered.

That retirement-saving message Master Sergeant Scanlon held in his hand, the message that was *Not Interesting* to Major Ricks, specified what was to be done with the M-14s the grunts of the three mechanized infantry battalions of the 22nd Armored Brigade would no longer be carrying. Those M-14s, suddenly surplus to the active-duty Army, were to be re-assigned (Pentagon's word) to Army Reserve and National Guard Units in Arizona and New Mexico where they would replace M-1 rifles left over from WW II. Little commands in small towns. Some as small as a single company. Not sophisticated outfits.

In the peacetime Army, the worst thing a soldier could do was lose a weapon. Woe betide the company armorer who could not account for every rifle. Lose one, just one that was supposed to be either in a soldier's hands or under lock and key, and some Spec-4 would meet a lot of people. Angry people. High-ranking people. Of course, the same held true for armorers in Army Reserve and National Guard units. Scrupulous accounting, by serial number.

But what if some of the replacement weapons never arrived at those unsophisticated commands? And what if there was no indication they had ever been destined to arrive? Weapons that had been hidden and never loaded on a truck. Weapons that were not listed on the manifest handed over by the driver of the M809 6x6 five-ton truck that delivered them to the Army Reserve and National Guard units. No need to account for those. No way to, either.

Officers considered. Sergeants delivered.

Master Sergeant Yannity Scanlon sat considering the detail work involved to deliver the suddenly-surplus rifles. Just not all of them.

There were three rifle companies in a mechanized infantry battalion in the new ROAD (Reorganization Objective Army Division) plan under which the 22nd Armored Brigade operated. In 1963, the ROAD battalions had replaced the old regimental structure of Pentomic Organization left over from the Korean war era.

The three mechanized infantry battalions in the 22nd Armored Brigade each had three rifle companies and a headquarters/heavy weapons company. That made a total of nine rifle companies in the Brigade. Each of those nine rifle companies had three rifle platoons for a total of twenty-seven rifle platoons. Each of the twenty-seven platoons had a weapons squad with an 81mm mortar, an M-60 machine gun, and three ten-man rifle squads. Each of those rifle squads was further broken down into the basic component of the infantry of the United States Army: two, five-man rifle teams. Each rifle team had three regular M-14 semi-automatic rifles, one fully automatic M14A1 rifle with tripod, and one M79 grenade launcher. That made two hundred and eight-four M14s, and one hundred and forty-two fully automatic M14A1s in the brigade. The 81-millimeter mortars, M-60 machine guns, and M-79 grenade launchers ('blookers') would stay. Only the M14s and M14A1s would be changed out.

The Army Reserve and National Guard units had not yet been reorganized into the ROAD battalion configuration. They still operated under the Pentomic regimental configuration of the Korea War era. Therefore, they had no idea how many weapons they should receive. Those Army Reserve and National Guard units, decided Master Sergeant Scanlon, could have all three hundred and twenty-four regular M-14s. They could even have ninety-two of the fully automatic M14A1s. But Sergeant Scanlon had plans for the other fifty fully-automatic rifles.

Those fifty were going to get lost in the paperwork shuffle by sleight of hand. Get lost because the sergeant remembered something an experienced armorer over in Bravo Company, Second Infantry Battalion, had done with one of them. One that had been worn out. Too many rounds down the bore. The rifling shot. No longer accurate and therefore replaced by a new rifle. The armorer, a bit of a gunsmith, approached the company commander for permission to try a modification. Just for fun. Just to see if he could. Permission had been granted, and the armorer created something fascinating. Something promising. Something compact and lethal.

Which led to the next step in the sergeant's thinking. Who would want fifty automatic weapons? Not only want them, but have the cash on hand to buy them? Only one specific large organization had both the money and the need for such weapons. It was a large organization with which Sergeant Scanlon had a passing acquaintance and a continuing fascination because he was Italian on his mother's side and hailed from Cicero, Illinois.

When Al Capone had finished building his criminal empire in Chicago during Prohibition, he moved his headquarters to Cicero to escape the reach of the Chicago Police. Sergeant Scanlon's mother and her family were related to some of the people who had worked for Capone and some who still worked for the organization that followed. She sometimes talked about the stories she heard from her cousins. And so, young Yannity Scanlon grew fascinated by the mob and soon began to keep tabs on the Mafia, avidly reading any news about it.

The sergeant, therefore, knew there was a Mafia war underway in Sicily. Knew that Cesare Manzella had been killed in Cinisi, and in retaliation, Mafia boss Angelo La Barbera had been wounded in Milan. Knew that one of the Five Families in New York had sent a triggerman to Milan to take out La Barbera, but someone from Sicily had struck first. Knew Emile Colontuono, one of Joey Gallo's people, had been killed in Manhattan in the Gallo-Profaci war, as had Al Mandello. It was clear the conflict had arrived on American shores.

It was inevitable that the war would spread to Las Vegas. Everyone knew that *Capo di tutti i capi* Vito Genovese and the Chicago Outfit were in competition for control of Sin City. Genovese ran his end from a cell in the Atlanta Federal Penitentiary. There was a good chance the Chicago Outfit would want to use the war as cover to take advantage of Vito Genovese's absence and take over his share of operations in Vegas.

That meant The Outfit would need guns. Real guns. Weapons with heavy-duty firepower. Of course, they couldn't walk around the street with the M14A1s, but what about a modified version of that weapon? One that could hang from a strap, undetectable, inside an overcoat, and be brought to bear and fired by simply tugging on a front folding grip connected by a rod to the trigger. A weapon that could fire twenty 7.62-millimeter rounds in less than two seconds. How about that for firepower?

Sergeant Scanlon sat and thought through the steps required for such a sale to come to fruition. First, he needed to find out if there actually was a market for such weapons. That would involve calling his mother in Cicero to track down a phone number for her cousin, Sammy Spinelli. If there were a market, he would need to get his hands on that modified M14A1. That would be easy. Then he'd have to get hold of some live ammunition for a possible demonstration. Once again, not difficult for a man of his talents with his connections.

Sergeant Scanlon was done thinking. He was ready to act.

"Gould, get your butt in here."

Spec-4 Gould was in front of the sergeant on the double.

"Get the jeep. You and I are going to take a ride. I have to talk to the man at Smoke Tree Hardware and Building Supply about some turnbuckles."

"Yes, Sergeant!"

That's the most enthusiasm I've seen from this clown since we got here, thought Sergeant Scanlon.

A little over an hour later, they pulled into the north end of Smoke Tree. Sergeant Scanlon began looking for a phone booth. He spotted one at the West End Shell and Diner.

"Turn around, Gould, and take me back to that diner."

"I thought we were going to a hardware store."

"We are, Gould, we are. But first, I'm going to buy you a nice hot meal. Might as well take advantage of our time in town."

They walked into the diner. The air conditioning felt wonderful. The waitress behind the counter said, "Welcome soldiers. Sit anywhere you'd like."

Sergeant Scanlon led Specialist Gould to a booth upholstered in red vinyl in the rear corner of the diner. A corner from which the phone booth outside could not be seen.

"Slide in there, Gould."

34

Specialist Gould did as he was told. He pulled the menu out of its clip in front of the booth's juke box selector.

Sergeant Scanlon sat down across from him and abruptly stood up again.

"Forgot. Something I gotta do. Go ahead and order without me."

He reached in his pocket and retrieved two quarters.

"Pick us out some tunes on that juke box. Something with some snap to it."

"Yes, Sergeant."

Sergeant Scanlon walked to the register. The waitress was just about to come around the counter with a tray holding two glasses of water.

"Need a favor, Miss."

"Sure, Sergeant."

"I need ten dollars' worth of quarters and dimes. Gotta make a phone call."

She put down the tray and hit "no sale" on the register. As the tray opened, "Wipe Out" by the Surfaris blasted through the speakers.

"God, I was hoping to get through my shift without hearing that one again."

She took the sergeant's ten-dollar bill and counted out his change.

"Take junior surfer over there a chocolate malt. Get him whatever he wants to eat. If he asks where I went, say you don't know. And don't say anything about the change and the phone call. There'll be a nice tip in it for you."

"Sure thing, Sergeant...," she peered at his name tag, "Scanlon."

"Thank you," ... "Debbie" he said, reading hers.

Outside in the phone booth, he piled the change on the tray and called his mother. She answered on the second ring. One good thing about having a mom who's a housewife, he thought. She's always around.

"Hi, Mom."

"Why hello, Yannity. This is a surprise. I thought you were out in the middle of the desert somewhere."

"I am, but I was lucky enough to get near a phone booth. Since I had the chance, I thought I'd call my favorite girl."

As they talked, they were frequently interrupted by the operator telling him to deposit more money. The third time that happened, his mother said, "This is costing you a fortune, Yannity. I'd better let you go."

"Okay, mom. Before you hang up, do you have a phone number for your cousin Sammy?"

"I'm sure I do, somewhere. Why do you want to talk to him?" Suspicion had crept into her voice.

"Got a question for him. Need to settle a bet. He'll know the answer."

He heard the receiver rattle as it was placed on the phone stand in the hallway of the row house in Cicero.

It was not long before it was picked up again.

"Here's his number, if he's not in jail."

She read off the number.

Sergeant Scanlon wrote it down.

"Is he still up to that kind of thing?"

"Are you kidding? That crowd he runs with? Last I heard, they had some big scam going out at O'Hare. He started to tell me about it one day, but I told him I didn't want to know. Your father doesn't even like to have him and Maureen over to the house. Says the cops are liable to kick down the door while we're carving the Sunday roast."

"Thanks for the number, mom."

"You're welcome. Yannity. It was good to hear from you."

"I'll call you again when this crazy exercise is over."

He broke the connection and dialed Sammy's number.

The phone was answered immediately.

"Whadya want?"

Maybe criminals are at home in the daytime as much as housewives, the sergeant thought. Must be the night work.

"It's Yannity Scanlon, Mr. Spinelli."

The surly tone disappeared from Sammy's voice.

"Oh yeah, Betty's boy. The one in the army. And hey, it's Sammy, okay? Enough with the 'Mr. Spinelli' stuff."

"Okay Sammy. I've got a little action you might be interested in. Would be a nice piece of change in it for you."

Sammy's tone changed from merely friendly to cautious.

"Give me the number you're calling from. I'll get back to you in ten."

Sergeant Scanlon read off the number in the center of the dial and hung up.

It was less than ten minutes before the phone rang.

"Yannity."

"Can't be too careful around here, kid. The Feds are known to tap a line or two since that Bobby Kennedy became Attorney General. Anybody with an Italian name in his little book, if you know what I mean. So, whatcha got?"

Sergeant Scanlon explained about the modified weapons.

Sammy let out a low whistle.

"Now that is very interesting indeed. You know, all hell is about to break loose."

"Good. Good for you and me. I'm out here in the middle of the desert. My unit is less than eighty miles from Las Vegas. Do you know someone who could get a message to someone way up in the Vegas end of the operation? Someone there who might be able to put together the money to buy the guns?"

"That could happen."

Sergeant Scanlon kept feeding the phone while he and Sammy discussed the possible value of the fifty guns, as well as what Sammy's end would be for putting the deal in play. By the time they had reached an understanding, he was almost out of change.

"Can you make that contact today?"

"Sure. I know a guy out there."

"Okay. I'm at a phone booth too, and I have to go do some Army stuff. If I call you back in an hour, do you think you can have a name and a phone number for me?"

"I'm on it, nephew."

"Okay, I'll call you exactly one hour from now."

When Sergeant Scanlon went back into the diner, he had sweat big circles under the armpits of his fatigues. He walked to the booth where the remains of a fried chicken meal were scattered on Specialist Gould's plate.

"Where you been, Sergeant."

Sergeant Scanlon put on his best master sergeant face.

"Gould, master sergeants don't tell specialists where they've been. I've been where I had to be. Got it?"

"Sorry, sir."

"And don't call me sir! I work for a living. Now, get outside and start up the jeep. I'll be right there."

"Aren't you going to get something to eat?"

Sergeant Scanlon did not reply. He simply sat and stared at Gould with the flat-eyed stare reserved for those lower in rank.

"Sorry, sorry. And Sergeant Scanlon? Thanks for the lunch."

The specialist lifted himself off the seat of the booth so quickly his fatigues did contact the vinyl before he got to his feet.

Sergeant Scanlon walked to the register.

"What do I owe you?"

The waitress pulled out the ticket.

"One fried chicken special with garden vegetables, French fries and gravy, one chocolate malt and one coffee. That'll be $3.37."

"Did he ask where I was?"

"No."

"Good."

Sergeant Scanlon handed her a twenty-dollar bill.

"This is for the bill and five dollars in dimes and quarters. The rest is yours."

"Thanks, sergeant."

She counted out the coins.

"Y'all come back again anytime, hear?"

"I may just do that."

When he got outside, Sergeant Scanlon gave Gould directions to the hardware and building supply. He leaned back in his seat and smiled. It had been a productive day, so far.

Forty-five minutes later, Sergeant Scanlon had put in a rush order for fifty turnbuckles. The owner of the store was delighted, and so was the sergeant. He had an excuse to come back to Smoke Tree with a purchase order another day.

"Let's take a quick ride through town before we leave Specialist. Let's see what delights Smoke Tree has to offer."

They drove down Broadway to the city limits at the south end of town and then circled back. On the return route, instead of staying on Broadway, the sergeant had Gould do down Front Street

They passed the carnival and continued on toward the Santa Fe Depot.

At the south end of the depot, Sergeant Scanlon saw a phone booth.

"Pull in here and park, Specialist. I might as well make a phone call while we're in town."

Gould steered the jeep into the parking lot.

"Sergeant, would it be all right if I called my mom?"

"Sure thing, Specialist. As soon as I get done."

He checked his watch. Coming up on one hour. He climbed out of the jeep.

Sammy answered on the first ring.

"Right on time, kid. This isn't easy. I'm working my way up the ladder. It may take a while."

"Why so long?"

"'Cause I don't want anyone but you, me, and the big shot in on this. Otherwise, other guys will want a piece of the action. I'm trying to get the number of his personal line in Vegas without exactly telling anyone what this is about. Like I said, it ain't easy."

"I appreciate that, Sammy. Give me a minute here."

He thought the schedule through.

"Okay. My unit's out in the middle of nowhere. Not a phone for miles in any direction. I'll arrange to get back in town on Saturday. Will you have the number by then."

"For sure. And kid? Call me at home. Don't say who it is. I'll recognize your voice. I'll give you a number and say goodbye. The number will be in code to confuse anyone who might be listening. Just drop the first and last number and add one to each of the remaining numbers. Got it?"

"I do. And Sammy, if the deal goes down, I'll get back to you about getting your money."

"Be sure you do, nephew. Be very sure you do. Family is family, but business is business."

"Understood."

He was whistling as he walked back to the jeep. Yes, it had been a very good day indeed. Things were looking up on the retirement front.

"Specialist Gould?"

"Yes, Sergeant?"

"Go call your mother. That's an order."

CHAPTER 8

Grief

When Captain Carlos Caballo, known throughout the Lower Colorado River Basin as 'Horse,' left the Smoke Tree Substation after six o'clock that evening, he was still shaken to his core. His good friend, Burke Henry, had asked him in May to come out to his place at the mouth of Piute Canyon on official business in early June, but Burke had hung up before Horse could ask him any more questions, including where he was calling from. Since there was no phone service where Burke lived, Horse had not been able to call him back. Nor had he heard from him since.

Burke had been closely involved as a volunteer with the department for years, both as a member of the search and rescue team and as a use-of-force instructor for Smoke Tree deputies. He was also Horse's best friend. In spite of everything going on in his huge area of responsibility in this busy time, he would have made the visit even without Burke's reassurance it involved official business.

Sadly, it was official business; death always is for a San Bernardino County Sheriff's Department substation commander. Burke Henry was dead. Horse had been stunned when he learned under what circumstances his friend had died. And what Horse had to do next.

First, he had to tell his wife, Esperanza. He had not told her when he returned to Smoke Tree earlier in the day. And he had not told her when he called to let her know he would be late for dinner. It was not something he could tell her over the phone. As he drove

41

home after work late in the day, he still wasn't sure how to break the news, for Burke Henry had been Esperanza's friend, too.

Horse drove past the Smoke Tree Airport. Normally the home of nothing but one sleepy hangar, a few single-engine planes and a small airstrip, it was now jammed with huge tents, military aircraft military vehicles and equipment, and soldiers. Lots and lots o soldiers. Smoke Tree airport had been transformed into the headquarters for the planners and strategists of Calonia and Nezona: two imaginary countries fighting a mock war in Join Operation Desert Strike. An operation that was a monumental pair in the butt for Horse and his busy deputies.

Two miles from the substation, he turned off Highway 95 onto a dirt road that ran west into the foothills of the Sacramento Mountains. At the point where the road curved south, he continued straight ahead on a two-track that led to his driveway. In another two miles, he saw the streak of green marking the line of cottonwood trees he had planted years before on the northern edge of his five acres to block the unrelenting winds of winter. The track was beginning to washboard in a number of places, and Horse made a mental note to bring his tractor down and run a blade over the worst parts.

Approaching the home he had built himself from cement blocks many years before, he noticed the white plaster covering the blocks needed patching in a few places. He added that to his 'to-do list. An oscillating sprinkler was gently spraying the neatly-trimmed Bermuda grass lawn in front of the house.

As he turned off the driveway onto the spot where he usually parked his cruiser, the front door to the house flew open. Two very brown children dressed in nothing but shorts and flip-flops came tearing out. The screen door banged shut behind them. Probably thought Horse with a smile, just after Esperanza had hollered not to slam it.

The children were at the open door of his car before he could get all the way to his feet.

"Pappi, pappi! We've been playing in the sprinkler."

His heart filled with such a feeling of well-being at the sound of his daughter's voice and the sight of her happy face that it almost pushed aside the sadness from earlier in the day. Straightening, he scooped up Elena and her brother Alejandro and started for the house, swinging the car door shut with his hip on his way past.

"What else have you two monkeys been doing today?"

Elena suddenly looked very serious.

"English lessons."

42

Esperanza was teaching their twins, adopted from an orphanage in Mexico, to speak English. At the same time, she was teaching them to read both Spanish and English. She was a wonderful and dedicated teacher, and Alejandro and Elena were quick studies. Horse was amazed by how fast they were picking up English. Their grammar was correct, thanks to Esperanza, and their vocabularies were growing daily.

By the time Horse had carried the two shrieking children through the spray from the sprinkler, Esperanza was on the veranda, her faced creased with the glorious smile Horse loved so much. Her brown eyes sparkled. She was so beautiful, so unconsciously elegant. He fell in love with her all over again every time he saw her. He had been doing that since the day they first met at Smoke Tree Junior High School.

"*Hola, mi esposo.*"

"Which in English means?"

"Hello, my husband," both children shouted at the same time.

"*Hola, mi amor.*"

"Hello, my love," they both said without prompting. Elena giggled and rolled her eyes.

Esperanza held the screen door open and followed Horse and the children inside. The big swamp cooler on the roof was keeping the indoor temperature around eighty-five, even though the high outside that day had been over a hundred and ten.

With effortless grace, Horse dropped to a knee and deposited the children on the tiled floor.

"Sweetheart, maybe you could give the twins some carrots to feed the horses."

Esperanza saw something in his eyes that gave her pause.

"Of course. And you two be sure to give them some hay first. They can have the carrots for treats. And give them fresh water."

Esperanza returned from the refrigerator and handed each child a brown paper sack filled with broken carrots.

"Remember, don't hold..."

"We know, mama. Don't hold the carrots with our fingers. Put them on our palms. You tell us that every time."

Esperanza laughed.

"Yes, I do. And you always do it the right way. That's why you both still have all your fingers."

Elena and Alejandro went out the back door.

"Don't..."

The door slammed behind them.

"...slam the screen door," she finished with a laugh.

43

She turned to Horse, suddenly serious.

"Carlos, what's happened?"

Horse sighed. There was just good way to say it.

"Burke Henry is dead."

Her hand went to her mouth, and she took a step back.

"Oh, no. That cannot be."

"When I went out to see him today, he wasn't there. His motorcycle and truck were in front of the house, but Pepper wasn't in the corral. I remembered when he called last month, he told me where to find the key to the house if he wasn't home when I got there. He said to go inside and get something cold to drink. Said there'd be pop in the refrigerator.

When Andy and I went in, it didn't seem like anyone had been there for quite a while. The house had a musty smell. When I opened the refrigerator to get us a drink, I saw two envelopes. One said 'Carlos Caballo. Read this one first.' The envelopes gave me a bad feeling, but I put them under my arm and got the sodas. Nehi grape of course. The only drink Burke ever had in that refrigerator. No beer, no wine, no Kool-Aid, no iced tea."

At the thought of Burke and his beloved Nehi grape, Horse's voice broke, and he had to stop for a moment before he went on.

"Because it was so hot in the house, I suggested to Andy we got out on the back porch. Andy wandered off toward the creek, and I sat down and opened that first envelope."

Horse stopped again and wiped his eyes with the back of his hand.

"I'm sorry. I'm giving you a lot of pointless details. It's just so hard to say what I have to say next. And I know how hard it's going to be for you to hear it.

"The letter said..."

His voice broke again. He struggled to regain his composure.

"The letter said Burke had pancreatic cancer. The cancer was both incurable and fast-moving, and he had decided not to die in a hospital. Said he had gone off to meet death on his own terms."

Esperanza's eyes filled with tears.

Horse spread his arms and she came to him. He folded her into an embrace, and they hugged for a long time. He could feel her tears soaking into his shirt.

She spoke first, her wavering voice muffled.

"If Burke Henry had made up his mind to do this thing..."

"That's right, *Querida*, then it has been done. I have no doubt our friend is dead. There is no reason to think otherwise."

"Where did he go to do this dying?"

"A cave out near the Providence. In his note he said Joe Medrano would know where it is. And he said he was going to walk there. Can you imagine that. A man dying of cancer walking all that way?"

"How could he carry enough water?"

"Burke knows the location of every spring for miles around. But still, a weak and dying man on foot with very little food and no help at all?"

"*Pero de nuevo.*"

"*Sí, entonces sin duda se ha hecho.* The letter went on to say his will was in the other envelope and named me as his executor. Said the original is in a lawyer's office in Barstow. The will leaves Joe the house and the property on Piute Creek. Leaves Pepper to the twins. Pepper is at the Stonebridge ranch. Left a fifty-dollar bill for me to give John for Pepper's board there. Left his motorcycle to Mr. Stanton and his truck to Ellis McCreary. Andy and I delivered both on our way home.

I talked to Joe this afternoon. He's working in town, over at Doc Hayden's place. Room addition or something. Joe said he knew the cave Burke was talking about."

"That's our Burke. Nothing overlooked. Will legally made. Nothing to chance. Did you tell Joe about Burke leaving him the house and land?"

"I did."

"He must have been sad when you told him what has happened."

"It's always hard to tell with Joe, but yes, he was."

Esperanza smiled through her tears.

"But there's more. That first letter is for the two of us only. I brought it home for you to read No one else is will ever see it."

"Why so secret?"

Horse took a deep breath.

"This next part is unbelievable. Burke left us over four hundred and twenty-five thousand dollars. It's buried in a metal box out in the canyon. There's a map in his safe deposit box in an envelope that says 'Carlos Caballo only'. The key to the safety deposit box was in the envelope holding the letter."

She stepped away from him and looked up into his face.

"That's crazy, Carlos. Where did Burke get that kind of money? And why did he leave it to us?"

"He doesn't say where he got it. He does say no one's looking for it, and that no crime was committed getting it."

"So, even in death our friend is a mystery."

"Even in death. He gave the money to us because he wants us to give it to the orphanage."

Esperanza was silent for a moment.

"That's so much like him. Lord knows, the orphanage can use it. They never have enough money. *México está lleno de huérfanos.*"

"He said to start them with fifty thousand and see if they put it to good use. If they do, we're to give the rest in similar increments. If they fail to use it well at any time, we're to give what remains to the Salvation Army. Said they helped him once when he was in Los Angeles."

"In all the years you knew Burke, did he ever mention being in Los Angeles? Or needing help there?"

"Never. The instructions in the letter are so like Burke careful, detailed, and not trusting others to do the right thing."

"Except us."

"Except us. He knew we wouldn't walk away with the money."

"He knows you, Carlos."

"And he knows you, but he also said if at any time we had an emergency and needed money to take it. As much as we need."

Esperanza shook her head.

"We have everything we need. Each other. The twins. This house. This land. Our life is good. So good it scares me, sometimes."

"Burke established trust accounts in the children's names at a Nevada bank. For college. You and I are the trustees. Twenty-five thousand dollars each and drawing interest."

"What do we do next?"

"I'll call a few of the search and rescue volunteers tonight. Joe and I will lead them out to Foshay Pass early tomorrow morning. We'll take Dusty Spires and have him declare Burke legally dead before we move the body. That's why he didn't just go off into the desert and die without telling anyone where he was. Said he wanted us to be able to probate his will, and for that he had to be legally dead."

"A meticulous planner."

"It's going to take most of a day I don't have because of a bunch of other stuff going on, but I want to get him out of that cave and have him cremated. I can't bear to think of him lying out there."

"That's what he wanted, to be cremated?"

"Yes. And no service of any kind. Ashes scattered on top of the New Yorks. I'll take care of that part when things calm down around here."

"You mean things like Desert Strike and the carnival and graduation parties with alcohol?"

"Plus, one more thing. On our way out of town, Andy and I saw a guy wearing sandals and a long white robe dragging a big cross down the shoulder of 66 toward Smoke Tree. On our way back to the station this afternoon, I saw the cross planted on the vacant lot at the south end of Palestine street. There was a tent going up on one of the big slabs. There were a couple of trucks, a generator and a searchlight. Looks like Smoke Tree is about to get its first outdoor revival."

CHAPTER 9

Caravans, Carnivals, and Circumstances

The Happy Times Funfest rolled into Smoke Tree at five o'clock in the afternoon. Six eighteen-wheelers with lettering on the trailers in red and gold led the convoy, followed by flatbed trucks with rides and a bevy of old pickup trucks pulling a variety of travel trailers.

The section of Front Street that paralleled the railroad tracks south of the Santa Fe Depot was soon clogged. The drivers of the show's transportation simply abandoned the vehicles and walked to the two-lot site to survey the markings to find out where their part of the carnival would be positioned.

Carlyle Evans, the owner of the show, strolled the lot with Danny Dubois, his combined 24-hour and advance man. Carlyle studied the layout.

"This is different."

"Yessir, it is. But I think it'll work real good."

"The usual perimeter but a diamond shape in the middle instead of a horseshoe shape?"

"That's right. Bottom of the diamond points at the arch, top points to the rides and tent shows."

"Why did you do it that way without consulting me?"

"Well sir, when I went to city hall to pull our permits this morning, I learned something we didn't know in Kingman yesterday. There are almost one hundred thousand soldiers spread out all over the desert. Most of them won't ever get to town, but five thousand are just south of the Smoke Tree Airport. Headquarters and planning and all that stuff. Five thousand bored soldiers, close to town!"

"Why are they here?"

"It's some kind of war game thing. Called Desert Strike. Lady in the City Clerk's office said it's a training exercise to get ready for nuclear war."

Carlyle thought that over for a minute.

"Hah! In less than five minutes I could train these G.I.s what to do in a nuclear war. Bend over and kiss your ass goodbye. But what have soldier boys got to do with this layout?"

"Actually, it's a combination of things. These lots are oddly shaped. They're narrow across the front but very deep. I remember it made it tough to set up our usual horseshoe configuration when we were here two years ago. When people come through the arch they just naturally move to the right. That will take them to the best joints, just like the horseshoe would. But because it's an elongated diamond, I think people will keep moving along the edges. Once they turn that corner and see the food booths, they may get something to eat and then go on to the rides and shows, but they may turn the corner again to see the other food booths. If they do that, they'll probably go on around and see the games they missed on the way in. Maybe. It's hard to tell how a crowd will move.

If we get just a percentage of these soldiers, we're going to have a huge crowd. With the old layout, the horseshoe would clog up. People would start milling around and be so jammed it would be hard for the shills to lead them out to make the tip for the tent shows."

"But kid, that's one of the reasons for the horseshoe design. We want them jammed up. I mean, that's exactly how we make the tip. Otherwise, the crowd doesn't go where we want it to."

"I know, but I've been thinking about some new scripts for the talkers. With all these people, if they say things right, they can take a bunch of people to every show and still have people going back around to spend more money on the games."

Danny pointed.

"The back of the show is a straight line instead of a curve. The tip of the diamond will point right at it, so people coming away from the diamond, either on their first or second time around, will be standing in front of the Ferris Wheel. Go left for the grown-up rides, right for the kiddie rides."

Carlyle turned in a full circle, taking in the design.

"I can see it, Danny. You did good here." He smiled and slapped Danny on the back. "Five thousand soldier boys, huh?"

"That's right."

"You know, kid, you're getting to be more of a showman all the time. Speaking of which, we're going to need extra outside talkers if the crowd gets as big as you think it will. You'll have to help out."

"Sure, as long as nothing breaks down. I'm a little worried about the clutch on the Tilt-a-Whirl; otherwise, I think we're in pretty good shape. And one more thing. Instead of putting the Genny in the middle, I marked it over there in the northeast corner. Benny the Bolt can alter some of the junction boxes to fit the new layout. That way, we can angle the searchlight and light up the top of the Ferris Wheel so the traffic over on 66 will be able to see it. Should bring us some extra business."

"That'll work."

Danny was relieved. If Carlyle Evans was happy, everyone else would have to be fine with the new arrangement. Carlyle was what people in the trade called a fence-to-fence owner: the entire carnival was his, not just the rides. That fact made his show more welcome in towns along the route than some carnivals because Carlyle ran a straight-up show. The games on the midway were gaffed, but not as much as with most carnivals. Gaffed just enough to give an edge to the jointees. That allowed Carlyle to make a profit overall, but it also gave the citizens a chance to win a bit and not feel like they were being swindled. Carlyle was a master of striking that delicate balance: the balance between being welcomed back and told to keep your show moving to the next burg.

The only part of Happy Times Funfest that still raised red flags in some towns was the hoochie-coochie show, but Carlyle would be more adamant than ever about not giving that up with a bunch of lonely soldiers in town. The biggest money maker, the coochie allowed him to keep the other games almost on the up-and-up. And Carlyle cut down on objections by having one hard and fast rule: the girls, the most pampered performers on the midway, were forbidden to have sex with the marks. Any girl who did and was found out was soon standing alongside the road, suitcase in hand.

"Danny, we've got a problem. When you left Kingman this morning, I didn't know how big it was. You know I gave everyone a little cash advance last night after we put the awnings up, right? We've been running pretty hard lately, and I wanted to give the crew a break. Especially since we were coming down into this heat. I should have known better. In fact, I did know better, but I did it anyway."

"You even gave the ride guys an advance?"

"Even them."

"Let me guess what happened. When it was time to tear down the show, they hadn't come back."

"No, a lot of the ride jockeys were late, but they made it. Hung over and marked up from fights, but that's a normal morning."

"What's the problem?"

"A lot of the prat boys didn't come back. I had to hire a bunch of gazoonies."

"Did any of the new ones come down the hill with you?"

"That's the rest of the problem. Just one came. That means we need at least eight more."

"I saw a couple of beer joints and a pool hall. I'll make a pass and recruit a few."

"Good boy. But you know what will happen."

"Yeah. When they find out how hard the work is, they won't show up to pack the pig iron when we leave town."

"We'll think of something."

"I have an idea. I can get us enough gazoonies for the tear down if you'll let me use a pickup at about seven-thirty."

"And go where?"

"Graduation practice. Smoke Tree High is having graduation tomorrow night. Practice will probably start after dinner this evening. Too hot to do it earlier. I'll bet I can scrounge up a few boys who want to make some extra money at the beginning of summer."

"Tell them we'll pay a bonus if it's a hot day."

"It's always hot here, Mr. Evens."

Carlyle winked.

"Yeah, but they don't know we know that. Let them think they're getting one over on us. Everybody likes to think they have an edge."

By the time Danny returned that afternoon with eight hastily-recruited workers, the show was setting up. Locals who had heard the carnival was in town had gathered to watch. Mothers were keeping a firm grip on their children to keep them from running onto the lot for a closer look, especially when the ponies were led off their trailer.

The spectators were seeing a production as carefully choreographed as any music-and-dance number Busby Berkeley ever put on the silver screen. Although it looked chaotic to an outsider, a pattern revealed itself as the pieces fell into place. A social anthropologist would have quickly spotted the strict social order.

52

Everyone worked, even the hoochie-coochie girls, but the hierarchy was revealed by tasks. Holding the lowest rank were the gazoonies: unskilled, temporary laborers who signed on to help set up or tear down the carnival. If they thought the job was going to be easy, they were soon disappointed. They had the dirtiest, hardest, most unskilled tasks and were worked like rented mules. Of course, if they thought they were getting more work than they'd bargained for, they were free to walk off the job, but then they wouldn't get paid. One rung above them were the prat boys: guys who had originally hired on as gazoonies and stayed with the show but never developed any useable skills beyond grunt work.

The next rung on the ladder was occupied by the ride guys, also known as ride boys or ride jockeys. These were the men, and they were always men, who did the dirty work of assembling the complicated jigsaw puzzles that were the rides and then operating them. Of all the people working for Carlyle, they were the most transitory and least reliable. They sometimes disappeared without notice, only to rejoin the show somewhere down the road. Such lapses were tolerated because ride guys had to be willing to do hard, greasy work requiring mechanical skills.

They were the easiest to pick out of a crowd because of their uniform: Levi's, black engineer boots, and white t-shirts with a pack of cigarettes rolled into the sleeve. The only variant seemed to be hair styling. Some favored Brylcream and a duck's tail; others leaned toward the Elvis Presley look with extra Vitalis. Danny had a theory that they put so much grease on their hair because they always had so much on their hands. Trying to find a ride guy with clean fingernails was like trying to find an albino crow.

Above the ride jockeys were the people who prepared the cheap food sold at the booths. They had to have enough flair to make an entertaining production of what they were doing so the lines of people waiting to order wouldn't get restless and leave. The best cooks graduated to the next step up: preparing the food for the crew. Their call of 'the flag is up' in the morning meant coffee and breakfast were ready.

Next were the jointees, the people who ran the games. Mostly, but not all men, they had to have people skills: the ability to lure marks to the games and deal with their disappointment once they got there. The most accomplished jointees were called agents because they were able to keep marks happy while coaxing ever more money from their pockets. The agents got the toughest games to sell: the ones that were the hardest and had the best-looking prizes, but prizes that were very hard to win. Agents were skilled at

53

talking marks into buying just one more chance in a losing game. The knife throw, the bullseye toss and the Pepsi-bottle ring-toss fell into that category.

Then came the shills, highly prized because they were the only innocent-looking people in a crew made up mostly of miscreants. Shills had to make winning the difficult games look easy (with the help of jointees). They also had to make up the tip, or crowd, and lead the marks to the tent shows to be enticed to buy tickets by outside talkers, the next rung up the ladder. Topmost were the inside talkers: those who coaxed additional money from the marks once they were in the tent, usually with the promise of seeing something they thought the general public wouldn't get to see.

The most important inside talker, of course, was the one in the hoochie-coochie tent. He was the man responsible for bringing in the most money. Marks who had paid to come inside because they thought they were going to see naked girls soon discovered they would be paying a premium at each step of the strip tease for such a privilege. In a sense, the inside talker had to convince marks to pay more and more for less and less.

Danny Dubois had a different status than anyone on the lot. He had started so young that he never worked as a gazoonie. Because of his innocent look, he had moved directly to being a shill and he was very good at it. He then skipped being a jointy and went straight to becoming an outside talker. In his upward progression he discovered he had a gift for repairing things and was soon the one who kept the rides, cooking equipment, and vehicles operating. That invaluable skill increased his importance and his pay.

Nor did it take Carlyle Evans long to realize that Danny had a good head for numbers and was absolutely honest and dependable. That earned him another even more important function doing accounting work in the office trailer late at night, tallying up the days take and making up the deposit.

The people who filled all these jobs represented a broad spectrum of American life. The ride jockeys were often ex-cons who found it hard to find legitimate work because of criminal pasts. Many were on the run from bail bondsmen and process servers, but just as often from IRS garnishments or child support payments. Carnival work paid in cash, therefore attracting the disenfranchised, the disadvantaged, and people who had to be paid off the books.

On the other hand, many of the shills, jointees and talkers were college kids working summer jobs that promised a chance to see the country and have a bit of adventure. Some of them returned for summers all the way through undergraduate and graduate school.

As the day moved toward sundown, and the jigsaw puzzle that was the midway began to fit together, Danny and Carlyle were conferring near the arch when Danny looked south down the sidewalk.

"Here comes your preacher man."

Carlyle turned. Jedidiah Shanks was walking toward them. Despite the heat, he was dressed in a white linen suit.

"Hello, Jedidiah."

"Hello yourself, Carlyle. A carnival is a quern, upon which are ground many souls."

Without hesitation, Carlyle replied, "A revival is a rivening stone, by which are laved away many a raddled role."

Jedidiah laughed and shook his head.

"Carlyle, you are the only man I've ever met who knows more archaic words than I. You even made yours rhyme with mine. You continue to be a mystery to me."

"Where did you learn your old words, Jedidiah?"

"College. You?"

"Years of toil and travail walking the highway of life, swimming the river of dreams and struggling through the slough of despond."

"See you're familiar with *The Pilgrim's Progress*."

"Among other sacred works."

"You should be in my business."

"Oh, we're in the exact same business, preacher. We earn our daily bread making people think they can have what they want if they just have a little more faith or part with a little more money."

Danny turned and walked away.

"Boy doesn't cotton to me, does he?"

"Doesn't seem to, and that's unusual. Seems to like most people. I don't think it's personal, though. Anybody starts talking religion, Danny leaves."

"How long's he been with the show?"

"Since he was thirteen. Came looking for work one spring. Was wore to a nub. Broke. Scared-looking, too. Don't think he would have got much farther. Normally, my dad wouldn't let someone that young travel with us unaccompanied, but he took him in. Said the boy would make a great shill. But he wasn't fooling anyone. He had a kind heart, my old man."

"So, you come by it honestly. Admit it, Carlyle, a soft heart beats beneath that vest, even though you wear it over a sweat-stained t-shirt. I'm curious about Danny, though. I think there's more to him than meets the eye. What do you know about his past?"

"Not much. Close-mouthed about it. Know he's from the lower peninsula. Can hear it when he talks."

"Anything else?"

"Nope."

Jedidiah pulled out a handkerchief and mopped his brow.

"Getting toward sundown, and it's about as hot as noon. When does it cool down in this place?"

"October. That's why I always try to get across the desert before the middle of June. That's when that brass heat hammer really pounds the Mojave. Appears I may have miscalculated this year, but I didn't want to bypass Smoke Tree. Town's full of railroad people who make a lot of money but are, by and large, a bunch of rubes."

"You think that makes it worth the stop in this heat?"

"Look how good we did in Winslow and Williams. Both railroad towns."

"I'm counting on your expertise, Carlyle. Never brought a revival out this way before, and I wouldn't have this year if we hadn't met up in Holbrook. I was about to turn north and head for Colorado. Cooler there."

"But not as profitable. Can't beat these little desert towns for turning loose of their cash. Plus, Danny just told me the town is full of soldier boys. We are going to rake it in. You are too! Soldiers need salivation as much as anyone. In fact, more than most."

"Carlyle, I've got to get out of this heat before I faint. I've been feeling poorly ever since I did my 'drag-a-cross' show. I just came down to tell you about tonight."

"You did walk in from the other side of town, right?"

"As usual. Never want anyone to associate the two shows."

"You're opening tonight?"

"Surely am. Smoke Tree Weekly came out this afternoon, and I had an ad in it. Hopefully, some of those people who saw me dragging that cross have mentioned it to their neighbors. We've already got the cross up and the searchlight will come on right after sundown."

"You don't waste any time. We're not opening until tomorrow."

"Are you going to have the coochie show."

"Why wouldn't I? It's our biggest money maker."

"I just thought you might not because Smoke Tree is so close to Las Vegas."

"What's that got to do with it?"

"Well, they have that topless show up at the Serengeti now. Drawing big crowds. I mean, men can see the same thing there, right? Big, fancy show. Beautiful women. They've probably already been up there. Why would they come to the coochie show at a carnival?"

"For a preacher, Jedediah, your knowledge of the male of the species is surprisingly deficient. Let an old carny educate you. That show is Vegas is about as sexy as a Doris Day movie. Those women go through five or six costume changes before they come out topless. And they don't even dance! They've got so much crap on they can hardly move. They just stand there. Don't even shake 'em. It's all so damned...boring."

That show is so tame, men take their wives with them! Now ask yourself, what guy wants to go look at half-naked women with his wife sitting right there beside him? To make it worse, he has to pretend he's not really interested. Pretend the girls aren't pretty. Men like to sneak around a little. Get away with something the old lady doesn't know about. But no, they have to sit there and fidget and pretend they came to hear the music and see the costumes. Like the guys who say they buy Playboy to read the articles!

A hoochie-coochie show, on the other hand, is nasty. Raw. Back alley, back window, back door, lowdown and dirty. And if those good ol' boys put enough money in the box, they get to see what they really came for–and it ain't some topless woman hidden by feathers with artificial fruit piled on top of her head. No sir, they get to see the real article."

Carlyle laughed

"Las Vegas is no competition for what I got."

"I get your point. How do you want me to play it?"

"Lay it on heavy. Say it's not bad enough the town is so close to America's answer to Sodom and Gomorrah, say you've just learned there's a hoochie-coochie show coming to town and it's worse than anything they'll ever see in Las Vegas. And don't forget to tell them to stay away. I mean, can there be a better way to whip up men than to tell them not to do something sinful? I guarantee you, when you get done, telling them to stay away, they'll beat a path to my show. And the next night, all the guys who snuck down here will be back at your place, bawling and sniveling and wearing out the knees of their britches trying to get saved again."

"And putting extra money in the bucket when the offering comes around."

"You got it, preacher. This has worked for us before. It will work for us here, Las Vegas be damned. We'll drive these guys back and forth two or three times before we head for Parker, and we'll both come out ahead!"

CHAPTER 10

Unintended Longings

At a quarter to eight that evening, Danny Dubois was behind the Smoke Tree High School gymnasium. He was looking out at the football field that stretched away from the concrete steps below him. Graduation rehearsal looked like it was just about over. After one last practice walk to 'Pomp and Circumstance' played by a very bored band, the seniors had climbed into the portable bleachers in the center of the field. He had already picked Mitzi Sodermeyer out of the group. She looked good. Just as pretty as he remembered. She was giggling with some friends, and Danny faintly heard some sharp words from a man who was probably a teacher.

As far as Danny could make out from this distance, the students were getting one last lecture about the proper decorum for Friday night, with special emphasis on what would happen to anyone who showed up smelling of alcohol. After that final warning, the class was dismissed and began to leave. Mitzi and her friends were the first ones out of the bleachers. Danny leaned against the railing above the steps and watched as they came across the grass toward him.

It was very hot, and the light, sundowner breeze provided little relief. The field lights had been turned on, and clouds of bugs swirled around every fixture. Bats and nighthawks swooped through the fluttering feast. The last light of day barely tinted the western horizon as this part of the planet turned very slowly into night. For the first time since stepping off the bus that morning, Danny Dubois felt at peace. The feeling surprised him. Peaceful was not a feeling that visited him often.

He wondered what it would be like to live in a little desert town like Smoke Tree. To go to school and take classes. To do whatever else kids did in high school. Play sports. Go to dances. Hang around with friends. Because this town was so isolated, it was very self-contained. Danny thought that might be nice, even though it was so close-knit many teenagers probably felt like they were suffocating and couldn't' wait to graduate and leave. He had observed that kind of restlessness in small towns all over the south and west. Danny didn't think he'd feel hemmed in like that. Though it might be nice to live in a place where everybody knew everybody else.

He wondered how many of the seniors had talked themselves into a corner by boasting about how they were going to blow this burg once they graduated. Wondered how many of them would leave and someday wish they hadn't. Danny had been on the road since the age of thirteen, and in some very fundamental way, every place he had been was the same as every other place he had been. The only difference was a new set of strangers. Carlyle told him some Roman guy named Horace once said, "They change their sky, not their souls, who rush across seas."

All this restless wanting to move around made him wonder. Wonder whether people ever walked outside at night and looked, really looked, at the stars. Looked and thought about the impossibly great distances the light from those uncountable stars had traveled before they saw it. Every time astronomers built a bigger telescope, what did they see? More stars beyond the millions of stars they had already seen. And what are all those stars doing? Moving away from each other.

Here we are, he thought, we little humans. Crawling around on our little planet, a planet which is going around our sun, an unimportant little star. A speck. And yet, we're always talking to each other about moving. Moving away. Moving on. Moving down the road. But compared to the distance the starlight we see at night has traveled, our movement, no matter if we go all the way around the world, is infinitesimal.

As he stood thinking, Mitzi and her friends came closer. She looked up and realized who was standing on the top step. A look o surprise crossed her face. Obviously, her mother had not told her about his call earlier that day.

"Danny!" she screamed as she broke free of her group and skipped up the steps.

He stepped forward to meet her and wrapped her in a hug. She leaned back from him, and he tried to kiss her. She turned her head aside at the last instant, and he ended up smooching her cheek. It was an awkward moment and very disappointing for Danny. He had been carrying this girl's picture for two years while he dreamed of kissing her.

Mitzi stepped back.

"You look good."

"And you are even more beautiful than the last time I saw you."

"How long have you been in town?"

"Since this morning."

"Why didn't you call?"

"I did. I talked to your mother."

"She didn't hang up on you?"

"I disguised my voice. Fooled her for a minute. When she realized who it was, she told me to leave you alone. Again. Where were you when I called?

"At work."

"Still part-time at Milner's?"

"Nope. Tuesday was our last day of classes, and I've been full-time since Wednesday. Also, been promoted to cashier."

"That's great."

"Yeah, big whoop-di-do. All the other employees hate me because they know I only got the promotion because dad's the manager. I'm probably the only eighteen-year-old cashier in the history of the store, but he thinks I should be over the moon."

"Aren't you?"

"Hardly. I don't want to work in a grocery store in Smoke Tree for the rest of my life, with lunch and two breaks for a smoke and a Coke the highlights of my day."

"I guess I've never thought about it that way."

"Well, I have. A lot. I want out of this place. I want to move to L.A., or even better, Hollywood."

"Hollywood is part of L.A., Mitzi."

She ignored his comment.

"The school play this year was Rebel Without a Cause, and I played Judy."

"Was that a big part?"

"Judy is the female lead. It's the part played by Natalie Wood in the movie."

"You never told me you were in a play."

"I guess I didn't. I was afraid you'd be jealous."

"Of what? Heck, Mitzi, I think it's great you had the lead."

"I mean jealous because of that scene where Judy kisses Jim for the first time. It's a pretty big scene."

"Jim was the male lead?"

"Of course. He's the character played by James Dean in the movie. Don't you go to movies?"

"Movies are at night in the small towns we go to. I work every night of the week, either putting up the carnival or taking it down or working as a talker or fixing something that just broke."

"Well, it's a great movie, and I think Natalie Wood is brilliant. I may be in love with her."

She blushed and turned her head.

"What about James Dean. You're not in love with him?"

Mitzi laughed.

"He's a wonderful actor, Danny, but no, I'm not in love with him."

"Then I'm not jealous."

"Not even if I tell you that Eldon, the captain of the football team, played the James Dean part?"

"Not even if, Mitzi. A play's just a play, and real life is real life."

As they talked, the seniors were climbing the steps and filing past. Some of them glanced at Danny with open curiosity. One boy did a double-take and turned to stare at them.

"Uh-oh. That's Eldon. He doesn't like you."

"That's just what I need. An enemy I've never met."

Mitzi gave an exasperated shake of her head. She seemed to think Danny knew everything that was going on in the enclosed world of Smoke Tree High.

"He's sweet on me, Danny. He knows you and I talk on the phone. Here he comes, and he doesn't look happy."

She turned.

"Eldon, this is Danny Dubois. Danny this is Eldon, the boy I was telling you about.

Danny extended his hand.

"You're that carny. Heard the carnival was in town."

"That's me. But I prefer 'Danny' to 'carny.'"

"You're all the same to me, and I don't shake hand with dirty carnies. What were you telling him about me, Mitzi?"

"About us being in Rebel Without a Cause together."

"Did you tell him about the kiss?"

"Just now."

"That's right, carny, I kissed your girl. Every time we rehearsed."

Eldon winked and leaned forward.

"And opening night, when I kissed her? She kissed me back."

Mitzi laughed.

"In your dreams, sweet pea!"

Eldon stepped closer to Danny.

"You know, I could have been going out with Mitzi all year if not for her mysterious man on the road. I had to settle for second best, and I didn't like it."

"Sorry I ruined your senior year, kid."

"Kid? Why, I oughta punch you right in that smart mouth of yours."

For seven years, Danny had been living the carny life. That meant he had been in his share of scrapes, sometimes with locals and sometimes ride jockeys. In the carny world, challenges were not ignored. Ducking fights invited bullying.

The easy humor went out of Danny's voice. It came out flat, flinty and uninflected.

"I don't see an anchor in your pocket."

Eldon was genuinely puzzled by the phrase.

"What the hell is that supposed to mean?"

"It means if you want to try something, there's nothing holding you back."

As he spoke, Danny had turned sideways. His hands were at his sides, but there was nothing casual about his stance.

To his surprise, Eldon found himself intimidated, but he didn't want to back down in front of Mitzi. He thrust his chin forward and gave Danny his best glare. It didn't work.

Eldon stepped back.

"Ah, if I knock you on your ass, they probably won't let me graduate with my class tomorrow night."

Danny knew the threat had passed. He decided to help Eldon save face and accomplish something for Carlyle at the same time.

"Look, Eldon, I'll fight you or finesse you or run you a foot race, but what I'd really like to do is hire you."

The sudden change of the subject flummoxed Eldon.

"Hire me?"

"Sure. How'd you and some of your friends like to make a bunch of money for a few hours work next Tuesday night?"

"How much money?"

"Let's say twenty-five dollars for about six hours work."

"Doing what?"

"Tearing down the carnival after we close."

"Well, ..."

"And a fifteen-dollar bonus if it's a hot day."

Eldon opened his mouth and then immediately closed it.

He was about to tell me it's always hot in Smoke Tree, but he thought it gave him an edge, just as Carlyle had predicted.

"Forty dollars for six hours work?"

Danny knew he had him. Eldon had factored in the fifteen dollar bonus.

While Eldon knew forty dollars was almost a week's pay at a minimum wage job, he didn't know it would be hardest, dirtiest six hours of work he had ever done. It would actually be closer to seven hours, and it would seem like twenty.

Eldon smiled

"You've got a deal."

"One catch."

The smile left Eldon's face.

"You were just goofing me. I knew it was too good to be true."

"The catch is, I need seven more guys. And I'll give you a five dollar bonus for every one you sign up."

It didn't take Eldon long to do the math on that.

"I'll find your seven."

He put out his hand and Danny shook it.

"Thought you didn't shake hands with dirty carnies, Eldon."

"Hands with money are a whole 'nother smoke."

He walked away.

During the conversation, the entire class had walked by When Eldon left, Danny and Mitzi were alone at the top of the steps The field lights had been turned off, and the weak, yellow light above the door to the girl's locker room was the only illumination.

"Danny, there's something I have to tell you. I wasn't going to but it won't be fair to you if I don't."

"Uh oh, that doesn't sound good. What's his name?"

"Not here. Let's drive somewhere."

They turned and walked toward the parking lot. When they got there, Danny's '42 Studebaker truck and a new Chevrolet Impala were the only vehicles left.

Danny opened the door for Mitzi.

"Still the gentleman, Danny."

"Still."

The inside of the truck was bare metal. There were no door panels and no roof liner. Mitzi looked dubious about the worn ripped and dirty upholstery but stepped onto the running board and climbed inside.

Danny got in the other side and slammed the door. Twice. The first time it didn't catch. He stuck the key in the ignition and pushed the clutch to the floor to mash down the starter button. The engine stuttered and stumbled before coming to life, the muffler roaring and rattling against the frame. Exhaust fumes began to leak into the cab from a hole in the floorboard.

"Got to get moving or we'll die of carbon monoxide poisoning. Where do you want to go?"

"The coolest place in Smoke Tree is down by the river."

"Tell me how to get there."

Ten minutes later, they were on a dark, badly-washboarded road atop a dike that paralleled the Colorado River. Inside the cab, it was noisy as a machine shop in full production.

Leaning toward him, Mitzi shouted loudly.

"Slow down. There's going to be a road that goes down off the dike to the river."

Danny eased off on the gas. The dust cloud rooster-tailing behind them caught up and began to fill the cab with silty dust as fine as talcum powder. He decided the dust was better than the oppressive heat, so he left the window rolled down.

"Right there, through those bushes on the left."

Danny made the turn and plunged off the dike into a ghostly, greenish-gray tunnel of tamarisk.

When the road ran out just short of the river, they were engulfed in dust again. At first, the weak headlights barely penetrated the cloud, but as it settled Danny saw the river, wide and black, ahead of them. He turned off the lights.

The river was moving fast, but Danny could also smell pooled-up brackish water somewhere nearby and the unmistakable odor of alkali. The moon was in the west and lighting a swatch of the dark waters. A great stillness settled around the truck. The only sounds were the river and the ticking of the cooling exhaust manifold. The lack of moving air made Danny sweat even more. He could feel it sliding from under his arms and down his torso.

Not very romantic, he thought. Still, he had been dreaming of such a moment, so he leaned toward Mitzi and started to put his arm around her, his damp t-shirt making an audible peeling sound as it pulled away from the ripped vinyl seat.

Mitzi squirmed away from his arm and scooted closer to her door.

"Talk, Danny. Talk. We came here to talk, remember?"

Feeling chastened and foolish, he leaned away from her. Although a veteran of many sexual encounters in his years on the road, he had zero experience with romance.

"All right, Mitzi. What is it that's so important we have to talk about it right now?"

"Let's get out first. The mosquitos will find us in a minute unless we close the windows, and if we do, we'll suffocate."

"Yours doesn't work anyway. They won't get us outside?"

"Not if we get close to the water. They don't like fast water plus, there's always a little breeze coming off the river. We just don't feel it over here."

Danny got out of the truck and started around to open her door, but she was already out and moving through the soft sand toward the river.

"There's a little point over here. If we walk to the end, we can sit on the big rocks. It'll be a lot cooler."

"Okay."

"But watch for sidewinders. They're out at this time of night."

"Great. Just what we need. Got any more surprises for me?"

"Yes, Danny, I do. A big one."

They walked to the promontory. They followed it to the end and sat down facing each other on two of the boulders that formed the revetment. Danny could hear the gurgle and flow as the fast-moving water collided with the outcropping and swirled out into the main channel. The gibbous moon reflected in the waters looked brighter here, and he could make out the Arizona side of the river. He and Mitzi sat quietly for a while, both of them staring at the water.

"The river is where Smoke Tree people come to escape the heat in the summer. There are beaches in the coves between the points all up and down the river. Jump in at the top of one, float down, get out, lie on a towel for a minute until you're dry and hot. Get up and do it again."

"Mitzi, you brought me here to tell me something. Something important. And it wasn't about how the locals beat the heat."

He turned back to find Mitzi staring at him, her face pale and sepulchral by the light of the moon. He eyes looked sad and haunted.

"I don't know where to start, Danny."

"Well, Mitzi, you're going to have to start somewhere. Just jump right in and let 'er rip."

"I want to start by thanking you."

"For what?"

"For being my boyfriend for the last two years."

"You're welcome, although I haven't been much of a boyfriend. I've enjoyed our phone talks though, when we could have them. Thinking about you kept me going, at times. The road is not an easy life."

Mitzi grew silent again. Twice she started to speak but stopped before she was able to get the words out.

"I'm going to tell you something I've never told anyone."

"Okay."

"I mean it. Not anyone. Not ever."

She hesitated again.

"How are you with people who don't fit the norm?"

Danny laughed. He laughed for so long Mitzi was worried he was making fun of her.

He caught his breath.

"You're asking the guy who travels around with bearded ladies, six hundred-pound fat men, sword swallowers, flame eaters, ride jockeys, hoochie-coochie girls, and an ape woman who sometimes scares people so bad they run out of the tent if he can deal with unusual people?"

Mitzi smiled for the first time since the encounter with Eldon.

"Okay, dumb question. Maybe that makes this easier."

She took a deep breath.

"I don't like boys."

"I don't either. They're rude, crude, crass, messy, and they smell bad. Plus, they pick their noses when they're driving."

"That's not what I mean. I mean, I like boys okay, just not that way."

Comprehension came quickly to Danny.

"Mitzi, I don't want to get you wrong here. Are you saying you like girls, not boys, romantically speaking?"

"I am. That's why I want to thank you for being my boyfriend for two years."

"I'm not sure I get that, Mitzi. If you don't like boys, why did you want a boyfriend?"

"I have always had lots of boy friends, Danny, but never a boyfriend. People were beginning to talk. You gave me an excuse to turn down boys who wanted to take me to a movie. Or homecoming. Or the prom. Or anywhere else."

Danny looked at this girl whose picture he had carried for two years. She was sitting with her knees almost touching his, but the distance between them was suddenly so great she might as well have been on the moon floating overhead.

"The boyfriend people knew about but didn't see. The boyfriend you were so in love with you couldn't go out with anyone else."

"That's right."

"I was a cat's paw."

"What's that?"

"Someone who gets used without their knowledge by someone else to accomplish something."

"Yes, I guess you were, then. I'm sorry."

"Why didn't you just tell me when we talked on the phone?"

"And take a chance my mom or dad would hear me?"

"They don't know?"

"Of course not. I just told you, I've never told anybody else what I just told you. Especially not them, and I hope they never find out."

"Why not? It's part of who you are. You're their daughter. Don't they love you?"

"They love the 'me' they think I am. They would hate the real me. I've heard my dad throw 'queer' and 'faggot' around all my life. My mom doesn't use those words, but I know she agrees with him. Homosexuals and lesbians are evil and must be stamped out before they corrupt Christian America."

"The sticks are full of hicks. Downside of small-town life."

"That part is. You know, I complain a lot about Smoke Tree. I was doing it earlier. But I do it for show. Something to set up my next move. To plant the idea that I can't wait to get away from here. The truth is, Danny, I love this silly little town. I know I'll miss it when I'm gone, but I can't stay here. I just can't."

She started to cry.

"I understand, Mitzi."

Her tears glistened in the pale moonlight. Like a line in a bad ballad, he thought. But his heart went out to her. He realized how terrible it must have been for her, carrying that around. And not just for the last two years. For a long, long time. And carrying it still. Suddenly, his hurt feelings seemed petty.

"You're being too good about this, Danny. Aren't you angry?"

"No. I don't mind the two years. Gave me something to dream about. I certainly didn't have anything else going for me, and I never will as long as I stay with the carnival. That gives me something in common with you."

"I'm not sure I understand."

"You can't stay in Smoke Tree and have the life you want and need, but you love the place. I can't stay with the carnival and have

68

the life I want and need, but I love the show and the people I travel with. In a way, they're my 'place.' They're certainly my family: the only real family I've ever had. I hate to leave them, but I'm going to have to."

"When?"

"I was standing at the stop of the stairs watching graduation practice this evening, and I had a moment..."

He stopped.

"What kind of a moment?"

"I don't know what to call it. A moment of peace? A moment when I suddenly felt... comfortable? I can't really explain it. It's just...for a while, being here felt right. Like I was home. As soon as I felt that, I decided that when the carnival leaves Smoke Tree, I won't be going with it."

"You must have been thinking about this for a while, whether you knew it or not."

"I don't know. Maybe talking to you on the phone. I've never had someone to talk to before who was anchored in one place. All my friends are constantly moving, just like me. But when I talked to you and you told me about what was going on at school and in town, it began to feel special to me. I've been getting the news from Smoke Tree for the last two years.

When I got here today, I realized I have been missing this place, even though I've only been here once before. I missed that old city hall. There's a library there, and I'd like to go there on a hot day and sit and read. And the theater. I'd like to go to a movie there. And I missed the high school, even though this evening was the first time I've ever seen it. Is any of this making sense?"

"Yes, I think I get it."

They sat beneath the moonlit sky and listened to the sibilant run of the river for a while.

"I can see why you'd want to move to L.A."

"More specifically, to Hollywood. I hear they're quite accepting there."

"But you don't want to be an actress?"

"That's my cover story. I don't have the talent. Or the looks. I just want to be in a place where people won't think I'm a freak."

"You might do better in San Francisco."

"I suppose, but I sort of have my heart set on Hollywood. I'm smart in my own way. Maybe I can get some kind of job at one of the studios. Secretary or something. I'd like to be around glamorous people for a while, even though I'll never be one of them. All these years of pretending have made me want to live in a place of make-believe. But how about you, Danny? What will you do in Smoke Tree?"

"Work. I can do lots of stuff. I'm a good mechanic and a welder and a decent electrician. I can machine parts on a lathe. I can fix just about anything. A guy with my skills can always work in a garage or a machine shop. I'll get myself a little apartment. Stop moving. I may not stay here forever, but I'd like to give the place a try."

Mitzi laughed.

"Who do you think you're kidding, Danny Dubois? The way you talk, you're going to be here the rest of your life. You'll probably join the Elks."

"And you, Miss Mitzi, are going to be in Hollywood! Promise me you'll stay in touch. I'll want to know everything you're doing."

They both laughed.

A weight had been lifted from Mitzi. She felt her secret was safe with Danny in a way it would not have been with anyone from Smoke Tree. Sharing her secret with him had eased her fear. For his part, Danny was a little sad. But only a little. He had come to Smoke Tree to meet a lover and come away with a friend.

CHAPTER 11

The Carny and the Charlatan

Friday morning, Danny was up before dawn. When he left the lot in the gray light, the flag was not up at the cook tent. He was dressed in shorts, t-shirt and tennis shoes. Because of the terrible heat, he had not slept well. Although it seemed almost as hot as when he went to bed, he thought a run might shake the cobwebs out of his head. The other carnies thought he was odd for running when he didn't have to, and they would think he was completely insane for running in this heat. One of the ride guys had once told Danny that if he ever saw him running it would mean the police were after him. It would have been funnier without the outstanding warrants.

He jogged south on Front Street to the point where it intersected with Highway 66. Traffic was light on the Mother Road in the pre-dawn, but there were already a few cars trying to get across the long stretch between Smoke Tree and Victorville before the heat reached blast-furnace levels: the kind of heat that splits hoses, boils radiators and vapor locks fuel pumps. He could tell the cars that had come from farther east from the ones pulling out of motels on the south end of Smoke Tree. The cars coming in from the east had their headlights on. The drivers probably wouldn't remember to turn them off when they stopped for gas in Amboy, Ludlow, or Barstow. The service station attendants wouldn't remind them. A dead battery meant the sale of a new one when the driver came back from the restroom. Or at least some money for a quick charge.

At the first break in the flow, Danny darted across the highway and continued to where the road snaked southwest on its way through town. He had no idea where the run would take him. He was simply moving his feet. Although the sun was just now clearing the mountains to the east, he could already feel it burning on his back. The temperature on the big Dr. Pepper thermometer at a service station was hovering near one hundred degrees.

He ran past the revival tent. The three blackened palms on the north side of the lot made an odd contrast with the cross planted out front. The generator was silent, and there were only two people on the lot. They had probably spent the night protecting the equipment. He recognized one of them and waved. The man waved back before pulling aside the tent flap and disappearing inside.

As Danny approached the Swank Motor Court, he realized the preacher was sitting on a metal Adirondack chair outside the first cabin. Danny didn't care for him, so he picked up his pace. The lanky, gaunt, bearded man rose and held up his hand as he came toward Danny. He realized for the first time that the preacher had a slight limp. He was wearing white pants, a tattered, white, long-sleeved shirt, and an L.A. Dodgers cap.

"Carlyle's right-hand man. Good morning."

Danny wanted to ignore him, but he had always found it difficult to be rude.

"I don't know about that."

"That's what he tells me. Says you could run the show without him, and you only twenty years old."

"That's an exaggeration."

"This partnership between the carnival and the cross has been through four stops now, and you and I have never formally met. I'm Jedidiah Shanks, and I know you're Danny Dubois."

He held out his hand. When Danny shook it, he was surprised at how calloused it was.

"You don't much like me, do you Danny?"

"Sir?"

"Come on. Every time I stop by to see Carlyle, you disappear."

"Got work to do."

"No, it's more than that. Is it me personally or is it the religion thing?"

Danny knew he wasn't going to get away without answering the question.

"It's the religion thing, Mr. Shanks. I don't like religious people."

"We should get along just fine then because I'm not religious."

"But you're a preacher."

"Being a preacher and being religious are not the same thing at all. Religious people have beliefs: preachers have occupations. But back to you. Mind telling me what you have against religion?"

Danny shifted from one foot to the other.

"Excuse me, Mr. Shanks, but I'm out for my morning run. Trying to get my engine turning over. Got a busy day today. Opening tonight."

He turned to go, but Jedidiah reached out and grasped his arm. It was like being clamped down on by an eagle.

"One minute, son..."

"Don't call me son! I'm no one's son."

The words rushed out, bitter and hot.

As he saw the reaction in the preacher's face, he realized for the first time there was a deep sadness in the man's blue eyes. It made Danny regret his harsh words. He regretted them more when the preacher apologized.

"Sorry, Danny. Didn't mean to offend you. But listen, now that the sun is up, it's going to be too hot to run without getting sunstroke. But it's not too hot to walk. I walk every day, and I was just about to go. What say we walk together?"

Danny felt like he had to make up for his angry words.

"Sure, Mr. Shanks, but you might want to get rid of that long-sleeved shirt."

"I read that the Bedouin have been wearing long white cotton robes in the Sarah for millennia. They think it's cooler than letting your skin stick out. Thought I'd try it."

Jedidiah moved quickly to his unit and locked the door before joining Danny.

"I'd like to walk by my tent. Then we can get off 66 and away from the noise. I'll bet the town is quiet this time of day."

The two men walked back the way Danny had come. When they reached the corner of Palestine and the highway, Jedidiah waved at the man in front of the tent and called out.

"Everything okay last night?"

"Fine, Jedidiah. Very quiet."

They turned north on Palestine. On the long two blocks between the corner and Nineveh, neither man spoke. Just two men walking: one middle-aged; one young; one almost preternaturally thin, with blond hair, pale, blue eyes, and a beard flecked with gray; one corded with muscle, clean shaven, with hazel eyes and curly, brown hair.

Two men, only one of whom thought he was very different from the other.

The blazing sun, burning fiercely in a sky that was already turning from pale blue to glaring white, was at an oblique angle to the horizon formed by the Black Mountains across the river. It made of the two men a single, elongated shadow that rippled across the lawns of the houses they passed. Sometimes the shadow had four legs, sometimes three. Sometimes two separate heads, one above the other, and sometimes the heads were superimposed, making one conjoined, amorphous blob as the shadow jerked and danced and changed size depending on whether the lawns were even with the side walk, terraced, or fronted by low, block walls.

Once they were across Nineveh, Jedidiah spoke.

"Good town for a revival. Religious street names."

"Yeah."

They walked on, their shadow now interrupted from time to time by the trunks of Chinese Elm or Chinaberry trees, their canopies providing precious shade to the tops of houses but not yet to lawns or the two walkers.

When Jedidiah spoke again, he did so without turning his head toward Danny.

"What turned you away from religion, Danny?"

"Too much Sunday school."

"Come on, don't con a con man. When you told me you weren't anyone's son, those words came out with hatred. Dark hatred."

"Okay, the truth. My father."

"The father whose son you are not."

"Yeah."

"He was some kind of fanatic?

"Among other things."

"What faith?"

"Nazarene."

"With that French-Canadian name, I'd have thought your family would be Catholic; that is, right up until you said 'Sunday school' instead of 'Catechism.'"

"My father hated Catholics. Called them papists."

"So, Nazarene. Evangelical but not Pentecostal. Closer to the Baptists than to The Assembly of God. Believe the Bible is infallible, believe in the Virgin Birth, believe Jesus is the Son of God and will be coming back soon. Believe in salvation through faith, not deeds. All in all, pretty mainstream stuff."

"Not for my father, it wasn't. We lived near Rogers City on Michigan's lower peninsula. Nazarene churches all around. But

74

every one we went to, Dad got in an argument with the pastor about doctrine. By the time he found a preacher he agreed with, it was a three hour drive each way. Up at five on Sunday morning to be at church on time. Stay for evening services. Sit in the car in the parking lot until they started. Last family out the door when they were done. Never got home before midnight. Add in that I got carsick, but if I threw up, I got smacked. Dad would say 'you don't see your mother or your sister throwing up, do you, boy?'"

"Okay, I can see how that would turn you off on going to church. And maybe even religion in general. But Danny, that was fury I heard in your voice. Want to tell me where that's coming from?"

"Are you Catholic, Preacher?"

"That would make me a priest instead of a preacher. Besides, Catholics don't have revivals."

"Reason I ask, you seem to want to hear my confession."

Jedidiah laughed.

"Make you a deal. You tell me about the hatred and why you ended up on the road, and I'll tell you how I got into the revival business."

"You said 'business' preacher."

"I did."

"What about your faith?"

"I don't have any. But I don't dislike religion. It's God I'm angry at."

Danny stopped walking.

Jedidiah turned and came back to him.

"I promise you that any of the sinful things you say or do can be forgiven, no matter how terrible those things are. But if you speak against the Holy Spirit, you can never be forgiven. That sin will be held against you forever. Mark 3:28-29."

"Goodness, you didn't sleep through those services in Michigan. And that's the second time since I got to Smoke Tree I've been accused of blasphemy. Must be something in the water."

Danny started walking again. Jedidiah moved with him.

"I remember, preacher man, that even doubting is a sin. The apostle Thomas refused to believe Jesus had appeared to the other apostles until he could touch Christ's wounds himself. Thomas had to become a martyr to redeem himself. How will you redeem yourself?"

"I won't. You tell me you don't like religion, so I'll give you my take on it. The whole thing is a scam. The Virgin birth, the Resurrection, fishes and loaves, the raising of the dead, all of it."

"I can't believe I'm hearing this from a man who preaches revival."

"Revivals revive, and I have no problem reviving belief in others. When you get right down to it, belief is hope. Hope is good for people. Helps them down the road."

"But not good for you?"

"I have no hope and no belief. Mine died long ago. At first, I thought I was having a crisis of faith. Then I discovered the crisis was that I no longer had faith. Not even enough to hang a crisis on."

"Then what do you have, preacher man, if you don't have faith or hope?"

Jedidiah laughed a rueful laugh.

"I have grief. I carry it with me everywhere I go. It haunts me but it also sustains me."

"Are you an ordained minister, preacher man?"

"I am. Degree in divinity from Duke University."

"Well, for all your blasphemy, you've got the preacher way about you. You invite confidences."

"Considering that I've just admitted to you I'm angry with God and think religion is a scam, facts I don't ordinarily reveal, I could say the same about you, Danny Dubois."

"That's what the girl I found out was no longer my girl told me last night down by the river."

"Mind telling me why she's no longer your girl?"

"She shared something with me, but she asked me never to tell anyone what it was, so I can't."

"This girl, she part of the carnival?"

Danny shook his head.

"Smoke Tree girl."

"You're full of surprises, Danny. Are you like a sailor with a girl in every port?"

"No. Just the one."

They crossed Gilead Street.

"You said I invite confidence, Danny. If that's true, you should tell me the rest of your story. It's obvious there's more."

"Not even Carlyle knows what I'm about to tell you, and I'd appreciate it if you kept it to yourself."

"You have my promise."

Danny took a deep breath.

"As soon as my mother died, my father, the self-righteous hypocritical sonofabitch, started creeping into my sister's room when he came home drunk at night."

"That must have been a heavy burden for a son to bear."

"No preacher, the heavy burden is that I should have stopped him, but I didn't. At first, I didn't even know what was going on. My sister was too ashamed to tell me. But I figured it out."

"How old were you when this started?"

"Nine. I was eleven before I tried to stop him. That's how big a coward I was."

"You weren't a coward. You were a child, and your father was a grown man. And vicious, unless I miss my guess."

"I tried to get my sister to leave, to just run away. But she was too afraid. Had nowhere to go."

"No other family?"

"No."

"Did either of you tell anybody about this?"

"Who would have believed us? People in Presque Isle County mind their own damn business."

"Where's your sister now?"

"She's married. At least she was the day I left, which was the day she got married."

"You left as soon as you thought she was safe?"

"I ran away. Ran all the way to Indiana, which is where I met Mr. Evans and Carlyle."

"You were thirteen, right?"

"How'd you know?"

"Carlyle told me. Tried to tell me they took you on because they thought you'd make a good shill. But we know better, don't we?"

"Yessir. Good hearts, both of them. Carlyle has the better head for business, though. When I first hooked up with the Evans family, the carnival was smaller. A fifty-miler. But Carlyle's dad died of a heart attack when we were back in winter quarters in Noblesville. Within two years, Carlyle had bought out a bigger show, and then another and another, and we went from being a fifty-miler to a hundred-miler to being a stringer through the south, the southwest, and all the way north to Oregon."

Neither man spoke for a while.

"Danny, I don't think you hate religion. I think you hate your father."

"They're the same thing in my mind. When I left home, I decided when I got big enough, I'd go back and kill the bastard."

"But you didn't. You see, you had absorbed more religion than you care to admit."

"That's not what happened. In the winter of 1958, a limestone freighter went down on Lake Michigan. The Carl D. Bradley. Big news. Thirty-three men died. Twenty-nine were from Presque Isle County. One of them was my enemy. Saved me a trip."

"Ever go back to see your sister?"

"Figured seeing me would just remind her of those horrible years after mom died."

They crossed Zion Street and walked on."

"Let's go west at this next corner. Want to see what they named the street that parallels this one."

They turned, enveloped in the increasing desert heat. The sun pushed their elongated shadows directly ahead of them.

"You're a different guy, preacher man."

"Why's that?"

"You listened to what I said. I didn't get the feeling you were just waiting for me to get done so you could talk."

"I can see how you'd recognize that trait in others, Danny since it's one you have yourself. That, and one other. You keep confidences."

"How do you know?"

"Last night your former girlfriend told you something that broke your relationship and maybe broke your heart."

"So?"

"She asked you not to tell anyone. When I asked what she had told you, you said you couldn't say. That means I can trust you too."

"Okay, I've told you all of my story. Now give me the rest of yours."

"You sure you want to hear it? It's pretty long."

"Something to talk about while we walk."

Down the street two houses from the next corner, a woman was watering her small front yard by hand. Jedidiah stopped in front of her house."

"Excuse me, ma'am?"

"Yes."

"Could you spare two thirsty pilgrims a drink from your hose?"

"Be glad to."

She brought the hose to the two walkers. Each drank their fill.

When Jedidiah thanked her and handed the hose back, she looked at him closely.

"You're the preacher having that revival, aren't you?"

"Yes ma'am."

"Saw your picture in the Weekly. Welcome to Smoke Tree. We need us a good revival here. Town is steeped in sin. Men chasing other's men's wives, women wearing bikinis to the river, teenagers fornicating. Why, did you know, preacher, this little town drinks more Coors beer than any small town in California?"

"Do tell. We'll see if we can't bring some of those sinners to Jesus, ma'am. We surely will. I'd be pleased to see you at services. I know you don't need saving. There's no doubt in my mind you've been washed in the blood of the lamb. But even among the devout, a little reinforcement is a good thing."

The woman beamed.

"Thank you reverend. Me and the mister will be there."

The two men walked on.

Danny noticed Jedidiah was smiling.

"What's so funny?"

"I believe that good Christian woman was proud of the thing about the beer."

Danny had to smile too.

"I think she was. But I have a question."

"Ask away."

"How could you talk to that woman about sin and saving souls when you don't believe? Are you really that cynical?"

"Danny, a cynic has been defined as someone who knows the price of everything but the value of nothing."

"That's not you?"

"No, it's not. I know the value of spiritual things. I just don't have them. But I don't begrudge them to those who do. Belief brings comfort, and I like to help people find comfort. I know it's hard living without belief because I do it every day."

"You take their money."

"I don't lie to them when I take it. I don't tell them it's for missionaries or for widows and orphans. I just ask them to dig deep and then have my ushers pass the buckets."

"And do they dig deep?"

"Oh my, yes."

"What do you do with the money?"

"Pay the crew, pay expenses, contribute a few bucks to the local churches so they don't complain about me. Spend a little. Save a lot."

"Save it for what? Pink Cadillacs?"

"That, and for when I'll need it, I guess."

"Okay, you were about to tell me the rest of your story."

"Not long after I was ordained a Baptist minister, World War II broke out. I joined as a chaplain. Some other chaplains and I went to jump school to bond with paratroopers. We jumped from planes in pairs. I was assigned to the 101st Airborne. Guys called me 'Holy Jumpin' Jesus'. Either that or preacher or father or padre. Being an Army chaplain teaches you something about universality. Men *in extremis* don't care whether you're Baptist, Methodist, Catholic, Holy Roller, Jewish, Muslim or Buddhist."

"It must have been hard."

"It was, but thinking of Elisabet Morgan, to this day the girl of my dreams and the girl in my dreams, kept me going. She was so kind, so wonderful, so humble. I loved her with all my heart and tried my hardest to bring her happiness, but in the best of times there was always a little sadness in her eyes."

"What was she sad about?"

"Not about herself. She was sad the world was not honest. Sad there were hungry, helpless children. Sad that somewhere someone was abusing an animal. Sad she could do so little to change things because there were cruel, powerful, arrogant people in the world who thought those with little counted for nothing."

Jedidiah stopped and smiled.

"But I'll tell you Danny, I still remember the first time I ever saw her. It was like Isaac seeing Rachel in the Old Testament."

"Isaac, the son of Abraham who was nearly sacrificed by his father. Isaac, who lived to be the father of Jacob, the man who wrestled with God."

"More biblical knowledge. Good memory!

When I returned from the war, Elise and I married. We wanted to stay in east central Alabama, but there were no Baptist congregations in the area in need of a minister. But the Calvary Church in Opelika needed one. Baptist and Calvary theology are not all that different, and the congregation was happy to have a pastor with a college degree. So, Elise and I settled down in our home town. We loved each other so much that I began to believe I might alleviate her sadness. Especially when, in 1952, we found out she was pregnant. I was the happiest man in Alabama.

I should have known it wouldn't last. No man is allowed that much happiness. Not for long."

Jedidiah sighed and stopped talking.

They arrived at Nod. It seemed appropriate to turn south on Nod. When they did, Jedidiah took a deep breath and resumed his story.

"Elise and our unborn child were killed on a country road by a drunk driver."

"Jesus, preacher."

"Jesus was nowhere to be seen. It took me a while to realize it, but when I answered the phone at the parsonage and an Alabama State Trooper told me what had happened, I didn't just lose my wife and unborn child. I lost my love of God. Whatever God is, wherever God is. Lost that love. Traded it for hatred. I tried to pretend I hadn't, but I think I suspected from the beginning.

Lost my moorings. The love of my life and my faith: the two things that mattered most to me. If one had remained, I might have coped, but neither did. It felt like the ground had fallen away from beneath my feet. The instant my eyes opened each morning, I knew there was no Elise in the world. I dressed and went outside into a world with no Elise. Went to sleep in a chair because I could not bear to get in a bed with no Elise

I could deal with what had happened if I was busy, but when I was alone in our house, I wanted to die. You ever hear a song by Ray Acuff called 'Blue Eyes Crying in the Rain'?"

"Sure. Heard Hank Williams sing it on the radio."

"Nearly wore that record out. Sat in that lonely house and played it over and over again. It was very close to more than I could bear, and I very nearly did not bear it. Wished fervently I had been in that car with Elise. Wished my heart had stopped beating the instant hers had. To this day, I would joyously give the rest of whatever life I have remaining for one more day with her, or one more hour. I began to think about taking my own life. Do you read Shakespeare, Danny?"

"No."

"Well, in 'Hamlet' he writes, 'O that the Everlasting had not fixed His canon 'gainst self-slaughter'. I kept thinking about that line, and I realized I had to get out of that house or I would die in it by my own hand. If I did, someone would have to clean up my mess. I couldn't do that to anyone.

So, I started walking. Miles and miles and miles. Every day, good weather or bad. As I walked, I talked to Elise. She didn't answer, of course, but I liked to think she could hear me, that she was near me somehow. It was the only thing that kept me sane. And as I walked, I asked questions. If God were a loving God, how could He take the best, most loving person I had ever known out of the world? At night I read Kierkegaard's 'Fear and Trembling,' Jean Paul Sartre's 'Being and Nothingness' and Camus' 'The Myth of Sisyphus.'

"Preacher man, I have no idea who those people are."

"They were men who had doubts. The final penny dropped one day when I was in my study. I was punching holes in the typewritten pages of my next sermon with a three-hole punch. I didn't get the pages all the way into the slot before I pushed down the lever, and it only caught the outside edge of the paper. Little quarter moons of paper clung to the paper when I pulled it out. I stood there staring at them. They looked like clippings from a baby's fingernails. Like my beloved Elise would have clipped from the nails of our child had she and that child not been killed in a senseless accident on a country road.

I threw that sermon away and wrote another. I poured all my doubts and rage and agony into it, and I preached it on Sunday. That sermon was not one my congregation wanted to hear. They wanted some comfort and something they could believe in. Wanted a homily before they went home for pot roast and football. The next day, when I came home from visiting Elise's grave, some women were in the parsonage folding up Elise's things. They said I had become obsessed with her death and they were going to take her things away to end my obsession."

"What did you do?"

"Went to the bank and took out my money and walked out of town. Just kept on walking. Never went back. Never will."

"Like me with Presque Isle County."

"Just like."

"Then what happened?"

"Walked for years. All over the place. New England, the Northwest, the Midwest. Everywhere I walked, I talked with my Elise. Talked to her out loud, and damn the people who thought I was crazy. Talk to her still. Every day. That first year on the road, I talked to God, too. Screamed at him. Raged at him. Cursed him. Then, one day, I realized there was no one there. After that, I just talked to Elise.

Picked up work. Washed dishes, bussed tables, pumped gas, worked on tracts of houses being built for the guys with their V.A. loans. Lived on the edges of towns. Barns. Shacks. Abandoned places. They're everywhere. And glory be to the Salvation Army for cheap clothes.

I was lonely. After sundown was the hardest. Sometimes I would go to a movie to pass the time. To be distracted. And it would work, sort of, but when the movie was over, there I was in an empty theater, alone with my sadness and hours to go before dawn. It didn't take me long to strike up a close acquaintance with Kentucky bourbon. I became the worst kind of drinker. I didn't frequent bars

82

I frequented liquor stores. Started drinking when I went out the door with my bottle and kept drinking until it was gone. I was an alcoholic. Still am.

"You hide it well, preacher. I never would have guessed."

"I'm a dry drunk. Haven't had a drink for five years, but I want one every minute. Want one right now."

"What made you dry out?"

"Stopped by a revival in a small town. I was drunk. I was going to confront the preacher about the failings of his God, but the man I met was so kind and good-hearted I could not. We talked so long I began to sober up. I told him about my education and ordination, and he offered me a position with the revival on one condition."

"That you stop drinking."

"That's right. I swore I would. I failed a couple of times, of course, but he was patient. And forgiving. Eventually I got sober. Been sober ever since."

Jedidiah took a long, shuddering breath.

"Lord, I miss it."

"Thought you didn't believe in the Lord."

"Figure of speech, Danny. Figure of speech."

"What became of the preacher?"

"He got old. The schedule and all the travel were too much for him. He decided to quit. He sold me the show: tent, truck, sound equipment and everything else. I paid him off, but I still send him a check every month. After all, he saved my life. Alcohol would have killed me by now for sure if I hadn't met him."

"Did he know you were a non-believer?"

"I think it was so far beyond the pale of his experience, he never suspected."

"I notice you call your revival a show."

"I do. Just like Carlyle's. Carnivals and revivals are both ephemeral things. They run on thin air and illusions."

"You're admitting that you're a charlatan?"

"Absolutely!"

They arrived at the corner of Nod and Gilead.

"Let's go west on Gilead. I want to see what they named the next north/south street."

When they came to Ezekiel, Gilead began to rise.

"Let's see what's up on that hill."

The sun was almost overhead. The heat had passed blistering and moved to ominous. They trudged up the hill, sweat pouring from them. Jedidiah was beginning to feel faint. At the top of the hill, they found Gilead Elementary School.

"I'm not sure whether that's a mirage or a drinking fountain over by that office."

They crossed the parking lot and drank their fill. The water was lukewarm and tasted of alkali, but it was wonderful for all that. When they finished drinking, they laved water over their faces and sat under a tree for a while before returning to the sidewalk.

Looking south from the top of the hill, they could see Smoke Tree and the Colorado River spread out below. The green of the town and the blue of the river stood in stark contrast to the dun-colored desert stretching away on all sides. The desert was so overwhelming the river appeared an afterthought. The town accidental.

"Interesting place."

"It is."

Jedidiah laughed.

"Danny, I've flat talked myself out, and that's not easy for a long-winded, blowhard preacher. I talked you into walking with me so I could hear your story and then told you twice as much about myself. Things I've kept inside for years."

He cocked his head as if searching for the answer to a puzzle.

"Maybe they should change the name of this place from 'Smoke Tree' to 'Epiphany': a place where two strangers can exchange confidences and thereby reach an understanding, each of himself."

"And I'd better get back. I've already missed breakfast. I'll miss lunch if I don't hurry."

They started down the hill at a brisk pace.

"Carlyle said you told him you were going to send people our way during your service last night."

"I did. I called out Jezebel and every other harlot I could think of in the Bible. Said they should all be dancing in your hoochie-coochie. Said the street where the carnival was set up should be renamed Sodom and Gomorrah Avenue."

"I don't see how that will get them to the show."

"Oh, but it will. The whole time I was preaching, I could see men glancing sideways at their wives or girlfriends, trying to figure out how to sneak away to the hoochie-coochie tent."

Danny laughed. "I'll say this for you, preacher man, you know how to chase the early morning cobwebs out of a fellow's head, even if it takes until nearly noon to do it."

CHAPTER 12

Finding Burke Henry

Very early Friday morning, Horse and Chemehuevi Joe were west of the Highway 66 / Goffs road intersection. On a siding south of the highway, soldiers were offloading armored personnel carriers from flatcars.

"Where do you think they're going to take those APCs, Joe?"

"North. South rugged, even for tracks."

"They'll have to stop traffic to get them on the other side of 66."

Joe nodded.

"Road blocks. Marston mats."

"Wonder why they didn't just use that siding at Fenner on Old 66 where they load cattle. Less inconvenience to the motoring public."

"Army doesn't care."

Horse laughed.

"Good point."

Horse turned off the highway onto northbound Essex Road. He slowed and checked to make sure all three of the pickups pulling horse trailers made the turn behind him.

The little convoy moved north. The Clipper Mountains turned on the western horizon as the Old Woman Mountains receded in the south. They were in classic low-desert country: creosote bushes interspaced with white bursage, cheese bush, and brittlebush with the remains of the spring-blooming yellow flowers jutting above the grayish-green leaves on the dried stalks that gave the shrub its name.

Fifteen minutes later, they were beyond the abutment that marked the northern boundary of the Clippers.

"Right about here is where Interstate 40 will be. They're talking about blasting through the Bristol Mountains with nukes. Twenty-two small A-bombs."

"Heard that."

"Part of Project Plowshare."

"In Hiroshima after the war. Japanese, no plowshares."

"Probably not. Hope we don't get any, either."

The Blind Hills began to slide past Joe's window as they entered the Clipper Valley.

"I wish they'd hurry and finish Desert Strike."

"Trouble?"

"All the time. Like that thing back there by the highway. Nobody told me they were going to block 66 today. Obviously didn't tell the CHP either. A colonel I met when this first started, one of the planners with that bunch out by the airport, told me there were seven thousand wheeled vehicles, eight hundred aircraft and one thousand tanks running around out here."

"Nine ninety-nine."

"Nine ninety-nine what?"

"Tanks."

"You counted?"

"Nope. One not running."

"Broke down?"

"Stuck. Drove up Trampas Wash. Narrows, fills with boulders."

"Up there by where we climbed out back in '60 when we were chasing Vickers?"

"Yeah. Tried to turn around. Wedged, big boulders. Half the hill on top of it. Sergeant said lieutenant thought the platoon was in the Stepladders, not the Chemehuevis."

"That's a hundred and eighty degrees off. How could that happen?"

"Shave tail lieutenant. Tried to orient map. Compass next to the tank."

"And the compass..."

"Yeah."

Horse started laughing.

"How are they going to get it out of there?"

"Cutting torch?"

86

Horse laughed so hard he had to wipe his eyes on his sleeve. When he recovered, he said, "Did you ever hear about the time one of Patton's tanks tangled with a train?"

"No."

"September of '42. I was just a kid. You had already joined up gone. Patton's boys were out here training for North Africa. Late one night this convoy of tanks was running blacked-out on Danby Dry Lake. Making a big dust cloud. Passenger train from Phoenix was coming north. Not too far past Rice, the engineer saw the dust, thought it was a wind storm. The tanks couldn't see the headlight on the train through the dust. One of them drove onto the tracks and the train hit it going full clip. Tore the turret and one tread off the tank. Flipped it over. Two of the tank crew were killed."

"Train?"

"Derailed, but stayed upright. The tank was an M-3. Twenty-seven tons. Don't know what would happen if a train hit one of these fifty-ton M-60s. Hope we don't find out."

The land rose as they moved on. Orange-hued desert mallow, at the tail end of its blooming season, began to appear along with shadscale, desert holly and a few scattered patches of struggling Indian rice grass. Just beyond where Black Canyon road came in from the north to join Essex Road, they came to where the powerline crossed Essex Road. Horse took the dirt road beneath the huge metal towers striding across the rocky desert on a northeast to southwest path. In the shallow wash beside the road, the celadon of desert willow and thorn-laden cat claw began to appear, many locked in an endless and losing struggle with parasitic mistletoe.

Soon they were at three thousand feet. It was cooler than the valley below. The dirt road was rough and rutted, sandy in some places and washboarded hardpan in others. The surface demanded much-diminished speed and would barely be passable for the trucks pulling the horse trailers. They reached the short, rocky hill that announced the beginning of the pass between the northern and southern sections of the Providence. Tall, slender yucca often mistaken for young Joshua trees climbed away from the road on both sides.

"This will be the end of the line for the trailers. They'll have to unload and ride from here. How much farther to the cave where we'll find Burke?"

"Beyond the summit."

When Horse glanced into his rear-view mirror to make sure all the trucks were coming, he could see the vast expanse of the Clipper and Fenner Valleys spread out behind them. An area so big it could hold all of Los Angeles and New York City. And yet, there were no more than fifty people living in the entire expanse. To most people, it looked drab at best and forbidding and foreboding at worst. To Horse, it was beautiful.

I love this place, he thought. Never want to live anywhere else.

At the top of the pass, the slender yuccas were more prolific. Ahead of them, the road dipped and rolled and climbed on its way onward toward the distant Granite Mountains. They drove a mile down the hill and came to a north-south drainage crowded with desert willow, catclaw, blackbrush, cholla cactus and varieties of yucca.

"Here."

Horse pulled off the road at the edge of the sandy wash. Just beyond the truck, Joe fashioned an arrow of rocks pointing northeast to let the oncoming riders know which way to go. He pointed up the steep hill.

"Near Finger Rock Spring."

They started climbing through rough country with bad footing. It would take the horses longer to traverse the path than the two men.

Far up the hill near a ridgeline short of the spring, Joe walked to a stand of intertwined blackbrush and cat claw. He picked his way carefully through the thicket of thorns. On the other side of the stand was a narrow opening in the side of the hill. It had been blocked off by rocks.

"Keep out coyotes, buzzards."

There was a canteen in front of the rocks.

Horse picked it up and shook it.

"He didn't drink all his water."

"Came to die. Water outside, walled himself in. Warrior."

"You're one too, Joe."

"Not like this one."

Horse and Joe began to disassemble the piled rocks. As the opening widened, the unmistakable smell of decomposition reached them. When they had moved the rocks aside, they found Burke Henry on his side, his face twisted in agony. His eyes were closed, hands in front of him, fingers knotted together. Joe picked up a rock and gouged a trough in the dirt. Reaching inside his shirt, he drew out a golden eagle feather and buried it. He chanted something in Chemehuevi, a language Horse did not understand.

When Joe finished, the two men knelt side by side for a long time, looking at Burke Henry. Horse was already filled with sadness over the loss of his friend; now despair over his agonizing death engulfed him. He cried silently, tears streaking the dust on his face. He had no idea what Joe was thinking; he rarely did.

The two men stood and threaded their way through the tangle of brush. They moved to a place where they would be able to see the coroner and the riders with the stretcher and body bag ascending the hill.

A dust devil danced across the pass below them.

Neither spoke again.

The sun had not yet climbed high enough in the sky to illumine the undercroft of the warrior, Burke Henry.

CHAPTER 13

Soldiers and Coochie Shows

Danny Dubois could not remember a more successful opening night. It was the soldiers. Hundreds of them poured through the arch, along with a good number of locals. The diamond layout worked. It moved people smoothly along the northwest-trending side of the diamond and on around the west-trending side. As Danny had hoped, when the crowd hit the top of the diamond, it did not head straight for the rides. Instead, people moved around the point and went southeast to see the other food booths and then turned to pass by the games they had not yet seen.

After one and a half turns around the diamond, most of the crowd headed for the rides, but even then, some groups swirled in eddies back to whatever games had interested them most. It was going to be a good night for the jointees and agents.

Danny worked the crowd, making the tips for the hoochie-coochie show. Sometimes a demanding job, on this night it was like shooting fish in a barrel. All he had to do was find a knot of G.I.s and say, 'have you seen the pretty girls they got back there?' Just that opening line got their immediate attention.

"What girls?"

"Dancing girls. Young ones. I'm telling you, I was just back there. They take all their clothes off."

"All their clothes?"

"Every last stitch. Man, you've got to see it to believe it. I'm one my way to see it again."

And off he would go, like little Bo Peep with her sheep, except his flock kept growing. Soldiers following him would see soldiers they knew and tell them about the show. By the time Danny reached the front talker next to the ticket booth, the guy just had to get out o the way so the soldiers could buy their way inside.

There were locals too. Danny wondered how many of them had come because of what the preacher had said on Thursday night These local men were easy to find and lead because they were in bunches. That was usual. It was as if they didn't feel as much like dirty old men if they were in a pack. Most of them were drunk, heads swiveling as they tried to figure out where the naked girls were.

Danny found them long before they found the girls. Found them and led them like the Pied Piper of Hamlin. Except these weren't children. They were men. Men who should have known better. And unlike the children of Hamelin, they would be seen again as they bounced back and forth between the revival tent and the hoochie-coochie show.

Between shows, Danny was free to wander the midway. Hal the lot was dusty with tramping feet. The other half had been so oiled by various petroleum products over the years it put up no dust at all. The dusty half smelled of manure with an undercurrent of the flux used by the blacksmith in his coal-fired forge; the oiled part gave off a chemical odor. Neither odor was appealing, but of the two Danny preferred the manure.

Although he knew what lay behind the illusion, he loved the midway. Loved the noise, the swirling, colored lights, the smell o hot grease and popcorn and cotton candy. The screams of people on the adult rides and the smiles of the little ones on the kiddie rides eyes wide with excitement and wonder.

If the Happy Funfest Show pulled out of Smoke Tree on Wednesday morning and he remained behind, he would miss it. But seeing the children made him realize again how much he wanted to be a daddy; however, he had no intention of hauling a wife and kids around with the carnival. The road would not be a good life for them and when he had children, they were going to come first.

He was worried about telling Carlyle if he decided to stay behind. The Evans family had been very good to Danny. They had taken a considerable risk by letting a thirteen-year-old boy trave with the show. What if his family had been looking for him? Or the authorities? Danny had not made their decision easier by his refusa to tell them where he was coming from or why he was running. They only knew he was desperate.

Carlyle had been like a father to him these last seven years He felt a stab of guilt as he remembered how proud Carlyle had been of his new layout idea. It seemed a lot like the pride a father would feel about a son who was growing into the family business. But, Danny reasoned, children grow up and move away. It happened all the time. He was just going to grow up and stay behind.

Just after nine o'clock, Danny led another easily-corralled crowd to the back corner of the lot where another session of the coochie show was about to get underway. He was heading back to the midway for more people-watching when Carlyle came hurrying toward him.

"The clutch went out on the Tilt-a-Whirl."

"I told that ride jockey to go easy."

"I know you did, but he just had to try to shake some extra change out of the riders' pockets. He'll be spending the rest of our stay in Smoke Tree going deaf from the calliope music at the carousel. I'm pulling him off the Tilt-a-Whirl."

"Why not put him on the kiddy rides? That's the worst you can do to a ride guy."

"Jake's too scary. Mommies would take one look at that ugly, tattooed kisser and yank junior right off the midway."

"Okay. I'll get on the clutch. Better have Billy replace me. He's over entertaining the lines at the food stands."

Danny hurried off to swap his talker clothes for mechanic's overalls.

At ten thirty, Danny was wiping the oil from his hands with a shop rag when he heard a familiar voice.

"Danny, I've been looking all over for you."

Danny turned to see Mitzi with a good-looking young man. One beyond high school age. His first thought was that she had fed him a line the night before about not liking boys.

"Danny, this is Aeden Snow. Aeden, Danny Dubois."

The young man beside Mitzi extended his hand. Danny held his up.

"My hands are greasy. Just finished a job."

"That's okay. Mine are greasy all week. No reason for Friday night to be any different."

The two men shook.

"Aeden's my cousin. College boy, home for the summer."

Danny relaxed.

"Where do you go to college?"

"Cambria. Up on the central coast. Come home to Smoke Tree to dry out."

"Everybody else in Smoke Tree tries to sneak away to the coast in the summer. Aeden comes home to soak up the sun. He's insane, of course."

Aeden shrugged and smiled.

"What year are you, Aeden?"

"A senior, come September."

"What are you going to do when you graduate?"

"The way Vietnam's heating up, I'll probably be drafted."

"Maybe you'll get lucky and be 4-F."

"I played football and ran track the last three years in college. It's hard to believe I'll be lucky enough to flunk the physical."

"Who's more likely to get us in deeper, Johnson or Goldwater?"

"Goldwater won't win, but having him in the election has made Johnson worry about being seen as soft on Communism. That's why we've got twenty thousand troops over there now. Whoever wins, it won't be long before we have a lot more."

"I didn't know that."

"Most Americans don't. I'm surprised you've heard of Vietnam already. It's pretty much been background noise."

It was Danny's turn to shrug.

"My boss reads the New York Times. I read it when he's done."

"When I started hearing about the domino theory, I knew we were in for it."

Mitzi interrupted.

"Okay boys, enough politics. Sounds like the dinner table at my house."

"Who's your dad going to vote for in November?"

"Goldwater, of course. You know dad. Says Goldwater will nuke the Commies."

"He thinks that's a good idea?"

"He says we should have nuked them before they got the bomb."

"What's your dad have to say about Vietnam?"

"Never heard of it, far as I know."

"There you go, Danny."

"Danny, Aeden came to my graduation this evening. When we were talking afterward, I told him you might be looking for work in Smoke Tree."

"Is that right, Danny?"

"Yeah. Do you know of anything?"

"Mitzi says you're a good mechanic."

94

"Pretty good. Just fixed the clutch in this ride. There's hardly a vehicle or generator or ride on this lot I haven't fixed a time or two."

"That's impressive. I work summers at the natural gas pumping plant south of town. Vacation relief for the maintenance crew. The crew keeps the engines and compressors running and does general repair work around the plant. Engines, pumps, valves, that kind of thing."

"What kind of engines?"

"Huge things. Bigger than a semi-trailer."

"How many cylinders?"

"Six."

"Man, those must be some big pistons."

"You could fit inside the cylinder wall. The engines and the compressors they drive are lined up side by side about fifteen feet apart in a big metal building."

"Must be easy to work on. No tight corners where you can hardly fit a wrench."

"Spoken like a true mechanic."

"Sounds like it would be right up my alley."

"There might be an opening. One of our crew members who was on vacation got himself a job with P.G.&E. in a cooler place. He won't be coming back."

"That happen often?"

"All the time. Lots of guys keep an eye out for a job with a different outfit or a transfer inside the company. The heat grinds on a lot of people. Summers are hot enough without working inside a big metal building that has six huge engines running and no exhaust fans."

"Yikes."

"Yeah. Let me tell you my favorite story about heat at the plant. When they built the place, they installed the engines and compressors, built the building around them and got everything up and running before they realized they should have painted all the pipes in the sub-floor first. That meant someone had to crawl around in the space down there and paint all the pipes. Hundreds of yards of pipes. All different sizes and all color-coded.

Since the construction outfit was long gone, the job fell to the maintenance crew. The foreman picked the two newest guys and sent them under there with paint, brushes and a diagram."

"Okay."

"Well, it was July. Hotter than blazes under there, and with only four feet of clearance, not enough room to stand up. The work

95

had been going on for about three days when one of the guys crawled out and headed for the parking lot."

"Where are you going," asked the foreman?"

"Forgot my gloves."

"Where are they?"

"Arkansas," said the man. He drove away and was never seen in Smoke Tree again.

"That's quite a story."

"It is. Not sure if it's true or not. Anyway, the pay is good out there, and so is the job security. Would you be interested?"

"Other than the heat, why aren't people lined up for these jobs?"

"The railroad pays a whole lot better, and the work isn't as hard."

"What are those jobs like?"

"Unless your daddy worked there, impossible to get."

"Then I'm definitely interested in the maintenance crew."

"Okay, I'm going to be out of town tomorrow and Sunday, but I'll be working Monday. I'll talk to my foreman, and he'll probably take it to the plant manager. I should have some news for you by Tuesday night."

"Thank you, Aeden. I really appreciate this. Where you headed for the weekend?"

Mitzi spoke up.

"Cousin Ade's a little weird. Every weekend since I can remember, he's been hiding out in the desert mountains about an hour and a half from here."

CHAPTER 14

The Calm Before the War

Saturday and Sunday were stand-down days preceding the start of the mock-combat phase of Joint Operation Desert Strike. The final off-loads of tanks, armored personnel carriers and other military vehicles would be complete on the Santa Fe and Union Pacific by Sunday morning. Once the mock combat began, re-supplies would be done by air only: helicopter, parachute drop or rough landings on crude airstrips gouged out of the desert.

On Saturday morning, Master Sergeant Yannity Scanlon drove his jeep over to Bravo Company and had a talk with the armorer, Spec 4 Sidney Salazar.

"Remember that modified 14A1 you showed me in garrison last month?"

"Sure do, Sergeant. Proud of that project."

"Did you bring it along?"

"I did. Wanted to see how it would work if I ran blanks though it."

"Perform okay?"

"Never missed a beat."

"I want to borrow it from you for a day or two."

"Okay. You want it right now?"

"Tomorrow, early. And I want you to make me some drawings and write a description of how you did the modification."

"That would take a while."

"Hundred and fifty bucks in it for you, Sidney."

"That's almost a month's pay. I'll stay up all night if I have to."

"That's my man. And this stays between you and me, got it?"

"Got ya."

"I mean it. Not a peep. Have the gun and the plans wrapped in a poncho when I come by."

"Wilco, Sergeant Scanlon."

Later that afternoon, Scanlon and Gould pulled into Smoke Tree ostensibly for turnbuckles and sledgehammers. They carried a requisition signed by Major Ricks. The major had been dubious about the order before Sergeant Scanlon explained the need.

"They're going to parachute in that 101st Airborne battalion."

"What's that got to do with turnbuckles?"

"Means more command tents, more tents for field kitchens."

"So?"

"Sir, I know those airborne guys. Great at fast deployment, not so great at long-term logistics. They won't have enough turnbuckles or sledgehammers, and there will be helicopters landing near their command tents. If they don't want their tents uprooted and blown all the way to Barstow, they'll need more. I'll have them. Their supply sergeant will be under the gun. Be willing to trade all kinds of equipment we can use here in brigade. We'll be on top of Command Maintenance Inspections for years after this. Guaranteed."

Major Ricks smiled.

"As usual, sergeant, you're ahead of everybody else. Go ahead to town, but stay away from that USO show."

"What USO show, sir?"

"More realism. Just like World War II and Korea. They're bringing in singers, comedians, dancing girls, the whole ball of wax. Putting the show on at the high school football field. But it's only for the headquarters troops out at the airport."

"Well, that is like the real thing. The REMFs get the goodies and the grunts eat dirt."

When Sergeant Scanlon drove away, Major Ricks had that slightly-used feeling he always got when dealing with his senior NCO. Still and all, the man got the job done. Lord knows he could cockroach supplies and parts like no supply sergeant the Major had ever known.

Sergeant Scanlon directed Gould to pull in at the West End Shell and Diner again. When they went inside, the waitress was very glad to see them. Big tips work magic in small town diners.

"Well, hello again, Sergeant."

"Hi, Debbie."

"Anyplace you like."

The two soldiers moved to the same corner booth as before. Gould ordered the same meal he had the last time. Sergeant Scanlon wanted only a milk shake.

"I'm going to hit the head, Sergeant."

Perfect, thought Sergeant Scanlon.

As soon as Gould left the table, the sergeant walked to the counter.

"Yes?"

"Same as the other day, Debbie. Change for a ten. Feed the kid. Don't make my milkshake until I come back in. If the kid asks where I went, tell him I had to make a phone call and said for him to wait in here for me. Give him these two quarters for the juke box. Flirt with him a little. Kid's a sucker for a pretty face. Your help means an even bigger tip than the other day."

Debbie beamed.

"You got it, Sergeant. I'll make that boy feel real special."

After Debbie handed him his change, he went outside and lined it up on the shelf in the booth. He dialed Sammy Spinelli's number.

"Yeah."

"It's me. What have you got?"

Sammy read off a number.

Sergeant Scanlon hung up and crossed off the first and last number he had written down before adding one to each of the remaining numbers.

He dialed the decoded number.

"Mazzetti."

"Yannity Scanlon. I was given this number by the friend who told you I'd be calling. He said I should tell you I'm the guy with the toys you wanted."

"Give me the phone number you're calling from."

"I'm calling from a phone booth in Smoke Tree."

"You damn well better be in a phone booth. Give me the number."

The sergeant read it off. The line immediately went dead. He pressed down on the receiver hook and got ready to look like he was having a conversation if anyone walked up to the booth.

It was fifteen minutes by his olive-drab plastic watch before the phone rang.

"Hello. The toy man speaking."

"You can cut the code crap. But let's make this quick. It's hot in this booth."

"Mr. Mazzetti, you and I have a great opportunity, but we have a very short window to take advantage of it. In four days, I'm going to be able to lay my hands on fifty fully-automatic rifles. Rifles that I will be in a position to render unaccountable."

99

"Wait a minute. I'm roasting my ass off to talk to a guy wants to sell me Army rifles?"

"That make you nervous?"

"No, but you must think it makes me stupid. I'm looking for a number of automatic weapons for a certain very important figure because of some possibly-coming unpleasantness, but what makes you think this man wants his guys walking around with Army rifles? Maybe you could get us a few mortars or a bazooka or two while you're at it. Jesus. If you're the best the Army's got, the Commies will be on Main Street before breakfast."

The sergeant smiled. He loved this guy's Chicago accent.

"I don't think you're stupid, Mr. Mazzetti, and I don't think your important figure is either. I'm assuming that would be Tommy Bones."

Eddie Mazzetti was temporarily speechless. He squeezed the receiver so hard it made his fingers ache.

"Where did you hear that name?"

"I grew up in Cicero, Mr. Mazzetti."

"Okay, okay, so you know your way around the pasta patch. That still doesn't mean I want to deliver a bunch of Army rifles to the party in question."

"These can be modified. It's simple, and I have the plans for the modification. Any gunsmith can do the work. I think I'm right in assuming Tommy Bones knows a few. I also have one rifle that has already been modified, and I'm willing to demonstrate it."

"I'm getting a little more interested, but I'm not convinced yet."

"It can be carried on a shoulder strap under an overcoat. Completely undetectable. No visible outline. The weapon, which is only twenty inches long, can be pulled up and fired in one motion. Twenty rounds in two seconds. Additional magazines carried in the overcoat pockets. Eject the spent magazine, slam in a new one in less than three seconds."

"What caliber are these magic guns?"

"7.62 millimeter."

"What's that in real life?"

".308."

"Ammunition and magazines included?"

"Magazines with the first delivery. Two hundred rounds for each gun to be delivered separately."

"Where can I see this gun?"

"Well, I think it's best we don't test fire it in your parking lot. Can you come to me?"

Eddie Mazzetti was silent again for a few seconds.

"I'm sure as hell not interested in coming to Smoke Tree. Or anywhere in San Bernardino County. How about somewhere on my side of the state line?"

"That can be arranged. Are you familiar with Searchlight?"

"Yeah."

"There's a road that goes southwest out of town. State Route 164. Goes to a place called Nipton."

"Okay."

"The state line between Nevada and California cuts across that road. I can meet you just over the line."

"That might work. When do you want to do this?"

"Tomorrow for the demonstration. I'll have the fifty guns in my possession on Wednesday, but there will be too many troops around for me to deliver them. A week from tomorrow for delivery and payment."

"Okay. See the gun tomorrow. What time?"

"Early morning. Let's say seven o'clock. All the troops out here will be on stand down for church services. No military aircraft flying in the morning, but recon flights will start up again at noon. They'll be taking pictures. We don't want to end up on Candid Camera."

"Where do we meet on that road?"

"I'll be in my jeep a couple miles past the Nevada State line. What kind of car will you be driving?"

"Chrysler 300. Black."

"Be there or be square, Eddie Mazzetti."

Smart mouth, thought Eddie. See how smart you feel after you meet a couple of the boys.

A few minutes after Sergeant Scanlon left the booth, he and Gould were on their way to pick up turnbuckles and sledgehammers.

CHAPTER 15

Seeking Guidance

Saturday morning just before sunrise, Danny knocked softly on Jedidiah's motel room door. Jedidiah came to the door with a cup in his hand.

"This is a surprise. What can I do for you, Danny?"

"I know it's early, but I thought you might be up. You strike me as a man who walks every day. If you're going this morning, I'd like to come along. I learned yesterday that talking comes easier when I'm walking. I've got some things I need to talk through, and I also need your advice."

"I'd appreciate some company. Would you like some Earl Gray tea before we go? It's made with tap water, so it's not real hot."

"Thanks, but I'll pass. As bad as the water is here, I can't imagine it makes a great cup of lukewarm tea."

"It doesn't, but I have to have something other than water in the morning. It used to be the hair of the dog to ease me past my hangover and into another day. If I don't drink something as soon as I get up, I start thinking about finding a liquor store. Let me dump this in the sink."

"I'll wait in the truck."

Jedidiah looked past Danny into the parking lot.

"You didn't run here this morning?"

"We're going to drive to our place to walk today. Up by the high school. Some nice streets up there where you can see even more of the valley, but it's too far to walk there and back before the sun burns a hole through us."

Ten minutes later, they parked the truck on Broadway at the point where Canaan Loop rose in a westerly direction. As they climbed Canaan, the sun crested the horizon above the mountains across the river. The temperature began to rise. They walked without speaking until they reached Smoke Tree High School. The parking lot was filled with military vehicles, and more were arriving. They walked on.

They passed a series of residential streets but stayed on Canaan Loop until it curved south before merging with Jordan Street and turning due west. They came to Reclamation Road, which cut to the north and ended in two streets lined with houses and cottonwood trees. They stayed on Jordan.

"I'm not ready to start back yet, preacher, if you're not."

"No, Danny, I'm fine. But you're eventually going to have to tell me what's on your mind, or we're going to run out of town and walk into the desert. Whatever you want to talk about, being out there where there's no water won't make it easier. I know, I was out there the other day. Darn near killed me."

"Okay, here's my problem. I want some advice on how to talk to Carlyle about something without hurting his feelings."

"That shouldn't be too awful hard. The man thinks you hung the moon, you know."

"That's why this will be so hard."

They continued on for a while before he spoke again.

"Preacher, I'm strictly a small-town boy. Don't like big cities. Never have. Never seen the charm of a place where people are afraid to talk to you. Heck, afraid to even look right at you."

"Go on."

"I like this town. I don't know why, exactly. Just something about it. I know most people would say it's a hell hole, especially in the summer, but I like it anyway. It's the feel of the place. And the people. I saw a lot of nice people last night on the midway. Of course they weren't the ones I was working with."

"Oh? What were you doing?"

"I was making the tip for the coochie show."

"Danny, I don't speak carny yet. I know what the coochie show is, but what is the tip?"

"Sorry. It's the crowd. The marks."

"I see."

"I'm talking about the families I saw at the carnival. And the town itself."

"For example."

"The other night, I was at Smoke Tree High graduation practice to meet up with my now ex-girlfriend. Maybe it was just the time of day, I don't know. The sun was going down behind those mountains ahead of us there, and for a minute the whole valley was filled with this kind of rose-colored light. And while it was that color the seniors were walking toward me across the football field on the

104

bright green grass. All of a sudden, I could imagine a Friday night football game there, you know? I'll bet football is pretty big in a little town like this. People in the stands cheering for the home team. Cheerleaders jumping up and down and the band playing and the pom-pom girls dancing and...

Ah, I'm not explaining this very well, am I?"

"You are, Danny. You're longing for something. Something you missed when you ran away from home. I'm not sure it's here in Smoke Tree, but I'm sure you're looking for it. Looking for a town where people smile and say hello to each other and there are rose-colored sunsets and bright green grass and young people full of hope. A town where friends and families matter. That's the heart of it."

"It is. I mean, in a way the carnies are my family, but in a way they're not. They come and go, you know. And a lot of them, the ride jockeys especially, are actually running away from family. Just like I was. But they're not running toward a new one. They're just running down any road that leads away from where they were."

"What you're telling me is, you want to settle down somewhere. Put down roots."

"Yes. I'd like to get my own place; one that doesn't have wheels. And maybe meet a nice girl and get married someday. Have a bunch of kids and take them to the river for picnics or swimming or fishing. I may have a chance to get a good job here. I talked to my ex-girlfriend's cousin last night. He says I might be able to get on as a mechanic where he works."

"You're afraid to tell Carlyle that?"

"Carlyle thinks people who aren't on the road three quarters of the year are squares or marks or something. He calls them citizens. Citizens generally look down on carnies, but what they don't know is the carnies look down on them right back."

"Danny, I think maybe deep down inside there's probably a little part of Carlyle that once wanted what you want. But he never got it. Sometimes, we make fun of what we can't have."

"Like you making fun of that woman who was going to come to your revival."

"What do you mean?"

"Well, she has something you used to have but can't anymore. Some kind of simple belief. Not something she learned at divinity school. Something she just feels in her heart of hearts."

Jedidiah walked a few steps before he answered.

"You know, kid, for a carny, you're a pretty sharp cookie."

They continued to walk west up Jordan Street until they reached Cross Street, a street that bled into Jordan.

"Another religious-themed street name."

"Maybe. But maybe someone had a sense of humor and gave it that name because it's a cross street. Remember that street we saw yesterday that ran on an angle? Well, it was Angle Street. Maybe we've run out of religious street names for a while."

Jedidiah was right. They soon reached Rio Vista. They had been walking for a long time without a drink, and when they turned east onto the street, the blazing sun was suddenly bleaching the color out of the sky directly in front of them.

"I see the ticky tacky boxes have reached even Smoke Tree."

"What's a ticky tacky box?"

"Stucco house. It's from a song by Malvina Reynolds. Came up with it when she saw tract homes in Daly City, up by San Francisco. Called them little boxes made of ticky tacky. Sang they all looked the same except for the colors."

Danny thought about it.

"She's right. I like the houses in the old part of town better."

"Me too."

They began looking for anyone who might be outside so they could ask for water. At the corner of Rio Vista and Desert, they came across a man sitting in a lawn chair and spraying a small patch of Bermuda grass.

"Pardon us, sir, but could we trouble you for a drink from your hose?"

The man got out of his chair and walked toward them, careful to keep the hose turned away.

"Did your car break down?"

"No sir. Just out for a walk."

"A walk, huh? Not many walkers this time of year in Smoke Tree. Give me a minute and I'll get you something better than hose water."

Dragging the hose, he walked to the door and called through the screen.

"Doris? We've got two walkers out here who looked pretty parched. Could you bring out a couple glasses of sun tea?"

He turned back toward the two men.

"Doris wants to know if you want mint, lemon, sugar or some combination of those things."

"Mint and sugar," said Jedidiah.

"Lemon," said Danny.

106

The man turned back to the screen door and relayed the orders before calling to Danny and Jedidiah again.

"Doris wants to know if you'd like to come in."

"Oh, no sir. Too much trouble."

The man turned off the water.

"Well then, let's get you in some shade. This time of morning, that little holly oak over there casts enough shadow to keep you out of the direct sun. Go on over, and I'll be right there."

Jedidiah and Danny walked over and stood in the shade of the small tree. Jedidiah examined the leaves.

"The bark looks like a holly oak, but these leaves don't."

Their host appeared beside them with two lawn chairs.

"It's the heat. The leaves are smaller, more pointed. Reduces the surface area. Save water, absorb less light. Everything out this way adapts to the heat. Adapts or dies."

He arranged the chairs side by side and retrieved the one he had been sitting on.

"Odd thing about this heat. If the humidity is low, like today, when you step inside the shade line, the temperature is ten to fifteen degrees cooler."

"What if the humidity is high?"

The man shook his head.

"Then it's Katy-bar-the-door. Most folks have swamp coolers. Price of electricity is too high to run a big air conditioning unit. When the humidity goes up, swamp coolers don't work. Can't move the air. It just gets damp, and hot. It can be mighty miserable for a few days when the monsoon clouds reach us in August. And if it actually rains? You can see the steam rising off the desert almost as fast as the rain is coming down. Feels like being in a steam bath."

As he was speaking, the screen door opened and a smiling woman in her fifties came across the lawn toward them carrying a tray with three glasses of tea. The melting ice tinkled as she approached.

"That one there is mint and sugar," she said with a nod of her head. "And that one is lemon."

Jedidiah and Danny rose to their feet and picked up their drinks.

Their host also stood,

"Gentlemen, this beautiful lady is Doris. If there's a better heart west of the Mississippi, I haven't come across it."

Doris looked embarrassed."

"Don't mind him. He always says that."

107

"And always mean it. And I'm John, by the way. John England."

"Jedidiah Shanks, Mr. England. My walking companion here is Danny Dubois."

John took the third glass of tea off the tray. As he did, he slapped his forehead.

"Doris, I forgot to bring you a chair. Let me get you one."

"No, John, I've got too much to do inside. I want to get caught up before we take the boat to the river. Nice to meet you both."

"You too, ma'am. And thanks for the cold drinks. They are much appreciated."

Doris nodded and turned away. John, Jedidiah and Danny maneuvered to settle in the lawn chairs without spilling the cold drinks.

"Don't think I've ever seen either of you gentlemen here in Smoke Tree before. Of course, I don't know everyone in town. But pretty near."

"We're out of towners."

"From?"

"Opelika, Alabama."

"Thought you might be from the south when you asked for mint and sugar. And you, young man?"

"Noblesville, Indiana."

"And you both wound up in Smoke Tree. I swear, I sometimes think half the country has been through this little town, and the other half is on its way. Well, welcome to you both. Going to be in town a while?"

"My young friend here is thinking about living here."

"Is that so? Did work bring you to town?"

"No sir. I came with the carnival, but I'm thinking about giving up the road life and settling down."

"Well, it's a fine place. Just fine. Friendly people who'll make you feel welcome. Little hot in the summer, as you may have noticed but beautiful in the fall and spring and not too cold in the winter."

"What about you, Mr. Shanks. Will you be staying?"

"No, I'll be moving on."

John smiled.

"That puts you in the majority. Few stop. Fewer stay."

Fifteen minutes, a lot of questions and another glass of iced tea later, they were back on the sidewalk retracing the route that had brought them to the England's yard.

"See what I mean, preacher? There's something about small towns. That would never happen in St. Louis or Cincinnati or New York City."

"You're right, it wouldn't. But there are some who would think John England went beyond being friendly to being nosy."

"I think it's nice when people are interested in their neighbors and newcomers too."

CHAPTER 16

Ground Rules

Just after noon on Saturday, Horse was waved through the temporary gate at the airport by an MP. The runway was crowded with helicopters and light, fixed-wing aircraft. The UH-1D choppers with their turbine engines were much sleeker than the 'giant grasshopper' piston-engine versions of Horse's Korean War experience.

He parked his cruiser near a large command tent. The sign planted in front of the entrance read "G-3".

There were two more MPs in front of the tent.

"I'm here to see Colonel Dulac."

"Is he expecting you?"

"No, but he knows me. I'm Captain Caballo, San Bernardino County Sheriff's Department."

"One moment, sir."

The MP ducked inside the tent.

He came back out and held the flap aside for Horse.

"The specialist will help you."

When Horse went inside, he noted the damp, musty odor of swamp cooler pads. A row of them sat on wood pallets at the far end of the tent, pushing cooler air forward. The generator that supplied the power was roaring some distance away.

The Specialist, a rank that hadn't existed when Horse was in the Army, was sitting at a portable field desk just inside the tent.

"The Colonel is expecting you. Have you been out here before?"

"First time."

The Spec-4 stood and pointed.

"Halfway down the tent, on the right side there, you'll come to an office sectioned off by canvas. The Colonel's there. Go right in."

The specialist watched the ramrod straight man carrying the Stetson walk away. That's what Texas Rangers must look like, he thought.

Horse walked deeper into the tent. He saw junior-grade officers and enlisted men of all ranks working at various tasks, most involving maps. As he drew closer to the center of the tent, the breeze from the swamp coolers grew stronger. He noticed that soldiers had piled rocks on top of files and maps on their desks to keep them from blowing away.

Horse found the office formed by tarps suspended from overhead cables. He pulled the front tarp aside and stepped inside. It was at least fifteen degrees warmer. None of the cold air was penetrating the canvas forming the Colonel's office. A lieutenant and a sergeant were sitting at separate desks. Both had sweated through their fatigue shirts.

The Colonel had the biggest desk. A huge, laminated map was suspended behind him. Unit designations were marked on it in black grease pencil. There were red arrows showing troop movements. The Colonel got to his feet.

"Captain, pleasure to see you again."

"Likewise, Colonel."

"Please, sit down."

Horse pulled up the rickety, olive drab folding chair. He sat and propped his hat on one knee.

"What can the United States Army do for the sheriff's department?"

"Share more information."

"Sorry?"

"Let us know more about the things you're doing that will have an impact on civilians. Sometimes, we can help. But, more importantly, sometimes we can head off questions and inconvenience for the people who live out here or are traveling through."

"For example."

Yesterday, I was in Essex. Troops were unloading APCs of flatcars on the siding out there. They were going to drive them across 66 to go north. I know your men put something over the road to keep the tracks from damaging the highway, and we appreciate that. But the point is, once those vehicles started crossing the highway, traffic was going to be backed up for miles.

If you had let me know, I would have contacted the Highway Patrol, and the patrol and my department could have assisted. Maybe made up some signs to explain what was going on. People

112

like to be informed, Colonel. Cuts way down on irritation and phone calls to my office when military personnel and civilians bump up against each other."

"We have a public information officer."

"And we both know he's here to do eyewash for the newspapers and television stations. Anytime you close down a highway, a little advance notice would be helpful."

He paused a moment to collect his thoughts.

"Sir, let me put this as diplomatically as I can. Americans love the military as long as they don't come in contact with it. They gladly allow a huge chunk of their taxes to support it. However, that doesn't mean they will tolerate the military inconveniencing their everyday lives unless they are told what's going on. I know, because they call my office at all hours of the day and night wanting to know what the soldiers are up to. They seem to think I have some kind of hotline to the Supreme Commander of Joint Exercise Desert Strike."

"What do you propose?"

"Assign a lieutenant to keep me informed"

"You said a lieutenant, Captain Caballo. Why not a sergeant?"

"Sir, you know and I know who actually does the work in this man's Army, and it's not the lieutenants, captains, majors or lieutenant colonels. It's the sergeants."

The Colonel smiled.

"I notice you did mention full-bird colonels."

Horse smiled back.

"Diplomacy, sir."

He reached in his shirt pocket.

"Here's a few of my cards. Might want to give them to whoever you assign to this function. I've written my home number on the back of each one. I don't mind being called at night if something important to people of Smoke Tree comes up. They rely on me."

"Your point is well taken. I'll assign someone the task."

"Be much appreciated, sir. For right now, will there be any more of this off-loading near the highway?"

"Late tonight and early tomorrow morning will be the last of it. One load on the Union Pacific line and one on the Santa Fe. The Union Pacific shipment will unload near Kelso."

"Certainly no traffic out there."

"The Santa Fe shipment is jeeps and trucks. Nothing tracked. It's coming all the way into Smoke Tree and will be unloaded in the rail yard. Anything else?"

"Yes. What's going on up at the high school? I'm getting calls from the neighborhoods up there. Military vehicles, including buses parked everywhere."

"Oh, that. It's a USO show. Touch of realism for the joint exercise."

"I see. Troops coming in from the field?"

"No. Just troops from the command centers here in town."

Horse laughed.

"That's real enough. Rear echelon guys get the entertainment. Front line guys get dust and C-rats."

The Colonel smiled.

"You've been in the military, Captain?"

"Korea."

"What unit?"

"Second Infantry Division."

"Indianhead. Good unit. Covered the strategic withdrawal o the Eight Army to the south. Saved it from annihilation."

"Was there for that."

Colonel Dulac looked at Horse with new respect.

"Is there anything else I can help you with, Captain?"

"If you have time, I'd appreciate a quick summary of the major events of the next few days?"

"Certainly. Stand-down tomorrow. Religious services in the morning and readiness evaluation in the afternoon. That extends to military aircraft. None of those annoying sonic booms as the reconnaissance flights go over until after noon."

"So that's what that's been about. I see flashes in the sky a night, too."

"Nighttime recon. Taking pictures."

"How do they get the photographs to you?"

"The film is in canisters. Parachute it onto the south end o the airstrip here."

Horse's curiosity was aroused.

"How good are those pictures?"

"The nighttime ones, not so great. But the ones taken in daylight? Read the name tag on a man's uniform."

"That's impressive. What happens after the Sunday stand down?"

"0400 Monday morning, the forces of Nezona are going to cross the Colorado River in a number of places between Davis Dam and Topock and invade Calonia."

"How will they do the crossings?"

114

"With temporary bridges put in place by the combat engineers and motorized barges."

"That's got to be difficult on a river that runs as fast as the Colorado. I'll get the word out to the marinas. The schools in L.A. got out this weekend. Vacations are starting. That means there will be a lot of people on the river from now on. Don't want any of your lads garroted by a tow rope pulling a water skier. Don't want a ski boat to run into a tank, either. Dawn is the favorite time for skiers. River is smooth as glass then. Anything else?"

"Part of the war against Calonia is a psy-ops campaign. There will be leaflets dropped all over Smoke Tree as the river crossings start."

"That should make our phones ring."

"There won't be any soldiers in town on Monday or Tuesday unless they're rolling through in a convoy. None of the people from up here will be allowed out of the airport area. Too much to do.

And here's something you might find interesting if you've got time to see it, even though it won't have an impact on Smoke Tree. Three mechanized infantry battalions that are part of the 22nd Armored Brigade are going to be supplied with the Army's new rifle, the M-16."

"By truck or rail?"

"Neither. That's the interesting part. They're going to come in via a touch-and-go airdrop by a C-123."

"Where will it happen?"

"Near Hayden siding, a little north of Kelso. A combat engineer battalion built a temporary airstrip out there."

"I heard there were a few of those on the desert."

"This one is more sophisticated. It's the only one built this way. After it was bladed, the engineers coated it with oil and then laid down a granulated asphalt they made out of oil, tar, and rock, sand and gravel they mined on-site. A C-123 could land on it, but the strip's not long enough for it to take off again, so the Air Force crew has strapped everything on pallets. The plane will come in with the ramp partially lowered and the crew will shove the pallets out the door as the plane touches down on the runway. The plane will just keep rolling. Chutes attached to the pallets will open and slow them down as they come out of the cargo bay so they don't splatter all over the desert."

"That sounds tricky."

"It is. And not just for the pilot. You wouldn't want to be on the wrong side of one of those pallets when the chute inflated. Take you right out the door with it."

"When is this happening?"

"It's scheduled for Wednesday at noon."

"I doubt I'll be able to get away, but I'll try. I'd like to see that Just out of curiosity, what's going to become of the M-14s the troops have now?"

"You'd have to ask G-4. I'm sure there's a plan."

"There's always a plan, Colonel. They just don't often work as advertised."

"I see you remember General MacArthur."

"Among others."

The Colonel went on.

"One more thing. I'm not sure exactly where or when it will happen, but a battalion of the 101st Airborne Division is going to parachute in. Men and equipment both."

"I hope you scout out a cholla-cactus-free zone for those boys to come down in."

"We'll do that when we know where it's going to happen. By the way, those APCs you saw being offloaded belong to the 22nd Armored Brigade. It's the one that will be re-supplied with the new rifles. It'll be held in reserve on the west side of the Providence Mountains and may be deployed to plug any holes when the mock combat heats up.

"One more question."

"Go ahead."

"You seem to know what both sides are doing. Doesn't that mean you can control who wins and who loses?"

"This shop is the observer. I oversee the operation for the General. Planning for the Nezona and Calonia forces takes place in separate tents under separate commands right here on the airfield. Both forces report their plans to me for analysis. I brief the General so he knows what both sides are doing at all times. Obviously Calonia does not know what Nezona plans to do, and vice-versa.

That's why the MPs are out front. Intelligence sections from Nezona and Calonia would love to get in here for a look at the map behind me."

CHAPTER 17

Have Another Drink

Smoke Tree has always been a town that likes a drink. Likes several of them, in fact. Especially on a Saturday night. Over the years, many hare-brained schemes have been born late on Saturday nights in the local bars.

The least outrageous plans seem to emanate from the Palms on Front Street, the oldest saloon in town, with its autographed murals of Lefty Frizzel and Hank Williams. Perhaps that's because the Palms serves only beer and wine, or perhaps it's because of Mac, the retired Marine Gunnery Sergeant who owns it. His stoic, non-nonsense approach to life seems to carry over to the line of stool-occupying beer drinkers who mostly spent their time cracking salted peanuts from the bowls that line the bar and trudging morosely to the restroom and back, their drink of choice burdening their kidneys more than stoking their imaginations.

The Boxcar, the Derail, the Highball, the Shoofly and the Rusty Spike, however, all serve hard liquor. Lots of it. Mixed, cut with soda, or straight up with a beer back. Sometimes, as midnight on a Saturday approaches and the cut-off for drinks looms a little more than two sad, short hours away, those who have spent their night dropping Jim Beam or Jack Daniels depth bombs into their schooners of Olympia, Hamms, or Coors begin to convince themselves that the truly outrageous and sometimes downright dangerous plans they have concocted are actually within the realm of possibility.

While many famously demented designs have emerged from those bars over the years, the record for lunatic ideas has always been held by the long bar at the Oatman Hotel in the Black Mountains of Arizona. The hotel itself has two claims to fame. First it is the oldest adobe building in Mohave County. Second, it was the honeymoon choice of Clark Cable and Carole Lombard. In fact Gable had liked the place so much that he often returned from Hollywood to play poker with the miners

But the bar that is located just off the lobby is famous in its own right as the place that has taken Mojave Desert insanity to its highest levels. Maybe the madness results from inhaling the blended odors of diffused burro dung and the coal oil burning in the lamps that illuminate the mining shacks dotting the hillsides of the town. Shacks that were abandoned early in the century. Shacks that lack not only electricity but indoor plumbing and insulation of any kind their warped planks shrunken so drastically by the arid desert atmosphere that there is little difference between standing outside in the cold winter winds and sheltering inside the porous walls.

Or, perhaps it is the influence of the sometimes squatters in those shacks: a collection of outcasts, cast-offs and misfits who pay no rent and pay no mind to the upkeep of the structures; who, in fact, burn one or two of them to the ground each winter while trying to keep warm. These squatters are people who go by first names or nicknames only and stare hard at anyone who tries to press them regarding whence they came, why they left, or how long they intend to stay.

But a Saturday night in June of 1964, the long bar produced the scheme that would depose all others for sheer, wanton stupidity It was conceived by two young men from Smoke Tree who had crossed the old wooden Bureau of Reclamation bridge at the southwest end of town and driven through the silty river bottom full of screw bean mesquite and dusky tamarisk and turned up the badly washboarded road of dirt and shards of volcanic rock that climbed to the ghost town four thousand feet above the valley below.

Austin and Braxton Banner, pride of their father, Fermin, and bane of their mother, Honour, were identical twins. Many identical twins are indistinguishable from one another in infancy. But then small but perceptible differences begin to appear as they grow. One for example, may grow taller than the other, or one turn out to be more intelligent. Not so with Austin and Braxton. They grew at exactly the same rate to the exact same size. Both were tall. Both had sandy, curly hair, gray eyes and protruding ears. Both were right handed. Both were well-muscled. Both could run fast, but neither faster than the other. Nor was there any clue to be found in the timbre of their voices. They sounded exactly the same. Even their dentition was identical. And they were both dumber than stumps. What no one could figure out was how Fermin and Honour Banner, both short, with straight black hair and dark eyes, had produced the pair.

Fermin's pride in his sons had been trumpeted four years before on a Saturday morning at the Smoke Tree barber shop. While getting his hair trimmed, Fermin had waited for a lull in the conversations around him before clearing his throat loudly. When he had everyone's attention, he proclaimed, "Proud a them boys a mine."

"Why's that, Fermin," asked someone?

"Brought their report cards home t'other day."

Men glanced at each other in surprise. Austin and Braxton were known to be as deficient in scholarship as they were adept at causing trouble.

"They do good?"

Fermin nodded, nearly losing a chunk of his earlobe to the clippers in the process.

"Yup. Straight Fs. Right across the board. Just like their pa."

No one knew what to say, so no one said anything, since Fermin, his diminutive size notwithstanding, had a reputation as a ferocious scrapper.

Later that summer, before the beginning of what would have been, by virtue of credits earned, their sophomore year at Smoke Tree High, the twins had announced they would not be returning to school for the coming year. Since they had turned eighteen and were therefore not in violation of any state laws, teachers at the school were relieved. But when the boys applied for work as trainmen on the Santa Fe Railroad, their father's place of employment, they were turned down.

Fermin had worked as a brakeman on the Santa Fe since coming west well in advance of fellow farmers from the area that became known in the 1930s as the Dust Bowl. It had been Fermin's good fortune to fail at farming even in the wet years that preceded the massive ecological disaster, thus beating the rush to California. The railroad had provided him steady employment from the day he was hired. When the Depression hit, Fermin had enough seniority that he was not affected. In fact, since he had a good-paying job when so many others had no work at all, his standard of living actually rose instead of declining during those terrible years.

When his sturdy sons were denied employment by the company that had sustained his family for years, he was spitting mad. He brushed aside questions from Emma White, the trainmaster's secretary, flung open the door of Mike Langford's office, and stormed in. Fortunately for Emma, the town gossip nicknamed the semaphore of the Santa Fe, the door remained open and she heard every heated word. The entire conversation was in the wind before Fermin reached the parking lot.

Mike, his ever-present-but-never-lit cigar screwed into the corner of his mouth and the fedora he never removed in public clamped on his head, looked up in irritation. That look alone was usually sufficient to make Santa Fe trainmen reconsider angry words with the man who controlled their livelihood, but it didn't deter Fermin. He stood fuming in front of the trainmaster's desk meeting Mike's look of irritation with a baleful glare.

Mike spoke first.

"I figured to see you in here sooner or later, Fermin. What I didn't know was that you'd make such an obstreperous entrance."

Fermin was so angry he didn't even ask for a definition of the smarmy, smart-assed word he had not understood and therefore assumed was insulting.

"What the Sam Hill is going on down here?"

"I assume you're referring to your sons' job applications."

"I sure as hell am."

"They're not qualified."

"Not qualified? Them boys is fit as mules."

"That's not what I mean. They're not high school graduates."

"So! Never made it past the fourth grade my ownself."

"That was back in the days of steam, Fermin. The Santa Fe has upped its standards. Need a high school diploma for a train crew job these days. You might have them apply for track maintenance."

Fermin exploded, his voice echoing off the walls, through the outer office, and down the hall.

"Work out there with them Mexes and ig'nrnt Mojaves? By God, no Banner's ever gonna do that."

He lowered his voice somewhat.

"How about yard clerk or dispatcher or some such?"

"High school diploma required."

"Well, that's just, just...stupid," spluttered Fermin. He turned on his heel and stormed out as ferociously as he had come in.

As are your boys, thought Mike before he returned to his interrupted work.

So Austin and Braxton, who Fermin had been counting on to add to the family income, were suddenly a liability. However, he had no intention of feeding them for the rest of their lives if they didn't contribute. He drove home and stuffed them into his new Chevrolet pickup and ferried them around town, seeking employment. They found it working for the person Fermin referred to as 'that junk yard Jew. As it turned out, the boys had mechanical aptitude. They were soon happily stripping the many totaled cars they towed in off Highway 66 for useable parts.

It was dirty work. Cold when the wind blew down the Colorado River from the north in the winter and blistering hot in the summer. Austin and Braxton loved it. They especially liked the junkyard dogs. They also liked to drive the tow truck, hoisting up wrecks from miles around and bringing them to Zack to admire: nuggets of profit panned from the flowing stream of commerce that was Highway 66.

Four years almost to the day after their hiring, they were still working for Zack. Life was good, but sometimes just a little boring. Which is why they were looking forward to an eventful Saturday night. They could get drunk. Maybe start a fight or two. Good stuff.

They started at the Box Car. It was full of soldiers. Not sure they wanted to take on soldiers, they visited the Derail, the Shoofly and the Rusty Spike in turn. Soldiers everywhere. They settled for having a boilermaker at each place before moving on. They thought about going to the carnival over on Front Street, having heard about the hoochie-coochie show there, but girls didn't really interest Austin and Braxton very much. Not as much as hunting, or fishing, or watching pro football on Sundays on Pa's new RCA color TV.

So, as they sometimes did, they wound up at the long bar in the Oatman Hotel. It was just after nine o'clock when they walked in, and the place was crowded. But Maggie, she of the snap-button shirts, turquois bolo ties, bouffant hairdo and gem stone rings, took a moment to make them feel welcome. They were good customers who actually tipped her and were, compared to some of her regulars, pretty normal.

The two young men, voluble and boisterous in the bars of Smoke Tree, kept their voices down and their eyes to themselves in Maggie's place. Men regarded as hard cases across the river had often been chewed up and spit out by the clientele of the long bar. One guy had a black widow spider, red spot and all, tattooed across his neck and the entire right side of his face, and the tattoo was not as scary as his eyes.

The Banners drank their first boilermakers in silence and were halfway through their second round when Austin suddenly slammed his open hand down loudly on the bar.

The room immediately went silent. Everyone turned to stare at the two young men at the far end of the bar. Austin ducked his

head, held up both hands, palms out, and spoke without making
eye contact with anyone.

"Sorry."

The silence lingered a moment before the two were dismissed
as non-threatening and therefore not interesting. Conversations
resumed around the room.

Austin turned his head toward Braxton and spoke in a fierce
whisper.

"Jeep!"

"What?"

"Jeep."

"What about a jeep?"

"We need one. We need something with four-wheel drive. You
know there's only two things in all of Smoke Tree with four-wheel
drive?"

"Is that right?"

"Yeah, Lee Hoskins' old Willy's pickup and one a them new
Toyotas (pronounced *Tie-yah-tahs*) owned by the guy runs the PG&E
plant. It would be so great to have one when we go quail huntin' up
the Providence. No more walkin' all over the desert. Just drive right
up them gullies until we find us a covey and jump out and blast 'em.
We need our own Jeep, Brax. They're all over the desert."

"Quail?"

"No, damnit, jeeps!"

"Yeah, but there's always soldiers close by."

"Yeah, but I been thinkin'. I know how we can get one."

"Here we go, Austin. The last time you wanted a jeep we sent
fifty dollars to that place advertised in Popular Mechanics.
Remember that?"

"I do. Still remember that there ad. 'Cheap Army surplus jeeps
you can buy brand new in the crate for fifty dollars.'"

"Remember what we got back when we sent in the money?"

"Yeah. A bunch of papers. Told you how to bid at a gummint
auction."

"That's right. Fifty dollars down the crapper. Didn't even say
where them auctions was, did it?"

"Nope."

"Didn't say how much a body'd have to bid to get one a them
jeeps if you found one a them auctions neither, did it?"

Austin was getting irritated. He hated to admit he'd been
hoodwinked.

"No!"

Louder this time, and delivered in an angry tone of voice.

122

"Know what, Austin? I don't think there ever was any a them jeeps."

Austin's shoulder slumped.

"I 'spect you're right about that. But I still want one!"

"Wantin's not the same as gettin'."

"I know, Brax, but I got me a idear."

"Austin, no way I'm goin' in amongst them soldier boys and stealin' no jeep."

"Me neither, brother mine."

"Then how you fixin' to get you one?"

"Gonna get ours where there ain't gonna be none a them soldiers."

Braxton shook his head.

"And where's that?"

"Off'n a train."

Braxton sighed.

"Austin, them jeeps is chained up on them flat cars."

"Cuttin' torch'd take care of that. And I know where there is one."

"Yeah, out at the yard. So, you're gonna jump up on a flat car with a hunnerd and fifty-pound acetylene bottle plus a oxygen bottle and just commence cuttin' chains."

"Not with no bottles. Just the torch. Bottles'll be on the truck"

"Which truck is that?"

Austin looked around to be sure no one was listening in on their conversation.

"Zack's wrecker."

"Zack won't like that!"

"Zack won't know. Where's he go ever Friday afternoon?"

"San Ber'dino."

"And when's he come home?"

"Sunday afternoon."

"Ever week?"

"That's right."

"So he's not at the yard right now, is he?"

"No."

"We take the wrecker. Go get us a jeep. Have the truck at the yard before he gets back."

Braxton sat thinking about what Austin had just said. He thought about it so long he finished his second boilermaker and ordered another one. Austin ordered one too.

Maggie brought their drinks and moved back to the middle of the bar where she was talking to a guy and his girlfriend. At least Braxton thought it was a girl. He looked a little closer.

Borderline, he decided.

He carefully lowered his shot glass of Jim Beam and let it slide to the bottom of his mug of Oly. He watched as the liquid blossomed and stained the beer a darker amber. He took a deep draught and smacked his lips.

"I guess we could do that. But, there's still a problem."

Austin let him think. He knew Braxton came along easier if you let him help puzzle things out.

Braxton took another drink and shook his head.

"We seen them cars being unloaded. Tanks and trucks and them boxy things the soldiers ride in."

"Armored Personnel Carriers. And jeeps."

"That's right. And jeeps. But, the soldiers unload 'em."

He shook his head.

"Austin, it won't work. We can't just roll up in the tow truck and commence cuttin' chains. Get ourselves shot."

"Okay, but what if there wasn't no soldiers around?"

"Not gonna happen. They're right there the minute the crew puts the cars on the siding, and they commence unloadin' right then."

"But I know for a fact there's a time when them soldiers ain't there."

"When's that?"

"When the train is a rollin' down the main line."

Braxton considered this piece of information.

"You're going to jump up on a flat car with a torch and cut the chains while the train is moving?"

"Nope."

Braxton was getting agitated.

"What then, damnit?"

Austin leaned closer to his brother and lowered his voice further.

"Before he went down to catch a westbound this afternoon Pa told me there was another trainload of Army stuff coming eastbound tonight. Should be here after midnight but before mornin for sure. That's what got me to puzzlin' this out. We're gonna cut one a them cars out of that train. Steal the whole damn car! Then, when the train is gone, we can cut the chains and drive off in our new jeep!"

Braxton finished his boilermaker while he pondered what his brother had just said.

"Say we could even do such a thing and get us our jeep. We can't be ridin' around in no jeep with 'U.S. Army' all over it. They'll catch us, sure as hell."

"First, Brax, we're gonna do this in the dark."

"I get that, Austin. Jeez, I know it's dark after midnight."

"Second, when we get our jeep, we drive it to Zack's place when we return the wrecker. We get a bunch a that black spray paint and paint her flat black. Then, we drive her out to the Sacramentos and hide her. In a gully. Cover her with bushes and what not. We leave her out there until them soldier boys is long gone."

A light went on in Braxton's head.

"And we tell everyone we went to one a them gummint auction things and bought it. In a crate!"

Braxton was warming to this idea, as he always warmed to Austin's ideas if Austin allowed him to follow along with the planning. The whole thing made him so happy her ordered another round, and the two men sat sipping their boilermakers and contemplating life with their new jeep.

Then Braxton's face clouded over. Austin knew his brother was fretting again.

"Won't work."

"Why not?"

"You say cut the car with them jeeps out of the train."

"That's right."

"How we gonna do that?"

"Already got her figgered."

Braxton brightened again. In spite of the accumulated evidence of all their past failures, he still thought Austin was just about the smartest guy he knew.

"Tell me, 'cause I sure want me a jeep."

"You know that grade where the tracks comes up the hill from Fenner?"

"Sure."

"Them trains slow way down as they get near the summit at Goffs, right?"

"Sure. Steep hill."

"We lay by across the highway, close to the top of the grade. Train's going not much more'n a jog up there. We ease out and pull out alongside 'er and match the speed."

"Okay."

125

"Now, you'll be standin' on the back of the wrecker holdin' the tow hook. You just reach over and snap that hook on that little ladder at the front of the flatcar."

"Wait a minute. I'm standin' out there with the hook?"

"That's right."

"Why not you?"

"'Cause, I'm the better driver. You know that, Brax."

"Oh, yeah. Got me there."

"Once you get her hooked, you step over onto that flatcar and walk to the other end and uncouple it from the cars behind."

"Why do I do that?"

"'Cause, brother, we just want the one car."

"Wait a minute. How do I uncouple them?"

"Brax, you've seen that done lots of time. Remember that summer we worked at the ice house?"

"You mean part of the summer. Nice and cool out there. Best job we ever had."

"That's right. Until that block got away and it busted that guy's hip."

"And they fired me."

"Yeah, and then I quit. You fire one Banner brother, and you by God lose the both of them!"

"Damn straight!"

"Anyways, there's a lever on the end of the car. You just turn her and she pulls up the pin holding the knuckle together and the coupling comes right open. You've seen the switch crews do it."

"That's right, but what about the air hoses?"

"When the cars uncouple, the ones behind our car will start slowin' down and then start slidin' back down the hill. When that happens, them air hoses will just pop apart."

"What'll become a them cars and the guys in the caboose?"

"End up down near Fenner somewheres, I s'pose. Hell, prob'ly asleep back there anyhoo."

"Then what."

"Well, by that time, the train has slowed almost to a walk. You hustle back to the front of the car and uncouple it, too."

"What keeps our car from going to Fenner with the other ones?"

"As soon as you uncouple her, the slack goes out of the towline and I hold her with the wrecker!"

Braxton smiled.

"I get it."

126

"You set the handbrake on the flat car. I jump out and commence cuttin' on them chains. Be through them in no time a'tall."

"How do we get the jeep off'n the car?"

"Just get one on each side and give it a push. Right off the end of the car."

"Let it hit the tracks?"

"Sure, Brax. Them jeeps is tough. That's why the Army makes 'em.

"Wait a minute. What about the flat car?"

"Handbrake's set. Leave 'er there. Let the Santa Fe figure it out. We crank up the jeep and drive it and the wrecker back to the yard. Paint the jeep, lock up the yard, drive our jeep into the Sacramentos. Walk back to the yard and get our truck. It ain't that far. Be home before Zack gets back from 'Berdoo."

He snapped his fingers.

"Done deal!"

The two brothers sat side by side and finished their drinks, secure in the knowledge they would soon be the owners of a four-wheel-drive jeep."

Austin climbed down off his stool. He lost his balance momentarily but steadied himself by grabbing hold of the bar. He looked at the clock. It was a little blurry, but he made it out as eleven o'clock.

"Brother, let's go get a jeep!"

CHAPTER 18

Early Morning Catastrophe

The sobering Banner boys were parked on the north side of Old 66. They were in Zack's wrecker at the mouth of a gully carved from the east-facing side of the Fenner Hills. There was no moon. The waxing crescent sliver had set before midnight. Pre-dawn light would not come into the sky until five. Austin had already made a few trial runs across the highway and onto the right-of-way access road without his headlights to get the feel of the terrain beneath a sky lit only by stars. He had also angled the mirror on the passenger-side door so he would be able to see the train as he drove alongside without turning his head and looking back over his shoulder.

It was two-thirty in the morning when Austin's voice came hesitantly out of the darkness.

"I been thinkin,' Austin. Maybe this ain't such a good idea. I mean, it sounded good in Oatman, but maybe it don't sound so good now."

Austin sat silently while he gathered his thoughts and tamped down his anger.

"Listen to me, Braxton Banner. We have planned this here operation to a fare-thee-well. Ever little detail. We got the wrecker, we got the cutting torch, and we got the steel nerves it takes to pull this off. Don't you crawfish on me now!"

Uh oh, thought Braxton. He only calls me by my full name when he's really mad.

He held up his hands in apology.

"All right, all right. No need to be gettin' all hop-skitty about it. I don't think that train's gonna show up before morning anyway."

"We know it ain't gone by yet. It wern't in the yard at Smoke Tree, and we didn't see it on the way out. It'll be along."

"What if it don't come until after daylight?"

"We take the wrecker back to the yard and go home and get us some sleep. Then we go check them trot lines we set down by Devil's Elbow."

"But..."

"Hush now. I hear something."

The brothers went silent. In the distance, they heard a train laboring up the main line toward Goffs. As the heavy thrum of the diesels grew louder, the headlight of the N2A pierced the deep darkness of the desert night as it rounded a curve to their southwest

"There she is! This is going to be a piece of cake, Brax. Look how slow that train's a goin'. Hell, I don't believe there's even a helper on t'other end. They're gonna be lucky to get that load up the grade Baby could crawl as fast as they'll be goin' at the top. As soon as the engine goes by, I'm pullin' across the highway."

The lead locomotive and its slave were laboring hard as they drew abreast of the Banner brothers' location. When the hulking outline of five box cars had trundled past, Austin started the engine and drove the wrecker across the highway and onto the access road. He stopped, facing the slowly-passing train.

There was sufficient light from the countless stars in the desert sky to see the outlines of cars humped like segments of some vast, prehistoric centipede crawling up out of the center of the earth in the darkness

"I don't see no jeeps."

"Patience, brother."

Another thirty-five boxcars passed their position before the flat cars carrying U.S. Army equipment began to appear. Six flat cars of deuce-and-a-half trucks crawled past. Then flatcars carrying jeeps emerged from the darkness.

"Thank you, Jesus! Here we go."

Filled with misgiving, but determined not to disappoint his brother, Braxton got out of the cab and clambered up onto the back of the wrecker. Austin turned onto the road and eased forward.

It was difficult to drive slowly enough. He had to continually feather the clutch to keep the truck from lurching and stalling Finally, the first flatcar loaded with jeeps drew up alongside them He accelerated slightly and pulled just beyond the gap between the flatcar with the jeeps and the one loaded with deuce-and-a-halfs.

In the mirror, he saw Braxton reach over and snap the towline hook onto the ladder at the front of the flatcar. When he jumped off the wrecker and onto the car, he lost his balance and went down on his hands and knees. He remained crouching for a moment before he stood and started toward the rear of the car, stepping carefully across the chains securing the jeeps.

Way to go, Brax, Austin silently cheered.

Austin was soon unable to make him out in the mirror. He tried to estimate how long it would take his brother to make his way to the end of the car and uncouple it.

Austin continued to crawl along, careful to keep the slack in the towline. Uncoupling the trailing cars seemed to be taking a long time. Too long, in fact.

Come on, Brax, come on, he thought. You must be done by now. Get back up here and pull the pin on the front knuckle. We're going to be comin' to the top of the grade soon.

Still, no Braxton came into view.

Unable to see him in the mirror, Austin turned his head and tried to see out the back window. When he did, the wrecker steered into the moving train. It shimmied dangerously before Austin could gain control. Sweat poured down his face as he snuck a brief glance at the mirror to see if Braxton was returning.

He was not.

Austin could hear the train blowing for the crossing at Goffs. Coming to the top of the grade now, he thought. Unable to stand not knowing, he flicked on his headlights and turned them right back off. The picture burned into his retina during the brief illumination confirmed his worst fears. The top of the grade was just ahead.

Where's that damned Braxton, he thought?

Braxton was still trying to turn the lever to raise the pin that allowed the knuckle joining the two cars to open. Never having worked as switchmen or brakemen, what he and his brother failed to understand was the tremendous pressure clamping the pin inside the knuckle when one car was pulling another up a grade. Ten men could not have rotated the lever that freed that pin. Nor a hundred. The pin could only be released if the pressure inside the knuckle was eased.

Sweating in the hot desert darkness, he pushed and pushed. Nothing happened. Afraid he would disappoint Austin, he continued to push as hard as he could until he saw, out of the corner of his eye, the tail lights of the wrecker flicker briefly and then go out.

In a flash of insight, probably the best piece of quick-thinking Braxton had ever achieved, he realized Austin was trying to see where they were. Trying to see if they were coming to the top of the grade. He yanked harder on the lever. Still, it refused to budge.

Then the flatcar he was riding on crested the grade, and he was suddenly thinking of other things. Other things like the fact that, having crested the hill, the train would now start gather speed In fact, as he crouched there, he could feel it accelerating.

It was time to un-ass this train!

Climbing onto the ladder, he jumped. It was so dark he could not see the ground rushing toward him. He landed off-balance twisting his ankle as he toppled to the ground. His head slammed into the railbed cinders.

He rolled several times before he came to a stop and sat up picking cinders out of his face.

In the wrecker, the situation was deteriorating. Now that a big section of the train was starting its long downhill run to Smoke Tree it was speeding up rapidly. So rapidly that, as he chanced a look out of the passenger side window, he saw something horrifying. The ladder with the towing hook attached, the ladder that had been well behind the cab of the wrecker when Braxton snapped on the hook was passing the truck! He turned on his lights again in the vain hope that he was wrong. He wasn't. Not only that, the ladder was picking up speed as it continued to move away from him.

Zack's wrecker was very big. It could pick up a semi-tractor But, compared to the momentum of a freight train picking up speed as it rolled downhill, it was a feather. Intuitively aware of the mismatch, Austin tried vainly to keep up with the train, but the condition of the right-of-way would not allow it. The truck began bouncing and sliding.

Austin was out of speed, time and ideas. The slack went out of the cable. It snapped taut. When it did, the wrecker slewed sideways so abruptly that instead of simply turning east-end-west it flipped onto its side and began to skid down the right-of-way on the driver's-side door at a steadily increasing rate.

Austin, suddenly stone-cold sober, managed to climb out from behind the steering wheel and crawl uphill to the passenger door. He squeezed through the open window and balanced precariously on the lurching wrecker before launching himself away from the unfolding catastrophe.

It was a small miracle he survived. As it was, he did a face plant in the cinders that easily surpassed his brother's. He tumbled twenty yards before coming to a halt. When he sat up, he could see Zack's wrecker bounding and bouncing away from him like a child's toy attached by a string to the door handle of a speeding car.

The wrecker had disappeared Austin's view when it struck a pile of railroad ties lying perpendicular to the tracks. The impact snatched the wrecker into the air. The bottles of acetylene and oxygen, held loosely against the truck by a chain, flew free. The oxygen tank struck one of the steel wheels of the rolling train. The impact ripped off the valve. The oxygen, under a pressure of two thousand two hundred pounds per square inch, blasted from the tank and encountered sparks coming from beneath the truck as it was dragged down right-of-way again.

There was a huge explosion. A flower of hot white light bloomed in the night air. The two-thousand-degree temperature reached by the oxygen caused the nearby acetylene bottle to erupt in turn. The result was a second, even louder explosion. The fireball changed color and grew larger. The combined temperature of the two gases briefly reached over six thousand degrees.

That ignited the gas tank, which changed the color of the fireball again and then added black smoke to the equation.

Uh oh, thought Austin.

Jacob Gruber, the hoghead driving the train that night, saw the first flicker of the wrecker's headlights.

"Thought I saw lights coming up behind us for a minute, but they're not there now."

The head-end brakeman had been almost asleep.

"On the highway?"

"No, on the right-of-way."

"Can't image why anybody'd be back there this time of night. Let me know if you see them again."

The trail rolled on and cleared the at-grade crossing where the mainline crossed Old 66 at Goffs. Jacob had almost decided he had been seeing things when the lights appeared again.

"There!"

Ted Lyford came to the engineer's side and stuck his head out the window to look back, losing his cap in the process."

"Damnit! Third hat I've lost this year."

"Do you see them?"

"Yeah. Can't image what's going on."

"See if you can raise the caboose. Maybe they know what it is."

Lyford returned to his side and picked up the hand-held radio.

"Never mind. The lights are gone again."

133

A few minutes later, the hoghead was watching the side mirror when he saw a bright, white light flare next to the train followed by a tremendous explosion. A reddish-orange fireball leaped higher into the air, followed by a second, louder explosion.

"What the hell? Tell the caboose we're goin' in the big hole"

And then there was a third explosion.

Jacob slammed the air-brake valve into the emergency position as Lyford keyed the hand-held.

Just as Austin had predicted, the men in the caboose were sleeping. There's something about the combination of desert heat, darkness, and a gently rocking train that make it very hard to stay awake. The conductor was nodding at his table. The rear-end brakeman was in the cupola. He was supposed to be watching the cars ahead for possible hot boxes, but he had dozed off as they began the climb to Goffs. Both men were jolted awake by an explosion followed by a second, much larger one, and a third a moment later. As they tried figure out what was happening, the train lurched as the air brakes engaged at full pressure. Almost simultaneously there was a frantic call from Ted Lyford telling them the train was going in the big hole.

They had already noticed.

It takes a lot of time and distance to stop a long freight train that has been picking up speed heading downhill. The wheels locked. Sparks began to fly. The train was essentially sliding down the main line, dragging the badly burnt remains of the wrecker alongside.

Dragged it far enough that it collided with, and caught against, the concrete foundation anchoring the mast, the signal and the already-lowered crossing gate on the west side of the Goffs at-grade crossing. Amazingly, the cable holding the wrecker to the flatcar did not break. Instead, the concrete stanchion was snatched from the ground, and the whole mess: wrecker, concrete stanchion, mast, signal and crossing arm, fetched up against the big electrical equipment vault on the east side of the crossing. The vault was immediately added to the accumulated junk being dragged eastward by a train in emergency stop mode but still moving steadily downhill.

There would, of course, be an investigation. There always was. Both the conductor and the rear-end brakeman would testify they had been wide awake at the time of the explosion. One man lying; the other swearing it was true. Of course, it wouldn't have altered the outcome one whit if they had been eyes wide. Someone had to be held accountable. Someone at whom the Santa Fe could

134

point the finger of negligence. That person would have to be "fired". That is, he would be laid off and begin to collect the job insurance all trainmen with any sense purchased. The insurance, while it would not pay as much as normal wages, would allow the "fired" individual a few weeks of fishing on the river and maybe even a few days escaping the heat at the coast before he was re-instated at his previous level of seniority.

The person held accountable? Why, the conductor, of course. Thus, the railroad rhyme known as the conductor's lament.

> I cannot blow the whistle,
> Or even ring the bell,
> But let the damned thing jump the track
> And see who catches hell.

It was the job of the hoghead to remain with the front of the train once it quit moving forward. It was the job of the head-end brakemen to run like hell for the nearest call box. Ted Lyford grabbed the carryall filled with flares and railroad torpedoes and started toward Goffs. He came to a stop after a few steps, realizing that whatever had caused the huge explosion had probably destroyed the call box. That left Homer, two miles distant, as the nearest Santa Fe phone. He set out to the east at a run. He made it almost a hundred yards before a pack of Chesterfields every day, a six-pack of Coors every night, and years of inactivity caught up with him. He stopped and bent forward as he threw up. He remained in that position a moment longer, catching his breath, before he straightened and wiped his mouth.

No need to be a damn fool about this, he thought. Won't do anyone any good if I have a heart attack.

Alternately walking and breaking into a shuffling jog, he finally reached Homer and called the Smoke Tree Dispatcher, who called the Barstow Dispatcher. He started back the way he had come, putting torpedoes on the rails and dropping railroad flares from time to time. This even though the Smoke Tree Dispatcher had told him there was nothing coming up the mainline from Smoke Tree. Maybe so, but you just never knew. After all, there would be an investigation, and head-end brakeman Ted Lyford wanted the trainmaster to see those burned-out railroad flares and unexploded torpedoes and know Ted had done his job.

Long before the conductor and the rear-end brakeman reached the place where the explosions had lit the night sky, Austin and Braxton Banner met and assessed each other's injuries. Braxton's sprained ankle was the worst, but he understood they had to clear the area and soon, pain or no. The brothers, one hobbling badly and assisted by the other, made their way north across Old 66 and disappeared into the desert night.

CHAPTER 19

Horse Sense

Horse lay awake in the pre-dawn hours Sunday morning. He had eased out of bed at four in the morning and turned the swamp cooler to the lowest setting, tired of the noise it made. There was a pronounced rattle in the squirrel cage when it was on high, and he had not had time to fix it. It was going to be his first chore when he and Esperanza and the twins returned from Mass. As he eased back into bed, careful not to disturb Esperanza, he could feel the barest whisper of a breeze moving across his body. The house wasn't really cool; it never was once the summer heat set in, but at least it wasn't break-a-sweat hot. That in itself was a Sunday morning blessing. Horse was hoping for more. Hoping for one quiet, peaceful day before the storm that Joint Exercise Desert Strike was sure to unleash on his area of responsibility over the coming week.

He curled onto his side and watched his dearest Esperanza as she slept, her lustrous black hair fanned on the pillow, her lips parted in a sweet smile. A smile that made him believe in a better world. He thought "Hope" was a good name for his beloved. Lord, he thought, I love her. She is my universe. My everything. I'm the luckiest man alive.

He might have watched her for a long time if not for the phone. He was off the bed and down the hall so quickly he was able to snatch the Princess phone off the dining room wall in the middle of the second ring.

"Carlos."

"Good morning, Captain. Colonel Dulac. Sorry to be calling so early, but you said you wanted to be informed of anything affecting the civilian population."

"No inconvenience at all. What is it, Colonel?"

"We have a situation. Are you familiar with a place called Goffs?"

"Yes."

"Dumb question. Of course, you are. Sorry, I'm still half asleep myself. There was an explosion next to a rail car carrying Army equipment. A big explosion."

"Railroad accident of some kind?"

"No. The report I got said it looked like some sort of sabotage."

"Sabotage, as in the Russians are coming?"

"We don't know yet. Anyway, some of our CID boys are out there."

"Any cinder dicks?"

"Any what?"

"Sorry. Railroad detectives."

"I don't think so, but someone did mention a trainmaster."

"Okay, Colonel. Thanks for the heads up. I'm on my way. If Mike Langford's there, the scene's in good hands. He's very competent."

When he hung up the phone, Esperanza was in the kitchen starting coffee. He walked up behind her and put his arms around her, taking in her delicious smell: a combination of Pears Soap and lavender.

When he let her go, she turned around and hugged him. He felt himself begin to stir. He back away reluctantly.

"Gotta run, *querida*. Some crazy explosion thing out by Goffs. Might be civilians involved with the Army."

She smiled up at him.

"Hate to waste your morning happiness. Was that your gun or were you just glad to see me," she asked in her best Mae West imitation?

"Very glad. And very sad to have to run. Rain check?"

"Sure thing."

"I hope the phone didn't wake the twins."

"Not a chance. Championship-level sleepers, our kids."

"Lucky for us."

He turned and started down the hall.

"I'll have your coffee in the thermos by the time you get dressed."

Before Horse's cruiser reached Goffs, he could see the front of an eastbound freight sitting motionless on the tracks east of the nearly nonexistent town. About twenty cars or so west of the engine, he saw a string of flatcars with U.S. Army vehicles. There were deuce-and-a-halfs with the canvas covers burned off on two of them. The frameworks were blackened but intact, looking like the rib cages of some giant, pre-historic creatures.

An MP sedan was parked in front of the idled train when he reached the at-grade crossing. The southside arm of the crossing barrier with its string of flashers was in the horizontal position. He got out of his cruiser and climbed between two of the cars and dropped down on the other side. Mike Langford was talking to two men in civilian clothes. Horse had never seen either of them before.

CID, he thought. Based on their ages, probably a wobbly two and a sergeant E-6.

Mike heard Horse crunching through the cinders of the railbed and turned.

"Mornin,' Horse."

"Mornin' Mike."

"Trying to help our Army friends. These gentlemen are CID."

"Gentlemen, this is Captain Carlos Caballo of the San Bernardino County Sheriff's Department. He's the man responsible for policing this huge desert, not to mention the town of Smoke Tree."

"I'm Herschel Nielsen," said the one on the left.

That's the senior guy, thought Horse.

"And I'm Carson Fitzgilbert."

"And you can call me Horse. Everyone else out this way does."

The men shook hands.

"I would guess I'm talking to a Warrant Officer two and a Sergeant."

The one he thought was the warrant officer spoke up.

"I take it you've been in the military, Captain?

"Korean war."

"Then you know CID personnel don't reveal their rank."

"I know, but a simple smile if I guessed right would do."

The warrant officer gave the briefest of grins. The sergeant gave nothing away.

Horse turned to Mike.

"Trainmaster Langford, have you figured out what happened here?"

Mike shook his head.

"Darndest thing I've ever seen. Me and the CID guys are trying to piece it together. We've already talked to the crew. Looks like the hoghead and the head-end brakeman had the best view. They were closer to the explosion than the boys in the caboose."

Mike smiled.

"And a lot more awake."

Horse made no comment.

Mike gestured eastward.

"Down there a way, we found the remains of the crossing signal that was ripped out of the ground, and the electrical vault that was on the other side of the road. Also found what was left of a big tow truck. Gas tank had exploded. It had burned so hot the tires were melted off the rims. Impossible to make out the name of the company."

Horse stood thinking. Something didn't sound right.

"Wait a minute. How could a tow truck do all that damage?"

Mike shook his head.

"That's one of the stranger parts of all this. The tow truck cable was hooked to the ladder on a flat car. When the truck hit the concrete pedestal holding the signal mast, it yanked the ladder from vertical to horizontal but didn't pull it off the car. Didn't break the cable, either."

"My, oh my."

"Way I figure, the train was headed downhill and picking up some pretty good speed, so the force was so great it just snatched everything off at ground level and kept on going."

"And the tow cable held."

"Yep. Who knew braided steel was that tough?"

"How about license plates on the tow truck?"

"One melted, one partially readable. I wrote down what I could make out."

"My radio won't reach the substation from here. I'll call it in on the way back. There aren't a lot of tow trucks around, so a partial should do."

"Let's take a walk, Horse."

They set off, the two CID men trailing. The sun had risen. The smell of the creosote coating the railroad ties was growing stronger as the temperature rose. It was not an unpleasant odor to men from a town that owed its existence to the Santa Fe.

At their first stop, Mike pointed out a huge area where desert plants had been burned off. Only some bare, blackened branches of creosote had survived. The tiny, oily leaves of the creosote and the entirety of all the other shrubs in the vicinity had flared into ash.

140

Be interesting, thought Horse, to see whether the creosote comes back. Probably be green on it by spring. Stuff is too tough to kill.

"There was a huge explosion here. We found pieces of shrapnel all up and down this area. Found more of it driven into the army vehicles on the flat cars."

They walked on, Mike pointing out drag marks along the right of way where the tow truck had been on its side. He stopped at some scattered railroad ties.

"Truck hit these ties. Bounced up, kept going."

They followed the drag marks farther to the west.

"The tow truck that destroyed the crossing signal probably flipped onto its side right here. You can see over there it was still on its wheels. The place where the truck drove onto the right-of-way is not far. Somewhere between where the truck flipped and where it came onto the right-of-way, someone apparently hooked the tow line onto the ladder of the flat car."

He turned and pointed back to the east.

"When the train crested the hill, it started moving too fast for the truck to keep up on this bad road. The ladder passed the truck, and the cable snapped tight. It yanked the truck sideways so quick it went onto its side. Maybe the rocks beneath the truck were throwing off sparks and they ignited the gas tank."

Horse stood quietly for a moment, turning his head from side to side to look both directions.

"This wasn't just a gas tank. It couldn't have made that big an explosion all by itself. Tell me, Mike, was the flat car the tow truck cable was attached to carrying military vehicles?"

"How'd you know?"

"Saw on my way here that something had burned some of them. It must have been the explosion."

"It was."

Horse stood thinking until he was sure.

"I know who did this!"

He turned to the CID team.

"My guess is, you guys can take off. This wasn't sabotage. This was stupidity."

"Who's that stupid?"

"The Banner boys."

The trainmaster stared at Horse. He lifted his fedora and wiped his head with his hand. It was the first time Horse had ever seen him take off the hat.

"Oh, crap!"

141

"Exactly. Who else has access to a big wrecker and is dumb enough to try a stunt like this?"

"No one that I can think of. But why did they do it?"

"They wanted a jeep. I've got the advantage of you on this Mike. Those boys came to my office about two years ago. They had sent fifty dollars to one of those 'get an-Army-jeep-in-a-crate-for-fifty-bucks, places that advertise in Mechanics Illustrated."

"I can see them falling for that."

"All they got back was a pamphlet. They came to me. Wanted me to go arrest the people at the post office box where they sent the money."

"Okay. But why such a big explosion?"

"Zack had a cutting torch at the yard. Austin and Braxton loaded the oxygen and acetylene bottles onto the back of the tow truck because they were going to use the torch to cut the chains holding the jeep to the flatcar."

"But that's insane!"

"Nope. It's Banners. They put the tow hook on the ladder because they thought they were going to uncouple it from the cars on both sides and hold it in place while they set the handbrake and then cut the chains."

"You can't pull the pin on a Janey coupling under load on a moving train."

"You know that, but Austin and Braxton don't. That is, they didn't. I'm pretty sure they know it now."

"But even if they could have uncoupled it, it would have rolled away before they could set the brake. You can't stop a railroad car with a tow truck."

Horse smiled.

"Once again."

"Right. I know that, but Austin and Braxton don't."

"They hooked on just before the top of the hill where the train was going the slowest, but whichever one climbed on the flatcar couldn't get it uncoupled. From there it was just like you said. The train outpaced the truck, the cable snapped tight, the truck started to turn ass end front but the tires bit when it got sideways, and the truck flipped onto its side. It got dragged along until it hit that pile of railroad ties and went airborne. The bottles went flying. When they hit the ground, the valve broke off one of them. Just like you said there were sparks from the rocks scraping the truck. Explosion."

Mike stood, shaking his head.

"This would be funny, if it wasn't so sad."

142

"Yeah. Those boys are going to end up in jail. At least they didn't kill anyone or wind up dead themselves."

"So where are they now?"

Horse put his hands on his hips and looked north and south. "Somewhere out on the desert."

"I can see how you might find where they walked off of the right-of-way, but how can you find them once they get on that open desert and find some rocks to walk on?"

"I can't, Mike, but I know someone who can."

CHAPTER 20

Demonstrations and Rebukes

Early Sunday morning, while there were church services during stand-down, Master Sergeant Yannity Scanlon drove a jeep off the west-facing slope of the Providence Mountains and picked up Macedonia Canyon road, a primitive two-track. He reached the Union Pacific Railroad line and took the right-of-way road north to where it intersected with the terminus of Cedar Canyon Road. He drove over the rail crossing onto Kelso-Cima Road and continued northeast.

Two roads went north out of Cima. He pulled over to the side of the road and consulted his topographic map before getting back on the blacktop and picking up Morning Star Mine Road. It gradually curved eastward, eventually terminating in a "T" intersection with Ivanpah Road. He went north on Ivanpah until he came to California 164, which took him due east to Nipton A short distance beyond Nipton, he was in Nevada and headed for Searchlight. Sergeant Scanlon glanced at the Jeep's odometer. He was curious to see how far into Nevada he would have to go before he met the person he was supposed to meet.

People, he corrected himself. This guy will not come alone.

As he drove, he wondered about Eddie Mazzetti's reasons for not wanting to enter San Bernardino County. Eddie probably had the Clark County Sheriff's Department greased and could do pretty much whatever he wanted as long as he stayed in Nevada. The sergeant thought it was a lot of unnecessary caution because he doubted the San Bernardino County Sheriff's paid any attention at all to the empty desert out this way.

Oh well, he thought, as long as Mazzetti can buy the guns, I don't really care where we meet.

He was a couple of miles inside the Nevada line when he saw a big, black sedan parked beside the road ahead of him. He stopped, climbed out, reached under the seat and pulled out the modified gun. He snapped the clip into place and pulled back the bolt to seat a round. He slung the weapon over his shoulder. Lifting a field overcoat off the seat, he shrugged it on, leaving his right arm out of the sleeve and the coat unbuttoned.

He immediately began to sweat.

He got back behind the wheel and drove to the sedan. He parked nose to nose with it. There was no one inside. He looked south of the highway and saw nothing but another desert wash. To the north, foothills rose to distant mountains. He was walking toward the hills when two men appeared.

Restroom break, he thought.

Sweating heavily under the coat, he continued toward them.

The two men approaching him began to drift apart. By the time he was thirty feet away, they had him triangulated.

Wow, he thought. Tactics.

The men stopped. Sergeant Scanlon smiled.

"What's so funny, soldier?"

"Just noticing you two have faced a man with a gun before."

"Once or twice," said the one on the right.

Dominant guy, thought Sergeant Scanlon. If this was a gunfight, I'd shoot him first."

"And it's not 'soldier, it's sergeant. Sergeant Scanlon. Now you know my name, so let's have yours."

"Why's it matter?"

"It matters if one of you isn't Eddie Mazzetti."

"Eddie, don't come out on the desert. Not his style. No air conditioning."

"I see. Then the three of us have nothing to talk about."

"I think we do."

Sergeant Scanlon shook his head.

"I came out here to demonstrate a weapon to a buyer. I don't see a buyer. All is I see is some local muscle. Some muscle, I might add, that doesn't seem too bright, since you're wearing loafers for a trip to the desert. I bet your shoes are full of sand and your socks are full of stickers. In the Army we call that PPP."

"What's this pee pee thing, soldier?"

"Piss poor planning."

"You should talk," said the one on the right. "You're wearin' a overcoat, and it's a hunnerd degrees."

"I have a reason for my choice of clothing. You bozos don't."

The two men glanced at each other, sweat rolling down their faces.

146

"It's too hot for this shit. Give us the gun to take to the boss, or we take it away from you."

As he spoke, the man on the left stepped toward Sergeant Scanlon, simultaneously reaching for the big automatic under his left armpit.

Sergeant Scanlon grasped the pistol grip of the rifle with his right hand and raised it into firing position as his left hand grasped the folding forward grip. When he pulled back on the grip, it pushed a rod attached to the trigger. Three quarters of the magazine emptied with a roar as bullets stitched the dirt road between the two men.

He eased the pressure on the lever but kept his hand on it.

Brass casings fell to the ground from beneath the overcoat. The man who had been reaching for his gun dropped his hand and stood with his mouth open. The man on the right looked like he had turned to run. The sudden silence was louder than the roar of the weapon.

"What the hell's wrong with you."

"Been through World War II and Korea. Shot at by experts. You think a couple goombahs with .45s are going to scare me?"

Neither man replied.

"You just witnessed the demonstration your boss was supposed to see. The clip in this rifle holds twenty rounds. Don't know how fast you two can count, or if you can even count at all, but if you think I burned the whole load, you can try again to take it away from me."

He smiled.

"C'mon, you boys are from Vegas. Wanna gamble?"

"Don't get your skivvies in a knot, Sergeant."

"Oh, all of a sudden I'm sergeant. Not just soldier."

"You' got the gun. You got the drop on us. Don't matter whether you're a private or a general. You win."

"Okay, now that we understand that, I'm willing to surrender. Here are my terms. First, tell me your names."

"I'm Malaleta Clemente. The other guy is Guido Battagliano. Eddie sent us."

"And the Eddie person I was supposed to meet with?"

"We told you, he ain't here."

"Maybe you guys've got him in the trunk. Heard you do that kind of thing."

"Real funny."

"Did this Eddie authorize you to meet my price and arrange for payment and delivery?"

147

"Nah, none a that. Told us to come and shoot the gun and bring it to him."

"Well, you've seen it, but I haven't seen Eddie. What say we go see him?"

"You and your gun?"

"It goes where I go. Got anything in that trunk where Eddie isn't that we could put it in?"

"Nothin' in there but our golf clubs, Clemente."

"Jesus, guys. That's bad for your image. Nobody's going to be afraid of you once they hear you play golf. But for now, that's perfect. I'll put it in the bag. Just some guys checking into the Serengeti with their clubs. Go real good with those Hawaiian shirts."

"And you in Army clothes?"

"Unlike you two, I planned ahead. Brought my civvies. I'll change on the way to Vegas. The weapon and the golf bag will be in the back with me. Anything tricky, I blow both of you through the windshield."

"What if a policeman stops us and sees that gun?"

Sergeant Scanlon smiled again.

"We'll just have to shoot him."

The smile went away.

"I'm willing to bet that license plate is on a "do not stop" list with the police up that way. One more thing. It's getting on toward noon. The reconnaissance jets will be up taking pictures soon. Don't want this jeep seen. I assume you guys know Searchlight. Is there a place we can hide it?"

Clemente and Guido looked at each other.

"Yeah, there's an abandoned mine on the edge of town. Couple of buildings. You can drive it right in. Won't be seen from the air."

Less than an hour later, the three men were at valet parking at the Serengeti. Sergeant Scanlon, dressed in his civilian clothes, was out of the back seat with the golf bag before the car came to a stop. Clemente and Guido, blue blazers now covering their shoulder rigs, climbed out. Guido handed over the keys.

"The usual place. In the shade."

Clemente and Guido led the way across the casino floor, Sergeant Scanlon in Khaki slacks, a guayabera shirt and loafers trailing with the golf bag. When they reached the executive elevator, Guido inserted a key.

The sergeant remained behind them while they waited for the car to come down.

"Clemente, you seem to be the guy in charge here, so you stay with me. Guido, you go up. Your partner and I will wait here for the elevator to come back down. I'm not getting in that elevator with both of you."

"Thought you wasn't afraid of us."

"I said I wasn't afraid. I didn't say I was stupid."

Guido stepped inside and the doors closed. While he and Clemente waited, Sergeant Scanlon set the golf bag on the floor beside him. He reached inside and got hold of the gun.

"Jesus, Sergeant. Don't be gettin' that thing out in here."

"Don't worry. I'm just getting ready for our ride."

When the lights above the doors showed the elevator had reached the top, Clemente inserted his key and turned. The elevator returned. When the doors opened, Sergeant Scanlon got in after Clemente.

When they reached the top, Guido was waiting for them.

"You first, Clemente."

Scanlon followed him into a beautiful reception area. The receptionist had apparently been told they were coming because she rose and opened one of the double doors behind her.

The three men, Clemente in the lead, walked in. Sergeant Scanlon saw a man behind a huge desk. He was wearing a white sport coat over a black shirt and white tie. There was a red carnation in his buttonhole. There was nothing on the desk but a phone.

The man did not get up.

"What the hell you doing hauling golf clubs in here? I sent you out to see some soldier about guns.

Sergeant Scanlon spoke.

"I see Guido hasn't reported to you yet. They found the soldier with the gun."

"Who are you?"

"I talked to you on the phone yesterday. That is, if you're Eddie Mazzetti. I'm the guy who can get the rifles."

Eddie did not look happy.

"I didn't tell you to bring this guy to the casino."

"They didn't have a choice, Eddie."

"It's Mr. Mazzetti to you. Why didn't they have a choice."

Sergeant Scanlon pulled the modified M14A1 out of the golf bag.

"What the hell..."

"You see, Eddie, I had this fully automatic weapon. They had some pistols. When I demonstrated the weapon, they decided their pistols weren't so special."

"That true, Clemente?"

"It is, boss. He had it under a overcoat. We didn't know it was there. We was gonna take it from him and shoot it and bring it to you, but he made this real quick move and let off a whole bunch o rounds. Right between us."

"That's right, boss."

Sergeant Scanlon pulled the magazine out of the weapon When he did, Clemente could see the copper gleam of the rounds remaining in the clip.

Jesus, Mary and Joseph, he thought. He did have more rounds in there.

The sergeant put the clip into the pocket of his Khakis and pulled back the bolt. A live round bounced across the white carpeting. He slung the weapon over his shoulder and turned sideways to Eddie Mazzetti. With one quick move, he pulled the gun into firing position against his shoulder. His right hand was on the pistol grip His left hand was on the folding forward grip attached to the trigger by a steel rod.

"You can see, Mr. Mazzetti, why Quick Draw McGraw here didn't have time to get out his weapon before I put a few rounds between him and his pal."

Eddie Mazzetti looked puzzled.

"Quick Draw who?"

"It's a cartoon, boss. Saturday mornings. Clemente and me ...″

"Shut up, Guido."

Guido ducked his head.

"Sorry, Clemente."

"As Clemente told you, they didn't know this gun was under my overcoat. When I lifted it and pulled on this lever, it fired on full automatic."

"Is that what happened?"

"Yeah. Made a hell of a noise. Then he told us we had to bring him to see you. We didn't have no choice 'cause there was no way to know if he still had some rounds in that clip."

Eddie wrinkled his face in disgust.

Clemente spoke again.

"Besides, when we seen what that gun could do, we thought you might want to talk to him."

"And you brought him to my place of business. Let him walk through the casino with a loaded gun."

Eddie turned on the charm and gave Sergeant Scanlon a big smile.

"Just can't get good help these days."

He looked at Clemente. The smile disappeared as quickly as it had arrived.

"You two get out of here."

"Don't forget, boys, I need a ride back to my jeep."

"Wait outside for the sergeant."

Eddie got up and walked around the desk.

"Can I see that?"

"Certainly, Mr. Mazzetti."

"Eddie, sergeant. All my friends call me Eddie. Now that I've heard about this gun, you and I are going to be friends. Someone who's name we do not speak in this room is going to be very happy. If he's happy, I'm happy."

Sergeant Scanlon handed him the gun. Eddie turned it over and looked at it from several angles.

"What's this thing in the front?"

"Rise suppressor. Keeps you from shooting holes in the ceiling before three rounds clear the chamber."

"This is an interesting arrangement where it fits against your shoulder."

"Guy who modified it cut the stock off right there behind the pistol grip. Then he fitted a steel rod into the stock at an angle. See? Makes sort of a 'y' there. And this is the folding forward grip. It's been modified by attaching this rod that connects to the trigger. You pull up the gun, tug on the foregrip, fire the whole twenty-round clip in less than three seconds."

"Will it shoot one round at a time?"

"If you want it to. Just move this selector switch here."

Eddie bent over and picked up the round that had ejected onto the rug.

"Man, that's a wicked looking bullet."

"It is. Full metal jacket. You shoot it at that wall behind me, it'll go all the way through the building."

"You say you can get fifty of these guns?"

"I can."

"But they're not modified like this?"

"No, but the deal includes the drawings that explain how to do it. Any decent gunsmith can make the modifications and remove the serial numbers."

"Okay, I'm interested. What's your price?"

"Why Eddie, you suddenly know my name."

Eddie turned flat eyes on Sergeant Scanlon, and he suddenly understood how the man could have risen to a position of such power in the mob.

"Checked into you. Checked into your family, too. Want me to recite your address in Cicero?"

"Do I detect a threat, Eddie?"

The hard look went away.

"Nah, just a couple guys talkin'. You knew so much about me I thought I should know about you."

He flashed the sparkling, insincere smile and then put it away.

"The price is fifteen hundred per gun."

Eddie did a rapid calculation in his head.

"Seventy-five large. That's a lot of money, Yannity. Here's my counter. One thousand per gun."

"Come on, Eddie, how many million dollars move across those tables downstairs in a day? I don't haggle. I'm taking a hell of a risk getting these rifles. I could be court martialed and spend the rest of my life in the brig at Fort Leavenworth. Besides, I got a lot of guys to grease along the way. In fact, if this falls apart, you're probably doing me a favor."

Eddie gave him the dead-eyed look again.

"What if we do what Clemente said and just take this from you?"

Sergeant Scanlon shrugged.

"Then you've got one gun, and no hope of getting any more. I don't think the man who wants them would be happy about that. Not if this war I'm hearing about spills over from New York to Chicago and maybe even Las Vegas."

Eddie walked back behind his desk and sat down and thought.

It was so quiet Sergeant Scanlon could hear the whisper of the air conditioning.

"Okay. We'll go the seventy-five Gs. How do we arrange delivery?"

"More importantly, to me at least, how do we arrange payment?"

"Pull up a chair, Yannity, and let's work out the details. Coffee? Iced tea? Something stronger?"

CHAPTER 21

Chemehuevi Joe

After walking east down the tracks and surveying the remains of the tow truck, Horse drove back to the substation and swapped his cruiser for the Search and Rescue pickup. He told Merle, the weekend dispatcher, that the station would be receiving a call around noon from Zack out at the wrecking yard reporting his tow truck stolen. He left instructions with Merle to tell Zack the wrecker had been demolished and that Horse would come by later to explain what had happened. Then he drove home and got a kiss from Esperanza and big hugs from the twins, so Sunday wasn't a total loss.

Esperanza stole a few moments with him while he hooked up the horse trailer and loaded Canyon and Mariposa. He brought her up to date on what had happened that morning and his suspicions about who was responsible and why he needed Joe's help. When he drove down the driveway, she stood waving at him until he was out of sight. Then she went in the house and said a prayer. She always worried when her Carlos went off on one of these searches with Chemehuevi Joe.

Horse drove south on Highway 95 until he was parallel to the back of the horseshoe the Chemehuevi Mountains formed as they overlooked the Colorado River. He parked and saddled both horses. Riding Canyon and leading Mariposa, he headed up Trampas Wash toward the hillside where Joe Medrano lived in the primitive place he had dug out of the mountain.

When Horse reached the spot where he intended to tie Canyon and Mariposa before starting the steep climb to Joe's place on foot, Joe appeared out of nowhere. It was like a magician's trick minus the smoke.

"Horse."

"Joe."

Joe climbed on Mariposa. The two men were almost back at the highway before Joe spoke again.

"Who we looking for?"

"The Banner boys. You'll be on the county payroll until we find them."

"Not hard to find. Go to stupid, turn left."

"I'm afraid they've really stepped in it this time, Joe."

As they rode, he explained what had happened.

When he was finished, Joe said, "Those two."

They loaded the horses and set off for the site of the explosions. Since there had been no derailment, Horse was pretty sure the train would no longer be blocking the main line at Goffs, so he took Old 66 instead of going around and coming up the hill from Fenner. As they approached Goffs, the engines and the part of the train with the army shipment were gone. The rest of the train had been backed onto the siding.

They left the pickup and the horse trailer on the north side of the tracks and walked west until Joe found the spot where one of the Banner boys landed when he jumped off the wrecker.

"Blood here. Cut himself."

"He's lucky he wasn't killed getting away from the wrecker."

They walked on. They passed the place where the tow truck had flipped onto its side and continued west until they reached the spot the other twin had landed when he jumped from the train. They followed his tracks northeastward.

"Hurt himself."

"Think so?"

"Limping."

The place where the two men had rendezvoused was easy to find.

"Banner boys for sure?"

"Yes."

"Know the country. Hunt it. Seen their sign."

"How could you tell it was them?"

"Peters shotgun shells. Blue. Them, Lee Hoskins, only ones Everyone else, Remington, Winchester."

He stared north for a moment and then turned and walked toward the truck.

"No horses yet."

"Why not?"

"Know where they're going. Two places for water, that way. Hackberry Spring. Von Trigger. Not Von Trigger. Someone might see them on Lanfair. One hurt, moving slow. Drive out. Ahead of them."

They walked back to the truck and drove to Lanfair Road. They continued north until they hit a two-track turning west. They stayed on it until it intersected another. They hadn't driven too far when Joe spoke.

"Here."

They unloaded Canyon and Mariposa and set off to the southwest toward the north end of the Fenner Hills.

"How far do you think they made it, Joe?"

"South of us. Hugging the hillsides, hoping for water. Isn't any."

After two miles, they saw the Banner boys. One was supporting the other. They weren't making good time. Horse and Joe rode over.

The twins didn't seem surprised to see the two men on horseback.

"Got water," croaked one of them? Horse couldn't tell which.

"Yes. You boys look like you could use a drink."

"Thought we was going to die out here," said the other. "Farther than we thought to the spring."

"Always is," said Joe.

Horse unhooked a desert bag from the horn of his saddle and handed it down.

The brothers drank for a long time.

When they were done, one of them spoke.

"Brax hurt his ankle."

"Jumping off moving trains in the dark will do that. Looks like you're the one went face first into the cinders."

"Yep. Can Brax hitch a ride on one a them horses?"

Joe climbed down.

"Put him up there. You and me walk."

Braxton spoke for the first time.

"I cain't wait to get home and have me a beer."

Horse shook his head.

"You boys aren't going home."

"Where we goin'?"

"You're under arrest."

"For what," said Austin?

"For a whole lot of things."

Austin deflated.

"Yeah, guess I knew that."

Joe helped Braxton onto the horse.

"Don't ride away. Horse shoot you, sure as hell."

The group set off across the desert.

When they reached the truck, Horse dropped the tailgate and they had the boys climb into the bed.

"Better cuff 'em. Might try to jump out."

"Jump out of a moving truck?"

"Banners."

"You're right."

He cuffed their hands behind them and then removed their boots. He took the laces from one boot and tied the cuffs together.

He and Joe loaded Canyon and Mariposa into the trailer. They drove the rutted two-track and then the slightly-less-rutted Lanfair Road to Goffs and then turned toward Smoke Tree on Old 66.

Joe hooked his thumb toward the back of the truck.

"Sunk in?"

"What's that."

"Trouble they're in?"

"Hard to tell what Austin and Braxton are thinking."

They did not speak again during the drive to town.

At the substation, Joe helped Horse lead the prisoners into the station in their stocking feet. They left them there to be booked fingerprinted and locked up for the night.

"No interrogation tonight," Horse told the desk sergeant. "I'l talk to them in the morning after I call the District Attorney's office and find out what all we should charge them with. If they voluntee anything, write it down, but don't ask them any questions. Don' want to screw up a case with a procedural error."

"Got it."

Horse and Joe went back outside and drove to the spot along 95 where Horse had parked before.

"Let me unload Canyon and Mariposa."

"No need. Walk. Riding made me tired."

"Okay, Joe. Thanks for your help. I'll get you paid for this."

"'Preciate it."

"Have you been out to look at the place Burke left you yet?"

"Been there before. Spirit needs time. Come to rest."

"I'm having the body cremated. Burke wants the ashes scattered off the New Yorks."

"Like to come."

"Be glad of your company."

"After that, go to his place."

"All right. I miss that man already."

"Me too."

Joe climbed out of the truck. As Horse drove back to Smoke Tree, he thought about how lucky he was to have known two men as unique as Burke Henry and Joe Medrano in just one lifetime.

CHAPTER 22

Zack

Zechariah Zucker thought it odd that in a town full of Old Testament street names, he was one of only two observant Jews. The other admitted member of The Twelves Tribes of Israel was Ariel Bachman, a dentist. Smoke Tree didn't know what to make of their two Jews. They thought of them as exotics, even though they read about Jews in their Bibles and heard about them every week in their church services. Somehow, the Jews in the Old Testament seemed different than the two men they referred to as "the Junk Yard Jew", and "the Little Jew Dentist".

Zechariah knew there were actually other Jews in Smoke Tree; he recognized a *landsmann* when he saw one. But, as they had chosen not to identify as Jews, he kept their secret. He would like to say to them, "Don't hide your essential Jewishness. This is not Germany. What happened there can never happen here." But he knew better. Knew the horrors of Germany could be replicated anywhere at any time. Knew human beings were not far enough removed from the exclusionary tribalism of pre-history that heads could not be turned by the seductive siren song of hate.

Zechariah felt no animosity toward those who betrayed their heritage. He felt sorry for them. They had anglicized their names: the Fains, the Lipsons, the Stainers, the Starks, the Clines and others. Many had joined Christian churches in order to blend into the mainstream; although, he noticed, none of them had become Catholics. If you're trying to avoid the stinging lash of prejudice, it is best to pitch your lot with Episcopalians, Presbyterians, Methodists, or Baptists. He did, however, wonder whether they told their children the truth about their roots. He suspected they did not but could not imagine what they must have told the children about their grandparents. How did they explain why Grandma and Grandpa had a different last name?

159

As for the dentist, he and Zechariah had very little contact and none at all of a religious nature. In their few conversations, most of which took place with Ariel's hands in Zechariah's mouth and were therefore limited to "uh-huhs" and "ahs" on his part, Zechariah had come away with the unavoidable impression that Ariel Bachmann thought Jewish dentists far superior to Jewish junk yard owners. Zechariah found it odd that a man who was himself subjected to prejudice would inflict the same opprobrium on the only other person in town with whom he shared a religious and cultural identity. Apparently, thought Zechariah, irony had not been part of the curriculum in dental school.

But the dentist was not from the Old Country. Zechariah Zucker was. Perhaps Ariel Bachmann had not seen fear in a handful of dust and was only trying to protect his precarious and practically non-existent social status, a status afforded only because he provided an essential service in the community.

But doesn't a junk man, thought Zechariah, provide an essential service? Perhaps, if they had to, repair garage owners and other people from Smoke Tree could drive to Las Vegas to find cannibalized, second-hand car parts. But if they could do that couldn't they also drive there for their dental work? It was a puzzle. As were people. Zechariah had seen the very worst of people.

On April 1, 1933, when Zechariah was a twenty-year-old in Bavaria, Adolph Hitler called for a boycott of Jewish businesses. Ironically, the call came on the Sabbath, and most of those businesses were closed. But seven days later, the other shoe dropped. A law regarding government jobs was passed. It contained anti-Jewish paragraphs stating, "Civil servants with no Aryan ancestry must go into retirement." The law specified that anyone who had a Jewish parent or grandparent was non-Aryan.

Zechariah could see the writing on the wall. Could hear it in the Horst Wessel song, now proclaimed by law a national symbol. Could feel it in the hostile glare the local brown shirts directed at him. His parents, apparently, could not. They thought it was silliness that would soon pass. The rest of his relatives, most of whom lived near Frankfurt in the Hesse district, felt the same. They chided Zechariah for suggesting they leave the country they had called home since fleeing the pogroms in the ghettos of Russia and Poland.

A year later, still unable to convince his family of the seriousness of the situation, Zechariah set sail for the United States. He carried with him a letter introducing him to his father's cousin Zev Fleisher. Zev owned a scrap metal business in New Jersey.

Zechariah went to work for him and stayed on for many years. The two watched with alarm as the situation in Germany deteriorated.

For a time, the Nazis encouraged Jews to leave. Then, Jews could leave but had to leave their money behind as a "gift" to the Fatherland. This made it hard to emigrate, since few countries would take impoverished Jews. Then the Jews could no longer leave at all. After all, if you want to maintain a regime based on hatred, you need someone to be the object of that hate, and while Gypsies and Jehovah's Witnesses made interesting targets, there simply weren't enough of them. Jews, on the other hand, were plentiful.

The first letters Zechariah received from home continued to espouse the hope that everything was going to be fine. As the years went by, the tone of the letters changed, and his parents lost their earlier faith in the innate goodness of the German people. The letters eventually made it clear his parents would not be permitted to leave the country, just as Zechariah had feared. In November of 1938, came *Kristallnacht*, and over a thousand synagogues went up in flames across Germany and Austria while police stood by and watched. Soon, Zechariah received no more letters.

Not long after *Kristallnacht*, he and Zev had a falling out over the sale of scrap metal to Japan. Since his adopted country was in conflict with Japan over control of the Pacific, Zechariah thought such sales were unpatriotic. Zev's response was, "Let me know when war breaks out. In the meantime, there's good money to be made from those people."

So, in January of 1939, Zechariah took the savings he had scraped together from his meager wages and headed west. He picked up Highway 66 in Chicago and set his sights on the wild west he had read about as a Bavarian boy in the stories of Karl May.

His Model A broke down just west of Smoke Tree. He walked back to town and stopped at the junk yard he had passed a few minutes earlier. The place was in such disarray that the owner, a very old man named Cecil Billingsworth, didn't even know if he had the part Zechariah described. With Cecil's permission, Zechariah wandered the acres of wrecked cars until he found and removed the part he needed.

He paid for it and walked the three miles back to his car and made the repair. On a whim, he turned around and drove back to Smoke Tree. He spent an hour looking over the town, which seemed nice enough when compared to living in a one-room shack inside the fence of a New Jersey junkyard. He had lunch at the Liberty Café and got back on 66 and drove on toward Los Angeles.

He made it as far as Klinefelter before he pulled over and stopped. He sat in the parking lot of a motor court sheltered in a stand of aethel trees and thought for a while. He turned around and drove back to Smoke Tree to talk to Cecil Billingsworth. Zechariah told the old man that, for a modest salary, he would put the junkyard in order and inventory all the engine and body parts on the premises and record them in a ledger.

"Zechariah, that's…"

"Yes," interrupted Zechariah. "I'm a Jew, Mr. Billingsworth. Do you have a problem with that?"

"Not if you work cheap."

A discussion about wages followed. Eventually, the two men reached an agreement.

"What's your last name, Zechariah?"

"Zucker."

"Zechariah Zucker is a mouthful. Do you mind if I just call you Zack?"

"Not at all, as long as you pay me."

The two shook hands, and Zechariah became 'Zack' in Smoke Tree forever after.

The arrangement included a place to stay behind the office and Zechariah Zucker found himself living in a junk yard once again. True to his word, he organized Cecil's operation, but the ledger he produced was for Cecil's purposes only. Zechariah had a prodigious memory, and he knew the availability, location, provenance and price of every part on the lot.

He had finally saved enough money to think about getting a place of his own when the Japanese bombed Pearl Harbor. He resisted the temptation to send a telegram to Zev telling him the war had started. Zechariah loved the country that had saved him from the fate of the rest of his family. Before the calendar rolled over to a new year, he had joined the Army to defend it.

When he returned to Smoke Tree after the war, he found Cecil Billingsworth in poor health. He and Cecil structured a deal and a payment schedule that allowed Zechariah to buy the junkyard and Cecil to spend his last few years in places other than the office.

He painted "Zack" on the corrugated steel panels on either side of the front gate and went into business for himself.

At noon on Friday, June 12, 1964, Zechariah left the Banner boys in charge of things for the rest of the day and went home to clean up for his long, weekly drive to San Bernardino. He had long worshipped with Congregation Emanu El, a reform congregation or

North "E" Street in San Bernardino. He was well known and welcomed there; sometimes gently ribbed as the man who weekly crossed the desert to the promised land, going west on his journey instead of east as his ancestors had on their way out of Egypt and without needing to part any sea, Red or otherwise, to reach his destination.

As he came down the west side of South Pass and let the big V8 under the hood of his Pontiac Grand Prix unwind, he looked out over the panorama spreading below him. He thought, as he often did on the trip, of the contrast between this place and the Bavarian Alps of his childhood. Alps whose peaks were covered with snow all year. And thought also about the contrast between the barren basins ahead of him from here to Barstow and the green foothills stretching from Munich to Salzburg.

And yet, he had no *heimweh*: no homesickness. The desert, sterile and forbidding to so many, had imprinted itself on his heart over the years. He felt a stronger attraction to the humble creosote than to any delicate edelweiss in its snowy *cirque,* and a stronger attraction to the blue Colorado than to any *bach* running rapidly over smooth stones ground round by the glaciers that had retreated from the Bavarian Alps after the last ice age.

Those heading west toward Los Angeles saw the drive he made every Friday as endless, boring, and monotonous. Zechariah saw it as a drive through stark beauty. Through places where nature was stripped to its bare essentials and the underlying skeleton of the earth was revealed on barren hillsides or in outcroppings of rock

The charm of the journey always ended for him when he topped Cajon Pass and dropped into San Bernardino. He was *kleinstadt gezüchtet*, and cities were cities. His time in New Jersey had eliminated any desire to live in one ever again. But while the appeal of the drive itself ended at Summit, the value he received by completing it began before sundown in the valley below.

Many years before, when he first joined the congregation, he had become fast friends with the Baerlein family, and they had adopted him for *Shabbat*. He had a long-standing invitation, which he never refused but never took for granted, to observe the Friday evening *kiddush,* including the lighting of the candles and the sharing of the braided bread and the special family meal that marked the beginning of *Shabbat* with the Baerleins.

Since Zechariah had been so long without family, he treasured the feeling of closeness he experienced with the Baerleins. He especially loved the ritual during which the parents placed their hands on the children's heads and recited, *Yisimha Elohim k'Efraim*

163

ukhiM'nash (May God make you like Efraim and Menashe) for their son, and *Yisimeih Elohim k'Sarah, Rivkah, Rahel v'Leah* (May God make you like Sarah, Rebecca, Rachel and Leah) for their daughter. When the blessing was offered, Zechariah always remembered his father reciting the same words.

After the ceremony and the meal, Zechariah always spent the night. The next day, he went with them to the Congregation Emanu El. The Saturdays he spent with the people there buoyed his spirit. Emanu El was a reform congregation, utilizing the Union Prayer book with its concept of Jewish Peoplehood and guided by the thinking of Mordecai M. Kaplan with his emphasis on Judaism as a civilization. The Rabbi had tilted away from Zionism and written that Judaism was not just the Jewish religion itself but a blessed blend of religion, culture, language and social interaction.

It was that blend that re-charged Zechariah. He loved the lively and joyous welcoming service, *Kabbalat Shabbat*, and was always saddened by the pensive farewell ceremony. *Havdalah* meant that the extra soul he had received on Friday night would depart his body when the braided candle was doused with wine and the song of the prophet Elijah was sung on Saturday evening. Even the sweet-smelling spices that were supposed to help him carry some portion of *Shabbat* into the coming week left him feeling lonely. Lonely because the following day he would return to Smoke Tree and resume the solitary existence divided between the wrecking yard and his little house.

Because he did not want the Baerlein family to see his sadness, he never spent Saturday nights at their home. They thought Zechariah drove to Smoke Tree after *Shabbat*, but he did not. Instead, he drove to Victorville and spent the night there in a spartan room at the Green Spot Motel. He viewed the Green Spot as a halfway house of sorts: a place to become accustomed to the loneliness that would be his lot until the next *Shabbat*.

Early Sunday afternoon, Zechariah Zucker arrived back at his wrecking yard. He fed the Rottweilers and went in the office to look through the receipts from Friday afternoon. He did a little routine bookkeeping and balanced the checkbook.

While he was working, he couldn't shake the uneasy feeling that something wasn't right, but he couldn't put his finger on it. Puzzled, he walked out outside and looked around.

The wrecker was gone!

Zechariah went back into the office and opened the metal cabinet where the keys to the wrecker were kept. Gone. He walked back to the front gate and examined the lock and chain that secured it. No damage. He couldn't imagine anyone climbing over the fence without being attacked by the dogs.

None of this made any sense. He walked back to the office and dialed the Smoke Tree Substation of the San Bernardino County Sheriff's Department.

CHAPTER 23

A Long Day Made Longer

When Horse got to the substation, he called Esperanza.

"I just got back from dropping Joe out near his place. We found the Banner boys and brought them in. I've got a couple more things to do, and then I'll be on home."

"I'm glad you're safe. Those boys weren't any trouble?"

"Mild as kittens. They were so tired and thirsty, I doubt they could have put up a fight even if they'd been inclined to. They're in the holding cell."

"Don't forget to get them something to eat."

He could hear the concern in her voice. Just like his Esperanza.

"I won't. I'm off to see Zack to tell him what happened to his wrecker. I'll pick something up for them on my way back."

"I'll have dinner for you when you get here. Hurry home. *Te extraño.*"

"*Y yo le. Eres el mejor, mi tesoro.* How are the twins?"

"Getting sleepy. If you're going to see them with their big, beautiful eyes open, don't be too long."

"Okay. I'll give you a rundown on the day when I get home."

"*Te quiero.*"

"Love you too. Keep well."

When Horse drove to Zack's house on Zion Street, Zack answered the door so quickly Horse thought he must have been watching out the window.

"Hello, Zechariah. Sorry about what happened to your wrecker."

Zack had a surprised look on his face.

"Horse, that's the first time anybody in this town has ever called me by my proper name."

"Zechariah Zucker. It's on your driver's license. Stopped you for fifty in a thirty-five ten years ago. Thought I'd use it today since this seems like a formal occasion. Or at least an official one."

"Where are my manners? Come in."

Horse took off his hat and followed Zack. He wondered if anybody else in Smoke Tree had ever been inside. The house was immaculate. The dark furniture looked European. There was a bouquet of flowers in a cut vase on the divider between the kitchen and a small dining room. A crocheted yarmulke was next to the flowers.

"Iced tea, hot tea, coffee?"

"I'm good, but thanks."

"Please, sit down."

Horse lowered himself to the couch. There were white lace antimacassars on the arms. He rearranged the holster holding his .357 so it wouldn't damage the stiff brocade fabric and propped his Stetson on his knee. Zack sat in an old rocker made of dark wood.

"Your dispatcher said you were out looking for Austin and Braxton. Did you find them?"

"Me and Chemehuevi Joe. Brought them in. They're in a cell at the station."

"Horse, I've been thinking. I'm not sure I want to press charges against the boys."

"Some advice?"

"Please."

"You're going to want to. Otherwise, insurance won't pay on your truck. If you don't press charges, it wasn't theft."

Zack looked crestfallen.

"I hate to make trouble for them. They're not bad. Just dumb."

"Zechariah…"

"Please, Zack. Otherwise I'll have to start calling you Captain Caballo."

Horse smiled.

"Okay. You're Zack again for the duration. Zack, stealing your wrecker is the least of their problems. There are going to be federal charges. I don't know what all of them will be yet. Interfering with interstate commerce, destroying railroad property, destroying U.S. Army property. It's going to be a long list."

"I see. What do you think will happen to them?"

"I'm not sure. I'll know more after I talk to the D.A.s office tomorrow. They're going to do some time, for sure."

"Sorry to hear that."

Zack thought for a moment.

"I'll pay for an attorney for them. Help them out."

"Okay, Zack, I'll let them know."

He rose to his feet.

Zack stood too.

"One more thing, Horse."

"What's that."

"I want you to know how sorry I am about Burke Henry. He stopped by one time to get a part for that old flatbed Ford. After that, he came by now and then just to talk. But never about himself. Things in general. It was something I looked forward to. I mention it because I know he was a good friend of yours."

"He was indeed, Zack. Best friend a man could wish for."

CHAPTER 24

News from Nevada

It was nearly eight o'clock by the time a very tired Carlos Caballo dropped off burgers, fries and milk shakes for the Banner boys before heading home. When he pulled onto the two-track to his driveway, a sunset the color of a railroad flare was burning across the western horizon above the Sacramentos. He stopped and stared at it in awe.

Must be clouds way out there beyond the horizon, he thought. Never get to Smoke Tree though. Not this time of year.

He sat for a moment thinking about how he never got tired of these sunsets. About how the Mojave could fill his heart and bring him peace in the unpeaceful world he had to deal with. He thought of the Banner boys in the holding cell at the station. He thought about Zechariah, a man he had never seen anywhere in Smoke Tree but his wrecking yard, the grocery store and the service station. And now, Horse had been inside his house. A tidy place, but stiff somehow, and cold, in spite of the summer heat.

He wondered whether Zechariah ever had moments of peace. He guessed he would never know. As for the Banner boys, maybe they had found peace at times down on the Colorado listening to the run of the river. Even though they were in jail, they had each other. As far as he could tell, Zechariah Zucker had no one. At least not in Smoke Tree. He wasn't surprised to discover Burke had stopped by to visit from time to time. It was the sort of thing Burke would do for someone he saw as lonely and isolated.

Horse took his foot off the brake and eased down the bumpy road. He smiled as he thought about the evening ahead. He would

171

help Esperanza get their twins to bed. Then he would have a cold beer and eat his dinner while he told Esperanza about his day in more detail. She always wanted to know what he was doing. And more importantly, she would tell him everything she and Elena and Alejandro had done. After that, he would get a nice, hot shower, and then perhaps they could enjoy what had been interrupted so early that morning.

It was nine-thirty before he and Esperanza got the twins to bed after lots of laughs, hugs and kisses. Because his job kept him away so much, he tried to compensate with extra affection. Affection that came easily because he loved those two so much. After that, Horse finally got to eat his dinner while talking with Esperanza. He was heading down the hall to get his shower when there was a knock at the front door.

He thought it was probably someone from the Army. With a deep sigh, he turned and headed back the way he had come. Esperanza raised her eyebrows and lifted her hands in a palms-up gesture when he walked past the dining room. When he opened the door, Aeden Snow was standing there in the pale glow of the yellow bug light.

"Good evening, Captain Caballo. Sorry to bother you at home late on a Sunday night, but I saw something today I think you should know about."

"No bother, Ade. Come on in."

Horse stepped aside.

Esperanza had walked into the living room.

"Hell, Mrs. Caballo. I apologize for interrupting your Sunday evening."

"No need to apologize, Aeden.

I believe you're twenty-one now, is that right?"

"Yes ma'am. Just turned."

"Then unless you want me to start calling you Mr. Snow, it's Esperanza."

"And I'm Horse. Sit down Ade."

Ade sat in the nearest living room chair, one with wooden arms and soft, brightly-colored-cloth cushions. Horse and Esperanza sat down across from him on a couch of the same design. He noticed how they settled close together and exchanged a brief smile before Esperanza took her husband's hand. Ade wondered if he would ever feel that kind of easy, comfortable closeness with anyone. He didn't think it likely.

"Tell me what you saw."

"A soldier in a jeep meeting two guys who drove a black Chrysler 300 with Nevada plates."

Horse leaned forward.

"What did you think was so special about that?"

"I've seen that kind of car out that way before."

"When you say, 'out that way,' are you still spending your weekends at Lee's place?"

"Yes."

"Been doing that a long time now. I hear you never miss a weekend when you're home from college."

"No sir. My favorite place in the world."

Horse felt another piece of an old puzzle fall into place.

"The first time you saw a car like that out there, it was at the Stonebridge place back in '62, wasn't it?"

"Yes."

"Was John there the day you saw the car?"

"No."

"How about Joe Medrano?"

"You'd have to ask Joe about that."

"Ade, this is a conversation, not an interrogation."

"It feels like one."

"I assure you, it isn't. Just questions to satisfy my curiosity about something. Here's the next one. Was a young Japanese woman there the day you saw the car?"

"She was."

Horse thought for a moment about how to proceed. There were some things he wanted to know, but other things he didn't want to hear about.

"Reason I ask, Ade, is that I was out at Joe's one day and he had a picture of a Japanese girl. It was lying on his cot. When I asked him where he got it, he told me he took it off some guys who didn't need it anymore."

Ade said nothing. Just sat and stared at Horse with the same kind of look he sometimes got from Joe Medrano when Joe didn't want to answer a question.

"Ade, I'm not asking you to tell me what happened to the guys who didn't need that picture, even though I think you know. I think Joe knows too, but he wouldn't tell me. I'm fine with that, believe me."

"Thank you, Horse."

"But I am wondering about something. And it doesn't involve anything that might be a crime."

"I'll answer if I can."

173

"First, let me tell you I know the woman's name. It's Kiko Yoshida."

"Joe told me last summer about you seeing that picture, bu he said he didn't tell you her name."

"He didn't. I recognized her picture because I'd had it in my hands long before the day I saw it at Joe's. Some bad actors from Nevada had been looking for her in Smoke Tree, and they went to the library to see if she had a library card. Told Mrs. Sensebaugh they thought she might have one since she was a college graduate and would be looking for books to read if she was living in town."

"I see."

"Well, Ade, that told me they knew a lot about her. A whole lot. And when I asked Joe, he told me she had something that the mafia was looking for."

"Okay."

"I arrested those two for carrying concealed pistols without a permit. They made bail at their arraignment, but they didn't show up for their trial. I never saw them again. But here's the thing. They were driving a black, Chrysler 300 with Nevada plates. When I ran them, I found out the car was registered to the Serengeti Hotel and Casino. So, I'm assuming the Kiko person had worked there."

"She had."

"You see, some guys driving that same car had been in Smoke Tree before and scared some of the locals, so I drove up to Vegas and told Mr. Mazzetti, the boss at the Serengeti, to keep his hoods out of San Bernardino County. He didn't. They came back. So, you see, I'm familiar with black Chryslers too."

"When I saw the meeting between the soldier and the guys in the black car, they were on the Nevada side of the line."

"Is there more?"

"Yes. The soldier fired an automatic weapon of some kind."

"Whoa. Now you've really got my attention. Let's start at the beginning."

"I was in Lee's Willys on that terrible two-track that runs over behind Crescent Peak. I left the truck up there and took a hike to poke around the old Nippeno Gold Mine. Took my binoculars along to glass the mountains for mule deer. Anyway, I was taking a break when I heard a vehicle coming up the highway from Nipton. Not many people ever on that road, but I didn't think much about it until it stopped and then started up and stopped again. I thought maybe someone was having car trouble, so I climbed a hill by the mine to get a look. That's when I saw the Chrysler. It was pulled off the road down near Bullion Spring on the edge of Big Tiger Wash. And it was nose to nose with the vehicle I had heard. An army jeep.

"How far were you from the vehicles?"

"About a quarter of a mile. Close enough to see the Nevada plates on the back of the car with the binoculars."

There was one soldier in the jeep. And here's where it starts to get strange. The guy was wearing an overcoat. I couldn't imagine why anyone would put on an overcoat when it was over a hundred degrees."

"Was there anyone in the black car?"

"No. The soldier walked north toward the foothills of the McCulloughs. I had the glasses on him when two guys stepped out ahead of him."

"Can you describe them?"

"Big. Dark hair. Slacks and Hawaiian shirts. Looked a lot like those guys Johnny Quentin and I saw up at the McPhearson place when we were in high school. But here's the thing. Both of them had shoulder rigs."

They moved farther apart like two gunfighters in an old western. I think they were talking to the guy in the overcoat, but I was too far away to hear anything. All of a sudden, one of the guys reaches toward his gun. The guy in the overcoat does something very fast and the sound of all these shots reaches me."

Ade stopped talking. Horse thought for a while before he spoke.

"The Army's on stand-down all day today, so right there it's weird you saw a jeep out there. But maybe the guy in the overcoat was shooting blanks. I guess that's all they're using out there in these war games."

"Blanks don't kick up dust and ricochet off rocks."

"What happened next?"

"The soldier took off the overcoat."

"Did you get a good look at the gun when he did?"

"At first, all I could see was a strap over his shoulder and partway down his back. He and the big guys talked some more, and then everybody walked my direction, but I still couldn't see all of it. I think he was making the Hawaiian shirt guys walk in front of him. When the soldier got back to the jeep and turned sideways, I could see the whole gun. It was about twenty inches long. Back of the stock had been cut off behind a pistol grip, and that part was just beneath his armpit. There was some kind of handle just below the end of the barrel, and a big magazine sticking out of the bottom.

The soldier stood at the jeep and watched the two big guys until they got into the car. It was like he expected them to try something. When they drove away, he unslung the weapon and climbed in the jeep. Put it on the seat and covered it with the overcoat."

"So now you could see his uniform."

"Yes sir."

"Could you see his rank?"

"He had a patch on his sleeve. Lot of stripes on it."

"How many."

"Three pointing down, three pointing up."

"Sergeant E-8. That's a pretty high rank. Anything in the middle of those stripes?"

Aeden thought for a minute.

"No."

"Could you read his name tag?"

"He was sideways to me."

"Go on."

"That's about it. The sergeant drove off the same direction as the Chrysler."

"Did you get a number off that Nevada plate?"

"I did. I scratched it in the dirt and memorized it."

He pulled a piece of paper out of his shirt pocket and handed it to Horse."

"Thanks. I'll run this in the morning. How about the jeep?"

"Some kind of number-jumble on the back, but I don't remember it."

"What did you do next?"

"Waited until I was sure they were gone. Drove down and picked up the brass."

Ade reached in his pocket and pulled out a handful of cartridge cases and handed them to Horse.

'7.62.' was stamped under the primers.

"NATO rounds."

"Look like the .308s my dad reloads."

"It's almost the same."

"Well, that's what I came by to tell you. I thought someone needed to know."

"Thank you for bringing this to me, Ade. Believe me, I'll look into it."

They stood up.

"One more thing before you go Ade, and once again, this is not an interrogation, just my curiosity about someone I never met. Joe said he never saw Kiko Yoshida again. Did you?"

Ade didn't answer for a moment. He felt reluctant, but he remembered how straight Horse had been with him and Johnny Quentin, and how he had gone out of his way to help Charlie Merriman.

"I saw her once more. Spring of my freshman year. She came by the college, and we went out for coffee."

"Do you think you'll ever see her again?"

"I'd like to Horse. I'd really like to. But I don't think I will."

He looked very sad.

"Well, I hope she's safe wherever she is. Those are very bad people she got mixed up with."

"Yes. Very bad people partial to big Black Chryslers."

While Horse showered, he thought about the question he had asked Colonel Dulac on Saturday. The question about what would happen to the old M14s when the M16s were airdropped. And the Colonel's disinterred response. And now a sergeant meets up in the Nevada desert with a couple of boys from Las Vegas. Interesting.

CHAPTER 25

A Walking Update

The pre-sunrise sky was brightening when Danny Dubois arrived at the Swank Motor Court. As he had been the previous three mornings, Jedidiah Shanks was sitting on the metal chair outside the door of his tourist cabin. The increasing intensity of the light was beginning to bring out the luminous pink of his Cadillac Eldorado.

As soon as Jedidiah saw the young man, he rose and stepped down off the low, cement slab that formed the miniscule porch and joined Danny in the gravel parking lot.

"Master Dubois."

"Preacher man."

"Wither goest we this morning?"

"Let's do the religious named streets we did on our first walk. I like that part of town best."

"Sounds fine. Helps me stay in contact with the history of the religion which I bring to others but no longer believe in myself."

They set off eastward on the shoulder of Highway 66. The horizon was slowly becoming suffused with the soft, red light that presaged the sunrise. Suddenly, two blasts split the sky.

Jedidiah ducked into a crouch, his eyes scanning the area for cover.

"Easy, preacher man. Just sonic booms from jet fighters."

Jedidiah straightened.

"Startle reflex. Twenty years old but still there. Common among combat veterans. Happens before they have time to think.

"I remember you telling me you had been a combat chaplain. If you don't mind my asking, what was that like?"

179

"Sometimes terrifying, sometimes sorrowful. Terrifying as in the moment you hook up your deployment bag and stumble out the door, your heart pounding as you make the four count."

"What's the four count?"

"If your canopy doesn't pop by the time you get to four, you have to cut away the main canopy and deploy the reserve chute. That's terrifying. Sorrowful is attending to dying soldiers. I'm telling you, Danny, those were brave and valiant men."

"You sound proud."

"Only of my comrades."

"I notice you limp a bit. From the war?"

Jedidiah shrugged.

"Just a little shrapnel."

By this time, the two men had walked north on Palestine into the residential neighborhoods on that street. The red fireball of the sun had lifted above the eastern horizon. They continued on in silence for two more blocks.

"Have you told Carlyle you will be staying behind when the carnival leaves?"

Danny shook his head.

"Not yet. I'm hoping to hear this evening about that mechanic's job, but the guy checking for me may not know until tomorrow."

"That doesn't leave a lot of time. The show is pulling out Wednesday morning, right?"

"It is, and I know I have to tell him. He'll need to send a new advance man ahead that morning. What about you? When's the revival leaving?"

"Wednesday morning, same as the carnival. Got to do my 'carry-the-cross' act that afternoon. I'll tell you what, though, I'm not having my crew drop me so far from town this time. That last haul took a toll on me. I never used to wear a hat when I took my morning walk, but now I feel sick out in the sun without one. Another reason for a shorter walk in Parker. I don't think it'll have the same impact if Jesus is wearing this Dodger's hat."

"How about an Angel's cap?"

Jedidiah laughed.

"You have a quick mind, Danny Dubois. I'm going to miss walking with you. We could have explored Parker and Blythe and then Banning and Beaumont up in the San Gorgonio Pass. Not to mention all those towns along Highway 99 in the Central Valley. By the way, have you found a place to live yet?"

180

"No. The Smoke Tree Weekly comes out on Wednesday, though. I might find something advertised in there. If not, I can stay at that old hotel on Front Street. I stopped by on Sunday afternoon for a look around. The place is a dump, but it's real cheap."

CHAPTER 26

Fitting the Pieces Together

Horse was in his office before six. He put a piece of poster board on his easel. He drew the "north" symbol at the top and oriented the easel to true north. Unlike Chemehuevi Joe, who carried an accurately-oriented, three-dimensional picture of the world in his mind regardless of his own personal orientation, Horse had always had to turn to the north to properly locate himself in relationship to the world around him. If he was working with a topographical map, he had to orient it to the ground before it was of any use to him. He found that fact embarrassing, but knew there was no point in trying to defy his limitations. He actually looked out his office window at the distant Dead Mountains to the north and imagined the geography beyond them before beginning to draw on the board.

He marked the approximate location of Kelso and the Hayden siding on the Union Pacific Railroad where the touch-and-go would drop enough M-16 rifles for three infantry battalions. From there, he drew a rough approximation of Kelso-Cima Road and on to Morning Star Mine Road. He connected that line to one representing Ivanpah Road as it led to Highway 164. He traced 164 through Nipton and on to Searchlight. He tagged 'Nipton' and 'Searchlight' and approximated the spot between them where 164 crossed from California into Nevada.

Horse picked up a red marker and drew a line to represent the two-track that cut away from Walking Box Ranch Road and moved west behind Crescent peak. He drew an 'x' to represent the spot where Aeden Snow had seen the Army jeep and the black Chrysler 300 parked nose to nose. He put in another 'x' to show

183

where Aeden had been when he witnessed the events on Sunday and a large circle that encompassed Nippeno mine, Bullion Spring, Big Tiger Wash, and the foothills of the McCullough Mountains. The 'x' for the meeting location was in the middle of the circle.

When he was done, he stepped back and looked at the crude map. The meeting had taken place on the Nevada side of the state line. Not far across the line, but enough that it removed the event from Horse's jurisdiction. He sat on the edge of his desk and thought.

Colonel Dulac said the 22nd Armored Brigade was going to get the new rifles. That would be the mechanized infantry battalions. And the 22nd was being held in reserve on the west side of the Providence. That would put their field headquarters close to the touch-and-go site. The master sergeant Aeden had seen was probably the top NCO at brigade S-4. Who else would be involved with the disposition of the M-14s that were about to be replaced? The officer heading up brigade S-4, obviously. Probably a major. A field-grade officer who would be very interested in the logistics of getting the new rifles in the hands of the Ten Bravos in the units, but who might well delegate the disposition of the old ones to his top NCO. Officers don't do routine detail work. Sergeants run the Army.

Horse got another poster board and put it on the other easel and oriented it correctly. He drew in Highway 66, the Providence Range, the Union Pacific rail line, Hayden Siding, and the airstrip the Colonel had described. He marked in red the movement of the APCs he and Joe had seen being offloaded near Essex. The most obvious route would take them north up Black Canyon Road, west on Cedar Canyon and then farther west to the foothills of the Providence near Hayden Siding.

He labeled the arrow 'Army Route.'

He returned to his position on the edge of the desk, studied the new drawing, and thought some more. He returned to the board and sketched in Cima Dome. He marked Kelso with an 'x' and drew in Kelso Cima Road and added Kelbaker Road to where it connected with the two-track to Foshay Pass bisecting the Providence. He drew line coming south off Cima Dome to intersect Kelso Cima Road. He labeled those lines, 'Observation Route.' He stood in front of the easels for a while, switching back and forth between the two poster boards.

Satisfied, he sat down behind his desk, dialed up an outside line, and called the California Highway Patrol. He recited the plate number Ade had provided and asked for information on the registration. He had an answer within five minutes. The Black

Chrysler 300 was registered to the Serengeti Hotel and Casino, Las Vegas, Nevada. Eddie Mazzetti's boys were back on his doorstep. They just hadn't quite stepped through the door. That complicated matters.

He hung up and looked at his watch. A little after seven o'clock. He got up and resumed his study of the two poster boards, trying to be sure he had not overlooked a higher probability.

He kept at it until eight o'clock. If he knew his friend and mentor, Pete Hardesty, the man was already at work. He dialed the administrative offices number of the San Bernardino County Sheriff's Department.

"Captain Caballo for Undersheriff Hardesty," he told the receptionist who answered and transferred his call.

"Undersheriff's office."

"Captain Caballo calling to speak to the undersheriff."

"One moment."

There was a click.

"Horse, what's happening in the desert wastelands of eastern San Bernardino County?"

"War."

"Oh yeah. Desert Strike. What's on tap today?"

"Nezona has invaded Calonia. Crossed the river in a whole bunch of places a whole bunch of different ways beginning at four o'clock this morning."

"Who are the good guys?"

"Darned if I know. Supposed to be a war about controlling the water in the Colorado River."

Pete Hardesty laughed.

"That war's been going on ever since they built Boulder Dam. All those river crossings sound exciting, though."

"Already had a lot of phone calls about them this morning. One was a fisherman calling to tell us the Army was scaring the trout. I'll tell you though, if you and I had a fraction of a tenth of a percent of what this thing is costing, we could each buy ourselves an island in the Pacific and retire."

"Yeah, it must be a staggering amount."

"When I was driving to the office this morning, sonic booms were waking Smoke Tree from its sleep and rattling windows. Jet fighters doing mock combat. Apparently, they shoot film that is developed and analyzed to see who shot down who. Aerial combat by Kodak. Lots of calls about that, too. Questions and complaints. I guess they want us to call the Air Force and tell them to knock it off."

The undersheriff laughed.

"Sounds like you've got your hands full. What can I do, send reinforcements?"

"Actually, sir, I'm calling to ask for your advice on a Desert Strike related problem."

"You can drop the 'sir.' I'm still just Pete."

"Undersheriff Pete."

"I know. Can't get used to it myself."

"Do you remember that little problem I had with those Las Vegas people back in '62?"

"You mean when you arrested two Mafia guys in the Smoke Tree library?"

"That's the one. Scared our librarian so bad she retired. Anyway, the day I arrested those mutts was the second time they'd been in town. The first time was a couple of months before. They had been pushy with a few of the locals, and it made me mad. I drove up the Serengeti Casino and told the manager, guy named Eddie Mazzetti, to keep his goombahs out of San Bernardino County."

"And he didn't?"

"Nope. The two I arrested in the library were driving a car registered to the same place."

"If I remember right, they were arraigned, made bail, and never showed for trial."

"That's right. Anyway, one of those black Chryslers those guys seem to favor showed up on the desert just over the Nevada line yesterday morning. Two guys in Hawaiian shirts and shoulder rigs met up with an Army sergeant. There was a discussion of some kind and this sergeant cut loose with a wicked little automatic weapon he was carrying under an overcoat. Put a bunch of rounds between the two guys."

"Hold on a minute, Horse."

Pete put his hand over the mouthpiece, but Horse could hear him yell.

"Hold all my calls until I tell you otherwise."

He came back on the line.

"You say this sergeant was wearing an overcoat?"

"That's right. The weapon was concealed underneath it. The person who told me about this said he didn't even know the sergeant had a gun until the shooting started."

"What happened after that?"

"The Chrysler drove off toward Searchlight and the jeep followed it."

"How'd you find out about this?"

"A young man who had seen a couple of these guys they last time they were in the county recognized the type of car. Wrote down the license number. Came by my house late last night and gave me the plate number and some cartridge cases from the weapon. 7.62 NATO."

"How come these guys didn't see the young man who told you all this?"

"He was a good distance away, watching all this through binoculars."

"What was he...never mind. I'm afraid to ask. I'll tell you Horse, you've got some strange folks out your way."

"This one's pretty sharp. College boy. You'll see a report later today about what two who aren't so sharp tried to do on the Santa Fe main line early Sunday morning."

"Give me the down and dirty."

"They tried to uncouple a car from a moving train and corral it with a tow truck."

"Oh, man. You really do have a full plate, don't you?"

"Seems so. Anyway, I ran the license number off that car this morning. The car is registered to the Serengeti."

"The Mazzetti guy again."

"That's right."

"Okay, what do you need from me?"

"Pete, I know this isn't strictly a San Bernardino County thing, but I don't like it. Two mafia types. An Army guy with an automatic weapon of some kind. I think we might be looking at a possible arms sale."

"You and I both know how hard it is to steal a weapon from the Army."

"Yes, and if I hadn't had a conversation on Saturday with the full-bird running the G-3 shop for the entire operation, I probably wouldn't have made a connection."

Horse related the information about the M-16 drop and the M-14s becoming surplus. He heard Pete scratching out notes during the story. He continued to write after Horse was done.

"That many troops, must be CID around."

"There are. Met a couple of them this morning. The railcar those two yahoos tried to bulldog was loaded with Army jeeps."

"Well, there you go. You've got a contact."

"I do, but I'm still worried."

"How so?"

"This sergeant was an E-8."

"That's a lot of stripes."

"It is. I think this guy's probably the top NCO in a brigade S-4 shop."

"Sounds about right."

"You were in the big war, Pete. Who really runs the Army?"

"Sergeants. Everyone who's ever served knows that."

"That's what worries me. Say I contact these CID guys. They start nosing around trying to figure out what's going on. How many seconds do you think it will take before this master sergeant hears about it?"

"About five."

"That's right. Pete, I think this sergeant's planning to cockroach a bunch of these rifles that are going to become surplus and sell them to the mob."

"Could be. But I'm confused about something. It's only the M14s that will be surplus, right?"

"According to the Colonel."

"An M-14 is a big rifle. I can't see Mafia muscle walking around with rifles."

"I can't either, but the young man who came by last night described the weapon to me. It sounds to me like someone took a 14A1 squad automatic rifle, cut it down, and turned it into something easily concealed."

"Beneath an overcoat. Sounds like a Humphrey Bogart movie."

"Here's what I'm thinking. This sergeant gave those gangsters a field demonstration. He's offering to sell them guns, plus the modification plans, for a big chunk of change.

"You might be right."

"If we tip CID, the sergeant will hear about it and the whole scheme will die."

"What's wrong with that? No guns for the bad guys."

"This is getting personal with me. I don't like this Mazzetti guy, and I don't like the people he works for. They own Las Vegas and the Las Vegas police and the Clark County Sheriff's Department. They think they can do whatever they want whenever they want to."

"I'm sure that's true."

"I want to put some of these guys away. We can take some bad guys off the board. That's where I'm asking for your help. I don't know people at the federal level, and this automatic weapons thing must be federal. I'm thinking FBI."

"Ordinarily, I'd be thinking the same thing, except this is about the Mafia."

"Why does that make it any different?"

"For reasons no one understands, Hoover doesn't want to mess with the bent-nose crowd."

"But I've heard Bobby Kennedy has a bee in his bonnet about the Mafia."

"He does, but Hoover stonewalls even the Attorney General. Apparently flat out refuses to cooperate. Told congress there's no such thing as the Mafia!"

"Well, that derails what I had in mind."

"Maybe not. Who brought down Al Capone?"

"Not the FBI. The IRS."

"That's right. And the IRS is part of...?"

"Treasury."

"And the responsibility to enforce federal firearms laws fall to who?"

"Treasury!"

"That's right. Department called the Alcohol Tax Unit."

"Do you know someone there?"

"I do. Met him at a conference. He's a real sharp cookie. Has a thing about the Mafia. Especially in Las Vegas. He thinks they're skimming money from the casinos. He'd be perfect for this."

"How do we get hold of him?"

"He's in the San Francisco office. I'll put in a call to him today and relay everything you told me. If he wants a piece of these guys, and I'm pretty sure he will, he'll call you. Probably tomorrow."

"Okay. If he doesn't bite, I'll go to CID."

"Either way, the mob doesn't get a bunch of machine guns."

"What's this guy's name?"

"Dave D'Arnauld."

"Can you spell that for me?"

"Not sure I can. Not correctly, anyway. French name. Nobody at ATU can pronounce it right, even though he's a bit of a legend over there. They just call him Darnold."

By the time he said goodbye to Pete Hardesty, Horse felt like he was getting a handle on the situation. He paced around his office, turning from time to time to look at the poster boards. He thought about the 22nd Brigade out near the west Providence, close to Hayden Siding. Now held in reserve but probably moving within the next few days. When it did, Horse was pretty sure S-4 would stay behind. Maybe still in a command tent, with a tracked vehicle, like an M114A1, close to the tent for the Major. Because somebody had to get the new rifles to the troops and collect and dispose of the old ones

Horse walked out into the main office and conferred briefly with Sergeant Kensington and the dispatcher. The number of calls about the day's mock combat had not diminished; in fact, they were increasing.

At a little after nine, he went back into his office and called the District Attorney's office in San Bernardino for charging instructions on the Banner twins. The D A told Horse there would be a wide range of charges, many of them federal. The seventy-two-hour arraignment clock was ticking; the D A wanted the twins in San Bernardino as quickly as possible. He was planning to have them in front of a Superior Court judge Tuesday morning.

Horse went back to the front office to have the desk sergeant arrange for an off-duty deputy to come in and get some overtime driving the twins to the county seat. With everything that was going on in his area of responsibility, Horse didn't want anyone pulled off patrol.

Dispatch took a call and motioned to Horse.

"Mayor Milner."

"Put him through to my office."

Horse pulled the door to his office closed as he went inside. He glanced at the poster boards one more time before he punched up the call.

"Morning, Mr. Mayor."

"Morning, Horse. I'm at City Hall. Staff called me at the store and asked me to come over and look at all these complaints that piled up on my desk while I was out of town."

Horse smiled.

"Teach you to sneak away to Oak Creek Canyon. What are the complaints about?"

"Some goings-on at that carnival."

"Have they rigged the games?"

"Would that it were that simple. The complaints are about some girly show at the back of the lot. Some of the calls are from pastors."

"That's odd. No one has called the substation."

"That's because they don't think you're in the morality business, Horse. However, they seem to think that I am."

"City father and all that."

"I suppose."

"And these calls, I assume they're about skimpy costumes on the girls?"

"Worse than that. Most of them are about no costumes at all."

"I can see how that would lift a few eyebrows. Mr. Mayor, this is new to me. This is the first time since the substation took over policing Smoke Tree that the carnival has been in town."

"For some reason they didn't come last year. I was hoping they'd dropped us off their route. You see, this kind of thing has come up before."

"You turned it over to Rettenmeir?"

"I did."

"Did that put an end to it?"

"He said it was hard to control."

"But it's been the Happy Times Funfest for quite a few years, right?"

"It has."

"How did Rettenmeir get on with the guy who runs the carnival?"

"Okay, I guess. They usually managed to work things out."

"I just bet they did. Tell you what, Mr. Mayor, I'll run down there and have a word with the guy. If he's not cooperative, I'll try to put an end to this without getting the city involved in a lawsuit of some kind."

"I appreciate it, Horse. I really do. I'm hoping not to hear anything more about it."

"I think I can make that happen."

"Good. And now, I have to go and get ready for some silliness of my own."

"What's that?"

"The military has appointed me Governor of the State of Calonia. I'm going to hold a press conference in front of City Hall at noon for the television news in Phoenix."

"My condolences, Mr. Mayor. Have a good press conference."

"Have a good meeting with the carnival guy."

Horse lifted his Stetson off the coat rack and went out the door.

"Sergeant Kensington, I'm off to see a man about an immoral act."

"That should be interesting."

Horse parked his cruiser on Front Street where the Happy Times Funfest had set up on two adjacent vacant lots. Horse had always thought it ironic that the occupants of those two lots had been a stable and the town's first service station. The stable south of the service station that would eventually put it out of business, and the station that would in its turn be put out of business when the

191

National Trails Highway was re-aligned as Highway 66 and moved two blocks west to Broadway. And now, Highway 66 itself was to be re-aligned and become Interstate 40. Local business owners were fighting to keep it from bypassing Smoke Tree, but it didn't look good for the town.

The carnival was shut down, but he saw people going about daily chores. Absent the flashing lights and swirling music, the midway was a depressing place. Horse saw peeling paint, stained canvas, and garish prizes that looked tawdry in the light of day. At one of the booths, he stopped to look at goldfish finning sluggishly in tiny bowls filled with colored water of various hues. He realized some of them had died and were floating on top of the water.

He walked closer.

A man was shaking the dust off of stuffed animals and re-arranging them on the shelf behind the rows of little fishbowls.

"Say?"

The worker turned toward Horse and took in a man over six feet tall, lean, but muscular. His face was brown, his eyes darker. He had high cheekbones, and his snowy white Stetson made his jet-black hair look darker. The badge on his shirt and gun on his hip completed the package.

The worker gave Horse what could have been a smile but might have been a smirk.

"Howdy, cowboy."

"Your goldfish are dying."

The worker surveyed the bowl.

"Some of them. There are more where they came from. Got a tank full."

"Must not be a pleasant way to die, gasping like that."

"Never thought about it before."

"Well, think about it now. Either put some fresh water in the bowls or seine the fish out and put them in the tank with the live ones."

"Okay."

The man returned to re-arranging the stuffed toys.

"I mean now."

The man walked over and planted himself in front of Horse.

"You law people are all the same. Throwing your weight around. Pushing at people. Well, I'm not breaking any law, so go peddle your papers."

Horse was slow to anger, but when the back of his neck started to burn and his fingertips began to tingle, he knew he had to take immediate action before the red dragon of rage overwhelmed

192

him. Not in haste, but to forestall haste, he grabbed the man's shirt and yanked him practically off his feet. Coca-Cola trays filled with ping-pong balls flew off the counter.

"I'm not talking about the law. I'm talking about respect for living creatures."

The man grabbed Horse's hand and tried to pull it away. It was like taking hold of a steel clamp. He let go and threw up his hands.

"Easy, easy, *hombre.*"

His breath smelled of alcohol, cigarettes and bacon.

Horse let go.

"I'm here to talk with your boss. I'll be back by in a few minutes. I better see those bowls either full of fresh water or empty of fish."

"Or?"

"*Compañero, usted no quiere saber.* And just in case 'hombre,' is the only Spanish you know, that means you don't want to find out.

Now, where will I find the boss?"

The worker straightened his shirt and gestured toward the northwest corner of the lot.

"Back there. Only Airstream on the lot."

Horse turned and headed off in the direction the man had pointed. As shabby as the game booths looked, the rides looked worse, but not as bad as the men working around them. He noticed a number of them quickly turned their heads when they saw his uniform.

Horse found the Airstream and knocked on the door.

"Come," said a friendly-sounding voice.

Horse removed his hat as he went in.

A well-muscled man in a t-shirt was sitting at a table drinking coffee. The table was littered with scraps of paper. He stood up.

"If you're looking for the owner, you've found him. Carlyle Evans. Cup of coffee?"

"No, Mr. Evans, I'm good. Please, sit down. This won't take long. I'm Carlos Caballo, head honcho at the Smoke Tree Substation."

"All right, Carlos, pull up a chair."

Horse sat down on the other side of the table and put his hat on his knee.

Carlyle waved his hand at the scattered papers.

"Tally sheets from last night. From the games and food booths. Just checking to see how much these people are stealing from me."

"They steal?"

"Is the Pope Catholic?"

He took in Horse's brown face.

"Oops. That popped out without thinking. No offense."

"None taken. The Pope can look out for himself."

"Yeah, they steal. Some more than others. The question's always, 'how much?' No way to watch them all, so I let them get away with about five percent. Get above that, I bust them to being ride guys."

"Like the people I saw on my way in here?"

"That's right."

"I'll tell you, Mr. Evans, you've got some rough customers out there. I'm betting if I look real hard, I've got pictures of some of them back at the station."

"You might, Carlos, you might. I don't exactly advertise in the Wall Street Journal to fill my openings. I take whatever comes along, and sometimes that's guys with beefs with the IRS, or ex-wives, or even law enforcement. As long as they don't act out on the lot, I don't cut them loose."

"If these ride guys are so dicey, don't they steal too?"

"I'm sure they would if I ever let them touch money. But I don't. Citizens buy tickets at the booths and turn them in to get on the rides."

"What about the people in the booths? What percentage do they steal?

"Zero. Tickets are numbered. Although, now and then I get a devious character who tries to slip in his own roll of tickets."

"How do you know?"

"Subtle difference in color. I can tell if I hold them up to that ultra violet light over there. Anyway, enough shop talk. I suppose you're here on business."

"I am."

"Okay, I'll give you the same deal I used to give Rettenmeir."

"Hold on there, Mr. Evans."

"No, no, Carlos. No more than that. It was a fair deal."

Horse held up his hat.

"Stop," he said loudly. "I don't want to know what kind of a deal you had with Rettenmeir. You're about to talk yourself into a charge of attempting to bribe an officer of the law. I'm here about the girlie show."

194

Carlyle Evans leaned back in his chair. He seemed to be re-appraising the man in front of him. A man who looked like one of the Aztec warriors he sometimes saw in paintings on the walls of Mexican restaurants.

"What about it?"

"The Mayor of Smoke Tree called me earlier. When he went in this morning, he had a desk full of notes demanding call backs. Some of them were from pastors."

"What did these people have to say?"

"They said the girls in your show are revealing a little too much. In fact, revealing everything."

"I don't know that's so, but I'll look into it."

"Mr. Evans, you strike me as a man who knows every single thing that goes on in every corner of this lot. I don't want you to look into it. I want you to put a stop to it."

"Look, Carlos, the coochie show is my biggest money maker. It allows me to run the games pretty much on the up and up. That keeps the citizens happy."

"Pretty much?"

Carlyle spread his hands.

"This is a carnival, not a charity. But, let me ask you a question."

"Go ahead."

"Did you drop by the USO show on the high school football field on Saturday?"

"Mr. Evans, I don't have much leisure time, what with you and your preacher friend and Desert Strike in my backyard."

Carlyle raised his eyebrows.

"What do you mean, my preacher friend?"

"The man who drags the cross around. The man who was seen on your lot in his ice cream suit on Thursday."

Carlyle smiled.

"I guess I'm not the only one who knows what's going on in every corner of my lot."

"Guess not. You boys think you fooled me because he came into town from a different direction than you did? That's easily arranged. I'll bet if I call my friend at the Mohave County Sheriff's Department in Kingman, he'll tell me you two were in town at the same time up there."

"Okay, okay. You got me. But let's get back to that USO show. Did you know they had dancing girls on the stage at that show?"

"And?"

"And, they weren't wearing much."

195

"Define 'much.'"

Carlyle reached into a drawer beneath his desk and brought out an envelope. One by one, he laid a series of photos in front of Horse.

"These are polaroid pictures of the dancing girls. Take a look at them. Pay careful attention to the last one on the right."

Horse scanned them. The girls were wearing very short skirts that did not even pretend to cover their panties. Their breasts were bare except for tasseled pasties. In the last picture on the right, one of the girls had lost a pasty. She was bending over to pick it up, and her right breast was bare.

"My show's no worse than this. And this is sponsored by the government of the U.S. of A."

"Colonel Dulac told me there would be no civilians at this show."

"And as far as I know, there weren't."

"Then how did you get these pictures?"

"Carlos, how much do you think it cost me to have one of the soldiers who was on the midway Friday night take my camera to that show?"

"I see."

"When I heard there was a new sheriff in town, so to speak, I knew someone would be by sooner or later. Actually, I'm surprised it took you so long to show up."

"Like I said, been busy."

"Well, I figured when someone came by, it would either be someone like Rettenmeir, who was willing to wink and nod and look the other way while pretending to do something, or, it might be a boy scout. I thought it would be a good idea to have some evidence to support my argument if I got a boy scout. So" he pointed at the pictures," exhibit A, sort of."

"Bad luck for you, Mr. Evans. You got the boy scout, and he doesn't much care what the Army did. Above his pay grade. What the boy scout wants is for what's happening here to stop."

Carlyle sat thinking for a moment before he spoke again.

"Carlos, the bulk of the guys coming to the coochie show are G.I.s. If they're not seeing much more than they saw at the USO show, what's the harm? Can't we come to some kind of an agreement here that doesn't shut my money-maker down?"

It was Horse's turn to think.

Here it comes, thought Carlyle. It was about money after all. Aztec warrior here is going to shake me down good. What the Captain said next surprised him.

196

"I don't think the people calling the Mayor's office care very much about what a bunch of horny soldiers are seeing here, so I've got a proposal for you. I'm going to have a deputy on the midway tonight. He'll be in uniform, and he'll keep an eye on who buys tickets to see the girlie show."

Carlyle frowned.

"That's going to scare away customers."

Horse shook his head.

"He'll just drift by often enough to check the make-up of the crowds going into the tent."

"Okay, I can live with that."

"I'm not done yet. Here's the deal. Only soldiers can buy tickets. I want a sign in the ticket booth. 'Soldiers only. Military I.D. required.'"

Carlyle mulled the offer.

"Well, it'll probably cut down some on the income, but it sounds workable."

"Does that mean we have an agreement?"

"It does."

Carlyle stood and extended his hand. Horse stood and extended his. The two men shook.

"That's all you want?"

"There you go, Mr. Evans, paddling your canoe toward dangerous waters again. Yes, that's all I want. Now, I'm assuming your handshake commits you to our deal. If I hear you've operated outside it, I'll shut you down. And not just the girlie show. The whole kit and kaboodle."

"Carlos, you'll find I'm a man of my word."

Horse nodded and turned and went out the door.

My God, thought Carlyle, will wonders ever cease? An honest cop. But still, there was something funny, some undercurrent to what he had agreed to. It bothered him, but if there was a hole in the agreement, he couldn't see it.

Horse returned to the station. As he walked in the door, he called to the dispatcher.

"Fred, where's Andy Chesney?"

"Out at Sunset Beach trying to keep the civilians and the U.S. Army from bumping into each other."

"Get hold of him and see if the river crossing is over yet. I'll be in my office."

He sat down in the swivel chair behind his desk. He turned toward his crude map and re-visualized the sequence of events

197

Aeden Snow had described to him. He remembered Aeden saying the big guys in the Chrysler had turned around and driven toward Searchlight with the jeep following them

He had asked the young man, "*What did you do next?*"

"*Waited until I was sure they were gone, then drove down there...*"

Horse realized he had a way to go before he got proficient at this questioning business. He should have asked Aeden how long he had waited. After all, 'until I was sure they were gone,' is a different unit of time for different people. Maybe not terribly long for an angry twenty-one-year-old. Horse didn't know enough about young Mr. Snow to grade him on his patience, but he remembered he had certainly kept his own counsel during that house of three murders business.

Horse looked at Searchlight on his crude map.

The jeep and the Chrysler could have been headed for Las Vegas, but Horse didn't think so. At least, not initially. A guy in fatigues with a lot of stripes on his sleeves driving an M151A1 jeep on the strip would attract a lot of stares. Why not just leave the jeep where it was and go to Las Vegas with the big guys in the Chrysler?

Horse thought about Colonel Dulac explaining the Sunday stand-down for church services and then for readiness assessment prior to the beginning of the mock combat. He also remembered what the Colonel had said about the reconnaissance photographs: "*The nighttime ones, not so good. But the ones taken in daylight? Read the name tag on a man's uniform.*"

That was the answer. Stand down for church services. No one around to see the Sergeant way out in the desert all by himself. No reconnaissance flights until noon. No eyes in the sky taking photographs for development and analysis by the intelligence people out at the airport. No chance that some eagle-eyed specialist would say, 'Hey! What's that jeep doing out there?'"

'*Read the name tag on a man's uniform*'.

If the analysts could read a name tag on a daytime photo, they could certainly read the unit designation on the bumper of a jeep.

No wonder the sergeant hadn't wanted to leave the jeep out there. It had to be put under cover and left there until after dark when the film quality was not so good. So why Searchlight? Would reconnaissance flights take pictures there? Sure, they would. Therefore, the jeep couldn't be parked on the street. In a casino parking lot, it would stick out even more.

So why take it to Searchlight? What was there?

Suddenly, it made sense. Abandoned mines.

Forty-five million dollars' worth of gold had been taken out of the mines. And that in a time when gold was less than forty dollars an ounce. Some big mines up there. Abandoned mines with abandoned buildings. Who would know about such places? Someone with a business in Searchlight. A business like a Casino. Who owned the casinos? Las Vegas.

He imagined the conversation they might have had after the sergeant let off the rounds on full automatic. The conversation Aeden Snow had witnessed but could not hear.

'Hey,' says the sergeant. 'I can't drive this jeep into Las Vegas, but we've got to put it somewhere it can't be seen from the air.'

'Know just the place. Follow us.'

Horse sketched some notes on a five by eight index card and got up pinned it to the poster board.

When he sat back down, the intercom buzzed.

"Yes, Fred?"

"Raised Andy. Crossings are over. Andy says water skiers and fishermen are once again in control of the river."

"Okay. Have him come to the station."

Fifteen minutes later, Corporal Andy Chesney was seated in front of Horse's desk.

"How'd it go out there, Andy?"

"Pretty interesting. I'll tell you, those combat engineers know their stuff. Moved all kinds of heavy equipment across that river, not to mention troops. Then tore everything down and hauled it off."

"Like to have seen some of that, but it's been one of those mornings. Andy, I've got a job for you tonight, and it involves overtime."

"That's always welcome for a man building a honeymoon fund."

"You two still determined to get married in August?"

"We are."

"You may be the only August wedding in town."

"Best time if you want to escape the worst of the heat by leaving town on your honeymoon. Are you still going to be my best man?"

"Of course. And Esperanza's still going to be Christine's maid of honor."

"Have you told the twins we want them to be ring bearer and flower girl?"

Horse smiled.

"We have. Alejandro still doesn't always understand English words too well. He thought we said, 'ring bear.' Said he knew what a bear was, but wanted to know what a ring bear was. When he's out of earshot, Esperanza and I now refer to him as the ring bear."

"That's cute."

"It is. Those kids are the joy of our lives. Elena's going to be the prettiest flower girl in the history of weddings. And Alejandro will be the best ring bear ever.

Now, about this overtime. I had a call from the mayor this morning. He's getting complaints about the girlie show at the carnival. I went down and talked to the owner about it. Man named Evans. At first, he thought I was there to get my palm greased and play along."

"What he did with Rettenmeir?"

"Apparently. When I pressed him, he told me about the USO show on the football field on Saturday. Part of the show involved some scantily-clad young ladies. Evans showed me pictures. Said his show was no worse. Said most of the guys coming to his show were soldiers, and if what they were seeing wasn't any worse than the USO show, what was the harm? It gave me an idea."

"What did you come up with?"

"Told him the show could go on tonight, but only for soldiers."

Andy smiled.

"And there won't be any soldiers in town tonight. While the exercise is going full bore, those guys can't leave the airport."

"He doesn't know that. He agreed to my terms. We shook on it. He says he's a man of his word, and I'll believe him until I see evidence to the contrary."

"Which shouldn't take long."

"Probably not. I need a set of eyes on things. Incorruptible eyes. Tonight, you're going to be on the midway. In uniform. You are going to circulate all night long, but you're to pay particular attention to the tent that has the girlie show. Your first job is to be sure the ticket booth has a sign that says something along the lines of, soldiers only, military I.D. required. If they don't, shut them down until they get one. And even if they do, you're going to watch to make sure no civilians are buying tickets."

"In other words, nobody will be buying tickets."

"Sounds like."

At noon, Horse was on his way to Searchlight. As he drove north on 95, to the west an enormous dust cloud swirled high into the desert sky as mechanized units headed across the Piute Valley, bound for Lanfair Valley and points west.

Patton hauled his boys out here to get ready for the North African campaign in World War II, he thought, and they tore the place apart. All these years later, the scars remain. He couldn't even guess how many years it would take to heal the damage caused to the hillsides and basins of the Mojave by this exercise.

A short while later, he turned off Highway 95 onto the streets of Searchlight. A boomtown at the turn of the century, the place was down to less than one twentieth of its glory days population. A profusion of abandoned properties littered the hillsides. Willie Martello had tried to raise the town up as a rival to Las Vegas in the post-war era, but the fire that destroyed his El Rey Club had put an end to the flamboyant promoter's dream in 1962. There were rumors that prostitution was still alive in the nearly-deserted town, but for all practical purposes, it had died the night Willie's bordello went up in flames along with his motel, diner and casino.

Like a lot of people from Smoke Tree, Horse and Esperanza routinely drove though Searchlight on their way to Las Vegas without stopping. Before they had adopted the twins, they had occasionally gone to the gambling mecca to see a dinner show, preferably a musical, at one of the big hotels. Esperanza loved musicals, along with music in general. But, since adopting the twins, they had not made the drive. Raising those two endlessly interesting rascals provided all the entertainment he and Esperanza needed.

Still, Horse smiled as he thought of the surprise he had planned for her on the twentieth of August. The first West Coast appearance of the Beatles would be at the Cow Palace in San Francisco on the nineteenth. The second would be in Las Vegas, and he had tickets for the show. Esperanza loved the mop-haired quartet. She would be doubly delighted when she learned the concert would be opened by the Bill Black Combo and the Righteous Brothers. He was going to take her to the Candlelight Room at the Flamingo Hotel for a gourmet meal after the show and had already arranged for his mother to take care of the twins. He could hardly wait to see Esperanza's face when he told her about the tickets.

As he drove slowly through the nearly-deserted streets, his first thought was of the Quartette mine. By far the largest mine in Searchlight's storied precious metal history, its main shaft was thirteen hundred feet deep, and the massive diggings at the two hundred, three hundred and one thousand-foot levels had honeycombed the earth beneath Searchlight with miles and miles of underground tunnels and ore-car tracks. Too obvious, he decided.

He nosed around the paved but badly potholed streets without finding what he had in mind. It was not until he drove the dirt roads on the edge of town that he saw it. He parked his cruiser short of a barely-passable two-track that led to three ancient, metal-roofed buildings slowly surrendering to the forces of gravity and weather. When he found tracks made on the badly deteriorated trail by the knobby tires of a jeep, he knew he had the right place. He headed toward the buildings for a closer look.

Little gray birds darted though the creosote and yucca. Desert grasshoppers with their camouflage-brown coloring whirled away from his path. Searchlight was at thirty-five hundred feet, and the summer sun, while fierce, did not produce the heat characteristic of the lower Mojave. It was a good day for a walk.

The vault of the desert sky was deep blue at this elevation, not bleached of color as it was on summer days in Smoke Tree. As he looked out over the Piute Valley, a flight of F105 fighter-bombers swooped low over the desert, making strafing runs against the armored columns moving westward. Fighter escorts flashed high above them locked in combat with interceptors from the other side. F-102s and F-104s.

As he watched the silver jets twist and flash in the afternoon sun, the sounds of the blanks fired in the strafing runs came to him like a series of staccato, shuddering coughs. Horse wondered why they fired the blanks. Surely the soldiers in the tanks and armored personal carriers knew they were toast when those impossibly fast machines shredded the sky as they roared a few hundred feet above them.

He thought again about the premise for the artificial war: water rights. Mark Twain had said, "Whiskey is for drinkin'; water is for fightin." Already the Colorado River Compact, forced on the disputatious seven Colorado River Basin States by Herbert Hoover in 1922, was showing cracks. As river yielded, year after year, flows far lower than the optimistic projections made to build Hoover Dam, the states began to fight about shares.

In fact, California and Arizona were arguing before the Supreme Court today. Arizona wanted to build the Central Arizona Project to take its full allotment from the river and pump it uphill to Phoenix. California was in opposition, claiming 'highest and best use' didn't include growing cotton, a water-thirsty crop, in the middle of a desert. Horse, familiar with the saying in the West, 'Water will run uphill to money,' wondered how the fight would end.

As a crescendo of sonic booms ripped through the azure sky, Horse followed the jeep tracks that led to the largest of the three buildings. It was unclear whether the dried, sunbaked boards attached to the deteriorating four by fours were being supported by the posts or were preventing their collapse. He stepped beneath the roofline to the place the tracks ended. Gravel was scattered about the cement slab that formed the foundation of the building. As Horse walked deeper into the shade provided by the rusty metal roof, he heard the scratch of a footfall behind him. Casually dropping his hand to the grip of his .357, he turned side-on to reduce his profile as he took in the source of the sound.

The man he saw behind him was almost a caricature of an old-time, hard-rock prospector. He had everything but the burro and pickaxe. Of medium height, he looked smaller because of his bent posture and awkwardly angled neck.

Too much time squatting in mine shafts, thought Horse.

The man's face was lined and cracked as a chunk of leather abandoned to the desert sun. Coarse whiskers covered his face below his pale-blue eyes and sunburned nose.

"Help you, deputy?"

"Yes, you can. Do you live nearby?"

"Up on that hillside."

Horse lifted his eyes to what he had thought was an abandoned storage shed.

The man turned and looked, too.

"Bought it, and the acre of land that came with it, in '52. Lived there ever since."

"Do you know the owners of these buildings?"

"I do."

"Do they live in town?"

"Nah. Salt Lake City. Haven't seen them in years. I keep an eye on the place for them. In return, they let me work the claim on this property for whatever I can find."

Horse surveyed the two much smaller buildings to the west. He realized one of them partially covered the opening to a mine shaft.

"Still gold in there?"

The man's look changed from helpful to suspicious in an instant.

"Might could be. Just a tad, though."

"Enough for you to live on?"

"Pretty near."

Horse wasn't sure what that meant. He also thought some would be hard pressed to call this man's existence in that mean shack 'living'. On the other hand, maybe the fellow was onto something. He thought of Hugh Stanton living alone behind his service station down at Arrowhead Junction. A man who would appear impoverished by the standards of most people, but one who was at peace with himself and in harmony with his surroundings. In fact, one of the happiest people Horse knew.

Thinking of Hugh made Horse realize he had been so busy of late he had not stopped by for a good, long visit with the old man for quite a while. He made a mental note to do that on his way back to Smoke Tree.

If the man standing in front of Horse were uncomfortable with the silence, he didn't show it. Time passes slowly out this way, Horse thought. This is a man used to long silences. Like a week or so.

"Were you home yesterday?"

The man lifted the straw hat off his head and waved it in an expansive gesture.

"All this here is my home, deputy. I'm always home."

"Did you see anybody down here?"

"Saw one guy twice."

"Mind telling me about it?"

The suspicious look left his face, and he walked closer to Horse.

"Not at all. I'm Klaus, by the way."

"And I'm Carlos. Pleased to meet you, Klaus."

"Likewise. Sort of on the wrong side of the state line here, ain't you?"

Horse smiled.

"I am. Following up on something that happened in my county yesterday. If you don't mind, tell me what you saw."

"Yesterday morning, a big black car came up the road and stopped right over there where you parked. A jeep pulled in behind it. The jeep driver walked over to the car and talked to the two men inside. Got back in his jeep and drove it into this building. Went back to the black car and got in."

"While he was parking the jeep, did anyone get out of the car?"

"Nossir."

"The man driving the jeep, what can you tell me about him?"

"He was a sergeant."

"You're sure of that?"

"Fought in the Great War. Know a sergeant when I see one."

The statement made Horse think of Mr. Stanton again.

"When he left the jeep, was he carrying anything?"

The man nodded.

"The gun he kept slung over his shoulder the whole time he was here. Had his hands on it when he first walked up to that black car. Stopped a little behind the door while he talked to the driver. Seemed like he wanted the man to have to turn his head to look back at him. When he walked up the road, he kind of crabbed sideways so he could keep an eye on the car."

"So, when he came back from leaving the jeep, he still had the gun."

"He did. But now he was wearing civilian clothes. Walked a big circle and kept that gun pointed at the car the whole time. Got in the back seat."

"Do you think the men in the car or the sergeant saw you?"

"Nossir. I was in my place, looking out between the boards."

"What did you do after they left?"

"I climbed down for a look at the jeep. Mighty fine vehicles, those jeeps. You know, you can just drive one off? No key needed."

"But you didn't"

The man looked surprised by the question.

"Weren't mine."

"But the jeep isn't here now."

"Nope. After dark, a car came back. Someone got out. Walked away in a big circle. Never got in the headlights. Waited until the car drove away."

"Was it the sergeant?"

"Don't know. It was too dark."

"Did the person still have the gun?"

"Couldn't tell."

"Then what happened?"

"He was in the building a while."

Changing clothes, thought Horse.

"How long?"

"Ten minutes or so. I heard the jeep start up, and it backed out to the road."

"Did he turn on his headlights?"

"Had these little peeper lights. Looked like cat's eyes in the dark."

"He drove away?"

"He did."

Horse was silent for a few minutes.

"Klaus, can I ask you a favor?"

"Sure."

"Some strange things may happen out here later this week. Probably not before Wednesday."

"What day is this, deputy?"

Once again, Horse realized how far out of touch with the rest of the world this man was. No electricity. No radio. No mailbox.

"It's Monday, Klaus."

"What's the favor?"

"Is there somewhere else you can stay?"

"For how long?"

"Ten days or so. I know this is your place, but it might get dangerous here. I don't want you to get hurt."

"I've got a little camp a few miles away. Claim I work, time to time."

"Will you go there and stay a while?"

"I can. I'll drift on over there tomorrow sometime."

"One more thing. Please, don't tell anyone about what you saw yesterday, or about talking to me."

Klaus broke out laughing.

"Carlos, this is the longest conversation I've had in a year. I don't have anyone to tell."

"Thanks for your help, Klaus. Much obliged."

"Before you go, what's going on down in the valley? And what's with all these jet planes?"

"Big Army and Air Force war game."

"Think they'll leave anything around when they go?"

"I think you can count on it, Klaus. Nobody can waste stuff like the military."

"What kind of stuff, do you think?"

"There's a lot of artillery out there. Knowing the Army, I doubt they'll collect the brass from those howitzer shells."

"That could fetch a lot of money at a scrap yard."

"It could. Hope you find lots of it."

Horse shook hands with Klaus before walking to his unit, driving back through Searchlight, and turning south on 95. When he reached Arrowhead Junction, he pulled onto the apron in front of Mr. Stanton's service station. The old man was not sitting in his usual chair off to the side of the building.

Horse pulled under the overhang and got out. A light breeze was pushing dust across the lot. Horse could hear the wind and another sound he couldn't identify: a very faint, scratchy hiss. He walked to the steps that led to the office. The door above the steps was locked. He couldn't remember a time when that door had been locked in all the years he had been visiting Mr. Stanton.

Horse began to get a very bad feeling.

He walked down the steps and started down the side of the building toward the living quarters behind the station. He paused beneath the kitchen window. The crackling and hissing sound was louder. He realized he was hearing a radio. Horse knew the old man liked to listen to KOA out of Denver or KOB from Albuquerque at night. Apparently, he had fallen asleep with the radio on. The sun was now heating the ionosphere. There would no reception of distant stations until sundown.

Horse hurried around the building. He dodged piles of engine parts, discarded batteries and empty oil cans. The Royal Enfield left to Mr. Stanton in Burke Henry's will was parked in back. Horse climbed the cement steps. The back door was locked too. He banged on it.

"Mr. Stanton? Mr. Stanton, it's Horse. Are you okay?"

Even as he said it, he knew the old man wasn't, but he knocked and called again.

He turned and scanned the area for something he could use to pry open the door. He spotted a piece of angle iron near one of the old car bodies. He retrieved it and wedged it between the jamb and the edge of the door. The desiccated wood gave way with one heave. Horse stepped into a small utility room with a soapstone sink on one wall. A shelf above the sink held boxes of laundry detergent and Boraxo. He propped the angle iron against the sink and opened the door to Mr. Stanton's kitchen. The radio was on a counter next to a Montgomery Ward toaster with a badly-frayed, fabric-covered power cord.

Horse turned off the radio. He crossed the room and opened the door on the other side and found Mr. Stanton. There was no point in checking for a pulse.

The old man lay atop a patchwork quilt. He had on a faded nightshirt that was so worn it was nearly transparent. His terribly thin lower legs jutted from the bottom of the garment. A pair of neatly folded trousers and an olive-drab t-shirt were on the straight-back chair next to the metal headboard. A pair of boots were arranged side by side beneath the chair.

Horse removed his Stetson and crossed himself. He stood in silent prayer for a few moments before he crossed himself again. We almost lost you three years ago, he thought. Would have, too, if young Aeden Snow hadn't happened by and seen you lying out front next to your usual chair.

Mr. Stanton's eyes were closed. He had apparently died in his sleep. The look on his face was one of equanimity. His mouth was partially open. Horse couldn't help noticing that the man had all his teeth. His hair was still raven black. The fact that Burke Henry's motorcycle was outside meant Mr. Stanton had died Sunday night or early this morning. Left there any longer, it probably would have been stolen.

Horse looked around the simple room. Walls painted the muddy orange of a Santa Fe reefer were papered with Santa Fe calendars that spanned decades. Many of them had the famous covers painted by Maynard Dixon. As if in respect of all the years Mr. Stanton had sat out front watching the trains go by, Horse heard the heavy thrum of diesel locomotives making the long climb up the grade from Smoke Tree.

There was an ancient chifforobe against the wall opposite the bed. The doors were open, and Horse could see several hangers holding trousers and t-shirts like the ones on the chair next to the bed. As the train came closer to the old service station, Horse heard the bells clang as the crossing arms came down. The empty wire hangers in the chifforobe began to dance on the rods.

Horse stood, enveloped in a sound Mr. Stanton had heard countless times in his life and thought about some of the things he knew about the old man. His time with Black Jack Pershing's boys in the Meuse-Argonne in World War I. The farm he and his father and brother had lost to the dust bowl. The long trip west with little hope and less money. The passing travelers in need who had benefited from his generosity. His closeness with Aeden Snow and Johnny Quentin. The time he had faced down two mobsters with his ten-gauge coach gun. His friendship with his distant neighbor, Burke Henry.

Hugh Stanton had taken Burke's death very hard. Horse had known the two men were friends, but didn't realize the depth of their friendship until he and Andy Chesney brought him Burke's motorcycle. The old man seemed to fold in on himself in his anguish. But it made perfect sense. Two men, both half-Indian. Both from Oklahoma. Both living life on their own terms.

Mr. Stanton's body was so thin it resembled a mummy retrieved from some ancient tomb in Egypt. It made him think of Burke's, rendered mummy-like by the limestone dust. The difference was that that Hugh Stanton had slipped away in his sleep, at home and in his own bed, while Burke Henry had died an agonizing death in a limestone crevice. A hillside crevice into which he had barricaded himself to protect his body from predators and make identification possible so Horse could have him declared dead. A barricade erected in such a way that his last remaining water was left outside because Burke had decided it was time. A man who accepted no quarter. Neither from any human agency nor from death.

Horse realized he was no longer hearing the train. He had been lost in thought for a long time. He walked back into the kitchen. He picked up the phone on the kitchen table, dialed the substation, and told the dispatcher to send the coroner and have Askew Funeral Home send the hearse.

CHAPTER 27

Sliding Toward Salvation

Monday evening's revival started well enough. In spite of the heat, the tent was packed. Although it was nearly sundown, the heat of day had hardly abated when the faithful and the want-to-be-saved began filing into the tent. Everyone was sweating. People were fanning themselves. Jedidiah was hoping no one would faint until it crossed his mind that such an event might be interpreted as religious ecstasy.

Faint on, he decided. Might ramp up the collection.

The crowd soon grew so large there were no empty chairs. People began to fill the areas to the sides of the aisles. As they continued to squeeze in, he signaled the choir. They opened with "Shall We Gather at the River?" At the chorus line, it seemed doubly appropriate for a dusty desert town on the banks of the Colorado River.

Yes, we'll gather at the river,
The beautiful, the beautiful river;
Gather with the saints at the river
That flows by the throne of God.

The woman who had accused him of blasphemy the day he dragged his cross though Smoke Tree was in the front row, her round face staring up at him in rapturous adoration.

I liked her better when she was mad at me, he thought.

As the choir continued, Jedidiah stood on the stage, Bible in hand, making eye-contact with anyone who looked his way. He could tell which men had attended the coochie show he had preached against on three successive nights because their eyes slid away from his. Some ducked their heads to avoid his gaze.

Perfect. It would fit right into his message: *Backsliding*. His sermon would suffuse the souls of those men with guilt. They would writhe with internal anguish. Seek forgiveness. Reach deep into their wallets to add to the offering. Desperately reach for redemption. Join him in praying the sinner's prayer: *Dear Lord Jesus, I know that I am a sinner, and I ask for Your forgiveness. I believe You died for my sins and rose from the dead. I turn from my sins and invite You to come into my heart and life.* They would answer the altar call and stumble down the aisles as the choir sang, "Just as I Am."

But tomorrow night, knowing it would be the carnival's last night in Smoke Tree, they would pay one more visit to the hoochie-coochie tent. Sweat in anticipation, even more than they were sweating now. Proffer funds well beyond the entrance fee in hopes of having one last glimpse of live, nude women other than their wives.

So predictable.

Because the flesh is weak.

Because 'forbidden' and 'illicit' sing a siren duet.

Because they were men. Grown men in some ways; infantile in others. Their sexuality barely beyond puerile pubescence. Incapable of unlocking the deep desires of their wives. Desires that they probably didn't know existed. Desires that would disturb, intimidate, and frighten them if they did. Staring and fantasizing were so much easier. So much less threatening.

The guilt such visits produced had been responsible for doubling and sometimes tripling the money collected by the Jedidiah Shanks Revival since joining forces with Carlyle Evans. Sheep to the shearer. What a sweet racket! Jedidiah almost felt sorry for these men. Almost. But not sorry enough to give up the lucrative association with The Happy Times Funfest.

The voices of the choir swelled with the last chorus of the hymn. The crowd began to grow quiet. Jedidiah waited until the only sound he could hear was distant generator powering the searchlight piercing the sky above the tent.

"Backsliding," he began. "Backsliding. Listen now to the word of God: *Thy own wickedness shall correct thee. Thy backsliding shall reprove thee. Know therefore and see that it is an evil thing and bitter that thou has forsaken the Lord thy God, and that my fear is not in thee, saith the Lord God of Hosts.* Jeremiah, 11:19."

"Backsliding," he said again, and paused.

"Backsliding, in God's eyes, is worse than if you had never given yourself to Jesus in the first place. Because it makes a

212

mockery of that surrender of yourself to the Holy Spirit. Because you offered yourself up to the Lord in exchange for salvation and He accepted you in all your sinfulness and gave you boundless love in return.

You intended to do right. You really did. But then the tasks and cares of day to day life settled down around you, and you forgot your commitment to Jesus. You surrendered to the routine. To the commonplace. To getting and spending.

'The world is too much with us,' the poet wrote. And indeed, it is so.

And so your soul, your soul that had been washed in the blood of the lamb, was soon stained with sin again. Small sins at first, but then bigger and bigger ones. And soon, you were as bad as you had been before you offered yourself up to Jesus and he so lovingly accepted you.

But now, you were even worse. Because you backslid. You broke the covenant you had made with the Lord, thy God."

Jedidiah stood silently on the stage. One minute. Two. Three.

"But perhaps, perhaps the person I just described is not you. Perhaps you are instead one of those who never fully committed in the first place. Oh, you pretended you had, but in truth, you were just doing it because everyone around you was. You didn't want to be left out. You came forward for the altar call and said you accepted Jesus Christ as your Lord and Savior, but you held part of yourself back. Did not become part of God's devoted family. As if Jesus was just some distant cousin thrice removed, living in a foreign country. Someone you'd heard about but never met.

When temptation showed up on your doorstep, you succumbed willingly. Surrendered to the same kinds of impure thoughts you allowed yourself to have before your incomplete conversion. And since you allowed those thoughts to creep into your mind, the actions such thoughts inevitably engender soon followed. You know who I'm talking about, don't you," he asked softly? The men he had looked at earlier refused to so much as lift their eyes.

"You gave up obedience to the laws of God. Obedience you had pledged but not honored. To you I say: Not every backslider is an apostate, but every apostate is a backslider!"

On he went. For over an hour, he pummeled the sweating crowd with his disdain. Threatened them with damnation. Told them of the agony of suffering for all eternity. Told them the heat they felt at noon on the hottest day of the year in Smoke Tree was refrigerated air conditioning compared to the fires of hell to which they risked condemning themselves. It was one of the best sermons he had ever preached.

When he came to the end. He stood silently again for a long time before saying, "Can I have an amen?"

There was a scattered response.

"That's the best you can do," he roared so loudly the veins stood out on his forehead? Sinners who now wish to return to Jesus Christ? Who long with all their hearts to make atonement and find forgiveness and bury themselves in the bosom of the Lord? That's the best you can do? Give me an amen!"

"Amen," the whole crowd shouted!

"That's better. Can I have a hallelujah?"

"Hallelujah," rose as one voice, fervent with frenzied faith!

"Can I have a 'praise God?'"

"Praise God," came back at him, louder even than the 'hallelujah' and full of guilt now tinged with hope.

"Praise God!" Jedidiah shouted again, holding the Bible above his head with both sweaty hands.

"Praise God," the crow thundered in a sustained wall of sound!

And as he stood there, triumphant, he readied himself to call for the offering. He nodded to the crew members standing in the aisles with their stainless-steel buckets. One more clarion call, he thought, and I will have this crowd in my hip pocket."

"Can I have an...."

But before he could say 'amen,' a terrible pain slammed into his lower back.

"Aargh," he screamed.

"Aargh," screamed the crowd in return.

Jedidiah stood there in shock. He felt like he had been struck by a sledgehammer. He was actually turning to see what had hit him when the terrible pain came again.

"Aargh," he cried again, falling to one knee, one hand relinquishing its grip on the Bible as he reached for his lower back.

"Aargh," came the response as some in the crowd slipped from their chairs and went to one knee in imitation of his pose.

The pain struck a third time. It was so intense, Jedidiah could not speak at all. Holding his breath against the pain, he toppled onto his side.

As Tyson, his crew chief, rushed toward the stage, several of the people rolled onto their sides in spasms of religious ecstasy. When Tyson charged up the steps and knelt beside Jedidiah, the crowd thought he was praying.

"Boss, what happened?"

Jedidiah managed to suck in a breath and speak.

"Felt like something broke in my back."

"Does it hurt right now?"

"It's eased a bit. Oooh," he groaned. "Spoke too soon. Here it comes again."

"What do you want me to do?"

"Get me to the motel. Maybe it'll be better if I stretch out on the bed."

As the pain struck again, he held his breath.

"And all of a sudden, I really have to pee. Get me off this stage before I wet myself."

Tyson stood and looked out over the crowd. Some of the crew members were near the rear exit. He motioned them forward and knelt down next to Jedidiah again.

"Have Pastor Cecil take over."

"Okay."

In spite of his agony, Jedidiah had a reminder.

"Have him be sure to call for the offering. This pain should be worth a fortune!"

In a moment of inspiration, Tyson rose to his feet. Lacking Jedidiah's booming voice, he crossed the stage to the pulpit and its microphone.

"Brother Jedidiah has been struck so forcefully by the Holy Spirit it has knocked him to the ground, just as it did the Apostle Paul on the road to Damascus. Jedidiah is overcome and can no longer speak. Brother Cecil is going to come forward and take over."

An earnest-looking young man who was sweating in a suit like Jedidiah's was moving toward the stage in the wake of the crewmembers hurrying forward.

"In the meantime, the ushers are going to circulate among you to accept your generous offerings to the goodness of God. Dig deep, brothers and sisters. Dig deeper than you ever have before. I ask that you pray for Brother Jedidiah while your reach into your wallet or your purse for all you can give."

Tyson turned away from the pulpit. He walked over and spoke to the choir director before moving to join three crewmembers now hovering around Jedidiah. They lifted him off the stage and carried him up the center aisle, creating a scene reminiscent of a *Pietà*. As they moved, the choir was already singing:

Throw out the lifeline! Throw out the lifeline!
Someone is drifting away;
Throw out the lifeline! Throw out the lifeline!

Someone is sinking today.

Jedidiah was in agony, his eyes squeezed shut as spasms of pain wracked his body. People would later claim he had been locked in Charismatic prayer. Calls of "Praise Jesus," and "Glory to God" followed Jedidiah's progress out of the tent.

At the motel, the crew gently lowered Jedidiah onto his bed. He turned onto his side, finding that position a little less painful. Tyson sat down on the only chair in the small room.

"You boys go on back to the tent."

Tyson moved his chair closer to the bed.

"How is it, boss?"

"Not as bad right now, but I've got that urge to pee again. Help me off this bed."

Tyson leaned forward. He lifted Jedidiah to an upright position and grasped his hands, tugging him gently to his feet.

Jedidiah twisted from side to side.

"All of a sudden, it doesn't feel so bad, but I've got to get to that bathroom."

He walked unassisted across the gritty linoleum floor and pulled the bathroom door closed behind himself. Tyson followed him to the door and remained standing outside in case he was needed. He heard urine splashing into the bowl.

"Oh, no!"

"You need help, boss?"

"I don't think so. I'll be right out."

When Jedidiah opened the door, his face was pale. He shuffled into the room.

"Tyson, something has busted loose inside me. I'm passing blood. A lot of blood."

"Okay, we've got to get you to the hospital. I can call an ambulance, but if you can walk to the car, we can get there quicker by ourselves."

"Let's take the car."

Tyson moved to Jedidiah's side. As he did, he caught a glimpse of the water in the toilet. It was bright crimson. He put his arm around Jedidiah's shoulders and helped him out of the room.

CHAPTER 28

One Road Ends Here

While his walking companion was passing blood in his motor court room, Danny Dubois was having no luck making up the tip for the first hoochie-coochie show of the evening. Carlyle had told him to recruit only soldiers, and that was a problem: there were no soldiers at the carnival. Fifteen minutes after the first show should have started, he went to Carlyle's Airstream to give him the news.

"No soldiers?"

"Nossir. Not a single one. And I don't think the deputy's scaring them off. They're not coming through the arch."

"The deputy?"

"Yeah. In uniform with his gun and *Deputy Dawg* hat and everything."

"That's right. I forgot. That other deputy told me there would be someone here. But it doesn't make sense there are no soldiers. That's not good."

"Maybe we should take that 'military I.D. required,' sign off the ticket booth. I've seen a lot of men turned away already. It'd be easy to put together a good crowd for the show."

Carlyle leaned back in his chair. Then he broke out laughing.

"Danny, I never expected to be out-maneuvered by a deputy sheriff. As much as it pains me to admit it, I've been flimflammed."

"How's that?"

Carlyle explained the agreement he had made with Carlos Caballo, beginning with the complaints from the Mayor followed by Carlyle's argument, supported by photographic evidence, that the hoochie-coochie tucked away in the back corner of the lot was no worse than the USO show seen on the high school football field.

When Carlyle was finished, he broke into laughter again.

"I'll tell you Danny, I misread that man from the get-go. He stood in front of me with his six-shooter and his white Stetson, and I said to myself, 'well, look at this small-town rube.' Was I ever wrong! And quick on his feet? When I trotted out the USO show, he immediately came up with the agreement to let the coochie continue, but only for soldiers. I walked right into that one. Somehow, he knew there would be no soldiers in town tonight. But I've got no recourse. I shook on the deal."

"What do you want me to do?"

"Go to the tent and tell them no shows tonight. Have the girls put on something decent and go help the jointees. Maybe a little eyewash will loosen the locals' wallets."

"The girls aren't going to like it."

"Doesn't matter. We're going to have to make up some of the revenue we're losing tonight. Tell 'em if they want to be paid, they have to work."

"Okay, I'll get on it."

Danny turned to leave.

"One minute."

"Something else?"

"Danny, is there anything you want to tell me?"

"About what?"

"There's been something different about you the last couple of days. In fact, ever since you started walking in the mornings with our preacher. He's not bringing you to Jesus, is he?"

"No sir."

"I'm only saying that because he's not with Jesus himself."

"He told you that?"

"Didn't have to. I know a con man when I see one. I've come across a fair number of these revival types in my years on the road. Some of them are sincere, and some are grifters. But even the bunco boys, if you drill down far enough, believe in the good book. Not Jedidiah Shanks. I don't mean he's a bad man. He's not. But there's something gnawing at him. Or he's gnawing at it. I haven't known him long enough to know which it is, just yet.

Anyway, back to you. Something's gnawing at you, too. You're turning something over in your mind. Something big. Sit down and talk to me."

Danny sighed and sat down across the table from Carlyle.

"Should've known I couldn't fool you. You see right through people."

Carlyle smiled again.

"Didn't see through that Mexican deputy."

"Exception that proves the rule."

"So, what is it?"

"I don't know where to start."

"As they say in the music business, 'take it from the top.' Am I right in thinking this has something to do with that girl you've been calling for the last two years?"

"No. That's over."

"Uh oh. She has a new boyfriend?"

"No. She's a fine person, and I hope she finds someone someday. It's just not going to be me. But she started me thinking, all those times I called her. You see, I began to get a feel for how settled her life was, if you know what I mean."

"As in, she was in one place and not on the road all the time?"

"That was part of it. She was always telling me about the people in Smoke Tree. What they were doing. About their families and such."

Carlyle shook his head, slowly.

"You're leaving the show, aren't you?"

Danny looked miserable.

"I am, Carlyle, and I feel terrible about it. You've been good to me. You and your father before you. I was a scared little kid when I showed up in Noblesville. All I had were some clothes in a sack. I don't know what would have become of me if your dad hadn't taken me in. Let me tag along with the show."

"Hell, Danny. You were the best shill we ever had."

Danny smiled.

"Don't try to downplay it. It was an act of mercy. He took a risk. And you, Carlyle, you've been like a father to me."

"And you've been a son to me. But sons grow up and move away. Happens all the time. Most natural thing in the world. You want to get off the road. Settle down. Have a family. That's it, mostly, isn't it?"

"It is."

"I'm going to miss you, Danny, but this is the right thing for you. You've got to be a civilian to have a family and do it right. I know that."

"But you're Dad had..."

"I never knew my Dad when I was young. He was the man who left my mother and I every spring and didn't come back until fall. And even when he was home, he wasn't really there. He was always off on trips to look at equipment someone was selling or to look for five-and-dimes or toy stores going out of business so he could buy cheap plush for the games. And sometimes he was even farther afield, signing contracts and renting locations for the next season.

I didn't get to know my Dad until I was old enough to go on the road with him. He missed so much of my life. Never taught me to swim, or hit a baseball, or catch a fish. None of that stuff."

"But you followed in his footsteps."

"I did, and I love this life. Love the road. Love the strange people who come and go. Love dickering for contracts. That's why I never married. I know this life is not one for a man with a family. So, you stay here! You seem to have taken a shine to this little town. Put down roots. Get married. Have yourself some crumb snatchers and ankle biters. You've got a good heart, Danny Dubois. You'll be a great father.

Now, go out and wrangle those coochie girls before I start crying and embarrass us both."

Danny's voice broke as he stood and said, "Same here boss."

After having a predictably acrimonious set-to with the coochie girls, Danny finally got them to put on some modest clothing and go out to help the agents in the game booths. He noticed that once they stopped grumbling, they seemed to enjoy dealing with the public fully dressed. And, just as Carlyle had predicted, their flirtatious presence cranked up the spending at every location.

There was nothing more for him to do, so he cruised the midway, chatting up people he might never see again. The carnival might return to Smoke Tree the following year, but many of the people he talked to would no longer be traveling with the show.

Like Whitey, real name unknown, who liked to work the flat rides. Children took to the man with the white hair and Santa Claus beard, and Whitey delighted in them in return. But when the midway was shut down, Whitey became an entirely different person from the smiling man who enchanted children: quick to anger and quick to lash out with his fists. There was something ominous in Whitey's past. Danny had heard talk of a fire that destroyed a small, wood-frame house outside of Kenosha, Wisconsin, one winter, killing a woman and three children while the father was out drinking, but he didn't know if the story was true or just another carny rumor.

And Glen, a jointy who was one of the best agents on the midway, but notoriously fickle. He often left shows without warning or notice but was always welcome at another carnival because of the way he could establish a rapport with civilians at his booth. A rapport that made them spend extra money, even if they won little or nothing.

And then there was Susie, the college student who had been doing the ape-girl act for the last three seasons. She would be graduating next year and was already planning to go on to law school. She was a hoot. Civilians often ran screaming in fear from her tent but came back to see the show again. Danny smiled as he thought of Susie someday 'going-ape' while cross-examining a witness.

As he continued around the midway, seeing people who were in some ways like family to him, Danny began to have his doubts. After all, he was, to a large extent, basing this on a strange feeling that had come over him at sunset above a football field. Perhaps he was being hasty. Maybe it would be better to continue on with the carnival until the circuit was finished and they returned home to winter quarters. There, he could make a more dispassionate decision. A little more logic. A little less feeling. But as he wavered, he chided himself. He had always been pretty good at making decisions.

Suddenly, he saw a way to resolve the issue. He put wheels in motion when he asked Mitzi's cousin to check on a job possibility for him. He would let fate decide. If Aeden had been successful, Danny would stay in Smoke Tree. If not, Danny would move on with the show and make his decision in winter quarters.

He continued on his circuit but had only been walking for another fifteen minutes when he saw Aeden Snow coming through the arch. Aeden saw Danny and lifted a hand in greeting.

Here we go, he thought.

"I've got news for you," said Aeden as he walked up.

Danny didn't want anyone but Carlyle to know he was thinking about leaving the show. If he did leave, he decided, he would slip quietly away after the tear-down, saying goodbye only to Carlyle.

"Let's take a walk."

He and Aeden stepped out onto Front Street and turned left toward the distant Santa Fe depot. A switch engine was at work in the rail yard, putting together a string of recently-iced reefer cars for an eastbound train.

"I told my foreman about you today. I really talked you up. Raved on your skills as a mechanic. He seemed interested until I told him your name."

"Then what happened?"

Aeden broke into a grin.

"He went from interested to downright enthusiastic. Said he knew you."

"I don't see how that's possible. What's his name?"

"John England."

It took Danny a moment to make the connection.

"How strange. Jedidiah Shanks and I met him when we were out for a walk on Sunday morning."

"Who's Jedidiah Shanks?"

"The revival preacher."

"After lunch, John went to the office and talked to the boss. The boss almost always defers to John on these maintenance crew hires. The upshot is, the boss wants to interview you tomorrow., but I think that's just a formality. Danny, I think you just got yourself a job!"

"That's great. I can't thank you enough."

"Mitzi thinks highly of you, so I'm happy to help. Now, on to practical things. Do you have a place to stay after the carnival pulls out?"

"Not yet, but I'll find something. I can stay at the Gateway for now."

"I've got a better idea. Why don't you stay at our house?"

"That's a generous offer, but what will your parents think if you haul some carny home?"

"Already talked to them about it. They're all for it. And how about a car? Have you got transportation to get back and forth to work?"

"No. I've always just banged around in one of the carnival trucks. I've saved up some money, though."

"How picky are you about the looks of what you drive?"

"Not at all, as long as it's mechanically sound."

"Good. There's a wrecking yard out on the west end. Zack cobbles cars together out of tow-ins and sells them. If you don't mind something that has doors and fenders of different colors, his stuff always has good engines, and he never sells anything with a bent frame. I'll take you out there."

"Sounds fine."

They stepped into a drug store just short of the depot and had ice cream at the soda fountain. While they spooned up their sundaes, Aeden sketched out directions to the compressor station on a napkin.

I'm glad things have turned out this way, thought Danny. I can't wait to tell Jedidiah when I meet him for our walk in the morning.

But Danny would not be seeing the preacher man in the morning.

CHAPTER 29

Resignation and Revelation

As they drove toward the hospital, Jedidiah began to talk in a calm, level voice filled with both resignation and relief.

"This is for the best, Tyson."

"What, driving to the hospital instead of calling an ambulance?"

"No. Whatever's wrong with me, it's for the best. When my Elisabet died, I wished I had died with her. But quick, you know? A bolt of lightning. Hit by a train. Shot by a mugger. Something like that. No long, lingering illness, just suddenly...gone. When I passed all that blood, my first thought was, this is it. My time is nigh. I mean, when you start leaking blood, the end must be near."

"But boss..."

"No, no, it's okay, Tyson. I mean it. I welcome this. Hoped for this for twelve years. You see, the great comfort and warmth of Elisabet's love once filled my heart, but it no longer does. She's gone, and where that love once was there's a hollow chasm that fills with sadness the minute I open my eyes in the morning. I am smothered in despair, day after day."

The intensity of Jedidiah's emotion made Tyson uncomfortable. This was a Jedidiah he had never seen. He only knew Jedidiah the planner. Jedidiah, the stickler for detail. Jedidiah, the man always in control and on top of everything as they moved from town to town. Jedidiah, the man who raked in the cash.

Tyson felt obligated to make some kind of a response. He couldn't just leave words like this fall flat to the ground, unremarked.

"You've never talked to me about the death of your wife before. In fact, I've only heard you say her name once or twice."

"I've only had two conversations about her death. The first was with the preacher who brought me into this revival and sold me all the equipment when he retired. That conversation was understandable. The second one wasn't. The second was with that Dubois kid from the carnival. I don't know what came over me, but I poured my heart out to that boy. I think that maybe, deep down inside, I knew my time was growing short.

You know what the worst thing was about the death of my wife, Tyson?"

"No, boss."

"The enormity of it was bad enough, but it was the terrible, awful, inescapable finality that drove me to the ground. The rock wall hopelessness. Knowing I'd never see my beloved again. Never. Never hug her again. Never talk with her again. Never walk with her again. Never hold her hand. Never kiss her beautiful face."

"But boss, you'll see her again someday. On the other side. You know that."

Jedidiah laughed.

"Brace yourself, Tyson. I don't believe any of that stuff. Haven't since not long after Elisabet was taken from me. I don't believe when the role is called up yonder she and I will be there. There is no 'up yonder,' Tyson. It's all a scam. A scam to fool the suckers. Like Carlyle's carnival. Like my revival show."

He leaned his head against the window and did not speak again.

The Smoke Tree Hospital was off Broadway just beyond the Civic Street intersection. When they pulled in, Tyson drove straight to the emergency entrance. He jumped out, leaving his door open, and ran to push the call button outside the door before returning to the car to help Jedidiah. As he opened Jedidiah's door, an orderly was wheeling a gurney toward them.

"What's wrong with him," he called as he approached?

"Internal bleeding. A lot of pain."

"Is he conscious? Can he talk?"

"Can I have a hallelujah," said Jedidiah?

"What?"

"He must be getting delirious."

"Help me with him."

The two of them helped Jedidiah out of the car and onto the gurney.

"I can handle it from here. Move your car in case the ambulance comes."

As Tyson drove toward the parking lot, the orderly was pushing Jedidiah through the emergency entrance.

By the time Tyson parked and hurried inside, the lobby was empty.

226

"Where's the man who was just brought in?"

The woman behind the desk pointed at the double doors. Tyson headed that way.

"Hold it! You can't go back there. Have a seat, and someone will come out and let you know how he's doing."

Tyson walked over and sat down on an uncomfortable chair next to a low table covered with well-thumbed editions of The Reader's Digest. He thought about what it would mean for the revival if Jedidiah died. Funny, Tyson thought, how fast life could change.

And then, in his mind he heard 'Ethel Merman sing the last line of "There's No Business Like Show Business." *And go on with the showwww!*

A doctor with a clipboard pulled back one of the green curtains around Jedidiah.

"Good evening," .... he looked down at the clipboard... "Mr. Shanks. I'm Doctor Hayden. I see your blood pressure's a little elevated, but that's to be expected. Pain will do that. Pulse is a little fast for the same reason. How bad is that pain?"

"Not too, right this minute."

He paused.

"Let's cut the small talk, Doc. Don't sugar coat it. How long have I got?"

The doctor looked up from the chart, mild surprise on his face.

"Until what?"

"Until I die."

"I have no idea. There are too many facets to longevity. And there's always the chance of an accident."

"But this terrible pain. And when I peed, it was full of blood!"

Doctor Hayden smiled, understanding why the patient was asking about imminent death.

"Mr. Shanks, you're not dying. Not even close."

"I passed blood. Something's wrong inside me."

"I apologize, Mr. Shanks, it's my fault. What's happened is so common around here, I assumed at your age you knew what it was. Let me put your mind at rest. I'll start with a question or two."

"Sure, anything you want to ask."

"Did you recently get extremely dehydrated?"

"Last Thursday. I was walking to Smoke Tree dragging my cross. I walked a long way without any water."

"Oh, you're that guy. The preacher. Heard about that stunt. How far did you walk?"

227

"Three miles, maybe closer to four."

"Around what time of day was this?"

"Around two in the afternoon."

"And you had nothing to drink that entire time?"

"No."

"And when you did get something, what did you have?"

"Iced tea."

"Anything to eat?"

"A half-gallon of chocolate ice cream."

The doctor let out a low whistle.

"That should about do it."

"Do what?"

"Mr. Shanks, you've got a kidney stone, and believe me, you earned it. You got very dehydrated and then drank iced tea followed by ice cream. Lots and lots of calcium. Lots and lots of oxalates. Because you were very low on fluids, when that combination arrived in your kidneys, you precipitated a calcium-oxalate kidney stone."

"But I didn't feel anything until this evening."

"That's because the stone was just sitting there. Tonight, it decided to come out. But it couldn't. It's too big. It's stuck at the entrance to your urethra. Do you know what your urethra is, Mr. Shanks?"

"The pipeline that carries urine out of the body."

"That's right. Kidney stones are rough, sometimes even spiky, and yours is trying so hard to get out that it has torn some tissue as it tried to move into that narrow pipeline. That explains the blood. The pain is caused by all the nerves in that sensitive part of your body.

How's the pain right now?"

"It has eased."

"It'll be back."

"So, what happens now? Do you cut me open and get the stone out?"

"Nothing that invasive. That'd be like dismantling engine of your car to change the oil filter. No, we'll give you something for the pain. That will allow your muscles to relax. We'll hook you up to an IV and start pushing fluids through your body. If you're lucky, those extra fluids will flush the stone all the way through the urethra. If that happens, the stone will pop out of the end of your penis."

Jedidiah thought about that.

"And if it doesn't? Pop out, I mean."

"You're a preacher, Mr. Shanks. I suggest you pray that it does. If it doesn't, we'll have to go get it."

"How do you do that?"

"We insert a little device that looks like a tiny basket into your urethra and go get it."

"And how do you...oh, no."

"Yep, right up through there. But I can assure you, it very rarely comes to that. Right now, we're going to admit you to the hospital and get you hooked up. Are you allergic to any medication?"

"Demerol makes me throw up."

"Well then, you've hit the jackpot. We're going to give you the gold standard of painkillers: morphine. It will take away your pain and put you to sleep. Eventually, the saline solution will reach your kidneys and make you have to pee. Hopefully, when you pee, you'll pass the stone."

"How will I know?"

"You'll feel it come out. By the time it has gotten that far, it won't even hurt. When you've passed it, you will fall into the deepest, most peaceful sleep you've ever had in your life."

"Thanks doc, and thanks for explaining everything."

"You're welcome, Mr. Shanks. Welcome to Smoke Tree, California, kidney stone capital of California."

Jedidiah was wheeled out of the emergency room and into the hospital. Once the orderly had him in a hospital gown and in bed, a nurse came into the room. She was carrying two plastic bags and some tubing.

"Mr. Shanks, I know you're in a lot of pain. We're going to take care of that. Doctor has prescribed fifteen milligrams of morphine. As soon as I get this cannula in your hand, I'll get you started on it."

The nurse found the vein she wanted on the back of his hand and swabbed the area with alcohol.

"This is going to pinch a bit."

"Compared to the pain in my back, 'pinch' sounds good."

Once she had the cannula inserted and taped into place, she hung the smaller of the two bags from the arm of a wheeled IV pole and ran a line from the bottom of the small bag to his hand.

Jedidiah started to speak, but she stopped him while she concentrated on her task.

"Have to count drops, Mr. Shanks. We want to send you to dreamland, but we want you to survive the trip. You're now getting the stuff that will stop the pain. Take about ten minutes for it to really kick in. Normally, I'd wait to put the larger cannula in your arm until the morphine was working, but Doctor says we need to get these fluids going right away. Make a fist for me."

When Jedidiah did, she found another vein, swabbed the area, and inserted a bigger cannula. She hung the fluid bag from the pole and set up the line to his forearm. Once again, she counted drops and made fine adjustments.

"Okay, it won't be long before the morphine does it job, so listen carefully while you're still alert. You're going to fall asleep. When you have to urinate, you'll wake up. All that fluid will be trying to push the stone out of your kidney. Because of the morphine, it won't hurt."

"The doc told me about that."

"He gave you the concept. I'm going to give you the details.:

The nurse went into the bathroom and game out with a one-gallon jug that had a funnel in the top.

"This will be sitting on the toilet lid. Urinate into the funnel. There's a little screen in there. If the stone comes out, the screen will capture it and we'll send it for analysis. Leave the jug in there when you're finished. Got that?"

"Yes."

"One more thing. When you get out of bed, be careful with these lines. Don't want to pull them out. The IV pole has wheels. Just roll it along with you when you go to the bathroom."

"Okay."

"Is that pain easing yet?"

"Oh, yes," Jedidiah said as he smiled benignly at the angel of mercy who had hooked him up to this wonderful stuff. He suddenly understood drug addicts.

"All right. Get some rest and let those fluids do their work. There's a call button on that side table. Push it if you have an emergency."

She left the room, dimming the lights before she closed the door.

Jedidiah's body began to take on a peculiar weightlessness. It was like being wrapped in an anti-gravitational cloud. He began to float far above the earth on that soft, billowy cloud. It was a place of warmth, rainbows, and tranquility. He felt wonderful. He understood how those soldiers he had attended to *in extremis* had borne the pain of their terrible wounds after being injected with this magic. Some of them had smiled at him as they lay dying.

In spite of the warm feeling, he longed for Elise, just as he did at the end of any day. Longed for her with a need so intense it pierced the veil of the potent painkiller coursing through his body.

Oh Elisabet, he thought, no matter how hard I tried to tell you, you never realized how wonderful you were. Never quite believed me. You always thought you were flawed in some way or other. You weren't! You were perfect. It was as if someone had written a prescription to save me from the unhappiness I brought home from the war, and you filled that prescription. Filled it every day. Then you died, and the prescription ran out.

He could feel wetness on his cheeks. He cried silently but unashamedly as he so often did, even after all these years. Sleep was overtaking him, and he knew if he were going to say the words he said every night, he was going to have to hurry before the morphine spirited him away.

When Jedidiah had been a pastor, he had prayed for many people. Prayed for them and prayed with them. Sick people. Dying people. People in pain, both physical and emotional. But without fail, the last prayer he offered up at the end of each day was for his Elise. First, he always thanked God for the miracle of having her in his life. Then he asked God to protect her from pain and disease and harm.

Perhaps 'asked' was too mild a word. For he had seen, in war, the sudden, arbitrary nature of death. Two men standing side by side. One of them struck and killed by a sniper while the other was lighting a cigarette. So, he pleaded. He begged. He beseeched God to protect the person who was the center of his universe. The one who gave his life meaning.

But Elisabet died. Killed in a senseless accident by a habitual drink driver with no more conscience than a chestnut. God had ignored the prayer that mattered most.

Jedidiah hadn't known at first, but his faith died with her. For a while, he thought he was feeling only grief. Raw, overwhelming, debilitating, cry-until-your-throat-is-raw grief. But gradually he realized it was more than that. He was angry with God. And what Jedidiah had thought of as his unassailable, unshakeable faith had been slowly chipped away, piece by agonizing piece, until there was nothing left but the trappings of that faith. And then the trappings, too, had fallen away.

When that process was complete, Jedidiah no longer believed in prayer. But old habits die hardest, and in some perverse way he felt he could not leave Elisabet un-prayed for. So, he modified the words he said each night for her. No longer a prayer, the words were more a recognition of sorrow and anger.

Incomprehensible, unknowable, unreachable, inscrutable force of the universe, I am but a speck. Less than nothing. A dust mote in a distant corner of an inconceivable void. I do not understand your relationship to the universe. I cannot grasp it. I never will. My intelligence is too limited. But I know one thing. I prayed to you. I begged you. I pleaded with you. Protect my Elisabet.

You did not, and she died.

I can no longer pray. I can only hope. Hope that she is safe and warm and free of pain, anxiety and fear. And hope that I will see her again someday.

As always, he neither began his words with "Dear Lord," or "Dear God," nor ended them with "amen." On this night, the morphine coursing through his veins, he barely made it through the last whispered words before he fell down a deep, black hole into unconsciousness.

It was not an urge to urinate that hauled him up out of that hole. It was pain. The pain was back. Almost as severe as it had been at the revival. It increased even as he tried to gauge it. He pushed the call button.

He was gritting his teeth and sweating by the time a different nurse than the one who had hooked up his IVs came through the door and turned up the light in his room.

"You rang?"

"What," he groaned?

"Sorry. Sometimes I make bad jokes."

She took the chart off the end of the bed and glanced at it.

"I take it the pain is returning."

"It is."

"How bad."

"Very."

"And you haven't urinated yet?"

"No."

"We've pumped a lot of fluids into you. You're on the second bag. You didn't wake up when I changed it. Something should happen soon, but we don't want that pain to tighten you up. The notes say you can have additional morphine after three hours. It's been longer. I'll get you more."

As she started toward the door, Jedidiah said, "Hey?"

"What?"

"Y'all hurry back now, hear?"

"A little joke. Very good, Mr. Shanks. You're getting the hang of this"

She was back soon and started a new drip. She stayed beside his bed, waiting for the morphine to work its magic.

"If that stone doesn't come out by morning, we'll to ship you to Las Vegas and have the urologist at the hospital there go in and get it. Either way, it won't be too long before you don't have the pain anymore."

As she stood there beside his bed, the pain backed off a notch. Jedidiah managed a smile.

"Doctor Hayden said I should pray about it."

"I would."

He began to slip away.

The next time he woke up, he did have to pee. He maneuvered himself to the edge of the bed and swung his feet onto the floor. He was afraid the IV pole would slide away if he put too much weight on it, so he used his left hand to lever himself off the bed. He felt a strange lightheadedness. He was not exactly dizzy, but colored lights seemed to flashing somewhere in the dimly-lit room. He steadied himself before beginning his cautious shuffle to the bathroom, pushing the pole ahead of himself.

Inside, he stood staring at the jug sitting on the toilet seat. It felt like his head was filled with cotton, and for a while he could not remember what the nurse had told him about the jug and funnel in front of him. Then it came to him.

He lifted the jug with his right hand, the hand with the cannula, and pulled up his gown with the other. Never peed left handed before, he thought with bemusement as he directed his stream into the funnel. He was fearful it would hurt, but it didn't. Suddenly, he felt the stone leave his body and heard it plop into the urine backing up in the funnel.

When he was finished, he lifted the jug closer to his face to look at the stone.

That little thing caused all that pain, he thought. They should call them pebbles, except they feel like boulders when they're trying to get out. Stone is probably the compromise word.

He left the jug on the toilet seat and slowly made his way back across the room. He carefully situated himself before swinging his feet back up onto the bed. He felt no pain, but he didn't know whether that was because the stone was gone or because of the morphine. He peered at the bag containing the drug. It was about half full. He considered calling the nurse and having her disconnect it, but he was afraid there would be residual pain if the morphine wore off. Best let the professionals make that decision he thought, and floated away for the third time.

Jedidiah was roused to consciousness by the smell of jasmine, a scent he had always associated with Elisabet. He opened his eyes.

She was standing at the foot of the bed. There was a young girl beside her. Around them was nothing but soft, white light. The rest of the room had disappeared.

"Hello, my dearest Jedidiah," she said in the beautiful, soothing voice he had thought he would never hear again. "Are you feeling better now?"

"Elisabet! Oh, Elisabet, my dearest sweetheart. I've missed you so much."

"I know, dearest. I've been watching you. I'm sorry you're so sad, but I love it that you've been talking to me all these years."

"You can hear me?"

"Of course."

"Who's that beside you?"

"This is our daughter, Olivia."

"Hello, Olivia. You're as beautiful as your mother."

"Thank you, Daddy."

Jedidiah struggled with a thought for a moment, his mind still fuzzy.

"You mean she was born after you, after you..."

"It's all right, Jedidiah. You can say it. After I died. Yes, she was. She's almost twelve now."

"How is that possible?"

"Everything's possible where we are."

"You mean you're..."

"That's right, my love. We're in heaven. You'll be joining us someday."

A horrible sadness swept over him. He began to cry.

"I can't Elisabet. I can't. Oh, this is too much to bear. To find you and then lose you for eternity. I've been wrong in such a terrible way."

"You're human, Jed. Humans are wrong about a lot of things. That's why Jesus died. To take away our sins."

"But I've blasphemed, Elisabet. I denied the Lord. I raged against Him. I cursed Him. The Bible says that is the sin that can never be forgiven, and the Bible is the word of God."

Elisabet smiled.

"It is and it isn't, dearest. It is the word of God as perceived by those who wrote down His words. People, Jedidiah. Humans. And humans have but an imperfect understanding of the ways of God. And of His word. Humans make mistakes. If you're a true Christian, and you are a true Christian, Jedidiah, although you think you're not, you can never commit a sin that is unforgiveable in the eyes of our Lord and Savior, Jesus Christ. He intercedes with God. He will intercede on your behalf. All will be well."

"I pray that it is so Elisabet. I yearn so to be with you again. And be with our daughter, who I already love with all my heart."

"I know all this is all hard to believe, Jedidiah, but it's true. Olivia and I are going to make you feel that truth. We are going to hug you, Jedidiah. We are going to heal your broken heart."

As she spoke, she was moving to one side of Jedidiah's bed. Olivia was moving to the other.

As Elisabet removed the IV lines from his hand and arm, he felt the tender touch of her hands.

"Oh, Elise, how I've longed to hold you again."

She and Olivia climbed onto the bed on either side of him. Elisabet curled up on his right and Olivia on his left. They encircled him in their arms. They hugged him. He could feel Elise's sweet lips against his cheek.

It was the most marvelous hug anyone had ever had in all the long history of hugs. Jedidiah could feel the sadness flowing out of his body. It sank through the bed, through the floor, through the desert beneath the building, and deep, deep into the earth. So deep it could never find its way back to him.

For such a long time, grief had been all he had left of Elisabet. As such, he had guarded it fiercely, ferociously resisting anyone who tried to pry it away. And now, the grief was gone! The only person who could ever take it away was here, and she had driven the grief from him. Into the empty space the grief left behind flooded joy. Warm, hopeful, wonderful, all-encompassing joy. He had never been so happy in his life.

Jedidiah grew alarmed when he realized consciousness was slipping away from him. He fought against the loss, struggling to stay awake. He wanted to lie here and feel this joy forever.

But sleep took him.

When he opened his eyes, the doctor was in his room. Jedidiah found himself smiling. He could not stop smiling. He burst out laughing.

"Doc, I've experienced a miracle."

"That's what it feels like when you've passed a stone. Suddenly, the pain is completely gone."

"Not a medical miracle. My beloved Elise was in the room with me last night. Elise and our daughter. Oh Doc, she's so beautiful. Just like her mother. Her name is Olivia."

"I don't think so, Mr. Shanks. The hospital doesn't allow visitors late at night. Sometimes people hallucinate when they're given morphine, and you were very active last night. That's consistent with hallucinatory episodes. You pulled your IV lines loose. When the nurse came in this morning, she found saline solution all over the floor."

"It was no hallucination. Elisabet and my daughter talked to me. They climbed in bed with me. I could feel the bed move."

"Morphine-induced hallucinations can be tactile and auditory, not just visual. Now, Mr. Shanks, we're going to release you. Thankfully, the stone has passed. There's no reason to keep you. You can go visit your wife and daughter."

"Doc, let me ask you a question."

"All right."

"Do you smell jasmine?"

Doctor Hayden tilted his head and sniffed. He got a strange look on his face and sniffed again.

"Now that you mention it, I do smell something. I'm not sure it's jasmine, though."

Jedidiah decided to say nothing more. If he told the doctor the wife who had visited him last night had died twelve years before, and the daughter who had been with her had not yet been born, the man would probably have him held for psychiatric evaluation. And Jedidiah wanted out of here. He had a sermon to write. A sermon about hope and joy and love.

A sermon that was going to change his life.

CHAPTER 30

Turning the Page

Danny Dubois left the carnival lot in the dimness of morning twilight and headed for the Swank Motor Court. When he got there, Jedidiah was not waiting in front of his unit. Danny wasn't sure whether he should knock on the door. Maybe preacher man was tired and had decided to sleep in, he thought. He was turning to leave when a man came out of one of the units across the parking lot and called out as he walked toward Danny.

"Looking for Jedidiah?"

"I was. He's usually outside. I don't want to disturb him if he's sleeping."

"You must be Danny Dubois. I'm Tyson. According to Jedidiah, you do pretty much the same thing for the carnival I do for the revival. Always glad to meet a fellow nuts-and-bolts man."

He arrived in front of Danny and extended his hand. Danny met the firm, calloused grip with one of his own.

"Jedidiah's in the hospital trying to pass a kidney stone. I'm going to go over and see him when visiting hours start."

"I don't know anything about kidney stones. Is that something real serious?"

"Not according to the doctor who talked to me. He said there was a real good chance Jedidiah would be fine by this morning. Apparently, once you pass one of those things, you're good as new."

"If he's okay, will he be preaching tonight?"

Tyson's expression changed.

"I'm not sure. He said some very strange things to me last night on the way to the hospital. I still don't know what to make of them. Don't know whether it was the pain or Jedidiah talking."

"What kind of things?"

"I'd rather not say. He might regret them this morning."

"Okay. Is this the revival's last night in Smoke Tree?"

"It is. Same for you folks, right?"

"Funfest will start breakdown when the show closes tonight."

"Well, nice to meet you, Danny. See you in Parker."

"The carnival will be there."

As Tyson walked back toward his room, he thought about what Danny had said. 'The carnival will be there,' not, 'we'll be there.'" Why was everyone saying odd things?

Danny turned and headed out on his walk. He decided if he could break away in the evening he would come and hear preacher man. It sounded as if something might have changed inside him during his time in Smoke Tree, just as something had changed inside of Danny. He remembered Jedidiah's remark that perhaps Smoke Tree should change its name to 'Epiphany.'

When he got back to the lot after his walk, the flag was up at the cook tent. He had a quick breakfast and then went to the trailer he shared with three jointees and put on a clean t-shirt and his cleanest Levi's.

He searched out Carlyle on the lot and told him about the conversation with Aeden the night before. Danny asked Carlyle if he could use one of the show's pickups to drive out to the compressor station for his job interview.

"No," said Carlyle, gruffly.

Danny tried not to show his disappointment.

"Okay. I'll figure something out."

Carlyle started laughing.

"Gotcha! I mean 'no, you can't take one of those junkers.' You have to take my Jimmy. It has air conditioning, you know. Don't want you arriving out there all sweaty and stinky."

Danny was soon southbound on 95 in Carlyle's 1964, fire-engine-red, GMC, the after-market air conditioner blowing cold air. It was the nicest vehicle he had ever driven. An hour after he stepped out of the truck onto the gravel parking lot in front of the office, he had been hired and was filling out paperwork. Thursday and Friday would be paid training days. He would join the maintenance crew the following Monday morning.

CHAPTER 31

Agent Darnold

Horse was at his desk Tuesday morning when the intercom buzzed.

"Some guy from Treasury on line one, Captain. You been fudging your tax returns?"

"Oh Lord, I was afraid this might happen. Go ahead and put him through."

Horse punched up the line.

"Is this Agent D'Arnauld?"

"Hey, nice pronunciation, Captain Caballo."

"Pretty good yourself."

"Now that we've got that out of the way, just call me Darnold, like everyone else."

"And everyone calls me 'Horse. Did Pete Hardesty fill you in on what's going on out here?"

"He did, and I have to tell you, I find it very interesting."

"Any chance you can come down?"

"I just got off the plane at McCarran. I want to get on top of this. If your estimate of what's going on is right, we just might catch these boys with their pants down. I'll pick up a pool car at the Las Vegas Treasury office and head your way."

"Great. I didn't expect such a fast response. Look forward to meeting you."

"Likewise."

After Horse gave Agent D'Arnauld directions, the two men ended the call. Horse sat quietly at his desk for a moment. Then he pumped his fist in the air and shouted, "Yes!"

"Yes what, Captain, no audit," came Fred's voice from the out office?

Horse got up and walked to the door.

"Small celebration. I've actually got the Feds interested in this gun thing."

"All right! Now, while you're still feeling good, the Mayor for you on line two."

Back to everyday life, he thought, as he returned to his office and punched up line two.

"Morning, Mr. Mayor."

"Good morning, Horse. You worked some kind of magic. I just got off the phone with city hall, and I don't have a single message this morning complaining about that girlie show."

Horse explained what he had done. When he was finished, the Mayor started laughing.

"Oh, that's rich. I'll bet we have an unhappy carnival owner on our hands this morning."

"I'm sure we do, but I'll say this for Carlyle Evans. He said his handshake was his word, and he stuck to the bargain we made. I had a deputy at the carnival last night. He told me that when no soldiers showed up, the man shut down the show."

"When is the carnival leaving town?"

"Tonight's the last night."

"What are you going to do? He's not going to fall for the 'soldiers only' thing again, and he's not breaking the law unless those women take all their clothes off."

"I have something else in mind. Something that might work just as well."

"Well, I appreciate what you're doing. Makes my life a lot easier."

"We aim to please, Mr. Mayor."

Horse got an outside line and called the Askew Funeral Home. Rupert Askew Senior answered. Horse asked him to hold Hugh Stanton's body until he could arrange for a military burial service.

"I didn't know this man had so many friends in Smoke Tree," said Rupert Askew Senior.

"All veterans have friends, Mr. Askew. They're called veterans."

Half an hour later, Horse was talking with Carlyle Evans in his office trailer.

"You know, Carlos, very few people get the best of me in a deal."

"Beginner's luck, I'm sure."

"I'm not. Severe case of underestimation on my part. Anyway, tonight's coochie show's not going to be for military only."

"Didn't think it would be."

"And legally, you can't just shut us down."

240

"I know that. They teach us a surprising amount of law when we go to work for the department. But my office will be monitoring your show."

"You monitored it last night."

"From the outside only. Tonight, from the inside."

Carlyle found it hard to keep from smiling.

"Certainly, Carlos. Certainly. I understand the pressure you must be getting from your mayor."

"I'm glad you do."

Horse got to his feet.

"Well, we'll see you tonight."

He was putting on his hat as he went out the door.

After he was gone, Carlyle allowed himself the broad grin he had repressed. The coochie show had been visited by uniformed law enforcement in other towns, and the girls knew just what to do. The thought of them draped over a red-faced deputy sheriff, in essence making him part of the show, made his smile grow even wider.

But then, he thought of what Carlos had said on his way out the door.

We'll see you tonight.

Surely, that had been just a figure of speech. The commander of the substation was not going to be inside the tent at the coochie show. Was he?

Back at his office, Horse dealt with daily details so he could have the decks clear when Agent D'Arnauld reached Smoke Tree. When he had everything under control, he put in a call to Nye Delft, freight conductor and commander of American Legion Post 913.

It was always hit or miss trying to reach a Santa Fe trainman. There was no way of knowing whether he would be home or out on the main line somewhere. Fortunately, Nye was home.

"Nye, Horse here. Can the post help me with a funeral for a World War I vet?"

"We'd be honored."

"As I understand it, the Veterans Administration will pay a stipend for the burial."

"It does. Bit of paperwork involved, but we have a fund at the post. We'll put up the money and get reimbursed. Where did this man serve?"

"In France with Black Jack Pershing."

"Okay, I can arrange an honor guard and a bugler for taps."

"That will be great. The city owns the cemetery. I'll talk to the Mayor about a discount on the plot."

"When do you want to do this?"

"The mortuary's holding the body, so there's no rush. How about next week sometime? This week's going to be crazy, and I want to give veterans in the department a chance to attend."

"Okay. I'm first out right now, but when I get back, I'll put the detail together. We still have a few World War I vets at the post, and they'll want to be there, too."

When Horse hung up and walked out into the main office, a handsome man, slender and casually dressed, was coming in the door. There was an air of authority about him.

"Darnold?"

The man smiled.

"That's me, and you must be Horse."

"I am, and this is Fred, our day dispatcher. Sergeant Kensington over there has the desk today."

"Gentlemen."

"Darnold is a treasury agent from the San Francisco office. He's here to help us with a knotty problem. Provide him with anything he asks for, including the use of my office if I'm not around. Have you eaten, Darnold?"

"Not since last night. Don't like to eat before I get on a plane."

"Well then, let's head for my favorite diner. We can talk over lunch, or breakfast if you prefer. Breakfast is served all day at the Bluebird Café."

Horse led the way to his usual booth. As soon as he and Darnold sat down, a waitress was at their table with mugs and a pot of coffee.

"Hi, Robyn."

"Hello, Horse. Coffee for both of you?"

Horse looked a Darnold, who nodded.

"Be great."

"You need a minute?"

"I'll be having my usual, Robyn, but maybe my friend Darnold here needs to study your menu."

"Just bring me the biggest breakfast you've got."

"How do you want your eggs?"

"Over easy."

"What kind of toast?"

"Sourdough, if you've got it."

"One Ranch Hand Special and one tuna salad on rye coming up."

"Pretty girl," said Darnold when Robyn walked away."

"She is. Good person, too.

242

Even though he had been briefed by Pete Hardesty, Darnold had Horse take him through the background information."

"And the air-drop is tomorrow?"

"Yes."

"Pete told me you think this sergeant is in supply at brigade level."

"That's right. 22nd Armored Brigade."

"How did you arrive at that conclusion?"

"Any military service in your background?"

Darnold shook his head.

"Too young for World War II. Number didn't come up in the draft for Korea."

"Okay, quick education. The guy had too many stripes to be at company level, unless he was a first sergeant. But Aeden said he there was nothing the middle of the stripes. If he was a first sergeant, would have been a diamond there. Not battalion level either. If he had been a sergeant major, that would make him an E-9 and there would have been a star in the center.

That leaves a straight E-8, which is a brigade-level rank in one of the 'S' designations: S-1, personnel; S-2, intelligence; S-3, operations; and S-4, supply and logistics. If this sergeant is in the middle of the weapons exchange, it follows he must be in supply and logistics. With me so far?"

"Go on."

"All brigade-level staff officers are field grade. The commander is a full colonel. The 'S' designation officers are usually majors. The officers are the big-concept guys, but the senior sergeants who work for them do the actual work.

There are three infantry battalions and one tank battalion in an Armored Brigade. The three infantry battalions are going to get the M-16s and turn in their M-14s. The Pentagon probably wants to see this done during a simulated combat exercise. That's why the touch-and-go field delivery.

Since this is a supply issue, the major at Brigade S-4 has the responsibility. He's the big-concept guy, and he's be very interested in the air drop and the new rifles. But probably not interested in the old ones. So, he turns this over to his senior NCO, as in 'here, Sergeant, handle the surplus guns.' I think that senior NCO is the guy Aeden Snow saw on Sunday morning.

Darnold, a supply sergeant at brigade level is a very crafty character. Always thinking about how to get rid of one something he doesn't want in exchange for two somethings his brigade needs. This particular supply sergeant has seen a big opportunity. There are suddenly going to be a lot of rifles the active duty Army doesn't care much about. The perfect chance to cockroach a few because nobody's counting. Nobody but him.

And somewhere in this brigade, there's a very clever armorer who has modified a squad, fully-automatic version of the M14, an M14A1, into the thing Aeden saw the sergeant shoot on Sunday morning. This sergeant thinks the mafia would be in the market for a bunch of these guns. I was hoping you would know something about why he might think that."

"A mafia war that started in Sicily has spread to the east coast. No reason to believe it won't move west."

"That's another piece of the puzzle. I have no idea how an Army sergeant knew how to get in touch with the mob."

"I don't either. We'll find out after we bust him, if we do."

"I don't know how many of these rifles he's planning to sell. A goodly number, but not so many he can't fudge the paperwork and make them disappear."

Horse looked up and saw Robyn bringing their food. The discussion ended.

"Goodness," said Darnold. "That's a lot of food."

"You wanted the biggest breakfast."

She unloaded a plate of scrambled eggs with sausage, bacon, and hash browns. Smaller plates with pancakes, biscuits and gravy. A bowl of applesauce followed. Over the next fifteen minutes, Horse watched in amazement as the slender man ate it all.

"How do you stay so thin?"

"Metabolism. My mom always told me it would slow down someday, but it never has."

Robyn returned, cleared the table, and left the bill. Horse reached for it, but Darnold waved him off.

"This is on Treasury. We appreciate any chance to take a chunk out of the mob."

"Speaking of which, what is the take on all this from people in your office?"

"I guess the best description is 'fascination tempered by skepticism.' I mean, this is both interesting and outrageous in a number of ways. First and foremost, as far as Treasury's concerned, automatic weapons are completely illegal. Second, there's the mafia connection, and third, there's the issue of weapons being stolen right out from under the Army's nose."

"What was the consensus?"

"There is none. It's running fifty-fifty. Half think it's nuts to contemplate an operation based on a wild story told by a college boy to a small-town deputy sheriff."

"And the other half?"

"The other thinks the story is just crazy enough to be true."

"And what about you? What do you think?"

"I know your Undersheriff and your Sheriff have a lot of respect for you. Pete Hardesty speaks very highly of your investigative abilities, and that carries a lot of weight with me."

"Your bosses don't know me from Adam, so they sent you to make an assessment. I'd do the same thing They're probably wondering why I didn't just go to CID."

"That came up when Pete talked to me. I passed on Pete's concurrence with you about what would happen if you did."

"How was that received?"

"A couple of my superiors have been in the military. They thought your point was well taken."

"But still, they just sent one man. That way, if it turns out to be a fool's errand, an airline ticket is the total operational cost."

"That's true, but they have a certain amount of faith in my judgment. I've been lucky on a few cases."

"You're too modest. 'Legend,' was the word Pete used."

Darnold smiled.

"An overused term."

"How much authority did they give you?"

"You get right after it, don't you?"

Horse leaned closer.

"I want this Mazzetti guy. He sent muscle into my county. Here, to little old Smoke Tree, and over to even smaller Baker. They leaned on people. Threatened one. Roughed one up. I drove up to Vegas and got nose to nose with Mazzetti in his office. Told him to keep his greaseballs out of my county. He didn't listen. Two of them came back a couple of months later. I arrested them on a concealed-carry beef on a Friday afternoon. In our library. Our library, for God's sake! Got them in court and arraigned. Some high-priced lawyer showed up and bailed them out. They never showed for trial. These are the kind of people Mazzetti sent to my town."

Darnold smiled.

"So that's why they met this Sergeant in Nevada. I'd say you've got their attention."

"Not good enough. Not for me. Not by a mile. I want to wipe the smug smile off Mazzetti's face. This is a chance to do that."

245

"You think he'll actually be there when the guns change hands?"

"Normally, I wouldn't think so, but apparently Mazzetti thinks the two guys who jumped bail found what they were looking for. A young woman who was apparently on the run from the mob with a bunch of their money. Mazzetti thinks they found her, killed her and disappeared with the money."

"That's why you think he'll be at the buy?"

"That's right. If his guys ghosted with the money, Mazzetti's boss is holding him responsible. He can't afford for that to happen again. I think he'll be there."

Darnold whistled softly.

"I thought we'd get lucky and arrest some guys who might flip on their boss, but you think the local boss himself will be there?"

"I do. You know a lot about these people. Do you think you could get Mazzetti to flip on the guy above him?"

Darnold shook his head.

"Never happen. His boss is known as Tommy Bones, and it's not because of his facial structure. If Mazzetti cut a deal, he'd never live to serve the reduced sentence. I'm a 'take what you can get' guy. I'll settle for getting Mazzetti."

"Me too. Which brings me to another question."

"Go ahead."

"Are you involved or are you committed?"

"Explain the difference."

"It's like the bacon and eggs in the breakfast you just had. The chicken was involved, the pig was committed."

"I'd say I'm involved because of Pete's estimation of you, but leaning toward commitment because of my own assessment so far. You've done some solid thinking on this. You may well turn out to be right."

Horse leaned closer.

"This is not an operation for two guys, one of whom is operating out of his jurisdiction."

"I agree. When do you think this might all happen?"

"The mock combat part of Desert Strike winds up on Saturday. After that, the army will stand down on Sunday, just like they did before this exercise began last Sunday. Everything else will be logistics: moving men and equipment out of here. But that won't start before Monday. That creates a very limited time frame for this sergeant. Saturday is too soon because the reconnaissance jets will still be flying. Monday is too late. Too much happening. Too many

246

people moving around who might see what's going on. I think delivery will be made on Sunday."

"By truck?"

"I don't think so. I think our sergeant is doing this alone. He drove to the demonstration alone. He'll set aside the guns he intends to sell and deliver them alone."

"Cuts down on the loose lips thing."

"Exactly. I'm estimating the number of guns he's going to sell can be put in a trailer he can pull behind a jeep."

"Where is this brigade right now?"

"Not sure. As of Saturday, it was being held in reserve near the temporary airstrip where the weapons will be dropped.

"This is your backyard, Horse. What should we do next?"

"Tomorrow, we stake out the high ground above the airstrip and watch the drop. See what happens after the rifles are delivered. The drop is scheduled for noon."

"How will we know if our sergeant actually plans to steal some of the old ones?"

"Observation. I think even if the 22nd Brigade has been pulled out of its reserve position, the S-4 section was left near the airstrip to pick up the M-16s, deliver them, and collect the M14s. The hard thing to figure out is where the infantry battalions will be when it's time to deliver the new rifles."

"What's your best guess?"

"From what I've heard, the Calonia forces are fighting a retrograde operation. That would involve the unit held in reserve. That should put the 22nd somewhere near the Fenner or the Clipper Valley on Wednesday at noon. The guns will be dropped a good distance from there, so you have to ask yourself how the operations people would think about this. What's easier to move, three battalions of mechanized infantry or the M16s?"

"The guns."

"Right. But the full-bird colonel in charge of the brigade won't want the re-supply done right in the middle of the fighting. The other side might capture the new guns, and that would be a real black eye for the colonel. I think they'll make a high-speed move with the battalions back toward Hole-in-the Wall, make the exchange there, and rush the units right back into action."

"What makes you think all that will happen?"

"Something else the Colonel told me. The 101st Airborne is going to parachute in somewhere out there. I think they'll provide the blocking action needed to allow the mechanized infantry time to move to the re-supply point and then come right back to the battle."

"How will we know if you're right?"

"When the new guns are picked up, they'll be loaded onto a truck. We'll be watching. If the truck heads north on the Cima/Kelso road and then turns east on Cedar Canyon, we'll know the re-supply point will be somewhere on Black Canyon Road."

Darnold smiled.

"I'm glad you know the terrain."

"Been tramping around out there ever since I was a kid."

"You say we'll be on the high ground to watch the drop?"

"That's right. A place called Cima Dome. If the truck takes off the direction I think it will, we'll take a two-track off the dome, turn south, through Kelso, and come in the backside of Foshay Pass to a place where we can look out over the Clipper Valley."

"And look for what?"

"Three battalions of mechanized infantry moving at high speed will raise a huge dust cloud. If we see the cloud moving north, we'll know we've guessed right."

"What then?"

"We head back to town and, hopefully, you'll be able to convince your superiors to send reinforcements."

Darnold sat thinking for a while.

"There's still a problem. This is all well and good for identifying where the new for old swap will happen, but that still leaves us with a basic question. How will we know the sergeant is planning to steal some of the old rifles?"

"Surveillance."

"Surveillance how?"

"We'll have a man infiltrate the S-4 to see what the sergeant's doing."

Darnold started laughing.

"Wait a minute. A small-town sheriff's department is going to infiltrate the U.S. Army?"

"Not exactly."

"Explain."

"A civilian will do the recon."

Horse thought for a moment Darnold was going to get up and walk out, but he didn't. He's very interested, thought Horse. He's moving toward commitment, even if this sounds outrageous.

"A civilian? Yikes, I'd get fired for even thinking that."

"That's one of the advantages of being out here at the edge of the world. They pretty much leave me alone as long as I get the job done. And this guy's the best man for the job. In fact, I don't think anyone else could do it."

"Who is he?"

"He's an Indian who lives the old way, and he knows every inch of those mountains. There are limestone caves there that are sacred to his people."

"What will you do if he gets caught?"

"He won't. He'll be in an out of there without a trace."

"Come on, Horse. You really think this guy can get in and out of a military unit completely unseen?"

"He served in World War II in the Pacific Theater. His job was to infiltrate enemy perimeters at night and leave a trail of dead soldiers behind. He was good at it. Psychological warfare. Scared hell out of a lot of enemy units."

Darnold sat thinking.

"I'll say this, Horse. You know how to put on a show. Mafia muscle, casino operators, Indians, guns, cash, old scores. We could take this to Hollywood."

He paused again.

"It can't hurt to do some looking and some planning. If Wednesday plays out like you think it will, I'll make the call and recommend more bodies. How many do you think we'll need to cover this exchange?"

"If Mazzetti carries the cash himself, I'd say there will be two cars. One in the lead with four guys and one with Mazzetti and three more heavy-lifters. Unless you think this Tommy Bones might show."

Darnold shook his head.

"Never happen. He's got to know all the ways this could go wrong."

"All right. Seven guys plus Mazzetti."

"How do you think they'll be armed?"

"Handguns. Maybe a sawed-off or two."

"*Lupara,* the Mafia calls those. All right then, we'll need at least that many. And ours will have automatic weapons. Tommy guns."

"Superior firepower. And we'll have the high ground."

"When can I see this place you think the exchange will happen?"

"Tomorrow morning. We'll stop by on our way to Cima Dome. But only once. Don't want to scare the antelope away from the water hole."

"And you think this sale will happen at night?"

"Only thing that makes sense, but we should be set up for any time on Sunday. Let's go to my office. I have a couple of poster boards and a topographical map you should see."

"Okay. And I'd better find a motel room."

"No need. I've arranged for you to stay with my mom. She's got lots of room."

"I wouldn't want to impose."

"No imposition. She'll be glad of the company. You'll meet her at dinner at my house tonight. Do you like chile rellenos?"

"Don't even know what they are."

"You're in for a treat. My Esperanza makes the best ones in the world."

Back at the office, he showed Agent Darnold the two poster boards and a 1:125,000 topographic map that covered the area displayed on the boards.

"My God, Horse. This is a huge chunk of geography."

"There are over seventy-five hundred square miles inside those margins. Lots of rocks and bushes."

After he had explained the boards and the topo, Horse stepped to his intercom and buzzed Fred.

"Yeah, boss."

"Where's Andy?"

"Just coming into town from the west."

"Call him in."

Horse went back into his office and explained how the poster boards fit the terrain on the topographical map. They were deep into the discussion when Andy Chesney tapped on his open door.

"Come in Andy. The man studying the map is Treasury Agent Darnold."

Darnold turned.

"Pleased to meet you, Andy."

"Likewise."

"Agent Darnold and I have a little something going. I'm going to let him continue to orient himself while we talk. Have a seat."

Andy sat down and Horse moved to the other side of the desk.

"Got another job for you tonight, Andy. More overtime."

"Okay. That was light duty last night. The only hardship was eating too many corndogs."

"I'm sending you back there tonight."

"Okay."

"It's going to be a little more complicated this time. The girlie show is going to be open to the public, and you're going to be inside the tent this time, making sure it doesn't get so raunchy that the Mayor gets more phone calls."

Andy looked worried.

"That could be a problem, Captain. Christine was real understanding about last night, but that was because she knew I wouldn't be inside where the show was going on."

"How do you think she'll take tonight's job?"

"Probably not well. I mean, if you and Esperanza were just about to get married, how would she like you being in a tent full of naked women doing provocative dancing."

"I get your point. I've already thought of that."

"I hope that means you'll consider sending somebody else."

"No. You're my best man, Andy. My most reliable, most honest, most incorruptible."

"I appreciate your confidence, Captain, but that's not going to help me with Christine."

"Let me ask you a personal question."

"Go ahead."

"Does Christine have a good sense of humor?"

"Sure."

"Take her along."

Andy almost came out of his chair.

"What?"

"Let me tell you about the tightrope we're walking here. Legally, we can't shut the girlie show down unless one of the girls does something indecent."

"Meaning?"

"Meaning she takes off all her clothes. So, I need a deputy in the tent to make sure that doesn't happen."

"And if it does, I shut down the show?"

"If it comes to that, but I don't want it to. I want these girls to keep their clothes on. If I send you in there alone, I've got a pretty good idea what they'll do. When I told Carlyle Evans about having a deputy there, his eyes lit up. I'm sure they've faced this kind of situation before, and the obvious solution is to fold the poor law enforcement guy into the act, somehow. Embarrass him and give the patrons a little something extra for their money."

"And maybe end the law enforcement guy's engagement."

"It won't come to that if you take Christine. It solves two problems. First, Christine sees that you're completely on the up and up."

"And second?"

251

"Second, I don't think those girls will get naked with another woman in the tent."

"Why not? They get naked in front of men all the time."

"That's not the same. I think they'll will refuse to do the whole act if Christine's there. One more thing."

"Yes?"

"I'll be there, too."

"Uh, Captain, what will Esperanza think about that?"

"Already discussed it with her. She's coming along."

Andy smiled.

"Date at the girlie show."

"That's right."

Andy's smile got wider.

"And if Christine knows Esperanza is coming, she's more likely to come."

"What I'm hoping. When those girls look out there and see two men in uniform and the two women with them, they'll put on a show about as sexy as a Gidget movie."

"Then why have Christine and I? Why not just you and Esperanza?"

"Because Esperanza won't want to be the only woman in the audience, just like Christine wouldn't."

"Okay, Captain. I'll ask her. But if she says 'no,' please, please give this duty to someone else."

"I guarantee you I will. But I think she'll surprise you."

After Andy left the office, Darnold moved away from the map and sat down in the chair the corporal had vacated.

"You have an interesting life out here, Horse. Now you've added a girlie show to the mix I mentioned at the cafe. Any other outrageous stuff going on?"

"Got a revival in town that I think is some kind of scam, but I don't have time to mess with it. The Christians are going to have to fend for themselves with that one."

"I'd like to see how things playout tonight."

"You're welcome to come along."

Darnold smiled.

"Thought you'd never ask."

"Right now, though, you and I have another stop to make."

"Where's that?"

"The basement at Milner's Market."

"Sounds ominous. What's down there?"

"Men's clothes. We've got to get you some Levi's and t-shirts and boots. We're going to be on the desert, and what you're wearing will get ruined."

Darnold smiled.

"I don't think my expense account will pick that up."

"Tell them you're making a trade. The clothing will be less than the motel room you're not going to rent."

"Horse, you're used to considerably more flexibility in your operations than the folks at Treasury."

CHAPTER 32

Into the River

Jedidiah had dozens of sermons he used for the revival. Some were completely his own. Others were drawn from the historic doomsday sermons of Cotton and Increase Mather, and some from Billy Sunday and Amy Semple McPherson. None of them were anywhere close to the message Jedidiah wanted. By three o'clock Tuesday afternoon, he had been through six drafts of a sermon for that evening's revival meeting. None of them were right.

The morphine that had saved him from agonizing pain was wearing off. As it did, it left him with an odd feeling. His head felt full of fog; but at the same time, he was agitated and nervous. It didn't help that his window-mounted air conditioner was rattling and groaning like a snare drum crossed with broken bagpipes. He decided to get up and get out. He wasn't sure where he wanted to go until he remembered Tyson telling him about Danny Dubois coming by early in the morning. He clamped on his LA Dodgers hat.

Outside, he forgot about the desert sun and burned himself when he tried to open the door of his Cadillac. He took off his cap and used it to protect his hand from further damage. Inside, he wrapped the cap around the blistering-hot steering wheel, turned on the engine, and got the air conditioner going.

He drove to Front Street. When he parked and walked through the arch onto the midway, the carnival looked like a medieval gypsy caravan dropped into the wrong time and place. The fierce glare of the afternoon sun highlighted its every imperfection. The grounds were nearly deserted, and the few workers he came across had not seen Danny Dubois. He walked to Carlyle's Airstream, but his GMC pickup was not there. He assumed the carnival owner was off on some kind of an errand, so he returned to his car. He managed to get in without burning himself and drove to the only part of Smoke Tree he had not walked: the neighborhood east of the Santa Fe Tracks.

As Jedidiah drove through streets with names like El Paso, Otero, La Paz, Las Cruces and Valencia and saw all the brown faces there, he realized Smoke Tree was as segregated as the South. He left the neighborhood, got back on 66, and drove to the Mojave Indian Village just beyond the city limits. He felt ashamed of his show-off car as he dodged potholes in the ruined streets, seeing poverty of a severity he had not heretofore seen outside rural Mississippi.

Restless and unsettled, Jedidiah returned to 66 and turned north once again. When the highway began its sweeping turn to the west, he continued north on a secondary road. He stayed on it until he saw a sign for Sunset Beach. He headed for the river. He parked his car at the Sunset Beach Saloon and Grill. Inside, he bought a large coffee to go from a heavy woman who did not look pleased about having to get off her stool for such a small order.

Jedidiah carried his coffee outside and found a seat on the covered patio. Probably not the best choice of drinks for a guy feeling restless and jumpy, but he thought it might blow some of the fuzz out of his brain. He sat, sipping hot coffee and sweating, as he watched the blue river roll by below. As his head began to clear, he began to relive the miracle of last night's visit from his dear Elisabet and their beautiful daughter. He recalled the scent of jasmine in the room. Remembered the bed moving as she and then Olivia climbed in next to him. Relived the sensation of sadness flowing out of his body and being replaced by the purest joy.

His Elisabet had come to comfort him. But why had she chosen Smoke Tree? Why not Opelika? Why not in any one of the many towns where he had wandered or pitched his revival tent? Shakespeare had Hamlet say, *there's a special providence in the fall of the sparrow...The readiness is all.* Maybe, he thought, that is the answer. Maybe he had not been ready. And hadn't he told Danny Dubois that Smoke Tree should consider changing its name to 'Epiphany?' Something had changed. Something was new. Maybe that was the message. Maybe tonight's sermon had to deal with the change.

And just like that, Jedidiah decided not to write a sermon. The Holy Spirit had been in his hospital room the night before. Why not let divine inspiration speak through him at the revival? He would climb that stage with nothing but the good book and wait for the words of the Lord to fill his heart and spill forth. One thing he did know in advance was the song the choir would be singing as people filed into the tent.

Amazing Grace.

Sure about what to do, Jedidiah got up and walked down to the floating dock. When he stepped on it, he could feel it shifting beneath his feet. He stood for a moment, thinking about the rivers in the Bible. The Jordan, the Amana, the Shihor, the Gozan, the Zered. Desert rivers. But surely there was not a river running through any desert anywhere that was more beautiful than this Colorado. One more message?

Jedidiah got down on one knee and trailed his fingers in the water. He was surprised to discover how cold it was. He took off his shoes and socks. The rough wood planks, cooled by the river beneath, welcomed his feet. He stared at the green of the mesquite forest on the other side of the river and the dark, volcanic mountains farther to the east, beyond the river valley.

Suddenly in a hurry, he took off his Dodger cap and put it next to his shoes. Unbuttoning his shirt, he folded it and set it next to his shoes and cap. His khaki pants followed, and Jedidiah stood on the dock in his boxer shorts. I am a new man, he thought. A new man with a mission as yet unknown. As I am re-born, I should baptize myself. He stood for a moment, listening to the sounds the river made as it rippled around the dock.

He jumped in. The frigid water carried him away and down as he said to himself, 'I baptize you Jedidiah Shanks, husband of Elisabet and father of Olivia, in the name of the Father, the Son, and the Holy Spirit.' It was about that time Jedidiah remembered he was not a very good swimmer. He struggled to the surface, his face breaking above the water as he took in air. He began to paddle furiously toward shore. Alarmed at how fast the current was carrying him downstream, he increased his awkward efforts. He was exhausted and panicking by the time he came to a place where he could stand up. Relieved, he took a step forward and dropped into a deep hole dug by the river between the submerged sandbar on which he had stood and the beach. He yelped in surprise and sucked in a huge gulp of water. Fortunately, while the hole was deep, it lacked current. He was able to paddle, coughing and sputtering, to the shore. He wiped water from his eyes and shook it from his hair as, laughing like a madman, he walked up the beach to retrieve his clothes.

Inside the saloon and grill, the heavy woman sitting on her stool inserted her eighteenth unfiltered Pall Mall of the day into an ivory cigarette holder as she watched Jedidiah walk her way.

"Lord," she said aloud, "Another out-of-town crazy. Drives a pink Cadillac and swims in his underwear. Shameless."

CHAPTER 33

Violence Begets Violence

In spite of the fact that they were on the brink of a demanding, difficult and perilous operation, Horse and Darnold had a relaxing dinner. The heat of the day had eased somewhat when they drove toward the home Carlos had built in the foothills of the Sacramento Mountains. As they came up the long driveway, the freshly-watered Bermuda grass glistened out front. An easy breeze ruffled the leaves of the cottonwood trees and made them flash and sparkle in the rays of the setting sun.

Horse parked his cruiser in the usual spot, and he and Darnold walked toward the house. As they drew closer, they heard voices from the back yard. Circling around that way, they discovered Esperanza had gone all out in preparation for the dinner guest who had never eaten a chile relleno. The white lights Horse had strung from the cottonwoods behind the house to the eaves had already been turned on and were just beginning to show against the fading light in the evening sky. Esperanza had hung delicate Japanese paper lanterns of all colors from the wires, and they were moving in the mild zephyr that often blew in from the west at sunset, as if the earth were exhaling the heat of the desert day down to the river.

She had also lined the edges of the patio with *farolitos*, but had not yet lit the candles stuck into the sand in the bottom of the paper bags. The big redwood picnic table was covered by *el mantel camino carmesí,* her best Mexican cotton tablecloth. Through the screen door, Horse could see her and his mother moving around in the kitchen.

The voices they had heard belonged to Alejandro and Elena. The twins were feeding carrots and apples to Canyon and Mariposa. They didn't know there would soon be a third horse in the corral. Horse had still not told them about Pepper. He was unsure how to explain the death of Burke, the friend they loved to chatter with in the hilarious mix of Spanish, English, and Kiowa Apache the three of them had fallen into whenever they were together.

Horse decided not to interrupt what was going on in the kitchen. Instead, he took Darnold over to meet the children. Usually shy around strangers, they warmed immediately to the slender agent and were soon competing, voices clambering over each other, to tell him about their day, which had apparently consisted of wandering around in the hills with a canteen of water looking for lizards and horned toads until it go so hot they hurried home to play in the sprinkler.

When Darnold accepted Horse's offer of a tour of the property, the twins came along. They ran in circles around the two men as they walked, Alejandro and Elena talking and laughing the entire time. Horse showed Darnold the tack room made of railroad ties, and with Canyon and Mariposa trailing along in hopes of more carrots and apples, they walked the perimeter of the recently-extended and solidly-constructed corral with its large, roofed section where the horses could shelter from the sun. They visited Esperanza's late-winter, early-spring garden, fading rapidly now because of the heat, but still with a few pole beans and even some stubborn tomatoes.

Horse pointed out the boundary of the five acres he bought in 1954 for next to nothing and the additional twenty he was in the process of buying. Those twenty sat directly to the west of the original five, forming a truncated T. When the owner put the land up for sale, he received no offers. He eventually offered it to Horse through a land contract for five thousand dollars that allowed him to pay off the property over eight years.

"The owner bought the land because he wanted a horse property, but when Esperanza and I built our place, he decided he didn't want Mexicans as neighbors."

"You're kidding."

"I wish I was. This town is full of old prejudices. Given what's happening now in the South, I'm hopeful things will improve as Elena and Alejandro grow up. Esperanza and I own the original parcel and the house outright, and we've only got three years remaining on the land contract. After it's paid off, we plan to build a bigger house. We're going to need it as the twins get older. When it's complete, we're going to give the smaller one to mama. She can sell or rent out the family home when she moves in out here.

I'm fortunate to have a good friend who is a master at building with adobe. He'll work with me to build an old fashioned, whitewashed adobe with a terracotta roof, solid-wood doors and double hung windows looking out on a small, interior courtyard. Sometimes I design and redesign the place when I'm falling asleep at night."

"Twenty acres is a big chunk."

"It is. I have a brother and sister who no longer live in Smoke Tree. I'm hopeful they'll come back some day. Esperanza and I have told them they can each have five acres to build homes. Reuniting the family is a dream of ours. We'd love to see all the children at play out here."

"I take it you're not planning on leaving Smoke Tree anytime soon."

"Nope. Started my career here and intend to be here rest of my life. The Sheriff was glad to find someone who wanted to be assigned here right out of the academy. Someone who grew up here and knew pretty much everyone in the area. It has worked out well for me. I never would have been promoted this fast if I'd been in the San Bernardino Valley."

"When I drove down from Las Vegas, I was wondering why anyone would ever want to live on this desert. But now, listening to your plans, with the sun setting on one side of us and the river below on the other, I'm beginning to understand."

"Maybe you could put in for a transfer to Las Vegas or Phoenix."

Darnold smiled.

"Let's not get carried away, Horse. As much as you're a small-town guy, I'm a city guy. Besides, I couldn't live without the ocean."

The twins in tow, they returned to the house. The twilight was fading, and the white lights were glowing, illuminating the Japanese lanterns. The *farolitos* had been lit, softly marking the perimeter of the patio and walkway. Esperanza and Consuela were carrying platters of food from the kitchen and arranging them on the tablecloth.

Horse hugged Esperanza and introduced Darnold to her and to his mother while the twins trooped inside to wash their hands. When Darnold said wonderful things about how much he had enjoyed his walk with Alejandro and Elena, he was well on his way to making two new friends.

Consuela smiled as she said, "I'm going to like having this one for a houseguest."

The twins came back outside.

"*Dos hombres lavan las manos también. Dar un buen ejemplo.*"

"Translate, Elena," said Esperanza.

261

"Grandma said, 'The men must wash their hands also to set a good example.'"

"Very good!"

"May I translate the next one," asked Alejandro?

"Por supuesto."

"Certainly," he said solemnly.

"*Una vez una madre, siempre madre.*"

"That one's too easy, *Abuela*," said Elena. You always say that."

"Say what, Elena," asked Esperanza?

"Once a mother, always a mother."

"And '*Abuela*' means 'grandmother,' added Alejandro.

"When my mother speaks, it's wise to listen if we want dinner," said Horse as he led Darnold inside.

When he and Darnold returned to the patio, it was clear the twins had arranged themselves so they would have Darnold between them. As he sat down, the two began naming all the dishes on the table, demanding that, as *el huésped,* he help himself first.

Darnold feasted on amazing food that was like nothing he had ever tasted before. He constantly complimented the cooks, adding to his status as a good guy. As full darkness came to the desert, June bugs appeared and began to circle the strings of lights. A number of bats veered off their route from desert mineshafts in the Sacramentos to the lights of Smoke Tree for a snack.

"*Cuando los murciélagos ven, es hora de ir de la casa.*"

Alejandro raised his hand.

"I think it's my turn. I only got to translate one word last time."

"Go ahead, *Mi hijo,*"

"*Abuela* said, 'When the bats come, it's time to go in the house.'"

"And '*mi hijo,*' means 'my son,' "added Elena.

And with that, everyone began to help clear the table. Inside, Consuela and Horse scraped plates while Esperanza made coffee and dished up the *flan.* As *el huésped,* Darnold was not allowed to help; instead, he found himself at the dining room table where Alejandro and Elena set up a checkerboard. They played him as a team until coffee arrived.

Everyone was having desert when the phone rang. Horse went to the kitchen to answer it.

"Horse here."

"Andy Chesney, Captain. Just wanted to let you know, when I told Christine what you wanted her to do, she looked doubtful, but

262

when I told her you and Esperanza were coming, she said she was in. In fact, she's still smiling."

"Okay. See you on Front Street at eight o'clock."

Horse returned to the table and told Esperanza of Christine's decision.

"That's good, *mi marido*."

"My husband," said the twins in unison.

Consuela knew she would be babysitting the twins this evening, but she didn't know why. When Horse explained, she didn't care for what her son and his wife were about to do.

"It's the best solution I could come up with, mama. The Mayor wants the girlie show toned down, and I think I have a way to do it."

"*Que us una* 'girlie show,' *Papi*," asked Alejandro?

"Bath time," said Consuela and hustled the twins away from the table.

At eight o'clock, Horse, Esperanza and Darnold met Andy Chesney and Christine Gehardy a few blocks from the carnival. Andy and Horse were both in in uniform and carrying their sidearms. Andy introduced his fiancée to Darnold.

The group strolled down Front Street and entered the midway, taking in the game booths and then the rides. They walked on until the they found a young man circulating among the men in the crowd and recruiting an audience for the coochie show. He soon headed off toward the back corner of the lot, a group of men in tow.

Horse and his accomplices wandered the midway for a while longer to give the men time to buy tickets and get settled in the tent before heading that way themselves. When they got there, they walked past the ticket booth. The woman inside said, "Hey. You can't go in there without a ticket."

"Sheriff's Department," said Horse.

"I'm not talking to you and the other deputy. I'm talking to that guy and the two women."

Darnold pulled out his I.D.

"U.S. Treasury. These women are auditors."

The group entered the tent.

The woman left the booth and locked the door behind her before hurrying off to find Carlyle.

Inside, there was a raised stage with a drawn curtain. *The Stripper* was blaring from speakers on either side of the stage. All the seats were full, so Horse and the others stood in the back.

The curtain opened, and four women came out onto the stage. The two in front were young. The two in the back had a few more

263

miles on the clock. All four were dressed in costumes that were clearly designed to be removed a piece at a time, and each of the women had a different colored feather boa.

They moved forward, launching into a bump and grind that was met with cries of, "Take if Off!" The first items removed were the knee-length skirts, revealing garter belts beneath to appreciative whistles. The girl at the front left was scanning the crowd, searching for the deputy Carlyle had told her to watch for. She smiled when she saw Horse and Andy. She stepped to the front of the stage and beckoned them forward with a languid, seductive motion of her index finger.

"Gentlemen," she said above the music, "We have deputies with us tonight. I'm inviting them down front because we have a special little entertainment planned for them."

As she finished speaking, Esperanza and Christine stepped out from behind the deputies. The girl covered her recently-exposed black panties with the skirt she had not yet tossed aside.

"Turn off the music," she yelled.

The music went silent. A man wearing a straw boater stepped onto the stage.

"What's the matter, Candy?"

"There are women in here!"

That got a laugh, which died away as heads turned to take in Horse and Andy.

The man in the straw hat was quick-witted. Talkers have to be. He decided to play it for laughs.

"Of course, there are, sweetheart, four of them. Right up here on this stage. Let's give these boys a show."

"No! I don't get naked in front of housewives."

At the word 'naked,' the audience began to yell and boo, impatient with the interruption and eager for the show to go on.

"What difference does it make?"

"The difference," said one of the older women, "is that we're not doing it in front of women who are going to look down their noses at us."

"Get on with the show," someone yelled.

"Yeah, get nasty!" yelled another.

"We paid to see skin," cane a third. "Take it off!"

Other voices chimed in, and soon the men were stamping their feet on the ground, raising puffs of dust, as they began to chant in unison.

"Take if off! Take if off! Take if off!"

The women turned and left the stage. The talker knew when he was whipped.

"Sorry, gentlemen. No show tonight. There will be a full refund."

"Damn straight there will be!"

The men began to file out of the tent. A few of them glanced at Horse or Andy, but they averted their eyes from Christine and Esperanza. As the crowd dwindled, Carlyle Evans came in.

"Where's the guy from Treasury?"

"That's me. Agent Darnold."

"I'm Carlyle Evans, the owner. What in the world is so important about a little carnival that Treasury would send an agent all the way out here."

Darnold put on his serious face.

"We're starting a push on businesses that deal primarily in cash."

"Well, okay," said Carlyle, his brain making high speed calculations of violations and their possible penalties.

Darnold broke into a smile.

"Just yanking your chain, Mr. Evans. I'm not with the IRS, although that's the first thing everyone thinks when they hear 'Treasury'. I'm in town on some other business with Captain Caballo. I'm just tagging along tonight."

Carlyle visibly relaxed.

"Well, as long as you're here, I'd like to register a complaint."

"Why? Someone passing funny money?"

"No, but Carlos here is getting in my pocket."

"You'd better explain that statement, Carlyle. It sounds like you're implying I'm on the take."

"Lord no. If you were, I'd be money ahead. Pardon me, ladies, but I'm going to speak candidly. This coochie show is my biggest moneymaker, and this is the second night in a row Carlos has managed to shut it down without giving me justification for suing this hick town."

"I promise not to do it tomorrow night."

"Because you know we won't be here tomorrow night. You win, Carlos, I surrender."

"Not really. You ran your girlie show for three nights before the Mayor called me. I'd say three out of five is pretty good."

Carlyle held up his hands. "I'll stop complaining if you'll do something for me."

"What's that?"

265

"As I was coming in, I heard some ugly talk from a few of the guys going out. I think there might be trouble later. Sometimes happens the last night we're in town, local toughs trying to bust the place up, but this time I think it's because the coochie show was cancelled. I'd like a little protection here, and not the kind I have to pay bribes to get."

"Okay, but I want to drop my wife off at home and I'm sure Andy wants to do the same with his fiancée. After that, we'll be back."

Twenty minutes later, Carlos and Darnold and Andy met up on Front Street again and walked to the Happy Times Funfest. There didn't seem to be any trouble on the midway. Horse thought troublemakers would want to wait until just about closing time before they made their move, so the three strolled the grounds, checking once to be sure the girlie show had not re-opened.

After an hour without any problems, they headed for Carlyle's office. He was sitting at the bottom of the steps on a folding chair. The chair next to him was occupied by a young man with sandy, curly hair and hazel eyes who had been telling him about the unusual sermon preached by Jedidiah Shanks earlier that evening.

"Officers," said Carlyle as they walked up, and then added "agent."

Everyone nodded.

"Carlos, meet Danny Dubois."

The young man got quickly to his feet.

"Danny will be staying in Smoke Tree when the carnival leaves. Hate to lose him. He's been with us for years."

"What are you going to do in Smoke Tree, Danny?"

"I've got a job at the Southern California Gas compressor station. Aeden Snow put in a good word for me."

Aeden Snow again, thought Horse. That guy pops up everywhere.

"Well, welcome to Smoke Tree, Danny. I think you'll like it here

A man run up to the group.

"Boss, we got trouble. Out at the arch."

"How many?"

"A lot."

Carlyle stood up.

"Have the ride boys all grab a wrench. Tell Steve at the shooting gallery to unlock the rod and hand out the .22s to the jointees."

266

The man turned to go, but Horse grabbed his arm.

"Hold it."

He turned to Carlyle.

"You asked us to come back in case this happened, and we did. We'll take care of it. Don't be handing out guns."

"All right, but I don't want any damaged equipment or injured employees."

"Who does?"

He and Andy and Darnold hurried off toward the entrance to the midway.

Carlyle pulled the messenger aside.

"Forget about the .22s, but put the word out to the ride guys. I don't believe these deputies will take on local citizens to protect a bunch of carnies."

The man headed toward the rides as Carlyle and Danny followed in the wake of the two deputies and the Treasury agent.

When Horse, Andy and Darnold arrived at the arch, a phalanx of men armed with pipes, chains and axe handles was gathered behind a large man with the build of a wrestler. The man was berating the talker who was trying to calm the group.

Jerking his thumb toward the men in a skirmish line behind him, he was saying, "We spent good money at this crap show you call a carnival. We put up with the rigged games, the Mickey Mouse rides and the food that'd gag a maggot, but the last two nights hit a new low. A bunch of us came for the girlie show last night, but it was for soldiers only. Only thing was, we didn't see no soldiers. Tonight, we got in, but we didn't get no show."

"And we gave you a full refund."

"Not good enough. We came to see some naked women and we aim to see 'em. Right now. If we don't, we're gonna bust this place up."

Horse stepped forward.

"Fat-mouth-Mickey McCoury. I should have known it'd be you in front of these yahoos."

"Well, well, the Mexican marshal is siding with these crooked carnies against his own citizens."

"No, I'm siding with the law. I'm telling you and your friends to clear off of this lot. These people have a living to earn and you're in the way."

McCoury stepped close, poking his very big finger toward Horse's face.

"The last time you and I had a set-to was a couple years back in front of the house where that Mex kid sniffing after a white girl

267

lived. You threatened to lock me up for inciting a riot. Said I'd do jail time. But this here is different. That was a private house. This is a carnival. It's open for business to anyone who wants to come in. And my friends and I are going to come in and give this place the business."

He laughed, pleased at his play on words.

Horse looked past Mickey at the group of town toughs gathered behind him.

"The bars must have closed early tonight. Are all you men here with McCoury?"

Shouts of "yeah," "damned right" came from the growing crowd. Odd, thought Horse, how there are already more people with Mickey than when I walked out here. Yahoos must have some of radar. They hone in on trouble like those bats finding June bugs.

He held up his hand to quiet the crowd.

"Gentlemen, I don't want to call for backup and see a bunch of people arrested or hurt, so let's try something different."

He turned to McCoury.

"I take it you are the self-appointed leader here."

Mickey McCoury, two hundred and sixty pounds of mean, bad-attitude bully, seemed to puff up even bigger.

"Sure as hell am."

"I'll make you and your bunch a deal." Horse raised his voice and addressed the entire group.

"Mickey here has been wanting a piece of me for years. Tonight, he's going to get his chance. If lard-butt here can take me, my deputy and I will step aside. You and the carnies can fight it out. We won't stop you. But, if I whip him, all of you turn around and go home.

Fair enough?"

"Damned right," roared Mickey.

"I'm not talking to you. I'm talking to your *compadres*. I want everyone here to witness the fact that I am taking off my gun and badge and witness the promise I'm making Mickey. If he takes me, I will not bring charges of any kind against him. But if I take him, you all leave. Is that fair?"

Shouts of assent came from the crowd. If there was anything they liked more than a fight, it was the chance to see an officer of the law get pounded.

Keeping an eye on McCoury, Horse unbuckled his gun belt and removed the badge from his shirt. He handed both to Andy. He took off his Stetson and gave it to Darnold.

"Hold my hat. This will only take a minute."

268

"It's a good thing you gave that guy your fancy white hat, beaner," said McCoury "'cause I'm about to knock your head clean off."

Horse locked eyes with Mickey. Something about his intense gaze gave the man pause.

"Talk is cheap, fat boy," Horse said quietly. He raised his voice again. "Everybody, back away and give us room!"

People on both sides of the conflict moved away.

Horse spoke loudly again without taking his eyes off of McCoury.

"Andy, while I'm tussling with fat-mouth, or after I put him down, you have my permission to shoot anyone in his group that comes after me. But, if he whips me, you're to step aside and let them by. That's an order."

"You got it, Captain."

"Enough talk," said McCoury, as he got into a boxing stance and shuffled forward.

Man's had some training, thought Horse, and I know he's had lots of fights, but he has no idea what's about to happen.

McCoury flicked out a pretty good left jab. Horse let it hit him, but turned his head just slightly at the last instant to minimize any damage and swung a right hand that purposely missed its target.

McCoury shuffled away, happy with his success. He moved back in and flicked out another jab. Once again, Horse took it, while minimizing the impact. He dropped his hands and shook his head as if he were stunned. Here comes the looping right, he thought, the punch that's supposed to put me on the ground so he can stomp me.

Mickey launched the roundhouse. Horse, his hands suddenly no longer down by his sides, reached up and snatched the fist in mid-flight. He twisted it and pushed sharply downward and in as he slid his left hand up behind McCoury's elbow. Using the momentum of the big man's punch, Horse pulled the elbow toward himself as he leveraged the fist the opposite direction, simultaneously turning his right hip into the larger man. In as balletic a move as anyone had ever seen him make, Mickey McCoury came off his feet, turned a flip, and landed flat on his back.

Red-faced, he clambered to his feet, lurching toward Horse. Horse swept his feet out from under him. This time, McCoury landed on his side. Horse moved quickly behind him, dropped to one knee, and put him in a choke hold. He steadily increased the pressure on McCoury's windpipe until the man's face turned bright red.

"Say, 'uncle,' and I'll let you go, but you have to say it in Spanish."

McCoury's face was edging toward a dangerous shade of purple before Horse spoke again.

"Okay, English will do. You're too stupid to know the Spanish word."

He eased the pressure slightly.

"Uncle," croaked McCoury, waving one hand in supplication.

Horse released the hold, stood up and stepped quickly away in the unlikely event there was any fight left in his opponent.

McCoury rolled onto all fours and struggled to his feet.

"You all saw that," he said, massaging his neck. "The greaser assaulted me."

Horse lifted his hands and took two quick steps forward. McCoury turned and ran. Absent their leader, his supporters melted into the night. Horse retrieved his gun and badge from Andy. He slipped the badge into his pocket and strapped on the gun. Darnold handed over his snow-white Stetson.

"Thanks for holding my hat, Agent Darnold."

"Lord, Carlos," said Carlyle, "I wish I'd a known you were going to do that. I could've put the two of you in a tent and charged admission! Made up what I lost on the coochie show. Think you might do it again when we come back next year?"

"Just so we're clear, Carlyle, you know if you come back, I'm not going to let you have your girlie show here?"

"I intend to visit Danny and see how he's doing in his new home town. For Smoke Tree and its honest sheriff, I'm willing to sacrifice. I'll put the girls at work on the games. Fully clothed."

Horse and Darnold said goodnight to Andy and drove home. When they walked in the house, Esperanza and his mother were sitting in the living room. Esperanza looked worried. She stood up and hugged Carlos hard for a long time before stepping back.

"Show me your hands."

Horse held them up and turned them over.

"Good. I see you didn't punch anyone. I was worried."

"He didn't have to," said Darnold. He laid two of the slickest moves I've ever seen on this really huge guy. The guy got up and ran away."

"It was Mickey McCoury, and he wasn't that good. Just a barroom brawler. He's lucky it was me instead of Burke Henry. If it had been, he'd still be on the ground."

He turned to Darnold.

"Burke is the guy who taught me what you saw back there."

"Oh *cariño,* you worry me so when you go off like this."

"I'm sorry, *querida,* part of the job. Better than hitting someone with a stick, or, *Dios no lo quiera,* shooting them."

"Too bad the twins are in bed, they could translate for Darnold," said Consuela, and that broke the tension. "What Carlos just said means 'God forbid,' more or less."

"Folks, my job is nowhere near as exciting as being the sheriff in this town."

"It's not always this exciting, Darnold. Now, you and momma should get on home. You and I have an early start in the morning. I'll be by at six."

Consuela got to her feet.

"I promise to have him up and fed by the time you get there. Have you ever had *huevos ranchero,* Agent Darnold?"

"Never, *Senora Caballo,* but if they're anything like what we had tonight, I can't wait."

CHAPTER 34

A New Way

Jedidiah Shanks, Bible in hand, stood on the raised stage watching people fill every folding chair in the tent. Behind him, the choir was singing *Amazing Grace*. They had been told to continue singing the song during the entire service, normal volume at the beginning, much softer while he was preaching, and loudest of all when he gave the altar call.

Jedidiah had never felt so unprepared to deliver a revival sermon. Ironically, he had always been meticulously rehearsed when his sermons were just part of a money-making show. His lack of preparation made him anxious as he looked down at the expectant faces of the growing assembly. The seats were full, and the side aisles so packed that those forced closest to the tent were pressed against the canvas walls, when a mother and father and their little girl managed to worm their way through the clot of people at the entrance. They headed down the center aisle, searching for seats. As Jedidiah watched them come closer, he realized the girl was blind.

When they reached the front row, the mother spoke to the people sitting directly in front of Jedidiah. They leaned forward, the better to hear. Whatever she was saying, it involved frequent pointing at the little girl who stood silently, face upturned toward Jedidiah.

She looks like an angel, he thought. And indeed, she seemed surrounded by the same pearlescent glow that had suffused the air around Elisabet and Olivia at the foot of his hospital bed. He could not tear his eyes away from the child, and, although she was sightless, it was if she were looking into the very core of his being. It was at once a discomfiting but also a pleasant feeling.

Whatever the mother had said, the three people closest to the aisle stood up and relinquished their chairs. The man and woman nodded and smiled in appreciation as they sat down, placing the angelic girl between them.

273

People continued to arrive. The area behind the back row was now jammed. Tyson was standing behind Jedidiah and to his left. Jedidiah turned and motioned him forward.

"Biggest crowd we've ever had, boss."

"And more arriving. Get some crew members and roll up the flaps at the back of the tent."

"Going to let in lots of noise and dust if we do that."

"Doesn't matter. I don't want to turn anyone away."

"Okay. At least it will make for a good collection."

"There won't be a collection this evening, Tyson."

Tyson gave him a puzzled look but hurried out the back of the tent to find some workers.

Jedidiah remained standing, his eyes returning again and again to the blind girl. Her face was still tilted upward, and now she was smiling. The smile magnified the aura of light Jedidiah perceived around her. He wondered if anyone else saw it.

He saw the back of the tent being rolled up. As the canvas rose, it revealed more people outside the tent than inside. And still, he could see more arriving. For a brief moment, he thought he saw Danny Dubois at the rear of the crowd, but then he either turned away or the shifting sea of faces blocked him from view.

Tyson waved his hands and gave Jedidiah thumbs up. He motioned Tyson forward. Tyson disappeared into the crowd and soon stepped onto the stage behind Jedidiah.

"How many more out there?"

"They just keep coming."

"Roll up the side flaps, too."

Tyson went out the back again. In a few minutes, the side flaps began to rise. By the time they were all the way up, the crowd outside had grown to three or even four times the number in the tent.

And still Jedidiah stood silent.

And still the choir sang.

And still the little girl's smiling face remained tilted upward toward him.

With the tent flaps up on three sides, the traffic noise from 66 was loud, but even louder was the sound of the generator powering the searchlight. He searched the crowd for Tyson for a few moments before he realized his crew chief was back on the stage with him. He beckoned Tyson for one last request. In a few moments, the generator shut down in a final clatter of pistons, rods, and valve train.

274

Jedidiah lifted his hands above his head. The white cover on his Bible matched his suit. The choir decreased its volume as the crowd grew silent. With no idea of what he was about to say, Jedidiah opened his mouth. Words burst forth.

"Brothers and sisters, I know what it is to stray from the Lord. I strayed from the Lord for twelve years! I thought I had strayed so far that I had been lost to the Lord, forever. I turned my back on God because I thought He had deserted me. I denied God. I rebuked God. I got up on my hind legs and howled at God in anger."

He stood silently a moment.

"I cursed God!"

A gasp rose from those assembled.

Jeddah remained silent. People leaned forward, stunned by what this revival preacher had admitted and eager to hear his next words.

"Imagine that. Imagine a man, once a man of God, having the temerity to deny, nay, not simply deny, but rebuke and curse his Creator. For twelve years, I refused to allow our Lord and Savior into my heart. Twelve years!

For the first two of those years, I continued to be a pastor of my flock in Alabama. Continued until my congregation began to fall away, not from the Lord, but from me. Fell away because I became a minister who would preach doubt of God's goodness, even as his congregation tried to bring him to his senses. But I refused to be reconciled. I fled.

For the next five years, I lived on the road. No home. No address. No friends. And no room in my hardened heart for the Lord. And I became a drunk. And then one day this very revival, with this tent and this choir and this crew and equipment, came to the town I was in. I stopped in one night, fully intending to tell the preacher he was a fool for believing in a God who was either nonexistent or noncaring. But when we talked, the innate goodness of that man shone through so brightly I could not bear to challenge his faith. Instead, when the revival left town, I went with it, assistant to this Godly man who wanted nothing more than to serve the Lord. When he grew too old to travel, I took over."

Jedidiah stood silent again, the crowd in the palm of his hand, hanging on his every word as the choir behind him sang at a level not far above a whisper.

"But," he roared, shaking the Bible over his head, "I did not believe!"

His voice dropped.

275

"In my heart, I denied the Lord daily. I reconciled my lack of faith and my soulless preaching by telling myself I was bringing hope to others. Hope, although I had none of my own. Hope for others. A lot of money for me."

He lowered the bible.

"My sermon tonight, brothers and sisters, is about reconciliation and redemption. My sermon is about the awesome forgiveness of the Lord.

I will heal their faithlessness. I will love them freely for my anger has turned from them. Hosea, verse 4

Imagine that. 'I will heal their faithlessness.'

Last night, I was carried up the aisle and out of this tent. I ended up in the hospital. I thought I was dying, but I was wrong. I was not dying. I was being re-born in Jesus Christ!

Before last night, I thought I was not only beyond reconciliation but beyond redemption. I was not. *Therefore, if any man is in Christ, he is a new creature; the old things passed away; behold, new things are from God, who reconciled us to Himself through Christ and gave us the ministry of reconciliation, namely that God was in Christ reconciling the world to Himself, not counting their trespasses against them, and He has committed to us the word of reconciliation.* Corinthians 5.17-20

I, even I, am He that blotteth out thy transgressions for mine own sake, and will not remember thy sins. Isaiah 43:15:

And Psalm 86:5: *For Thou, Lord, art good, and ready to forgive; and plenteous in mercy unto all them that call upon Thee.*

I have preached all those verses many times over the years in my cynical sermons. But now, the understanding of those words has been returned to me by a merciful God.

Brothers and sisters, we are all the beloved of Jesus Christ, our Lord. I had to wander this land for twelve years before I stumbled onto this desert with my burden. Last night, I came up out of the wilderness and had my faith restored. I found my salvation in Smoke Tree."

Suddenly, the man sitting next to the little girl with her face still upturned sprang to his feet.

"Preacher, you are preaching a miracle. My wife and I brought out our little girl here tonight because we hoped you might be a worker of miracles, not just a preacher of them. We need a miracle, preacher. Our little girl has been without sight since birth. We brought her in hopes you might lay hands upon her and heal her."

The man stood in a position of supplication, head bowed, hands spread to the sides, palms up. His wife stood and assumed the same position.

"I am sorry, mother and father and dear child, but I am not numbered among those who have the healing power."

"Please, preacher, please. Even if you have never done it before, please try now."

Jedidiah could not refuse the piteous request.

"Bring her onto the stage. And bring her chair. I am willing to try, but I ask you, and everyone here, do not be disappointed if I fail."

How strange, thought Jedidiah, that this should happen tonight.

The parents complied, and soon the child was seated in front of Jedidiah in profile to the audience, her parents behind her.

"What is your name, precious child?"

The crowd, those who had been seated now on their feet, pushed forward to catch the little girl's response.

"Alicia," she said, in a clear voice.

"Alicia, have you ever in your life been able to see?"

"No."

"That's very sad. Alicia. As I told your father, I have never had the power to heal, but your mother and father love you exceedingly, and they have asked me to try. But what about you, Alicia, do you want me to try?"

"I think so," Alicia said in the same clear voice.

A smile spread across Jedidiah's face and the faces of many of those in the gathering.

"That's a very honest answer, Alicia. Is it all right with you if I place my hand on top of your head?"

"Yes."

Jedidiah stepped forward, transferring the Bible to his left hand. He placed his right, palm down, atop Alicia's head. When he did, she shook her head. He took his hand away. Alicia turned her face up to him and continued to shake her head, a puzzled look on her face.

"Alicia, can you see me?"

"No, Mr. Preacher, but I saw light around the edges of the darkness in my head."

"Have you ever seen a light inside your head before?"

"Once, when I fell and hit my head on the sidewalk."

"Was it like the light you saw just now?"

"No, Mr. Preacher. It was much brighter."

277

Jedidiah quickly scoured his memory for anything he had learned about the optic nerve in his college biology class. There was something there, he was sure, something about physical and mental trauma, but he could not call it forth.

"Is the light still there?"

"No. It was there a minute ago, but it is gone."

"And you can see nothing at all?"

"Nothing."

Jedidiah spoke to Alicia's parents.

"I am truly sorry. I have failed and thus have no reason to believe you will grant me a favor, but I ask you for one nonetheless. Would you and your daughter remain on the stage with me and allow her to help me with something?"

"Of course."

Jedidiah looked down at Alicia. It seemed to him the soft light surrounding her face had intensified. Once again, he wondered if anyone else could see it but thought it best not to ask.

"Alicia, there may be hope in the light you saw in your head just now and the bright light you saw when you fell. I promise you, Alicia, and I promise your mother and your father, I will help you follow up on that hope."

There was a stirring in the crowd. Someone said, "hallelujah," and then another, followed by an "amen," and several more after that.

Jedidiah turned to the crowd and raised his hands.

"When I stood on this stage tonight and watched you arrive, I had no idea what I was going to say, but I wasn't worried. For the first time since I began falsely preaching 'revival,' I felt the Lord would fill my head with right words, and true, and He has. And He has sent Alicia. I am going to ask her to help me understand something."

He turned back to Alicia.

"Child, I am going to put my Bible in your hands. All I ask is that you open it and let me take it back. Will you do that for me?"

"Yes, Mr. Preacher."

Jedidiah put the white Bible in her small hands. She opened it. He took it back and turned to those assembled.

"I read to you from the page to which this child has turned.

Now when Job's three friends heard of all this evil that was come upon him, they came every one from his own place; Eliphaz the Termanite, and Bildad the Shuhite, and Zopher the Naamathite: for they had made an appointment together to come to mourn with him and to comfort him.

278

And when they lifted up their eyes afar off, and knew him not, they lifted up their voice, and wept; and they rent every one his mantle, and sprinkled dust upon their heads toward heaven.

So they sat down with him upon the ground seven days and seven nights, and none spoke a word unto him: for they saw that his grief was very great.

That was indeed my past in some ways. My wife, Elisabet, was ripped from me by a drunk driver. When she was killed, our unborn child died with her. Like Job, I was tested. But unlike Job, I was found wanting. I screamed at God and turned my face from Him in anger. Until last night. Until last night.

I have told you of my past, and this child has opened the Bible to a passage that illuminated that past. Now, I am going to ask Alicia, this precious, unsighted child, to help me understand what happened to me last night.

He put the Bible in Alicia's hands again.

As before, she opened it, and again he took it from her. When he read what was on the page, he turned, swaying, to face those who were anxiously awaiting his words.

"I am overcome. Alicia has turned to Acts 9: 1-22. These verses are about blindness. They describe how Saul, who was on his way to Damascus to persecute Christians, saw in a vision a bright light which felled him to the ground. In Saul's vision he heard a voice say *Saul, Saul, why are you persecuting me?* After he got up, even though his eyes were open, he could not see. His accomplices led him to Damascus, where he remained blind for three days. He remained blind till Ananias went to him and, placing his hand on Saul. told him, and I quote from scripture to you, *Brother Saul, the Lord Jesus, who appeared to you on the road you were traveling, has sent me so that you can regain your sight and be filled with the Holy Spirit.* It is further stated in the same Acts: *At once something like scales fell from his eyes, and he regained his sight.*

Then Saul, this non-believer, this man who was on his way to persecute Christians in Damascus, got up and was baptized. As we all know, he was baptized as the disciple Paul and devoted the rest of his life to Jesus Christ.

My friends, today I drove to your beautiful river. As I stood on a dock and listened to it run, it came to me that, as I had been reborn, I should baptize myself. And I did. I took off almost all my clothes and jumped in and baptized myself. Even as I sank down into the Colorado, my spirit soared. There is a woman in that restaurant at Sunset Beach who can attest she saw me when I emerged from the river, nearly naked. I'm quite sure she thought I was crazy."

There was laughter, mixed with cries of 'hallelujah' from those assembled.

Jedidiah waited for the crowd to grow silent once more.

"I am going to ask this child for one last bit of guidance."

He turned back to Alicia and leaned down and placed the Bible in her hands.

She opened it, and he took it from her.

He faced the expectant crowd.

"I read to you from Mathew 16-18: *And I say also unto thee. That thou art Peter, and upon this rock I will build my church, and the gates of hell shall not prevail against it.*"

A buzz of conversation passed through those assembled.

Jedidiah lowered his head and stood silent for a long time. The crow quieted.

He lifted his head and spoke.

"When the Jedidiah Shanks traveling revival departs Smoke Tree tonight, Jedidiah Shanks will not go with it. I will remain in Smoke Tree, the town where I found salvation and was reborn in Jesus Christ. I will buy the property upon which we stand tonight, and upon this slab I will build my church, and the gates of hell shall not prevail against it. I will live out my life in Smoke Tree, ministering to any who come to that church and helping any who come out of the desert on highway 66 and find themselves in trouble or in need.

I am a man of considerable resources. I have bank accounts scattered all across this country. Accounts, I am ashamed to say, filled with money raised through my false preaching. I will call those dollars to Smoke Tree to help in this ministry, and, as I promised Alicia and her mother and father, I will find the best doctors that can be found to see if Alicia can be given the gift of sight.

This is my promise. I make it freely and without reservation, for all to witness, and with my heart filled with love of God."

The crowd broke into applause. Alicia was smiling a smile of such magnitude it illuminated her entire face and Jedidiah's soul. He let the joy swell around him and inside himself for a long time before he raised his hands for silence.

"And now, in my last act as a travelling evangelist and my first act as the minister of The Church of the Highway in Smoke Tree, I call all those who would receive Jesus Christ as their Lord and Savior forward to the altar."

Amazing Grace swelled to full volume behind him. People were soon lining the rail five and six deep.

By ten o'clock that night, the equipment in the travelling revival show had been sold to Brother Cecil on terms that allowed repayment over the next ten years. The heavy cross Jedidiah had dragged into town after town during his career as an evangelist was not included. It would remain in Smoke Tree to someday be mounted atop The Church of the Highway.

With the transaction complete, Jedidiah stood in darkness in the empty tent. We all like to believe there's some magical something somewhere, he thought. Something that will make everything right again. Elisabet and Olivia delivered my magical something to me in the hospital.

Of course, there is still ordinary life to get on with, and ordinary life can grind away at a person like a stone. Not the quern I mentioned to Carlyle our first day in Smoke Tree, but the stone that works the grain in the circular pattern above that quern. Smoother, but abrasive nonetheless, turning and turning relentlessly as it renders grain into meal.

I have a lifetime of work ahead of me, he thought. A church to build. A little girl's blindness to address. Countless people to help. But I have been reunited with my beloved after all these years. And she has healed my broken heart and restored my faith. And no skeptical, know-it-all doctor can destroy my belief in the miracle that filled me with such joy. Knowing that at the end of my life I will be reunited with Elisabet and Olivia will sustain me and give me strength to do that which has to be done to serve the Lord in Smoke Tree until I draw my last breath.

CHAPTER 35

Observations

Horse was up before the dawn Wednesday morning. As was his habit, he walked the property in the morning twilight. The only ill-effect from his encounter with Mickey McCoury the previous night was a slight soreness on the right side of his face where he had allowed McCoury to land a pair of glancing jabs.

Shortly after sunrise, a quick breakfast and two cups of coffee under his belt, he was at the substation checking the overnight log. There was a notation about a huge crowd at the revival that had threatened to spill over into the street. He wondered about that one, but the deputy who had called in the report had gone off shift at midnight.

He told Merle, the overnight dispatcher, where he was headed that morning. He also left instructions for the desk sergeant to assure Mayor Milner, if he called, that last night's girlie show had been cancelled and the carnival was leaving town.

By six o'clock, he was at his mother's house to pick up Darnold. He apologized to her for not staying for coffee but gratefully accepted the paper sack filled with *besos*, *cuevos*, and *ovejas*. She also handed him a child's lunchbox containing chili verde burritos she had wrapped in wax paper.

"Mama, I should have known you kept my elementary school lunchbox."

"*Porque no?*" I've got your sister's around her somewhere, too. *Tal vez Elena y Alejandro pueden utilizarlas cuando comienzan la escuela en septiembre.*"

Darnold was walking into the kitchen, and Horse translated for him.

"Mama said the twins can use my school lunchbox and my sister's when they start school."

He turned back to his mother.

"*Gracias mama, eres el mejor.*"

283

Consuela was too embarrassed to translate what he had said.

"Did mama feed you yet?"

"Best breakfast I've ever had. My mouth is still burning. And your mama's coffee!"

"Her secret blend of cinnamon and dark chocolate."

"I almost forgot," said Consuela. She went to the kitchen counter and came back with a big thermos. "To have with your *pan dulce*."

Darnold smiled.

"I'm tellin' you, there's no food like this in San Francisco."

"Take a ride over to the Central Valley some weekend. Head south on Highway 99. You'll find lots of it in little towns over that way."

"I ran Darnold's new Levi's through the washer last night so they won't be so stiff he can't walk."

Horse stepped back and took in the Treasury agent's outfit of Levi's, t-shirt and sturdy boots.

"You look pretty darn local."

"If Esperanza and your mom keep feeding me like this, I'm going to have to get bigger Levi's."

Consuela looked pleased.

The two men headed out the door. When they got settled in the truck, Darnold asked Horse what was in the canvas bag."

"A powerful spotting-scope. Eighty millimeters. And a collapsible tripod to keep the image from bouncing all over the place."

They were on the long, straight stretch between Arrowhead Junction and Searchlight when the search and rescue truck was buffeted by shock waves and a tremendous explosion. Simultaneously, an F-100 flashed overhead, less than five hundred feet off the deck. It did a barrel roll and arced upward in a nearly vertical climb.

"Jet jockeys," laughed Horse. "Just can't resist scaring the civilians."

A half hour later, he parked the truck near the abandoned mining operation. He and Darnold walked to the building where the sergeant had parked his jeep the previous Sunday. Horse pointed out the tracks from the knobby tires. They turned and climbed the hills to the west and walked the ridgeline.

"This is the place to set up the Thompsons if we do this. You and I will be down there behind that big boulder."

Darnold nodded.

284

"Maybe we could put a few guys in that abandoned shed."

"That's not abandoned. Guy lives there."

"Someone lives in that?"

"Beats sleeping on the ground."

"Do you think he's in there right now?"

"I told him to stay away from here for about two weeks. He agreed and went off to work a claim he has a few miles from here."

"If we get backup, we're going to have to rehearse, but I remember you said something about not scaring the antelope away from the waterhole."

"Too many prying eyes here. A bunch of strangers crawling around this hillside would light up the cactus wireless. I know a place where we can almost duplicate this layout, and it's closer to Smoke Tree. We can practice there."

"If we decide to go ahead with this."

"If. A lot depends of what we see today."

They drove across Highway 95 to Nevada 164 and reversed the route the sergeant had taken From Cima to Searchlight. At Cima, Horse took Cima Road northwest, almost paralleling the road they had come in on. After two miles, he turned due west onto a dirt road that ran across the slope of Cima Dome just south of Wildcat Butte.

"This is the Edison High Line maintenance road."

After two jarring, swaying, sliding miles, Darnold asked, "Are you sure this is a road?"

"By desert standards, this is a freeway. Wait until we hook up with the Old Mojave Road."

Seven miles later, they turned off the High Line road and took Aiken Mine Road south. It was much worse than the High Line road, and they had to slow considerably.

"Sorry I complained about that other road."

After another mile and a half, they arrived at the Old Mojave Road. Horse stopped and put the truck in compound low and they proceeded at little more than a walk.

"Now this, Darnold, is a bad road. I want to show you Marl Spring so you can get a feel for how rugged the people who used to travel this road were."

They lurched and crawled onward until they reached upper and lower Marl Springs area.

"We've got time for a stretch and a stroll before we head for out lookout point."

Absent the sound of the truck's engine and the constant scratching of bushes against the sides of the vehicle, Darnold was taken by the depth of the silence on the hillside. They walked to a concrete water trough.

"After all those dry miles we just drove, I can't believe there's this much water here."

"If it hadn't been here, there wouldn't have been an Old Government Road, which is what most of the locals call it. Some of them call it the Old Mojave Road."

'What do the Mojaves call it?"

"What they've always called it. The trail."

He pointed off to the east.

"The next water on the road in that direction is Government Holes, thirty miles away. The next water to the west is at Soda Spring, another thirty miles. Sometimes there's water before that, at a place called Paymaster Mine, but it's not reliable."

As they stood thinking about the hardships endured by those who had traveled this road before the turn of the century, a loud, coarse cough came from behind them.

Darnold whirled around.

"What was that?"

"Burro. They do that sometimes."

Even after Horse pointed toward them, it took Darnold a while to locate the three burros standing motionless in the rocks.

"They're all over the place out here. They ran away from the old prospectors or just got left out here, I don't know which. But they multiplied. No shortage of them."

They walked back to the truck and Horse returned the way they had come until they hit Aiken Mine road again. They turned south and drove slowly down the broad drainage. After three bumpy miles, they reached the final southwestern outcropping of the Marl Mountains.

"We'll leave the truck here. I doubt anyone could see it from down below, but why take a chance?"

They got out of the truck with the spotting scope, water, food and coffee and set up in the rocks."

Horse oriented Darnold to the terrain.

"Those big mountains to the southwest are the Providence. That's where the 22nd Armored Brigade was supposed to be waiting in reserve. Obviously, it's been pulled out of reserve and committed to the battle. But I think our supply section, the S-4, is still bivouacked in the foothills. The big mountains to the southeast are the Granites. If things go the way I think they will, we'll be up near there later today."

He swung his arm to the right.

"That's Kelso down there. We'll probably get a closer look later. And that big brown area southwest of there is the Kelso Dunes and the Devil's playground. Beyond that to the west is Soda Lake."

"My God, Horse, this area's so big. Forbidding, almost. Wouldn't be a good place for someone with agoraphobia."

"That's for sure. Most people who drive across it don't stop to look. They just want to get across as fast as they can. I think the emptiness makes them skittish."

"There's a lot of beauty here."

"Could this be a desert rat in the making?"

"Maybe so."

"Anyway, the Army has agreed to keep their tanks and APCs and other vehicles out of the dunes and the Devil's Playground, thank goodness, and there for sure won't be any infantry moving through there on foot, so that makes it the west boundary of the exercise. We're just beyond the northern boundary. There won't be any vehicles or troops up here.

We're at about thirty-five hundred feet. You can make out the airfield down there to the southwest beside the railroad tracks. It's at about twenty-three hundred feet, so we've got a bird's eye view. I think those objects by the tracks are grading equipment."

Horse attached the scope to the tripod and trained it on the airfield."

"Yep. Graders and some other kind of machine. Looks like one of those things that sprays oil or tar. I don't see any engineers down there. They must have moved on to do something somewhere else."

He moved so Darnold could take a look.

"How far is it to the field?"

"Six miles or thereabouts."

"Looks closer."

"Everything does on the desert. It's the sameness, I suppose. Plays tricks on the eyes, or the brain: I've never figured out which."

Horse looked at his watch.

"Just coming up on nine o'clock. We're very early. Plenty of time for mama's coffee and *pan dulce*."

When the coffee and rolls were gone, the conversation stopped and the silence of the desert seeped in around them. Ants showed up to scavenge the crumbs that had fallen from the *pan dulce*. One group was red, and one was black. Soon, there was open warfare between the groups.

Bad as humans, thought Horse.

Occasionally, they heard quail call as they fed somewhere in the drainage. Intermittently, the silence was broken by the boom of

287

far-off artillery and tank rounds. They could not see the source of the sounds. Horse could differentiate between the hundred- and fifty-five-millimeter howitzers and the main guns of the tanks. Both took his mind back to times he did not like to relive lest the memories reappear in his dreams tonight.

The guns all sounded the same to Darnold. They also seemed alien; as if they had no business in this place. As if they should be forbidden by some fiat from the spirit of the Mojave. Fighters sometimes streaked overhead, and they too seemed to Darnold like intruders. He smiled. He was beginning to feel proprietary about the place.

An eastbound freight labored up the grade from Kelso to Cima below them. Not long after, a westbound thundered down. Then another, this one much longer, struggled toward the summit. It moved so slowly, Darnold almost expected it to stop and give up. The little engine that couldn't.

Time seemed to stand still. He looked at the rocks. He looked at the sky. He listened to the soft wind. As the sun neared its zenith, he asked a question.

"I thought there were buzzards on the desert."

"There are."

"I haven't seen any yet."

"Grounded by the Air Force. Buzzards might be ugly, but they're smart. They're not going to ride the thermals with all those jets swooping around. That probably makes the jet jockeys very happy. Can you imagine what would happen if one of those F-100s sucked in a five-pound turkey vulture?"

At noon, they ate their chili verde burritos. They were wonderful, but Darnold was glad they had lots of water. A few huge flies showed up. The sound of their buzzing seemed very loud in the stillness. The ants returned.

Horse and Darnold took turns glassing the area with the scope, and it was Darnold who picked up the first dust cloud.

"Something on the move."

He relinquished the scope to Horse.

Something was coming down Cedar Canyon Road.

"Not our guys. Must be other units retrieving supplies that will come off the airplane."

He kept the dust cloud centered in the scope until it hit the short, paved section of Cedar Canyon just before the railroad tracks. Following a single jeep was a string of five-ton and deuce-and-a-half trucks.

"You sure it's not ours?"

"Too many vehicles."

Before the convoy reached the intersection with Kelso/Cima Road, it bumped down off the side of the road and headed west along the railroad tracks. Horse knew where it was going, so he stopped watching it."

"Keep an eye out a little more to the south. That's where our guys will come from."

Fifteen minutes later, another dust cloud appeared. Horse trained the scope on it.

"Two trucks. Two jeeps. One jeep for the major, one for the sergeant. Two trucks to carry off the new guns and bring back the old ones. They're on Macedonia Canyon Road. That's why we can't see the bivouac. It's in that little valley between the hills. I don't think it will be long now before the show gets underway."

In another twenty minutes, the smaller group reached the rail line and turned south toward the airstrip.

"That's us, for sure."

He leaned away from the scope.

"I'm impressed, Horse. Starting with a rumor from a college kid, you figured out what was going on.

"I hope so. But now that you're starting to think this is possible, I'm getting nervous. I don't want to drag you too far out on this limb with me. I mean, what if you ask for all this backup and the whole thing goes bust? How will that make you look at Treasury?"

"You're asking the wrong question, Horse."

"What's the right one?"

"What if I get all this backup, the deal goes down, and Treasury catches Mazzetti with his hand in the cookie jar? We'll be one up on those publicity mongers over at the F.B.I. My boss will be delighted, and so will my boss's boss."

Horse smiled.

"And the Legend of Darnold will grow even bigger."

It was just after two o'clock when they heard the heavy drone of a cargo plane inbound from the northeast. The C-123 rumbled into sight, light from the west-tilting sun reflecting off its massive fuselage. As it turned and approached the airstrip from the east, it slowed so much it looked like it would stall. It did not. In fact, when Horse tried to track it with the spotting scope, he found it impossible to keep the plane inside the narrow field of view. It was moving faster than it looked.

From their position, they could not see the opening of the cargo bay, but they saw parachutes begin to blossom from the rear of the plane at the instant the wheels touched the ground. The giant plane continued to eject chuted pallets as it rolled down the runway. The pallets skidded and created dust clouds as they broke through the thin coating of the temporary strip. Most remained upright, but two collided and spewed their contents.

"Think that was our guns?"

"I don't think so. I think they'll be last thing out the door."

The plane rolled on, trailing roiled dust. Three final chutes deployed. The pallets attached were smaller than the others. The engines roared as the pilot applied full power, and the gigantic airframe began to rise into the air.

"I think that's the rifles," said Horse. "They saved them for last so they would be clear of everything else. Didn't want anything to happen to the Pentagon's latest toys."

The plane left the ground and began to ascend with agonizing slowness. Trucks moved onto the vacated airfield. The group from the 22nd Armored Brigade, led by the two jeeps, headed for the pallets with the rifles. The pallets were quickly unstrapped, and individual containers filled with rifles were loaded onto the trucks. Horse noticed the pallets and strapping were simply cast aside and abandoned.

When the tailgates went up, the trucks trundled across the airstrip directly toward Horse and Darnold. Horse could make out a driver and passenger in the lead truck. The scope's magnification was not strong enough that he could make out their features. The jeeps followed, and as they turned east, Horse could see that each of them also had a driver and a passenger.

The other trucks were still on the airstrip when the small convoy went by. The four vehicles from the 22nd turned east along the railroad right-of-way. They did not turn south onto Macedonia Canyon Road, but continued northeast instead. Horse watched their progress until they climbed up onto Cedar Canyon Road and turned in the direction of Black Canyon Road.

"There go the new guns. The old ones will come back in the same trucks."

Horse waited impatiently for the other soldiers on the airstrip to finish loading supplies. Finally, the last of the vehicles moved onto the railroad right of way and turned east.

Horse and Darnold hurried to their truck, and Horse drove back toward Aiken Mine Road. When he reached it, he turned directly south.

"Hang on to something," he yelled as they picked up speed. "We've gotta move. We're going the long way around."

They slammed and bounced and bounded down the hill. A number of times, Darnold thought Horse was going to lose control and turn the truck over, but he didn't. When they reached Kelso/Cima Road, Horse turned west and jammed the accelerator to the floor. They raced toward the distant depot. As they approached, Darnold saw a Spanish mission-style building fronted by palm trees in the middle of the surrounding desert. It looked like something from a North African desert oasis.

"That's quite a building," he yelled over roar created by the pickup's screaming engine and the wind whistling through the open windows."

"A long time ago, steam engines stopped here to take on water on the way to Salt Lake City. If it was a passenger train, the people got off and had lunch in the dining room."

"Those little houses we drove past, people live in them anymore?"

"Union Pacific employees, but fewer every year."

Horse braked hard to slow for the left turn that took them across the railroad tracks. Darnold was surprised to see gray-green trees lining both sides of the rail line far off into the west.

"What are those?"

"Salt cedars. Brought from North Africa to make wind breaks for the railroad. Keep the sand from covering the tracks."

Kelbaker Road headed straight toward the heart of the Granite Mountains. Horse thought about taking the old Vulcan Mine Road, but since it had not been graded in years, he was afraid there might be washouts. Instead, he continued on another five miles to the next dirt road that cut off to the east. He yelled at Donald again over the noise.

"This one's not as bumpy, but it has lots of dips and rollers."

Six miles later, they were south of Fountain Peak and near Foshay Spring when they reached the high point in the pass cutting through the southern Providence. Horse pulled over and stopped. Both men climbed out into the sudden silence.

Horse was thinking about the crevice above them where Burke Henry had died as he and Darnold looked out over the vast expanse of the Clipper Valley spread out. It was obvious there was some sort of large maneuver taking place. A line of tanks and APCs was streaming north while an equally large unit was spilling out of the Fenner Hills into the western edge of the valley. The tanks with the northbound unit swung off the road and turned their turrets to the southeast. The APCs continued speeding north.

As Horse and Darnold watched the movements of the two units, separate dust devils originated and twisted and danced their way across that valley floor as if in counterpoint to the dust clouds floating high into the sky above the armored forces.

"Well," said Horse, pulling his eye away from the spotting scope, "there goes the 22nd Brigade toward the re-supply point. That unit tearing in from the east will be one of the Nezona units that crossed the river Monday morning."

"Those trucks we saw leaving with the rifles must be up that road somewhere."

"The trucks are probably waiting at a flat area just east of Hole in the Wall. The battalions would like to stage the rifle exchange there, but it looks to me like the unit coming in from the east is going to spoil the party. The fog of mock combat. I don't know how the 22nd can stop to do the exchange without being overrun."

As they watched the scene play out below, they heard airplanes approaching from the west. Big turboprops. Lots of them. Fighters appeared, streaking in from the east, but a larger group of fighters swooped down from the north to intercept them before they could reach the inbound C-130s. Aerial combat was underway when C-130s passed over their position and began spewing parachutes. Most of the chutes had a paratrooper attached, but there were also twin and triple chutes attached to large supply pallets.

Horse detached the scope from the tripod and focused on the larger chutes.

"Jeeps. Some with one hundred-and-six-millimeter recoilless rifles. Some with .50 caliber machine guns. Mules with ENTACs. Any of them can penetrate an armored personnel carrier. The 106s and ENTACs can take out a tank."

He swung his scope toward the northbound unit. The tanks from the 22nd were moving toward the oncoming Nezona forces as the airborne troops and equipment began to hit the ground.

"The guys dropping out of the sky are 101st Airborne. That's the blocking force to allow the 22nd time to exchange the rifles. Looks like they're going to come down in Black Canyon Wash. Not much cholla over that way. The air recon planes and the intelligence photo analysts did their jobs."

Horse lowered the scope and turned to Darnold.

"Well, it's fish or cut bait time. Call for back-up or back out?"

"I'm a believer."

"Okay. We'd better get back to Smoke Tree and recruit an infiltrator."

An hour later, they were driving down through Willow Springs Wash between the Bristol and Marble Mountains on Kelbaker Road heading for Highway 66. Darnold had been silent since getting on the paved road, but now he felt compelled to speak up.

"I feel like I have to say something."

"Go ahead."

"I know you've got a lot of latitude out here, but are you sure you want to bring a civilian into this?"

"There won't be any blowback."

"How can you be so sure?"

Horse pulled onto the shoulder of the empty road.

"I want to show you something."

He and Darnold got out of the truck."

"Look off to the east there."

"Okay."

"Tell me what you see?"

"Mostly green bushes of some kind."

"That's creosote."

"Okay, creosote. Lots and lots of it."

"This guy could be out there, and you wouldn't know it."

"I can see that. It's a huge area."

"See the ones about twenty yards in front of us?"

"Yes."

"He could be right there among them and you still wouldn't see him."

"I'm not sure I believe that."

"Let me tell you two stories. The first is from history. You know who Geronimo was, right?"

"Apache chief."

"Not a chief, exactly. Medicine man. In 1881, he and a band of about fifty Chiricahua Apaches left the San Carlos Apache reservation and went on the run. General George Cook, a decorated veteran of the civil war, was sent by President Grant to bring him back. For five years, Crook and his soldiers chased Geronimo and his band, which, by the way, included women and children. At one time, a quarter of all the soldiers in the U.S. Army were involved in the hunt. They never caught him.

And Geronimo didn't just run. Occasionally, at times and places of his choosing, he would turn and fight. And win. I've always remembered what one of Crook's lieutenants said about one of those

293

encounters. 'We were standing on the edge of a barren stretch of land. There was nothing to be seen in any direction. Suddenly, Geronimo and his warriors were on us. It was like they rose up out of the earth.'

The second story is from my own experience. I once dropped the man off a few miles from where he lives in the Chemehuevi Mountains. The place he got out of my car is a lot like the place in front of us. He said goodbye and headed for home. I was watching him. He disappeared."

"You mean you lost sight of him."

"No, I mean he disappeared. One minute he was walking away from me; the next he was gone. That's as well as I can explain it. And that's why I'm not worried. The Army won't see him coming, won't know when he's there, and won't know he's been there when he's gone."

"I'd like to meet him."

"Best you don't."

"Why not?"

"If you meet him, you'll have to put him in your report. I don't want that to happen. I want him to be 'unidentified source'. It's best for him that way."

"What makes you think he'll do it?"

"He has a score to settle with Eddie Mazzetti."

"He knows Mazzetti?"

"Doesn't even know his name. But he once met some friends of his. Didn't care for them."

Later that day, while Darnold was on the phone in Horse's office explaining his request for more agents, Horse drove to Doctor Hayden's place. He found Joe Medrano and ask him to take a day off from the job he was doing for the doctor to do some sheriff's department work. He explained, in detail, everything that had happened so far and then told Joe what he wanted him to do.

Joe listened intently without saying anything. But then, Joe rarely said anything. When Horse had finished the entire recitation, Joe thought for a while.

"Tonight?"

"Yes. By now, our sergeant is back at the bivouac with the old rifles. If he wants to steal some of them, he's got to move a bunch of the A1s to a place where they'll be safe until he moves them again next Sunday."

"Take me out there?"

294

"Of course. Time it to arrive after sundown. The quickest way, and the way that would leave you the easiest walk, would be to drive through Lanfair to Cedar Canyon and then take Wild Horse Mesa Road through the Mid-Hills. But I'm afraid if we go that way we might run into some Army units."

"Other way, up Kelso Road?"

"That would be best. The bivouac is in that little valley between Macedonia Spring and Columbia Mountain."

Joe stared off to the northwest, lost in thought. Horse waited patiently He knew Joe had a better map of the Providence in his mind than any topo ever printed. A map built step by step, visit blending into visit, of a range sacred to the Chemehuevi.

"Get me up Globe Mine Road?"

"Yes."

"Good. Ridge southwest to the plateau north of Wild Horse. Down to camp from there."

"That's a lot of climbing and walking in the dark."

Joe shrugged.

"Get close before the moon sets. Inside after it goes down."

"You'll do this?"

Joe nodded.

"I have to go by the office and do a couple things. Be back for you later. I'll bring a canteen."

"No need. Water at Mexican Spring."

"What about food? I've got C-rations."

"Chia seeds, pocket."

"I'll get you paid for this. Bill it as tracking. Just tracking rifles instead of people."

Joe shook his head.

"No payment."

"Why not?"

"For the missy."

"The missy being Kiko Yoshida?"

"And Aeden Snow."

"What's Aeden got to do with it?"

Joe seemed to search for the right words.

"Bad people drove the missy away. The missy took his heart."

"There was something between them?"

"Not between them. Him, for her."

"He's young, Joe. He'll meet someone else."

Joe shook his head.

"Saw him look at her. Raven, that one. No other. Ever."

295

When Horse returned to the station and stepped into his office, a disappointed Darnold was just hanging up the phone.

"Best I could do was a partial commitment."

"Meaning?"

"My supervisor was on my side all the way, but he hit resistance upstairs. We're getting one agent from my office and two from Denver. That's all. The Denver lads are bringing Thompsons, so that's a plus, and Beauford Butler, from my office, is bringing an M-3 with infrared scope, another plus."

"How'd you get hold of one of those?"

"They're now surplus to the Army. We put in our paperwork. Only took us three years to get one."

"I'm familiar with that weapon."

"But you're not going to be there."

"I wasn't, before your higher-ups wouldn't authorize the numbers we need. I don't like the idea of four of you against at least seven heavy-lifters from the mob, plus Eddie Mazzetti."

"What about the jurisdictional problem."

"Sometimes, I just forget exactly which side of the state line I'm on. Can be hard to tell out that way."

"You sure you can get away with that?"

"If we're successful, I can get away with anything."

"That's been my experience. Didn't know it was the same in local law enforcement."

"It's the same everywhere. When are these men coming?"

"Early tomorrow morning. The two from Denver will get there first and wait for Beauford. When he lands, they'll get a pool car and head down. Should be here just after noon."

"Good. I'd better put in a call to the Mohave County Sheriff's Department in Kingman and let them know we'll be in their county tomorrow."

Darnold started to get up from behind the desk, but Horse waved him back down as he dialed.

"Mohave County Sheriff's Department."

"Captain Caballo in Smoke Tree for Captain Taylor."

There was a click as the call was transferred.

"Bill Taylor."

"Afternoon, Bill, Horse here."

"Hey, how are you making out with the Army down there."

"The Nezona boys came across the river early Monday morning and attacked us. Kicked our butts. The Calonia crew has been conducting retrograde operations. Heavy fighting yesterday in the Lanfair Valley."

296

"I have no idea where that is."

"Out in the big empty way west of town."

"There's nothing but big empty west of Smoke Tree."

"And east of Kingman."

"True enough."

"Reason I'm calling, I've got Agent Darnold from the U.S. Treasury Department with me. We're getting ready for a little war of our own over in Searchlight. We'd like to set up a practice run on the edge of Oatman."

"California, Arizona, Nevada, ghost towns: sounds interesting, Horse."

"It's strange and getting stranger. Anyway, I wanted to clear our rehearsal with you in case you get phone calls about sinister government agents occupying abandoned buildings."

"Glad to accommodate you."

"Good. Here's Agent Darnold."

Darnold introduced himself and gave a bare-bones outline of the number of agents involved and a phone number where the captain could contact Darnold's supervisor to confirm the operation.

"Won't be necessary, agent Darnold. If Horse vouches for you, you're good with me. By the way, you Treasury people take good care of him. Horse and me, we've done some good work together, time to time. I don't want to have to break in somebody new."

"We'll do it, Captain."

"And one more thing."

"Yes?"

"Thanks for checking in. My experience with federal guys is they blow into town, do whatever they want, and leave without so much as an introduction. It's nice to have some warning."

"This was Horse's idea."

"I'm sure it was, but you went along with it."

With the liaison work with Mohave County worked out, Horse called Esperanza to let her know he would be home very late. He dropped Agent Darnold at his mother's house and doubled back to the heights to pick up Joe.

Little was said during the long drive to Globe Canyon. People who live on the Eastern Mojave are used to traveling long distances, and neither man thought the drive was the least bit unusual. When Horse stopped just over the mountain from the 22nd Brigade S-4 bivouac, the remains of the sunset were bleeding out of the western sky, and the waxing, gibbous moon was almost directly overhead. It occurred to Joe that when he crossed the mountain and circled the encampment, he would pass very close to the mine shaft where he and Aeden Snow had disposed of the bodies of the two hit men from Las Vegas three years before. Helping bring down the very man who had sent those two would give him deep satisfaction.

Things come around, he thought. For good or for ill, things come around.

On the edges of the wash, the yellow blossoms of the bladderpod, one of the few flowers still blooming this late in spring, were closing. Not so the nearby datura, which would bloom, white and creamy, throughout the night.

Moonapple, thought Joe. Powerful flower of dreams. Flower of death to those who don't know how to use it.

The two men stepped out of the truck to wait for total darkness, each of them enjoying the change as the desert transitioned from creatures of the daytime to creatures of the night: Bats and nighthawks taking to the air as hawks and buzzards relinquished the sky; coveys of quail and chukkar and flocks of smaller birds, thirst sated from one last visit to a spring, going silent; mule deer bedding down beneath junipers and pinyons after feeding in the twilight; pygmy rabbits seeking burrows; an elusive and secretive bobcat moving on padded feet; competing coyote packs beginning their forays; burrowing owls emerging to begin their night-long hunt; lizards slipping into nighttime torpor, tarantulas on the move now that tarantula hawks were no longer airborne; scorpions, vinagaroons and solpugids searching for a meal of smaller bugs; balloon spiders settling languidly to rest on bushes and shrubs as the last of the evening sundowner exhaled a final breeze across the desert landscape.

Horse and Joe stood quietly until the daily desert shift change was finished.

"Tomorrow after dark?"

"It will be very late. I'm going to get the treasury guys ready for an ambush. Couple of dry runs over by Oatman. Two of them after dark."

"Midnight, then. By the railroad."

Joe de-materialized in the moonlight. That was the only way to describe it. He was simply gone, trailing no sound to mark his movement, leaving no sign by which he could be followed.

It was after ten when Horse drove the truck up the long driveway to his home. He and Esperanza sat side by side on the couch for a long time, her head resting against his shoulder, the weariness of his long day eased by her presence. They were glad to be together in the peaceful house, the cooler whispering on low; twins asleep in their beds.

Esperanza was the first to break the silence.

"Consuela came by with Agent Darnold. She brought dinner for all of us. Alejandro and Elena could hardly finish eating for wanting to drag Darnold out to the corral to ride Mariposa."

"I didn't know Darnold was a rider."

"He isn't. Knows nothing about horses. Couldn't even put the saddle on. I did it."

"City boy through and through. How did he do once he got on?"

"Oh Carlos, he was so stiff. It was like he expected our gentle mare to turn into a bucking bronco at any moment. He only did it because the twins wanted him to. He rode her around the corral a few times with Elena and Alejandro running along outside and shouting instructions, none of which he followed because he had a death grip on the saddle horn. He was very happy to climb down."

"The twins have really taken to him, haven't they?"

"They have. They were so excited, I could hardly get them to take their baths and go off to bed. If Consuela hadn't taken Darnold home, I think they'd still be up. Now, tell me about your day."

Horse ran through everything that had happened since his arrival at the substation early in that morning. Esperanza listened intently, taking in every detail. Everything her *marido* did was of great interest to her. Always had been. Her days were of equal interest to him.

When he finished, she sighed.

"*Te extraño cuando han desaparecido en estos largos días.*"

"*Y yo le.*"

"And I'm worried about Joe. There are sentries out there. Soldiers. Soldiers have guns."

"I doubt they have live ammunition. But, even if they do, *él pasarán por ese grupo como un fantasma.*"

"I hope you're right. I don't think I could bear it if something happened to him. We've already lost Burke and dear Mr. Stanton."

"Speaking of that, when this whole operation is over, we're going to have to hitch up the horse trailer and bring Pepper home."

"Which means we'll have to tell the twins about Burke. *Ni soy. Van a ser tan triste.*"

299

CHAPTER 36

In the Shadows

There were no sentries, but Joe Medrano was cautious and patient, nonetheless. It was two thirty in the morning, the moon well behind the western horizon, before he was inside the bivouac area. He had been waiting for moonset so he could follow his nose to the water. Inside the camp, he found the lister bag suspended from a framework. He drank quietly before moving on.

He had less than three hours before the twilight preceding the sunrise came into the sky. He could hear the murmur of a diesel generator, its only load a few metal-mesh encased red bulbs inside the tents. He circulated through the area counting the sleeping soldiers. Most of them were outside on cots.

Eleven personnel to be accounted for.

As he moved among them, he recalled his time in the islands of the Pacific during World War II. Gliding past armed sentries. Penetrating perimeters and entering areas where soldiers slept. Leaving some of them dead, killed soundlessly as they lay sleeping. Leaving them with the symbol for 'four' painted on their faces, because four is an unlucky number to the Japanese. When pronounced *shi*, it means death.

Joe had no regrets about those deaths. Not then, not now. His nighttime forays had caused the enemy to sleep poorly. Caused more men to be put on sentry duty. Those things combined to erode readiness and fighting spirit. Perhaps saved the lives of an American or two. Although the many men he had killed sometimes visited his dreams, he had no fear of them when they appeared.

He found a jeep with a small trailer attached. Horse had predicted the sergeant would use it to move the stolen guns. It was covered by a tarp. He lifted it. Empty. He moved to the largest tent, and there found many rifles packed in completely unsecured, olive drab boxes. He opened and re-closed all of them. He soon discerned a pattern established by the separate stacks of boxes. So many regular M-14s, so many of the special ones with the tripods in each group. Already been sorted for delivery.

Once, he heard someone outside. The person drank noisily from the lister bag. Joe melted into the part of the huge tent barely reached by the dim, red light. Became a shadow among shadows. The soldier came inside and moved around the tent. Perhaps looking for something. Perhaps an insomniac prowling the area as he waited for first light.

Joe was not concerned about being discovered by this clumsy person, but he had decided that if he were, he would not harm him. Joe could hear the man breathing. Heard his audible sigh of relief when he passed gas. Heard him leave the tent, apparently taking nothing with him.

Joe went back to work. He found paperwork at a small desk and carried it to a spot directly beneath the light. The name of a Major, 'Ricks,' was on the bottom of each sheet. He had signed off on each allocation. So many M14s and M14A1s to an Arizona National Guard unit in Prescott, Arizona. A smaller number to an Army National Guard unit in Lordsburg, New Mexico. And so on. Joe put the papers back on the desk.

When daylight came, Joe would find the guns the sergeant had hidden. Either that, or he would discover Horse had guessed wrong and there were none. Joe hoped Horse was right. He wanted bad things to happen to the man who had sent the men to kill the missy. The man who had sentenced the missy to a life on the run. A life of day-by-day survival. A life of fear. A life without love, hope, or peace.

The man who had sentenced Aeden Snow to life without a mate.

CHAPTER 37

Making Plans

Thursday morning, Horse was in his office early, catching up on routine matters: reports, timesheets, the allocation of resources to patrol his huge area of responsibility, overtime for the extra man-hours required to deal with Desert Strike. As he worked, he could not help thinking about Chemehuevi Joe in Macedonia Canyon. Horse had great confidence in Joe's capabilities, but that didn't mean he was not concerned. There were always things that could go wrong; contingencies that could arise. If Joe's search for stolen guns continued during daylight hours, the chance he might be discovered would greatly increase.

A little after seven, he looked up from his desk to see Darnold in his doorway.

"Didn't expect you here this early."

"Came in to do some planning before the cavalry arrives."

"You mean the cavalry that's short a few horses?"

"That one. Speaking of horses, I rode one yesterday for the first time in my life."

"Heard about that. What do you think?"

"I think they're huge, powerful animals, and it's a long way to the ground when you're on one. I mostly just hung on while the horse walked around the corral."

"Esperanza said the twins were delighted."

"And delightful. What great kids. And your petite wife? She picked up a saddle and tossed in on the horse like it weighed nothing. I carried it to the tack room later. It weighed a ton."

"That's my Esperanza. Dynamite in a small package. Did mom feed you?"

"Sure did."

"Okay, give me a few more minutes here and we'll get started."

"No rush. Now that I've been on the ground out there, I want to study those diagrams and the topo."

Horse got up from behind his desk.

"Let's take the boards and maps down to the conference room. There's a cork board in there for maps and a chalk board where you can make some notes for briefing the other agents."

Horse picked up the topographic map and the diagrams and headed down the hall. Darnold followed with the easels. In the conference room, Horse pinned the laminated topo to the cork board. Darnold set up the easels and positioned the diagrams

The day dispatcher rapped on the open door.

"Yes, Fred."

"Mayor on the phone for you. I told him you weren't in your office, but I'd see if you were in the building. Are you?"

"I'll take the call."

"Line one."

When Horse left the room, Darnold was at the table. He was glancing back and forth between the poster boards and the large-scale topographic.

"Mr. Mayor."

"Good morning, Horse. I wanted to thank you for your help on that carnival situation."

"Glad to be of service."

"I heard a rumor you picked on a guy who outweighed you by a hundred pounds."

"We had a brief discussion. He fell down. Got up and left."

"I know you were out of the office most of the day yesterday, so I wondered if you'd heard the news about the revival preacher."

"I saw a notation on the overnight log yesterday. Something about a big crowd. The deputy who'd made the report was still out on patrol when I left the office, so I didn't get the details."

"It seems we've gained a man of the cloth. The man, Jedidiah Shanks is his name, claims he's going to build a church in Smoke Tree. He visited the planning department to check on the requirements. Later in the day, he was trying to contact the owner of the vacant lot where he held the revival. Intends to buy the land for his church. Also intends to buy a house in town. Cash deal, according to the realtor he talked to."

"Can always use another church."

"That we can, but the best part is yet to come. Seems the church will be dedicated to helping travelers in difficulty."

"We've always got plenty of those. He's going to be a very busy man. I've got some ideas about that, myself. Once we get the Army out of town, I'll hunt him up and see if I can help."

"How's the war going?"

"It's now concentrated in two areas. Lanfair, Fenner and Clipper Valleys on the north and Danby and Bristol Dry Lakes to Sheephole pass on the south."

"But mostly away from Smoke Tree?"

"Thank goodness. By the way, how did your press conference go on Monday?"

"Great fun. I made the six o'clock news in Phoenix."

"I hope this doesn't mean you'll be running for Governor of California."

"Hardly. Honorary governor of Calonia was excitement enough for me."

"Mr. Mayor, I don't mean to be rude, but I'm in the middle of something here. Is there anything else?"

"Just one more item. I hear we've got a Treasury agent in town."

Horse smiled.

"Mayor Milner, does anything happen in this town you don't get wind of?"

"Very little. Can you tell me what's going on?"

"That's what I'm in the middle of. When it's all over, I'll fill you in. But since you'll probably hear about it just after they hit the city limits, three more agents from Treasury are arriving today. The good thing is, none of this has anything to do with Smoke Tree."

"That's a relief. Okay, I'll let you get on with it."

Horse rummaged through the collection of seven-point-five-minute maps in his map closet until the found the one that included the abandoned mine. When he carried it down to the conference room, Darnold had circled the town of Searchlight and marked highway 95 on the topo.

Horse stepped up to the cork board and tacked up the seven-point-five-minute map below the larger one. On the big map, he put an 'x's where Aeden Snow had witnessed the demonstration of the modified rifle, the place where he and Darnold had witnessed the touch-and-go drop and the location of the bivouac for the S-4 section of the 22nd Armored Brigade. He used red grease pencil to show the route he assumed the sergeant would take to deliver the rifles to Mazzetti and noted an estimate of the travel time to Searchlight.

"That'll give your guys an idea of how far-flung these locations are."

"Good idea. I think it will be helpful if you write a time-line on the board from the time the college kid saw the weapon fired to your estimate of when the exchange of guns for cash will take place."

"Sure."

"And one more thing. I don't know how many of these guys understand a topographical map, so if you could explain the contour lines and what they mean, it'll help them visualize a place they're not going to see until very early Sunday morning."

"I have a request. When you're doing your part of the briefing, don't mention our infiltrator."

"I won't. And when I write up my official report, I'll refer to him the way you suggested. 'Unidentified source.'"

"Much appreciated."

Horse unrolled the smaller map he had brought into the room.

"I'll use the seven-point-five-minute to explain the contour lines. They have forty-foot intervals on this smaller map. That will give them a clearer picture of the exchange and conflict zone."

Darnold looked at the clock.

"The Denver guys should be on the ground by now, and Beauford will be there soon. Before we design an operational plan, we should decide how to handle briefing the other agents."

"Good idea. I'll give the background, through the rifle drop. You brief them on the operational side."

"You'd be better at that than me."

"I'm not sure that's true, but even if it was, your fellow agents will accept it with fewer objections from one of their own than from a guy they're going to see as a small-time deputy from some hick town in the desert."

Darnold thought for a moment.

"You're right, but I'll bet you've got the whole plan already mapped out."

"Now that we know our resources, I do."

"Take me through it."

"Okay."

Horse picked up a red grease pencil and made a number of circles on the map as he spoke.

"Here's the building. Here are the two smaller buildings. Here's the boulder we'll be behind, and here's the ridgeline and that old shack. This is the asphalt road and this line is for the dirt road that runs to the buildings."

Horse moved to the large topo.

"Way over here is Highway 95, and over here is Nevada 164."

He moved back to the smaller map and added a number of 'x's.

The 'x's closest to the building where we saw the jeep tracks are you and I. We'll be in the declivity behind the boulder. I'll have the M-3 carbine with the infrared scope and battery pack, and you'll have four of the high-powered, portable search and rescue spotlights."

"That's awfully close to the exchange for the guy out of his jurisdiction."

Horse shrugged.

"Can't be helped. The three 'x's on the ridge are your fellow agents. The ones on the flanks will have the Thompsons. The one in the middle will be behind the ridge between them. We will not move to these positions until after dark."

He put two large squares with four circles inside each of them at a point beyond where the asphalt road and the dirt road to the buildings intersected.

"Here's where I think the bad guys will park. The first car will have four heavies. My guess is that Mazzetti will be in the second car with three more."

"When do you think they'll show up?"

"Sundown is around eight. They'll be there at least an hour before that to take a good look around before the sergeant arrives. That's why we won't move into our positions before dark."

"Where will we wait before we move there?"

Horse drew another line on the map.

"Back to the south here, there's a second, higher ridge. It's almost half a mile from the one we'll move to after dark. I'm sure Mazzetti's guys won't scuff their pointy-toed loafers walking that far during their inspection, so we'll be there before the sun comes up on Sunday morning. We'll have a good line of sight from there to where they'll park when they show up. The sun will be far to the west by then, so there won't be any reflection off the binoculars while we watch.

The sergeant won't leave the bivouac with the guns until nightfall. Even though the surveillance planes are supposed to stop flying Saturday at last light, he won't take a chance there might be a stray in the air during the day on Sunday to wonder why a jeep is way out there by itself."

"What will the moonlight be like Sunday night?"

"Directly overhead at ten o'clock. Waxing, ninety percent visible. A very bright desert night."

"And we're going to walk half a mile across the desert by moonlight?"

"Won't be that hard. We'll move very slowly. I'll be in the lead. I'm assuming your men will be wearing ball caps."

"That's right. With the ATU symbol on them."

"I'll have a cap too. Everybody will have reflective tape, two stripes, on the back of their cap. The moonlight will provide more than enough light to reflect off the stripes. Single file. Follow the stripes in front of you. When we get to the top of the ridgeline, head quietly for individual locations. We'll practice this up in Oatman tonight after dark."

"Good, so far. What happens when the sergeant shows up?"

"This is guesswork, but I think it's sound. He's been in the Army a long time if he's a master sergeant. He will not want to make this exchange out in the open. I think he'll drive his jeep and trailer right past the parked cars and into the building where we found his tire tracks. I'll turn the infrared on when he shuts down the engine."

"What do you think the mafia guys will do when he drives by?"

"They'll already be as far up the two-track as their luxury sedans can go. When he drives around them, they'll turn on their headlights, get out and start walking."

"What makes you think that?"

"These aren't people used to being in the dark out in the country. They're used to city dark: always full of ambient light, especially in Las Vegas. They'll be nervous. Thinking about snakes and stuff."

"Oh, I wish you hadn't said that."

Horse shrugged.

"What they don't know is their lights are going to shine up on an angle. They won't light up the exchange area. And when they get to the top of the incline, they'll have to stop and get their night vision before starting down the other side. Believe me, these guys will not want to put their feet anywhere they can't see.

When they reach the trailer, the sergeant will have the tarp off the trailer so they can see the goods. He'll have a flashlight to show them the rifles. I think the money will change hands in the dark, but I'll see the exchange through the infrared. When it happens, I'll cue you to put one of the spotlights on top of the rock. You turn it on, duck right back down, and identify yourself as a federal agent. Tell them to throw away their weapon, put their hands on top of their heads, or whatever treasury agents yell at bad guys in a bust. But that's when things will get interesting."

"What's your best guess about what will happen?"

"If at least one of them has a shotgun with double aught, he'll blow the spotlight off the rock. That hostile act against a duly identified government agent will be all the justification the guys with the Thompsons need to open fire. I assume they'll have the fifty round drums?"

"Right, and three extra clips with twenty rounds each."

"They should burn the whole drum and two clips each. Save the last clip for part two of the show. Concentrate on the engine blocks. Destroy the cars so the help has no hope of driving away. I think when the Thompsons open up and the muscle hears the slugs destroying the getaway cars, they'll undergo an attitude adjustment.

When the Thompsons stop, turn on another spotlight. I don't think these guys will shoot again. I don't know about Mazzetti, but there's one thing none of these foot soldiers ever wants to do: kill a federal agent. They'll reflect on that while they're trying to burrow into the desert."

"What's the contingency if they do shoot again?"

"I turn on the infrared again and shoot one or two of them. That should put an end to any foolishness. They won't have a chance in the dark. I don't think it'll come to that, but if it does, I'll keep shooting until they surrender.

"What do you think our sergeant will be doing while all this is going on?"

"He's the wild card. The least predictable. If he's a combat veteran, he's not going to panic. He'll probably be down behind the jeep trying to figure out how to escape. He can't back up, so maybe he'll leave on foot."

"Do you think he'll have a weapon?"

"I doubt it. He knows going in he's going to be outgunned. Why bother to bring one?"

"You're serious about shooting these people, aren't you?"

"Dead serious."

"Okay, back to the plan where they don't shoot out the second light. What happens next?"

"You're the arresting officer. That's your call."

Darnold thought for a moment.

"I'll turn on another spotlight. Call the agents down off the ridge. Last clips loaded in the Thompsons. We'll take the spotlights and move toward them while you watch them through the infrared."

"And shoot anyone who makes a hostile move."

"For sure."

"We'll move in teams of two on separate arcs. Get behind them. Tell them to stay on the ground and spread their feet and extend their arms. Cuff them and pat them down."

"Something else you might consider."

"What's that?"

"Tie all the cuffs together with a rope. That way, no one can do a runner."

"Good idea. Then, I'll send two guys for the sedans. Cut the rope in half. Jam half of them in one car, half in the other. One driver in each car, one agent with a gun turned toward the guys in the back. Haul them off to the Treasury office in Las Vegas. Call the U.S. Marshalls. Hold them there until the Marshalls pick them up.

"Good thinking. Don't want these clowns anywhere never the Las Vegas Police Department. A couple of them might just accidently escape.

The sergeant will be my responsibility. If he leaves on foot, it'll be easy to find him with the infrared. When I get him, I'll cuff him and bring him back to the jeep. Tie him to the seat. Drive the jeep and the trailer full of rifles to Smoke Tree. Call CID to come and get him and the evidence. I can go back to Searchlight the next day for the pickup."

"Anything else?"

"Yeah. Don't forget to roll down the windows or the garlic fumes will kill you."

Darnold leaned against the conference table and stared at the small topographic map. Finally, he nodded.

"It sounds to me like it could work."

Horse smiled.

"Let me tell you what we used to say in the Army. 'Sound tactical plans are only sound until the first shot is fired.' This could all blow up. Just be ready if it does."

It was just after one o'clock when the three additional Treasury agents showed up at the substation. Two of them had wooden gun cases. The third was straining to handle a wooden box almost the size of a footlocker. He put his burden down, and he and the others stepped up to the desk and displayed their I.D.s. Sergeant Kensington led them down the hall to the conference room where Horse was completing the timeline on the chalk board.

Darnold introduced the man in the lead, a tall man with sandy hair and freckles. His wire frame glasses made him look like an accountant. The hard eyes behind the glasses made him look like something else entirely.

"Horse, the man in the lead is my compatriot from San Francisco, Beauford Butler. Beauford, this is Captain Carlos Caballo. He's in charge of the station. He's also the guy who got this whole thing rolling."

"Captain Caballo is too formal. Just call me 'Horse."

Beauford nodded.

"Pleasure to meet you, Horse. The guys with the heavy artillery are from Denver. Wilton Tamm and Creighton Ames."

"'Wilt' around the department," said the short, wide shouldered man. "Because I'm so tall."

"And I'm Crate," said a much taller version of his companion.

"The guy who introduced me to Horse is Darnold," said Beauford to the two Denver agents.

"Oh, we've heard of him."

"My, yes."

Handshakes and smiles were exchanged.

"Horse, have you got a place we can secure these guns? It would cost us our careers to lose them."

"Especially the big box out in the front office," said Beauford.

"Just leave them. Sergeant Kensington, how about locking these things in a cell?"

"Sure thing, Captain. Let me get some help."

The three men were looking at the maps and poster boards.

"Horse and I have been making plans for the big night. I know you've had a long drive down from Las Vegas, so if any of you need to use the restroom before we get started, now's the time."

"Down the hall on your left," said Horse. "And while you're gone, I'll get coffee for anyone who needs it."

"Now you're speaking my language," said Beauford. "But tell me, are we talking the usual cop shop brew?"

"Not at all. My mother's secret recipe."

Darnold smiled.

"Beauford, you're gonna love this. What about you two?"

Both men nodded.

When the agents were seated at the conference table, coffee in hand, Horse stood at the chalkboard and opened the briefing with the timeline and background. He took them through the information on the chalk board while referencing the marked areas on the large-scale topo. He also took the agents who had not worked with topographical maps before through some basic map interpretation on the seven-point five-minute topo, including some basic understanding of contour lines and what they represented.

Darnold took over and, using the same seven-point five-minute map, took the agents through the plan of action step by step. He was pleased to note that when he was finished and asked for questions, nobody said "are you out of your mind?"

Horse took over again.

"We've thrown a lot at you. It's a lot to digest in one bite. Here's what we're going to do next. We'll go get something to eat and then get you gentlemen over to the Travelodge where we've reserved a room for each of you. You can change into your rough-country clothes and meet us back out here. At the risk of taxing your patience, we'll run you through the entire briefing again. After that, we're off to Arizona for two practice runs in daylight and two after dark."

Wilt raised his hand

"I thought this was happening in that little place in Nevada we drove past on the way down here."

"Sorry. Darnold and I have been working on this for so long we're starting to assume everyone has all the information we do. The buy will happen in Searchlight, but we can't practice there. It's a wide spot in the road full of curious people with a lot of time on their hands, and some of them may know Eddie Mazzetti. We can't take a chance he'll get wind of this. I'm going to take you to Oatman, Arizona, another former mining town that has a place with a similar layout. We'll practice there.

I need to emphasize that what I'm basing this operation on is subject to additional verification. We know the automatic weapon demonstration took place. We know the sergeant who demonstrated it went off in a car registered to Eddie Mazzetti's casino with a couple of guys. We know the touch-and-go drop delivered the new rifles and our sergeant picked them up to a make the exchange. We didn't see the exchange itself, so we're waiting for evidence it happened and the old guns are back at the bivouac area. I'll know by morning whether that happened and whether the sergeant has pilfered some of them.

If we get verification, at daylight on Sunday morning we'll be in a position on that second ridge and you can each study the exchange area. You will have all the time you want to familiarize yourselves with the terrain because we don't expect Mazzetti until late afternoon and the sergeant until after dark."

CHAPTER 38

The Unseen

The hunter's eye reacts to movement. The rabbit, unnoticed, though standing in full view, darts away. The deer, previously perceived only as a pattern of dappled sunlight, suddenly erupts from the tree line. The pheasant explodes from the dried cornstalks. The hunter's sympathetic nervous system reacts before the conscious mind is aware of the event. The hunter does not think 'pheasant!' and raise the gun. The gun begins to rise before the pheasant's action has been consciously processed by the hunter.

But what if nothing triggers the sympathetic nervous system?

A nothing like Chemehuevi Joe, for instance. His skin the color of the desert, his pants the color of his skin, his hair the color of volcanic rock, his shirt the grayish-green of creosote, the shine of his eyes blocked from view by the brim of his tan patrol cap, his white teeth not visible because he rarely smiles at the best of times and never at all at times like these. Immobile to the point of invisibility most of the time, he cautiously traverses the bivouac area almost as easily in the daytime as in the night. But not quite.

Not quite, because he has to change position from time to time in his search for the fully-automatic rifles. But he moves only when fully aware of the location of every soldier. That awareness of where each and every one of them is comes not only from vision but from senses other than sight. Preternatural hearing. An abnormal sense of smell. By noon, Joe has not just read the name tags of the master sergeant, two specialists, three pfcs and five privates. He also knows their voices, their breathing patterns, their mannerisms and their footfalls, along with the distinct odors of their perspiration, hair tonic, and in two cases, deodorant.

But such surreptitious movement and close observation require time as well as care. It is nearly sundown before Joe finds the rifles. They are buried in a silt-and-sand-filled side channel leading into the main wash. An easy place to quickly dig a deep hole with a standard issue entrenching tool. He has to admit the sergeant with the name tag that reads 'Scanlon' has done a good job of concealing what he has done. Joe might not have found the rifles at all if not for jeep tracks. Not jeep tracks that lead to the hiding place, but jeep tracks that don't. Tracks that stop abruptly. Not only stop but double back the way they came. Terminate in the middle of the wash.

Because there is no sign of the jeep and trailer turning around, the doubled tracks are an anomaly. Joe lies motionless for a long time beneath a big creosote, scanning the area beyond the termination point. He solves the mystery. Finds the marks. The marks where the tracks have been brushed away. A job well done, but detectable to someone who knows how to look.

His senses on high alert, Joe moves slowly and patiently up the section of the main draw containing the brushed-out tracks until he finds the narrow side wash where the weapons are hidden. Upstream in that channel, he locates the place where the run-off pattern from the last storm of spring has been altered.

He probes the ground with his skinning knife until he hits something solid. Solid, but not rock. He scoops away the sand and finds an olive drab box. A box like those in the tent. Opening the lid, he finds the rifles with the tripods. He assumes there is another box, or perhaps two, but it doesn't matter. He has seen all he needs to see. He closes the lid and re-covers the box, smoothing the sand into the same pattern as before.

Moving slowly, he begins his horseshoe-shaped arc to Mexican Spring. He is very thirsty. He is hungry too, but he knows the chia seeds in his pocket should never be chewed without water. Not unless he wants to choke and perhaps cough and reveal his position. He will stay near the spring and wait for nightfall before moving back to Globe Canyon and down the road leading to the railroad tracks and the agreed meeting place.

By five o'clock, Horse and the Treasury agent are standing in front of a group of mining buildings on the side of a hill on the edge of Oatman as Darnold gives them one more verbal run-through of the operation, this time including an orientation to the terrain. They follow that with two complete run-throughs, including the approach walk. After dark, they do two additional practice runs, this time carrying weapons and making the single file approach walk by following the reflective tape on the back of the cap of the man in front.

314

In those practice sessions, they park one of the sedans on the rise approaching the buildings so the headlights point upward on an angle. The lights do not provide enough illumination for the operation, and Horse is glad to see he will have a significantly better view through the infrared scope than Mazzetti's group will have. He is confident the light angle will be pretty close to the same in Searchlight. By the end of the second trial, everyone is becoming increasingly confident in the plan.

They are back in the conference room at ten thirty that night when Darnold addresses his fellow agents.

"I know your day started very early this morning in airports far away, and Horse and I have hauled you up and down rough terrain, twice in full darkness. You performed like true professionals. Go back to your rooms and get some well-deserved rest. You're on your own in the morning, but be back in this room at three o'clock in the afternoon. We're going to replay everything we did today, from the briefing forward."

"Are you at the Travelodge too," asks Beauford?

"I hit the jackpot. Horse put me up at his mother's house. She's a wonderful lady, and she feeds me like a king."

At midnight, Horse is at the point where Globe Mine Road intersects the Union Pacific tracks. He turns off his headlights and engine and steps outside beneath the moonlit desert sky. He is about to call for Joe when he hears a voice behind him.

"Ready."

Horse has to smile.

"Where were you when I pulled up?"

"Waiting."

"I know but...never mind. Any luck finding the guns?"

"Yes."

Horse makes a 'K' turn on the road, and they head home. They are silent until they reach highway 66 and turn toward Smoke Tree."

"Where were they?"

"Buried in a wash."

"How many?"

"Don't know. Opened one box."

"Did you learn the name of the sergeant?"

"Scanlon. Boss is Ricks. Major."

"Thanks, Joe. What you did really helps."

"For the missy."

Horse nodded.

315

"For the missy, Joe."

CHAPTER 39

Where's Willy?

Friday morning, when Horse returned to the house from his pre-dawn walk of the property, a worried Esperanza was at the kitchen table with a cup of coffee.

"You're up early this morning."

"I am. I woke up in the night worrying."

"That's my habit. *Cuál es en tu mente, amor?*"

"We didn't see Willy at the carousel. He never mises a night when it's in town. Watches and listens from opening to closing. That's what woke me up. Willy wasn't at the carnival Tuesday night."

"You're right. Do you think he might have left for a while for some reason?"

"Did you see him when you went back?"

Careful not to get the grounds in his cup, Horse poured a cup of cowboy coffee from the pan on the stove and sat down across the table from Esperanza. She put her hands on the table. He covered them with his.

"I did not, and I would have noticed. Would have talked to him."

"Will you check with the guys at the station and find out if anyone has seen him lately?"

"Of course."

"Are you thinking the same thing I am?"

"Don't worry until I ask around, *querida*. It may be nothing."

Esperanza shook her head.

"I can't help it, Carlos. First Burke, then Mr. Stanton. Have we lost Willy, too?"

Willy Gibson was a badly disfigured veteran of World War II. He was a familiar figure in Smoke Tree, but very few knew anything about him. The skin on his face was a mass of scar tissue that looked like melted tallow stained with red ochre and iron oxide. He had neither eyebrows nor any other hair on his face or head. His ears had been so badly burned the lobes were missing, and the remaining skin had shriveled and curled tightly against his head. His eyelids had a crepe-like appearance and failed to cover his gray eyes completely.

Staff Sergeant Willard Gibson had been a tank commander in Patton's 3rd Army during the Battle of the Bulge. On Christmas Eve, 1944, his Sherman was escorting two squads of infantry along the edge of a tree line when a German Tiger IV, known to Allied forces as a King Tiger, topped a rise less than one thousand yards from his M-4. The Tiger commander spotted the American tank and immediately accelerated toward it. Sergeant Gibson knew his much smaller and more lightly armored Sherman was no match for the giant Tiger. The only thing he could do was try to draw the monster away before it got close enough for its MG-34 machine gun to decimate the men he was escorting. He ordered his driver to turn at an oblique angle to the left of the oncoming Tiger's path.

Private Dale pulled back hard on the lateral and applied full throttle. As he accelerated to top speed, he pushed and pulled the laterals, moving the Sherman in an erratic, evasive pattern that gave the appearance the Sherman was trying to flank the German tank. Since there was absolutely no chance a round from the Sherman's smaller gun could penetrate the frontal armor of the Tiger, it was a convincing ploy.

The G.I.s who had been following Willy's tank scattered into the forest as the King Tiger came to a full stop. Its turret rotated ominously toward the American tank and opened fire. It was a credit to Private Dale's maneuvers that the first two rounds from the Tiger's eighty-eight-millimeter gun missed. The third, however, found its mark, striking the front of the M-4 on an angle. The driver, main gunner and machine gunner were killed instantly, and the tungsten-tipped round ignited the Sherman's ammunition supply. The explosion blew Sergeant Willy Gibson out of the open hatch. The Tiger turned away from the burning tank and lumbered off in pursuit of the infantrymen that Sergeant Gibson's sacrifice had given precious time to seek cover in the forest.

Willy Gibson spent the next year and a half in military hospitals: first in Europe and finally in Massachusetts. The war and welcome-home parades were long over when he was discharged, terribly scarred and with most of his fingers and half his left foot missing.

When Horse reached the office, he had the night-shift dispatcher broadcast a request for response from any officer who had seen Willy in the last few days. There was no reply.

When the day shift came in for the morning briefing, Horse went in the squad room and asked the same question. No one had seen Willy, not even Andy Chesney, who had been at the carnival for five hours on Monday night. Horse left the briefing to talk with the day dispatcher.

"Fred, the swing shift guys should be waking up by nine. I want you to call all of them. Ask if anyone has seen Willy Gibson rattling doors the last few nights."

Willy had set out from Massachusetts on a bitter-cold winter day in 1946 with nothing more than his accumulated pay. A native of Harlan County, Kentucky, he had no desire to return home to the curious stares of friends and relatives. He decided to head for California and warmer weather. To save money, he rode the rails.

Two years after he climbed down from the gondola car in which he had nearly frozen to death between Belen, New Mexico and Smoke Tree, he was still living rough in tamarisk thickets along the river. His back pay exhausted, he began coming into town after dark to scrounge for food in the trash cans behind the businesses on Front Street.

In those days, Smoke Tree had its own police department. It was led by a man who had never risen beyond patrolman on the LAPD before he retired and applied for the job of Chief of Police in Smoke Tree to supplement his pension. The Smoke Tree City Council, impressed by the fact that Oscar Rettenmeir had once worked for the great William H. Parker, awarded him the job.

The crew he inherited was a rag-tag bunch, many of them cut loose from other departments because of incompetence, brutality or corruption. Interested mostly in fishing and the bottle he kept in his lower left desk drawer, Chief Rettenmeir did nothing to raise the standards. The department had a few good officers, but they were far outnumbered by the bad apples in the barrel.

The most rotten of all the bad apples was Officer Vernon Nichols. A bigoted and cruel man, when he learned the badly damaged man scrounging for food in the alleyways of Smoke Tree was of diminished mental capacity, Officer Nichols organized a late-night ceremony behind the police station. In what passed for humor among such men, he and his friends pinned a dime-store badge to Willy's shirt, clamped a cast-off STPD hat on his damaged head, and strapped a gun belt and holster around his waist. The holster held

319

a rusted revolver with no firing pin and a cylinder that could not turn. They tossed in a cheap flashlight for good measure.

To their great amusement, Willy took the charade seriously. He would walk the downtown late at night, carrying his flashlight and wearing his hat, badge and revolver. Shining the flashlight through darkened windows, he rattled doors to make sure the businesses were locked up tight.

Eighteen years after his nearly-frozen arrival in Smoke Tree, Willy was receiving a modest disability check from the Army thanks to the persistent efforts of Mac, the retired Marine gunnery sergeant who owned the Palms. And he continued to make his nightly rounds, without fail. If it turned out no one on the swing shift had seen him, something was very wrong.

Horse went into the conference room and closed the door. He studied the diagrams and topographic maps and turned the plan for Sunday night over and over in his mind. Even if everything went right, it was going to be a difficult operation. The assembled team lacked the numbers to pull it off smoothly if something went wrong. Not for the first time, he wondered if he had allowed his hatred of Eddie Mazzetti to override his best judgement. He had to admit it was a possibility, Nonetheless, he was determined to forge ahead.

At nine o'clock, Horse left the conference room and returned to his office. While he waited for Fred to contact each of the off-duty members of the swing shift, he called Pete Hardesty and gave him an update on what the Treasury agents were doing. He purposely did not acknowledge his role in the coming operation. Nor did he mention Chemehuevi Joe. If the whole thing fell apart, he wanted the Undersheriff to be able to say truthfully that he had not known in advance what Captain Caballo had in mind.

At nine-twenty, his intercom buzzed.

"Yes, Fred."

"Called them all, boss. No one's seen Willy in a while."

Horse was on his way out the door before Fred had finished the last sentence.

He drove to the San Bernardino County landfill where Willy lived in a squat, square building made of concrete blocks. It stood just outside the landfill gate on property owned by the county. In 1962, at Horse's urging, Willy had become the unofficial occupant of the unofficial building. When he first moved in, Joe Medrano built him a heavy-duty door of laminated two by six planks and burned *Willy Gibson Landfill Supervisor* into the wood before sealing it with marine varnish. Landfill supervisor meant Willy got first picks on anything discarded at the dump. When Joe and Horse installed the door, they included not only a keyed door knob but also a deadbolt. Horse also provided Willy a number of his business cards. On the back, above his signature, was typed, "This card will introduce Willy Gibson, my authorized representative at the San Bernardino County Landfill."

Horse pulled up next to Willy's place. When he knocked on the heavy door, there was no response. He tried to turn the knob. Locked.

"Willy."

No answer.

"Willy, it's Horse."

The answer came faintly through the heavy planks.

"Orse?"

The door opened slightly. Willy scanned the area behind Horse's shoulder before opening the door wider.

"Ih. Urry."

Horse stepped into the single, immaculately-kept room. When Willy first moved in, the place had a dirt floor. Burke Henry had hauled his cement mixer to town, and he and Horse poured one of cement. A large portion of that floor was now covered by a rug Willy had stitched together from pieces of carpet discarded at the landfill. It gave the appearance more of an odd quilt than a rug. How a man with only a thumb and finger on one hand and two fingers on the other had managed such a feat remained a mystery. Willy had also scrounged items of furniture over the years, and three huge oil lamps that had once swung inside Santa Fe cabooses in the days of steam engines sat on mis-matched end tables.

"Esperanza is worried about you, Willy."

"Eseranza?"

"That's right. She thought you might be sick. None of my deputies have seen you downtown at night. Are you okay?"

Willy hung his head.

"Nah oin ma jo."

Horse was sixteen years old when he first met Willy in the park in front of the Santa Fe depot. Over the years, the two had forged a bond. As a result, Horse was very familiar with the limitations of Willy's speech. Damaged by the inhalation of tungsten fumes and superheated air, his tongue and soft palate could not produce hard consonants and struggled even with soft ones. Horse was the only person in town, with the exception of Esperanza and Mac, who could understand what Willy was trying to say. Therefore, he knew Willy had just said, "Not doing my job."

"It's all right, Willy. The deputies have been covering for you. Where have you been?"

The ochre and iron oxide tint of Willy's face deepened as he struggled to bring forth the words.

"Ahns! Ahns ah ower!"

Suddenly, Horse understood. He felt stupid it hadn't occurred to him before. Willy was afraid of the tanks.

"Those are our tanks, Willy."

Willy shook his head.

"Oo ihj! Oo ihj!"

"Too big?"

"Ess! Nah Sehmans."

"No, they're not Shermans. But they're not German tanks either. They're American tanks. M-60s. Pattons."

Willy got very excited.

"Shehnerah aon ess ear?"

"I'm afraid not, Willy. General Patton has been dead for many years, but these new tanks were named in his honor."

"Ooo ess ahns?"

"That's right. U.S. tanks."

Willy's face lacked the ability to be expressive, but Horse could see relief in his gray eyes.

"Ahn oo Orse."

"You're welcome, Willy. I'm glad you're okay."

"El Eseranza?"

"I'll tell her. And Willy? I'm in the middle of something right now, but when it's finished, we'd like to have you over for dinner."

Willy pursed his lips in a Willy smile.

"Eenhilahas?"

"You've got it, Willy. Enchiladas it will be."

"Wins?"

"Sure, the twins will be there."

"Oh oy!"

As Horse drove back to town, he realized he had one more person to tell about Burke's death. Willy's circle of friends had been up to five: Horse, Esperanza, Mac, Chemehuevi Joe and Burke Henry. Horse hated to tell Willy that one of them was gone, but sooner or later, Willy would ask about Burke.

When Horse returned to the station, he had a message from the lieutenant who had been assigned the job of keeping Horse informed about Desert Strike developments that might affect civilians. The message was brief: *The Calonian forces have turned the tide of battle and are now driving the Nezonian army west. Lord,* thought Horse, they'll be at the river in another day. Will we never get these people out of our hair?

Horse began the three o'clock briefing by telling the assembled Treasury agents he now had confirmation Master Sergeant Scanlon had withheld a number of fully-automatic rifles from the inventory of weapons to be transferred to reserve and national guard units. The rifles had been hidden in the desert.

"How do you know this," asked Beauford?

"Agent Butler, do you reveal your confidential sources in the course of an investigation?"

"Of course not."

"Nor do I."

"Do you mind if I make a guess?"

"Not at all."

"You've got someone inside that unit. I mean, you not only know the sergeant has hidden the weapons, you know his name. I don't believe you knew it when we got here yesterday. And you know what the Army has planned for the old rifles. You didn't know that yesterday, either."

"You're right about that."

"You mean right that it's a soldier?"

"No. The part about not knowing the sergeant's name and what they were going to do with the rifles."

"You're not going to confirm that your source is a soldier?"

Horse shrugged.

"Not going to deny it, either."

Darnold took over. He ran his fellow-agents through a reprise of every step of the coming operation. He then had Horse repeat the background information that had led to Undersheriff Hardesty's call to Treasury.

By six o-clock, the daylight rehearsals were underway northwest of Oatman. By ten that night, they had completed both of the full-darkness run-throughs. Before they left the practice site, Horse checked to make sure the M-3 scope and carbine were accurate at the distance he would be shooting. He set a candle in the sand in front of the hillside, lit it, and stepped off forty yards: his best estimate of the distance between Mazzetti's men and the boulder where he and Darnold would be positioned. He powered up the scope and took a kneeling position. Wrapping the sling tightly around his forearm, he pulled the carbine against his shoulder and snugged his cheek against the stock. Assuming the carbine had been sighted in with a battlefield zero of one hundred yards, he centered the reticle below the bright red signature of the candle flame and squeezed the trigger. The rifle sounded very loud in the stillness of the desert night. The thirty-caliber round split the candle. The heat signature from the snuffed wick persisted in the scope.

The team packed up its gear and adjourned to the Oatman hotel. The bar was almost empty, unusual for a Friday night, and the bartender did not seem glad to see them. The Treasury agents ordered a pitcher of beer to wash down the desert dust. Horse asked Maggie if she had a Nehi grape in the cooler. He was rewarded by a strange look accompanied by an annoyed shake of her head. He settled for a glass of tonic water.

"Why the sour look, Maggie?"

"If I'd known it was you out there yesterday, I'd have called your office to find out what was going on."

"Why would you care?"

"You're kidding, right? Two plain-vanilla Dodge sedans with government plates in the hills outside of town? A bunch of guys in baseball caps, two of them carrying Tommy guns and one with something that looked like a space ray stomping around the desert?"

"What about it?"

"What about it? Horse, does this bar look normal to you for a Friday night?"

"It does look sparse. And don't you usually have a band on Fridays?"

Maggie laughed.

"Oh, that's rich, Horse. I called Kingman and cancelled the band."

"Why?"

"Because two thirds of my customers have left town. Didn't hang around to hear what the government types were up to."

"Where'd they go?"

"Jerome, some of them said. Randsburg and the Panamints west of Death Valley. Some place down by the Salton Sea for some others."

Maggie sighed and leaned on the bar.

"I'll tell you Horse, you and these *federales* are ruining my trade. And then you come in and ask for a Nehi grape!"

Horse spread his hands.

"We cleared our little exercise with the Mohave County Sheriff's Department, but I've got to admit I never thought of checking in with the bartender at the Oatman Hotel."

"Obviously. I'm not sure it would have helped anyway. A lot of these squatters are real skittish. The least you can do now is send us some of those soldiers you've got down your way."

"Maggie, you have no idea how much it would please me to send you the whole bunch."

When they got back to Smoke Tree, Horse advised the agents to get well rested on Saturday because Sunday was going to be a very long day.

"Well meet here at the station at two o'clock Sunday morning and saddle up."

"I sure hope you mean that metaphorically," said Darnold. "I haven't recovered from my little saunter around your corral yet."

"You went horseback riding," asked Beauford?

"It was more like horseback-hanging-on."

CHAPTER 40

One Deep Breath

While Saturday may have been a day off for the Treasury agents, it was just another workday for Horse. As Joint Exercise Desert Strike moved east, the number of jets in the skies above Smoke Tree increased. There was another dusting of leaflets: this time from the Calonia forces. The statement in the hyperbole-filled pamphlets could pretty much be reduced to, *Fear not, people of Smoke Tree! The Calonian forces will soon drive the dreaded Nezonians into the river.* It sounded to Horse like something Rufus T. Firefly would have said in the Marx Brothers' *Duck Soup*. In any event, it was unwelcome news to fishermen and water skiers. They immediately began calling the substation. Horse advised Merle, the day dispatcher, to counsel patience and remind callers the whole mess would be wrapped up before Sunday morning.

He had been out of the office a lot in the past few days and had a lot to catch up on. One thing led to another, and once again he didn't get home until late. When he got there, the twins were fast asleep. He walked into their room and stood for a while, watching them sleep. For all their joyous energy, the speed with which they surrendered to sleep amazed him. It was a welcome change after their first year with him and Esperanza. In those days, they had been restless sleepers, often waking from nightmares.

That was no longer the case. Horse and Esperanza loved it that Elena and Alejandro now felt secure. So secure they did not even wake up if they fell asleep on the couch and Horse carried them down the hall to bed. He leaned over and planted a light kiss on each forehead, slightly damp in the still-warm house.

Horse could have caught an hour or two of sleep, but he chose to spend the time with Esperanza. He knew how worried she was about what would happen in Nevada on Sunday. He knew trying to shelter her from the risks involved would only stoke her fears, so as they sat together on the couch, his arm around her and her head on

327

his shoulder, he laid out the operation from beginning to end with no attempt to sugar-coat the difficulties.

"I know it's pointless to tell you not to worry, querida, but I'm confident we can control the situation.

"But there are going to be eight of them and five of you."

"That's true, and I don't like that. But I'll be able to see them and they won't be able to see me. That's a big advantage. Also, Wilt and Crate have the Thompsons. Those are devastating weapons."

"And this Sergeant Scanlon?"

"Hard to account for, I agree. He'll probably be the coolest customer there."

"No, I don't think so."

"You think it'll be Mazzetti?"

"No, it will be my Carlos. It always is."

CHAPTER 41

The Real Thing

At two o'clock Sunday morning, the team gathered in the conference room at the substation. They reviewed the operation one last time.

"Horse thinks we've rested so much we've lost our edge," said Wilt.

"Well, I know you government types. Bunch of bureaucrats. Let you off the job for twenty-four hours, have to retrain you.".

The agents laughed, and the pre-operation tension in the room eased. Horse liked these men. They were professional and competent. They had confidence in their abilities, but not so much confidence they were a danger to themselves or others. They made a good team.

Remembering what Maggie had said about government plates, when they went out to the parking lot, Horse had the agents replace them with California plates the station had confiscated over the years. No doubt this was illegal in some way, but it paled in comparison with the cross-jurisdictional foray Horse was about to make.

By three in the morning, Horse was leading his little caravan north on 95 in the search and rescue pickup. They rolled into Searchlight and left both sedans parked on side streets less than a mile from the mining buildings. Darnold got in the front seat of the pickup with Horse, and Wilt and Crate climbed into the bed. Horse drove on to a point a mile south of the mine site. He pulled off the road and steered the truck up a desert wash and into the cover of a stand of desert willows.

The moon had set. The men quietly retrieved their gear and moved out beneath a sky so dense with stars they seemed to bleed into the horizon on all sides. The team gave the appearance of a guerrilla group moving into position for an ambush. Horse led. The others followed the greenish glow of the twin stripes of glow-in-the-dark reflective tape on the back of the cap in front of them.

Horse bore the heaviest burden: carbine with infrared scope; twelve-pound battery to power the scope in a canvas bag strapped on his back; spotting scope; C-rations that would serve as breakfast and late-afternoon meal. Wilt and Crate carried wooden boxes containing the deadly Thompson sub-machine guns, fifty-round drum magazines, and three twenty-round clips each. They also carried one-gallon, fabric-covered canteens. Darnold had two more canteens. He also carried four spotlights, a rope, and two pairs of binoculars in a burlap bag. Beauford packed four additional canteens. Horse knew two gallons for each man would be more than enough for the coming eighteen to twenty hours in the desert, but far better to have too much than too little.

When Horse led them to the two-track climbing the back of the ridge where they intended to set up for the day, the going got easier. While they moved as soundlessly as possible up the hill, Beauford and Darnold were thinking about the fog that would be rolling in off San Francisco bay at this hour, and Wilt and Crate thought about loved ones back home in Denver. For his part, Horse continued to think about the operational plan, turning it over in his head, analyzing and re-analyzing, thinking about all the ways it could go wrong. But also thinking how good it would feel to see Eddie Mazzetti in hand cuffs.

When the sun rose above Fourth of July Mountain just after five thirty in the morning, Horse had the spotting scope on its tripod and was studying the wooden shack Klaus called home. He saw no sign anyone was there. He surrendered the scope to Wilt, who would pass it on to Crate so the two men could locate their firing positions. Darnold was glassing the supposed exchange area through binoculars. Horse picked up the other pair. He had a clear view of the building where Sergeant Scanlon had parked his jeep a week ago today.

After giving everyone an hour chance to scan the entire area, Horse pointed out the location on the two-track where he anticipated Mazzetti's crew would be forced to abandon their cars.

"The moon will rise just after five this afternoon. Sunset is at eight. I think we can expect the sergeant at around nine-thirty, or maybe a little later. By the time he arrives, the waxing moon will be almost directly overhead, just a little larger than it was last night in Oatman. There may even be some moonlight reflecting off the windshields, and Wilt and Crate will have clear lines of fire. By the time they empty the fifty-round drums and two of the twenty-round clips, those cars will be ready for the scrap heap. I don't expect Mazzetti's guys to be carrying anything other than pistols and maybe a couple shotguns. Wilt and Crate will be sixty yards away in prone positions with just the gun barrels poking over the hill. That will limit their exposure to hostile fire.

Darnold, we can't see the two small buildings and our position from here. The south end of the ridge blocks the view, but you've seen the area before. When we get down there tonight, you can practice balancing a spotlight on top of the big boulder we'll be hiding behind.

Gentlemen, you have all day to study the area. Memorize it. You can never know too much about the terrain where you'll be risking your life."

CHAPTER 42

Theory and Practice

Time passes slowly on the Mojave, and it seemed even slower on the longest day of 1964. In the absence of jet fighters, buzzards returned to the skies. They soared high above Duplex Hill and over the broad Piute Valley below on dihedral wings, gently manipulating their outer primaries and making subtle adjustments to alter their paths along fluctuating trails in the sky only they could discern. Soaring so high they sometimes could not be seen by the naked eye.

Occasional red-tail hawks circled at lower altitudes. When the hawks were no longer visible, coveys of quail emerged from hiding to feed along the edge of the ridges, making burbling sounds as they fed, a distinctive four note call if separated from the main covey, and an urgent *chip-chip-chip* if something suspicious appeared. A horned toad climbed languidly onto a rock near the men and regarded them.

Horse rolled onto his back, pulled his cap down over his eyes, and caught up on some of the sleep he had missed over the last three nights. Beauford sat and wondered why anyone would live out here. Darnold decided he liked the area near the Providence Mountains better. The two agents from Denver thought the desert mountains looked small and badly worn compared to the Rockies.

Horse slept until it was time for a late breakfast. He opened four cans of scrambled eggs with the P-38 he carried on the chain around his neck. He distributed plastic spoons and one chocolate disc to each agent. When everyone was finished, he gathered the cans, flattened them, and buried them. Dave D'Arnauld, Wilton Tamm and Creighton Ames appreciated someone who didn't litter. Beauford Butler thought it an odd thing to do; not everyone thinks the desert worthy of protection.

Time slowed again. The water in the canteens got warmer. At four o'clock, they split up the remaining C-rats: turkey loaf for Beauford, ham slices for Wilt, beefsteak for Crate, more scrambled eggs for Horse. After their meal, Horse buried the remaining cans, the spoons, and the wrappers from the chocolate discs.

"Can I ask you something," asked Beauford?

"Go ahead."

"Why do you bury the cans?"

Horse shrugged.

"Deserts are clean. Leave them clean."

"Clean? All this dirt?"

"Clean. As in dry, uncluttered. Swept by winds daily. Disinfected by sunlight. You can take your potato salad out of its container, your sandwiches from their wrappers, your celery and carrot sticks from their Saran Wrap and eat your picnic off the top of a baked boulder. Try that on any San Francisco sidewalk."

The men sat on the hillside. The buzzards continued to soar. The quail had moved on. The horned toad had disappeared. Too hot in the direct sun. An occasional zebra-tailed lizard skittered by, tail curved forward as it ran.

A giant hairy scorpion emerged from its burrow to see if it was time to come out and hunt yet. It freaked Beauford out.

"They don't eat much," Horse reassured him."

"What about rattlesnakes?"

"Have you seen any?"

"No."

"And we probably won't."

"What if we do?"

"When a rattlesnake sees you, it thinks one thing. Can I swallow that? If it can't, it loses interest. They only strike if you get too close and they feel threatened."

"How do you know if you're too close?"

"That's why we call them buzz worms."

Just after five o'clock, the pale, waxing moon cleared the eastern horizon.

At five-thirty a black Chrysler 300 rolled up the road near the mining site and turned onto the two-track. It made it partway up the hill before stopping. Horse watched through the spotting scope. Darnold and Beauford watched through binoculars.

"That's about as far as I thought they'd get."

Four men got out, all dressed very much like the individuals Aeden Snow had described to Horse. Although the team on the ridge was nearly a half mile away, the sound of the car doors slamming was very clear. The men walked over the rise and down to the building where the sergeant had parked. They circled the building, two on each side, and met up again in the front. Then they disappeared from view, blocked by the lower ridge when they moved west to examine the two smaller buildings.

The ridge also blocked sound, and Horse could no longer hear their voices. Then three gunshots boomed. Little gray birds in the wash below burst into flight.

"What the hell?"

Horse put his eye to the spotting scope.

He could see bats in the air above the ridge.

"They shot into the mineshaft. Bats flew out. Since they probably think all bats are rabid, we'll see them again real soon."

Sure enough, all four men appeared, hurrying away from the area blocked from sight by the ridge. Two of them were holding handguns. One raised his and fired in the direction of the mineshaft until the slide locked back.

Horse, his eye still to the scope, said, "Forty-five automatics. Both of them."

"Why are they still shooting?"

"Probably embarrassed they were run off by creatures smaller than sparrows."

In a moment, the group turned north and disappeared from view again. They re-emerged as they reached the ridge near the shack Klaus called home. One of them pulled the door open. Horse could hear their voices again but, as before, was unable to make out what they were saying. All four went inside. Several items came flying out the door. The men emerged laughing.

They walked a portion of the ridgeline. At one point, one of the men looked directly at the ridge where the team waited. The spotting scope was so powerful Horse could see the angling sun glinting off the oil on the man's hair. He turned in a slow circle.

Never been soldiers, thought horse, skylighting themselves on a ridge.

Within fifteen minutes, the four had returned to the car. The signature clatter of a Chrysler-product starter carried clearly in the stillness. The car backed down the hill and onto the road. The driver made a "K" turn and drove off toward town.

When it had disappeared, the team relaxed.

"Scouts," said Darnold.

"A couple of them looked like the real deal. First team. I'm glad they showed up. It means the sale is set for here. Mazzetti is probably still at the Serengeti. They'll call him from Searchlight and give him the all clear. He'll be here before sundown to see the place for himself in the light, but I don't think the transaction will take place before dark."

"Weren't very thorough, were they," asked Wilt?

"Didn't think they would be. City boys."

"Hey," said Beauford, "I'm a city boy."

Horse laughed.

"Sorry. I'll rephrase. Stupid city boys. You're a smart city boy."

The desert grew quiet again as the sun moved westward.

Horse took another short nap.

"How can you sleep at a time like this," asked Beauford when Horse sat up?

"Soldier's rule. Sleep when you can. Might be a while until your next chance."

At seven o'clock the black Chrysler returned, followed by another. The lead car stopped in the same place as before. The second car pulled up almost against its bumper.

Tactically stupid, thought Horse. If the back car can't move, the one in front is blocked.

He focused the scope on the lead car. Looked like the same four men. He angled it to the second. Four men. Probably Mazzetti behind the driver, but Horse's view was blocked by the man on the passenger side in the front seat.

The four men in the second car got out. One of them was Eddie Mazzetti.

"Got you," whispered Horse.

The men walked to the point where the two-track crested the rise. They stood there talking and gesturing as they surveyed the building below.

Horse turned the scope over to Darnold.

"Any chance one of those guys is Tommy Bones?"

Darnold studied the group and shook his head.

The four returned to their car and climbed in. The car doors slammed. Both cars started up again.

"Think they're leaving?"

"Nope. Too hot for them. Turning on the air conditioning."

In ten minutes, both cars shut down.

"Now what?"

"Overheating."

Horse watched through the scope as windows were rolled down. The two men in the front seat of the lead car lit cigarettes.

The desert went quiet again.

At seven-fifty, the sun touched the top of six-thousand-foot Crescent Peak, and the western horizon flared magenta. In the eastern sky, the rising moon turned mercurochrome red. Twilight gathered. Bats appeared overhead. A nighthawk pursuing an insect pulled out of a dive with the characteristic roar that gave the bird its nickname: bull-bat.

The driver of the lead Chrysler got out and turned away from the car. The spotting scope gathered enough light that Horse could see him but not make out what he was doing. The man turned back to the car, zipping his pants.

The "chunk" of the slammed door did not carry as well as it had earlier. There was just enough incremental increase in humidity to change the sound.

The evening zephyr washed across the land, heading downslope toward Lake Mojave and the Colorado River to the east.

More time passed. It seemed to move more quickly now that confrontation was near. Twilight descended.

Horse looked at his watch. Full dark in fifteen minutes. That's when the sergeant would leave the bivouac and retrieve the rifles. Ease down Macedonia Canyon Road. Head for Searchlight. Arrive at their location, rifles in tow, about fifty minutes later.

When fifteen minutes had passed, he tapped Darnold on the shoulder and twirled his index finger. Darnold signaled the others. Equipment was gathered. Horse strapped the battery pack to his shoulders. Wilt and Crate picked up the Thompsons, fifty-round magazines locked and loaded so there would be no sound of the drums snapping into place and bolts shooting forward to seat rounds when they were closer to Mazzetti and his men. They tucked the twenty-round clips behind their belts. Darnold wrapped the burlap bag containing the four spotlights and the rope around his hand. Canteens, binoculars and spotting scope were left behind.

Although it was full dark, they crawled over the ridgeline. Horse in the lead, they set out for their positions on the next ridge. The moon, now nearly overhead, was sufficiently bright they did not have to home in on the reflective tape of the man in front. They did anyway. Because that was what they had practiced. Follow procedure. Control what you can control. Besides, if there were a snake, they wanted Horse to get the news first.

They eased down the slope, one slow step at a time, and moved quietly across the broad wash separating the two ridges. Climbing the south side of the one that was their ultimate goal, they slowed even further because every step brought them closer to Mazzetti and his men. Near the top of the rise, they got down on their stomachs and crawled to the edge. The Chryslers were shadowy bulks, moonlight reflecting weakly off their windshields.

Good targets, thought Horse.

Darnold tapped Horse on the shoulder and whispered.

"Want to turn on the scope and make sure they're all in the cars?"

Horse powered up the scope. In the viewfinder, the hoods of the cars burned reddish-orange: the one in the rear more reddish than the lead car. It had driven all the way from Las Vegas. The windows were still down, and the heads of the men looked like blood oranges: red in the center, orange at the edges. As he watched, one lit a cigarette. The match blossomed bright as a railroad flare.

All the men were in the cars. The only heat signature outside was a coyote twenty-five yards to the west. It was not moving. Horse couldn't be positive, but it seemed to be sitting down. Coyotes knew humans. They knew cars. They knew humans sometimes threw unwanted food out of car windows. The coyote was willing to wait.

Horse respected coyotes. Liked them, even. He resisted the insane urge to fire a round to scare it away before the Thompsons opened up. It was unnecessary. The coyote would bolt at the first sound of a car door being cracked.

Horse turned off the scope.

"Everybody's inside," he whispered. "Let's go."

Wilt and Crate crawled back below the ridge and moved west toward their firing positions. When they got there, they pushed their guns over the ridge and sighted in on the faint gleams. After they were in position, Beauford moved toward his spot on the backside of the ridge behind the shed.

Horse and Darnold crawled over the ridge and moved slowly down the hill. They were so close to Mazzetti's crew that if one of them slipped the sound could possibly be picked up by the men in the cars. When they reached their position behind the boulder, Darnold carefully placed one of the spotlights on top. He practiced getting it balanced and angled so it would illuminate the exchange area. When he was satisfied with the location and felt he had it memorized, he removed the light and dropped back down.

Horse powered up the sniper scope again. He stood and scanned the ground between their position and the largest building. It's metal roof still held a strong heat signature from baking all day in the desert sun. He could see background glows from the darker rocks. As he expected, he could not see the Chryslers parked beyond the rise at all.

Horse was pleased with the team's performance: stealthy approach march, everyone in position. He crossed himself and offered up a silent prayer in the darkness. When he was finished, he crossed himself again and leaned against the boulder. He thought of Esperanza and hoped she was not too anxious.

338

By his estimation, Sergeant Scanlon would be passing through Nipton, bound for Searchlight. Nothing to do now but wait. He hoped the others on the team were as good at waiting as he was. It might be a while.

In the deep stillness of the desert night, Horse heard the jeep. He heard the engine first, then the tires kicking up rocks on the two-track, then louder noises from the tires as the sergeant left the narrow path and drove through the desert around the parked cars.

He ducked back when he saw the cat's eye lights appear. He listened from behind the boulder as the jeep accelerated down the hill. It skidded to a stop. From beyond the rise came the sounds of car doors slamming. Tilting his head back, Horse could see headlights piercing the night sky.

Horse powered up the scope and eased the carbine around the side of the boulder. The sergeant was out of the jeep and at the rear of the trailer. It was impossible to make out his features. Part of his heat signature smeared in the scope as he moved his arm. Apparently, the sergeant was pulling back the tarp on the trailer. The front of the jeep was inside the building, but Horse could see the reddish orange heat from the engine bleeding through the cracks in the weathered boards. The end of the tailpipe glowed flaming red.

The figure in his scope pulled something from the back of the trailer. Something that held no heat. He could tell the blobs that were the sergeant's hands were wrapped around something as he turned to face west.

Horse nudged Darnold out of the way and pushed the M-3 around the other side of their hiding place. Mazzetti's crew was cresting the hill. Eight blurry figures that looked like ghosts of red bleeding into orange floating just above the ground.

"Evening, Eddie," came from his right. It was the first time Horse had heard Scanlon's voice. Deep. Assured. Calm.

Sergeant for sure, thought Horse.

The blobs on the hillside stopped moving. Hovered. Then two on each side began to ease away from the other four.

"Sergeant Scanlon?"

Horse remembered that oily voice. Mazzetti.

"You were expecting someone else?"

"Where are you?"

"Down here by the building."

"I can't see you."

"I don't want you to. Not just yet. I have a little speech to make."

There was a momentary silence. Then the two blobs on each side continued their lateral movement.

"Go ahead."

"Just in case any of the heavies you brought with you get any funny ideas, I'm holding one of the guns. It's locked and loaded. Twenty rounds in the magazine. Another magazine in my pocket. Selector switch set to automatic."

"Thought we were friends, Yannity."

That oily, insinuating voice again.

"Oh, we are, Eddie. You and I. But you've got a couple of guys on either side of you already trying to flank me."

For an alarming moment, Horse thought the sergeant had a night vision device.

"What makes you think that, Yannity?"

"Because I can hear the clumsy bastards. Tell them to come back to you."

"Okay, okay," said Mazzetti in his most soothing tone.

"Now!" yelled the sergeant. The voice of authority. A drill sergeant yelling at a recruit.

"You heard my friend. Get back over here."

The four blobs began floating back.

Sergeant Scanlon waited until they stopped moving.

"Much better, Eddie. I'm getting some real good vibrations down here. Now, you come forward all by yourself. Bring the money, and I'll show you the rifles. Your boys start moving again, I'll shoot them. And Eddie? There's a good chance you'll get hit if I open fire."

The blob that was Mazzetti detached from the others and floated down the road alone. A dark spot swung back and forth across the blurry figure as it moved.

The bag with the money, thought Horse.

He was inclined to give Mazzetti grudging respect for being brave enough to walk in the dark toward a man with a loaded automatic rifle when he realized why he was doing it. Tommy Bones wanted those guns. Eddie Mazzetti dare not return without them. Horse wondered how dangerous a man had to be to make you fear him, even in his absence, more than a guy with a loaded gun.

Two reddish-orange ghosts melded into one as the men spoke at the rear of the trailer. Horse could not make out what they were saying, but it seemed apparent Sergeant Scanlon had no fear Mazzetti could take the rifle away from him.

"Scanlon's turned on a flashlight," whispered Darnold.

Horse pulled his eye away from the scope. The sergeant was playing the flashlight beam over the contents of the trailer. The M-3 had not registered the flashlight because the tiny bulb was behind glass, and infrared cannot detect a heat source behind glass.

Mazzetti was leaning forward.

Counting rifles, thought Horse.

As he watched, Mazzetti straightened up. Scanlon played the flashlight on the ground. The money. Mazzetti picked up a gym bag up and held it open so Scanlon could shine the light inside. Apparently satisfied, Scanlon turned off the flashlight. Horse returned his eye to the infrared scope. The dark spot that was the bag of money was in the middle of the Scanlon blob when the Mazzetti blob turned away from the jeep. The exchange had been made.

"Now!" said Horse.

Darnold placed the spotlight on top of the rock. He hit the switch and dropped back down as the beam speared Mazzetti and Scanlon.

"United States Treasury agents," He shouted. "Throw down your weapons. Lift your hands over your heads."

And everything came undone.

Sergeant Scanlon was indeed, as Horse had described him, a wild card. Realizing in an instant everything that was at stake, including his freedom for the rest of his life, he dropped the cash. Grasping the pistol grip in his right hand and the folding forward grip in his left, he lifted the full-size M14A1 rifle to his shoulder.

Putting the front sight blade on the bright light and centering it in the peep sight, he pulled the trigger. The spotlight shattered, but as the rifle climbed, the rest of the shots sprayed the hillside behind the boulder.

Wilt and Crate opened up with the Thompsons. Even over the roar of the weapons, Horse could hear the heavy rounds slam into the cars. The headlights blinked out as the guns continued to hammer.

As soon as Sergeant Scanlon realized those rounds were not coming his way, he turned to pick up the money. It was gone. Eddie Mazzetti had snatched it up and climbed into the jeep. Unfortunately for him, he had no idea how to start it. His right hand still on the pistol grip, the sergeant stepped toward him and swung the rifle in a vicious arc, clubbing Mazzetti on the back of the head. Mazzetti's head bounced back off the steering wheel and Scanlon came back the other way, butt-stroking the mobster on the left side of the face, breaking his jaw and knocking out most of the teeth on that side of his mouth.

Sergeant Scanlon flung the rifle into the back seat. He wrapped his left hand around the collar of the unconscious man, grabbed the back of his belt with his right and levered Mazzetti out of the jeep. He climbed behind the wheel and started it up.

When Wilt and Crate had burned through the fifty-round drums, Darnold did a very brave thing. Hoping Scanlon had emptied his clip, and counting on the Thompsons to have driven Mazzetti's crew to the ground, he put another spotlight on top of the boulder and flicked it on as he dropped back down.

"United States..."

Which is as far as he got. Two of Mazzetti's men armed with sawed-off shotguns fired almost simultaneously. Another spotlight disintegrated. Double aught buckshot splattered the rock. Shards from the light flew into the night. Echoes of the twin blasts bounced around the hills.

Horse braced himself for rounds from Sergeant Scanlon's M14A1. There were none. The Thompsons had stopped, momentarily. Then, Wilt and Crate opened up with the first of their twenty-found clips, firing in bursts of three to four.

Inside the building, Sergeant Scanlon revved the jeep's engine until it screamed. Popping the clutch, he slammed the jeep into the back wall of the ancient building. The wall trembled but held. Horse poked the M-3 around the side of the rock and focused the infrared on the building. Through the gaps in the boards, he could see the heat from the jeep's engine. He could have estimated the location and snapped off a shot at the driver's position, but he was unsure who was behind the wheel.

He held his fire, a decision he would come to regret.

Sergeant Scanlon backed up for another attempt, running over Mazzetti's legs in the process. Wilt and Crate paused to reload again. Scanlon revved the engine and popped the clutch for a second assault on the building, running over Mazzetti's legs again. This time, the back wall gave way. The jeep shot into the air, the roof collapsing behind it and covering Scanlon's retreat. Horse rose to his feet and was about to start toward the remains of the building when he heard a new sound. A big handgun. Then another.

Mazzetti's men.

Every bone in Horse's body ached to pursue the jeep, but the team needed his help. Horse stepped back behind the boulder and balanced the rifle on top.

Two men were firing from a kneeling position. In the scope, the rounds exiting their automatics were trailed by crimson flames. Horse knew they were automatics because he could see the red-hot, ejected cases spinning away like tracers. It was obvious the two men were firing toward the muzzle flashes of the Thompsons. And then the two men with shotguns stood and fired the same direction. The hot gasses following the buckshot blossomed like poisonous flowers.

Twelve-gauge, double-aught buck rounds hold thirteen pellets, each of them over a third of an inch in diameter. Even cut behind the choke and thus with an increased spread pattern, a sawed off firing them could be deadly out to fifty yards. Wilt and Crate were sixty yards away and mostly concealed behind the ridge, but that didn't mean the shotgunners couldn't get lucky.

Even as he aimed, Horse was counting in his mind the seconds it would take the men with the shotguns to reload: swivel the lever to the right, crack the breech, tilt the gun backward with the left hand, dump the empties while fishing the pocket for two more rounds. Insert them in the dark.

While he was calculating, Horse was putting the center of the reticle on the thigh of the closest shooter with a forty-five. He squeezed the trigger. The impact of the thirty-caliber round knocked the man flat.

One of the men with a shotgun turned toward Horse. Horse shot him in the knee. He screamed and collapsed, his finger contracting in a spasm of pain on one of the double triggers and sending a three-foot tongue of flame and the double aught pellets into the ground directly in front of him.

Wilt and Crate stopped shooting. Empty again. Reloading their last clips.

Horse could see the elongated orange shapes of all but the two remaining shooters flattened on the ground.

He called out.

"You two! Get on the ground! I'm watching you through an infrared scope."

A shooter with a forty-five turned toward Horse. Horse fired a round into the ground beside him.

"The next one blows out your lights."

"All right, all right," came from the orange blob that dropped to its knees and elongated as it stretched out on the ground.

Horse yelled again in the sudden silence.

"Listen to my associate. He's going to tell you exactly what to do, and you're going to do exactly what he says. If you don't, you will die here tonight."

Horse watched the men on the ground through the scope. The shapes were very still, except for the two he had shot, and he wasn't worried about them. They were now living in the world of pain, all

343

the fight knocked out of them and replaced by a burning desire to survive.

"I think these guys are done, Darnold," said Horse in a voice as calm as someone asking for the salt at the table. "Put up another spotlight."

Darnold placed a third spotlight on top of the boulder and turned it on, angling it toward the men on the ground in front of the rise.

When he had it just right, he called out.

"The two men on the ridge with the machine guns are on their way down. They can see you clearly. If anybody moves, they'll shoot. They might hit the shooter, or they might hit all of you. Not easy to control a Thompson."

"Don't nobody move!" yelled one of the men on the ground.

Horse turned away and set out cautiously for the collapsed building, scanning with the infrared as he moved. Toward the center of the building, a heat source was bunched on the ground. He kept the reticle focused on it.

"Don't stand up. Stretch out flat."

There was no response. He pulled his eye away from the scope. In the light spill from the spotlight, he could see Sergeant Scanlon's olive-drab plastic flashlight. Transferring the M-3 to his left hand, he unholstered his .357 and cocked it. He lowered the M-3 to the ground, picked up the flashlight and hit the switch. The motionless heap was Eddie Mazzetti,

Horse swept the flashlight's beam in a circle.

The rifle was gone.

The money was gone.

Horse walked slowly toward Mazzetti. The man was unconscious. There was blood on the back of his head, and the left side of his face was badly damaged. The kind of damage done by a rifle butt. His legs were twisted at odd angles. After watching him carefully for a moment to make sure he wasn't faking, Horse knelt beside him. Returning his .357 to its holster, he reached back and pulled a set of cuffs from his belt.

He cuffed Mazzetti and then checked his pulse.

It was there. Strong and steady.

Probably has a concussion, thought Horse, and maybe broken legs.

He shoved the flashlight in his pocket and retrieved the M-3. Scanning the area ahead of him with the scope, he moved slowly along the east side of the building. Nothing lit up until he reached the back of the building and poked the gun around the corner and saw a long, red line connected to a large, high-heat source.

He pulled back and thought about what he had seen.

Exhaust system, he thought. Exhaust system and engine. The jeep is on its right side. I'm seeing the bottom.

He pushed the gun around the corner again and stood watching. Nothing moved. He pulled back and returned to the front of the building and went down the other side. Once again, nothing lit up until he reached the back of the building and poked the gun around the corner.

Orange, where the engine would be.

He scanned the area all around the jeep.

No other heat.

In case the sergeant was hiding in front of the jeep, he moved out in a half circle, continually scanning all around the jeep and listening intently for the sound of someone moving to keep the jeep between himself and any pursuer.

He circled the jeep and trailer twice at a safe distance. When he was convinced the sergeant had left the area, he put down the M-3, got out the flashlight, and turned it on. As he swept the beam from the jeep back to the rear of the building, what had happened became clear.

The building had been built into the hillside. While the front of the slab was level with the desert, the back was five feet above grade. When the jeep burst through the wall, the angle on which it left the slab had been altered. Perhaps there had been more resistance on one side of the back wall than the other. The jeep twisted in the air as it dropped toward the ground and ended up on its right side: fortunately for Sergeant Scanlon; unluckily for Horse. Had it landed on its left, the sergeant would have been killed or badly injured.

The trailer had turned on a different angle. More rifles on one side than the other? The result was a badly twisted hitch that made it impossible to unhook it from the jeep. Even if Scanlon had been somehow able to right the jeep, he could not have driven away.

The rifles he had intended to sell were scattered all over the ground.

Horse played the flashlight over the inside of the jeep.

No cash. No loaded rifle.

Carrying both, Sergeant Scanlon had left on foot.

Horse picked up the M-3 and went back around the building. Mazzetti was still unconscious, but his pulse was strong. He walked up the two-track toward where the Treasury agents were at work.

With the exception of the two he had shot, all Mazzetti's henchmen had been cuffed, searched, disarmed and roped together. Crate had come up with an interesting improvement to Horse's original idea: joining the men by linking their ankles. A man with his hands cuffed behind his back and an ankle secured by a rope to the man next to him was not going to make a run for it. Wilt was making a tourniquet for one of the injured men with a piece cut from the rope. The man screamed when Wilt pulled it tight.

"How bad is he?"

"He'll live. Through and through. Missed the artery. The other one wasn't so lucky. Be walking with a cane for the rest of his life. They'll both make a mess in the back of the car."

Horse turned to Darnold.

"Mazzetti's inside the building. He's all yours."

"Thought he went with Scanlon."

"Looks like he tried to run off without the sergeant and got bashed in the head and run over. He's unconscious. Probably a concussion, broken legs, but his pulse is strong. Going to be eating soft food for a while though. Scanlon smashed in the side of his mouth."

"Ouch."

"Double ouch. One on the back, one on the side. The jeep and trailer and almost all the rifles are behind the building. The jeep is on its side. The trailer's damaged. The sergeant left on foot."

"When you say 'almost all the rifles.'"

He's got the one he shot at us with. And maybe the extra magazine he told Mazzetti about."

"He was the wild card, wasn't he?"

"For sure."

"What are you going to do?"

"Horse turned and looked off into the night."

"He's out there, somewhere. I'm going after him."

"Why not let the Army do it?"

"I put this in motion. I'll bring it to an end. He has a wicked weapon. He could kill someone."

"He could kill you."

"He's good, but he's not that good. I'm going to have to borrow your carbine for a while longer."

"I'll come with you."

"You can't. Need two of you in each of the sedans. One to drive, one to watch. When I get him, I'll take him to Smoke Tree. Turn him over to the CID. The weapon he's carrying and the money will be evidence."

346

"We'll take the rest of the rifles to Las Vegas with us. Call me at the Treasury office when you get to Smoke Tree. You have the number."

Horse turned to go.

"Horse? One more thing."

"Yeah?"

Thank you. You were right about this from start to finish."

"Not quite. I underestimated Scanlon. I didn't think he'd come armed. And I sure didn't think he'd drive the jeep through the back of the building."

"It's just like you said. 'Once the first shot is fired.'"

In spite of the M-3, Horse could not see much better than the man he was pursuing. While the infrared could detect Scanlon if it were pointed at him, it would not pull up enough detail of the ground to make Horse's footing any easier than Scanlon's. A background glow from the warm ground, yes. Volcanic rocks that had absorbed more heat than the ground around them, yes. But neither declivities nor angled footing showed up in the scope.

As a result, Horse had to break his pursuit into a pattern. Scan the terrain a good distance ahead for a warm body. Finding none, and hoping Scanlon was not hiding behind something, turn the flashlight on and off quickly. Drop to the ground and recreate the after-image. Had there been any sign? A footprint? A disturbance.? If there had not, move sideways a bit and flash it again. But be erratic about the interval. And erratic about moving right or left after the first flash. Don't be predictable. Scanlon was not a man who hesitated to shoot at people.

An hour later, the inevitable happened. Horse scanned with the M-3. Detected nothing that looked like a human. Flicked the flashlight on and off. Moved to his right. Dropped to the ground and thought about the after-image. No footprints. No disturbance. Stood up, flicked the flashlight again and moved back to his left. Dropped to the ground to consider the after-image.

And heard bullets pass overhead. Close. He was already hugging the ground when he heard the sound of the gun. He realized he had forgotten to begin counting from the *crack* of the rounds passing overhead to the *thump* of the shots fired.

He lay in the sandy wash, trying to reconstruct the interval in his head.

Three hundred yards was the best rough estimate he could come up with.

He thought for a moment longer.

The sergeant had lain in wait. He had far more than a three-hundred-yard head start, given the time Horse spent searching around the jeep and then talking with Darnold. So, Scanlon had seen the flashes. Known what they meant. Set up somewhere and watched. And waited. Maybe watched two sets. Even waited for a third. Opened fire, but distance was hard to estimate in the dark. He had shot high, but not that high. It could have turned out differently if Horse hadn't been on the ground.

Horse crossed himself and offered up another silent prayer. This one that Esperanza and the twins would be all right if he didn't make it home. He crossed himself again and rose to a crouch. He stayed crouched as he moved. He knew it was silly, but he couldn't help it. Those bullets had made a nasty sound. A sound he had heard many times in the frozen hills of Korea

As he moved, he remembered something Winston Churchill had said: *Nothing in life is so exhilarating as to be shot at without result.* Horse didn't agree. As far as he was concerned, there was nothing exhilarating about it. Terrifying was more accurate.

Sergeant Scanlon had not been planning an ambush. He was simply exiting the area as fast as he could, moving steadily eastward. His goal was to reach the river, but he wasn't sure exactly how far away it was. If he could get there before sunrise, he could get into the tamarisk and mesquite thickets bordering the river. It was his only hope of evading the helicopters he was sure would be in the air at first light.

Escape and evasion, the Army called it. Escape and evasion it would have to be. Get to the river. Bury the gun. Bury his clothes, all except the boxer shorts. They would look like swim trunks to a distant observer. Stay in the bushes until nightfall the following night. Float down the river on his back all night with the money balanced on his chest. Get out before daylight. Repeat as many times as necessary. Maybe end up in Yuma; Float into Mexico.

Sergeant Scanlon's knowledge of the Colorado River was incomplete. He knew about Hoover Dam and Lake Mead. He knew about Lake Havasu and Parker Dam, but he knew nothing of Lake Mojave and Davis Dam. Nor did he know it had been years since the Colorado River had reached Mexico as more than a trickle.

An hour later, he was beginning to believe he might make this work. Then he had seen a light flicker far behind him. He realized he hadn't looked back for a long time. He dropped to the ground and waited. After a few minutes, he saw another light. It seemed to be in a different spot.

He decided to wait.

He waited a long time.

A light flickered again. Something about the pattern made him think it was only one man. If he could take him out, he'd be home free. He extended the tripods and took up a prone position. Keeping the gun pointed in the general direction of the last flash he had seen, he pushed off the safety and waited some more, trying to estimate the distance between himself and the approaching pursuer.

The light flickered, much closer now. He waited. It flickered from a slightly different position. He angled the rifle toward where he estimated the light was and squeezed off a burst.

He held his position, hoping the man would return fire so he could zero in on the muzzle flash. Nothing happened. He waited. Still nothing. He couldn't delay any longer. His pursuer had made up too much ground. He got to his feet and moved on, thinking as he went. He had no illusions he had scored a hit. But he was sure he had slowed the man down. Bullets will do that.

Since he was sure the man following him was moving much slower now, he decided to pick up his pace, even though that meant risking a hard fall or even a turned ankle. Then, he thought of something else. The more often the pursuer had to stop to search for tracks, the less ground he could cover. Especially now that he would be more sparing in his use of the flashlight.

Sergeant Scanlon started looking for just the right thing.

Fifteen minutes later, he found it. A broad wash trending southeast. Deviating from his original plan of moving directly east, he would move from side to side in the wash. Climb out on one side, travel on the rocky ground for a while, drop back down into the wash and remain in it for a short time before climbing out on the other side. Keep repeating that procedure, slowing his pursuer even further by forcing him to find the places where the man he was hunting had left and then re-entered the wash. It was a good plan.

A half hour later, Sergeant Scanlon had moved in and out of the wash three times. He decided it was time to up the pace by staying in the sandy bottom for a longer stretch. He was in the center of the wash, moving at a good clip, when suddenly there was someone beside him! Impossible! he thought, but he didn't have time for such thoughts.

Greed made him hesitate another fraction of a second before dropping the money, and that sealed his fate. When he let the bag fall and reached for the folding forward grip of the rifle with his left hand, he felt a searing pain in his right bicep. Suddenly, his right arm didn't work so well. Worked so poorly, in fact, that he could no longer keep his grip on the rifle, and it fell to the ground. He bent down, picked up the money and broke into a run.

Immediately, he felt a pain very similar to the one he'd felt in his arm. Except this one was in the back of his right leg. He managed one more step before the leg buckled. Since his right hand no longer worked, he grabbed the back of his right leg with his left hand, throwing himself off balance. He fell heavily on his side. His hand was wet when it came away from his leg. He tried to see it in the moonlight.

"Blood," came a voice.

"What?"

"Cut you."

"Who are you? Where'd you come from?"

"Don't hold still, cut you again.

Horse knew he was losing ground. It had been clear for some time that Scanlon was moving in and out of this southeast-trending wash, forcing Horse to flick the flashlight on and off more often as he searched for the places the sergeant left and then re-entered the wash. He couldn't rely on the man to return to the wash every time he left it. If he did, and the sergeant struck off in a new direction, Horse would lose even more time backtracking to find the trail.

Adding to this new problem was his continuing worry about being shot. He was now holding the flashlight closer to the ground and shielding the beam with his hand when he looked for sign. While this technique had resulted in no additional rounds coming his way, it limited the range of the light and made searching for tracks as slower process.

Horse was debating with himself as he forged onward. Should he give up and return to the truck and drive to Lake Mojave? Patrol the interface between the desert and the thickets? Perhaps. But while he was sure he could retrieve the truck and get to the lake first, he had no way of knowing exactly where along the shoreline Scanlon would emerge from the desert and plunge into the brush.

Plus, there was a part of him that hated to give up. He wanted to haul this guy out of the desert. Tonight. He had just resolved to keep moving but speed up by using the flashlight more often when he realized Joe Medrano was standing in front of him.

"Horse."

"Joe! How did you get here?"

"Trailways bus to Searchlight. See that Mazzetti guy."

He held up a pair of army boots.

"Got your guy."

"Where is he?"

"Behind me. Hands, ankles tied with laces. Fancy gun."

"Infrared sniper rifle."

"Heard you shoot it."

"You were there?"

"Close by."

"How'd you find the place?"

"In town first. Followed you. Found cars, buildings."

"Did the sergeant have the money?"

Joe held up a gym bag.

"How'd you track him down in the dark?"

"Didn't. Went with him."

"All this way?"

"Yep. He got careless. Noisy. Cut him."

"How bad?"

"Pretty good. Will live."

"Let's go fetch him."

It took two hours to get Sergeant Scanlon back to the pickup. He lost a lot of blood and complained bitterly all the way. Complained even more when they manhandled him into the bed and took his boots again.

"Don't want you jumping out."

They drove into Searchlight. Horse stopped at a pay phone.

Esperanza had the phone of the hook before the end of the first ring.

"You were right next to the phone."

"You knew I would be."

He could hear the relief in her voice.

"Sorry to worry you, *querida*. It's all over. Got the bad guys. Darnold is in Vegas by now with Mazzetti and the others. I'm in Searchlight with the sergeant. I'll take him to CID at the airport when I get back to town.

"And the agents?"

"All fine."

"Y *mi marido*?"

"Had to shoot two men. Hurt them more than it hurt me. I'll be home soon. I'm going to run Joe out his way after we turn over the sergeant."

"Joe was there?"

"Apparently, Joe is everywhere. He got the sergeant."

"Is he okay?"

"He's fine. I'll tell you all about it."

"Carlos?"

"Yes."

"*Te quiero.*"

"*Y yo le.*"

Horse hung up and dialed the Treasury office in Las Vegas.

"Agent Darnold."

"High-dollar operation like you Feds have, thought there'd be a night receptionist."

"Nobody here but us out-of-towners."

"Sad. Beauford will have to make his own coffee."

"Did you get Scanlon?"

"Our mystery man did."

"The same guy that infiltrated the bivouac?"

"The very one. Another thing to leave out of your report. Where are the bad actors?"

With us. The marshals are on their way to pick them up, minus Mazzetti and the ones you shot. They're at the hospital. Mazzetti's still unconscious, but the docs think he'll live. Wilt's standing guard outside the room.

Nice shooting out there tonight, by the way."

"Thanks. Your guys too. Really hammered those cars. I'll talk to you later. I'm still in Searchlight. Heading for Smoke Tree."

CHAPTER 43

The Handover

On the way back to town, Horse told Joe about Eddie Mazzetti's concussion, missing teeth and broken legs. Joe came very close to smiling. When they reached Smoke Tree, Horse drove directly to the airport and pulled up in front of the sentry gate.

"Let me turn this guy over to CID, and I'll run you home."

Joe climbed out of the truck and stood beside the open door.

"No thanks. Use a walk. Head to Doc Hayden's. Finish that job."

"Aren't you tired?"

Joe shrugged.

"Little bit."

"Thanks, Joe. Thanks for everything."

"Thank you, Horse. For the missy."

"For the missy, Joe."

Horse got out of the truck and checked his prisoner. The sergeant's eyes were closed. There was a lot of blood, but his pulse was good. Horse walked over to the MP.

"Sir, you can't park there."

"Captain Carlos Caballo, San Bernardino County Sheriff's Department. Call CID for me."

"You don't look like a captain."

"Tactical gear, corporal. Call CID. Officers Nielsen and Fitzgilbert. Tell them Horse is here."

The MP looked toward the pickup.

"You have a Horse?"

"Corporal, just call them."

"Wait one, sir."

Ten minutes later, the sleepy warrant officer and his sergeant drove up to the other side of the gate in an Army sedan. They climbed out and ducked under the barrier.

"Horse?"

"Got something for you. You might want to get the Commanding General out here for this."

"At five o'clock in the morning? I don't think so."

"Your choice. Got a notebook?"

"I do."

"Get it out. You're going to have to write this down. It's complicated."

The sun was just above the Black Mountains when Horse finished his report. Warrant Officer Nielsen looked up from his notes.

"Let me get this straight, Horse. You've detained an active duty sergeant in the United States Army on suspicion of stealing rifles and trying to sell them to the Mafia?"

"Great summary."

"But you didn't arrest him?"

"That's your job. I'm just a bounty hunter."

Nielsen gave him a quizzical look.

"Little western lore, Warrant Officer Nielsen."

"Have you got any evidence of this alleged crime?"

"Follow me, gentlemen."

Horse led them to the pickup and opened the door.

"That's one of the rifles. And that gym bag there has the money I watched Mazzetti hand to the sergeant. And by the way, I want a receipt for my files."

Warrant Officer Nielsen reached into the cab and pulled out the rifle.

"Careful. That's loaded. Safety's on."

Nielsen extracted the clip and examined it.

"Not a full load."

"He fired on the Treasury agents. Fired on me in the desert."

"How much money is in this bag?"

"Don't know. Haven't counted it."

"Why didn't the Treasury agents do that?"

"Because, like I told you, the sergeant ran off into the desert with it. Agents didn't come with me when I went after him."

Nielsen handed the rifle to Fitzgerald and picked up the gym bag.

"I'm going to count this before I give you a receipt."

Horse smiled.

"I was hoping you'd say that."

Warrant Officer Nielsen unpacked the money and counted it. When he was finished, he wrote Horse a receipt for seventy-five thousand dollars and the rifle."

"Is there anyone who can corroborate any of this?"

"Four United States Treasury agents?"

"Where are they?"

"There in Las Vegas. They're holding the Mafia guys for the U.S. Marshals. They'll be charged in federal court."

"Which one?"

"No idea. Beyond my pay grade."

"Captain, I'm pretty sure this whole thing is beyond your pay grade. How many rifles are we talking about?"

"I don't know. I took off after the sergeant before the Treasury agents had counted them."

"How do we get in touch with these Treasury people?"

"Give me your notebook."

Horse scribbled the Las Vegas number on the inside cover and handed it back to Nielsen.

"Ask for agent Darnold. Tell him you've got sergeant involved in the sale of the stolen automatic weapons in custody. He'll give you a final count on the rifles."

Nielsen looked doubtful.

"And where are you holding this Sergeant Scanlon."

"Back here," came a weak voice.

The three men walked to the back of the truck.

Most of the blood on the Sergeant's uniform had dried, but he still made a gruesome sight lying trussed on his side with his own bootlaces in the light of the rising sun.

"Get me away from this guy and that other maniac," said Sergeant Scanlon in a near whisper before his eyes closed again.

Nielsen turned to Horse.

"Who's he talking about?"

Horse didn't want Chemehuevi Joe brought into the discussion.

"Who knows? One of the treasury guys, maybe?"

"If Treasury backs your story, you'll have to testify at the proceedings."

"Fine."

"This is the second sergeant your department has turned over to us today."

"It is?"

355

"You didn't know?"

"Officer Nielsen, I've been out on the desert for over twenty-four hours. I brought the sergeant straight here. I didn't' stop at my office."

Nielsen produced the notebook again and thumbed through the pages.

"One of your deputies, a Corporal Chesney, hauled an artillery sergeant out here after midnight. A Staff Sergeant Miller. Seems Miller assaulted a civilian at a place called The Derail. Busted him up pretty bad. Man's in the hospital."

"There you go, then. Sale on sergeants today. Will the Army prosecute him?"

"Certainly."

"I'll want him when you get done."

"Why?"

"He assaulted someone in my jurisdiction. I'm responsible for these people. He'll be prosecuted by the San Bernardino County District Attorney."

"I'm not sure about that."

Horse was silent for a moment. He was very tired, but he could feel the red dragon of anger trying to get out of its cage. He took a deep breath.

"Officer Nielsen, you just told me the Army will need my testimony to try Sergeant Scanlon"

"That's right."

"Unless I get a written assurance from the United States Army that San Bernardino County gets a crack at this artillery sergeant after his court martial, you won't get it."

Warrant Officer rolled his eyes.

"Are you blackmailing the Army, Captain?"

"Not at all. Just doing my part to foster mutual cooperation between the Army and local law enforcement."

"I'll tell you this, Captain. There are some interesting people out here. Couple guys try to pull off the great train robbery, and now an officer of the law wants to blackmail the Army."

"We've got interesting people? You're the bunch with a sergeant who tried to sell machine guns to the mob."

Nielsen smiled.

"Got me there. Anyway, I can't wait to get out of here."

"Then we're in agreement about something, Officer Nielsen, because I can't wait for this circus to be gone."

356

The CID officers summoned more MPs. They none too gently unloaded Master Sergeant Yannity Scanlon and took him into custody.

Horse picked up the sergeant's boots and handed them to Nielson.

"Your man's boots."

Horse was very weary, but he drove to the substation. He checked the overnight log. He talked to the desk sergeant about the incident at The Derail. Talked to the night dispatcher. When he was satisfied there was nothing that could not be handled without him, he headed home.

Esperanza was out the door and running toward the truck before he stopped. They hugged for a long, long time, rocking back and forth. They went in the house and sat on the couch while Horse told her everything that had happened.

When he was finished, Esperanza hugged him again.

"You could have been killed out there. I'm so glad you're safely home."

"I'm glad to be here, *querida*."

He stood up, and they hugged again. Esperanza was trying not to cry, but she couldn't help herself. Horse felt like crying, too. Crying with happiness for all the love in his heart for his wonderful wife, the twins, and their life together. Crying with sadness for Burke Henry and Mr. Stanton.

"I'm going to go get a shower and climb in bed for a few hours."

Esperanza wiped her eyes.

"I'll try to keep the twins quiet when they get up.

Horse laughed.

"Don't bother. I could sleep through a nuclear explosion."

CHAPTER 44

Hoping for Better Things

On Tuesday evening, Horse and Esperanza sat on the couch, each reading a copy of the Los Angeles Sentinel that had arrived, as all L.A. papers did, on an eastbound passenger train. Smoke Tree got the morning papers about eight hours after everyone on the coast, and Horse had always felt that was fitting somehow.

Because it broke after the deadline, news of the Treasury Department operation in Searchlight had not made the Monday paper. But it was featured in the Tuesday edition. It was not the headline story, but it rated a front-page sidebar. It must have delighted Agent David D'Arnauld's bosses at Treasury. The story lavished praise on the agency for keeping dangerous weapons out of the hands of the mob. And while it named Eddie Mazzetti and his associates, it did not name the Treasury agents who had carried out the operation, referring to them only as, "two agents from San Francisco and two agents from the Denver Field Office." It also mentioned "an unnamed captain from the San Bernardino County Sheriff's Department" as having been part of the investigation leading to the arrests."

Horse looked up from his copy of the paper.

"And so, the legend of unnamed Agent David D'Arnauld grows ever larger."

Esperanza smiled.

"As does the legend of the unnamed Captain Carlos Caballo."

"Don't want to be a legend, *mi amor*. Just want to be your husband and the twin's father."

"The twins who are fast asleep and will not hear of how dangerous their father's Sunday and early Monday was. Has the Sheriff called you?"

"No, but Pete Hardesty has. Told me Treasury wants to send a letter of commendation for my file."

"What did you tell him?"

"Told him I don't need it. Told him getting Mazzetti was enough."

"What did he say?"

"Said I was getting it anyway."

"Well, it can't be a bad thing, in case you ever want to move higher in the department."

"I'd have to leave Smoke Tree to move higher, and I never want to do that. Never want to leave the life we've made for ourselves here. There's no place I'd rather be."

"Good. I feel the same."

Horse returned to his newspaper. Reading on, he found a disturbing story buried at the bottom of page nine. Three members of the Congress on Racial Equality working with the Freedom Summer campaign to register African Americans to vote in Mississippi were missing. James Chaney, Andrew Goodman and Michael Schwerner had reportedly been kidnapped by the Ku Klux Klan in Neshoba County, Mississippi. The F.B.I. had been called in and opened an investigation. The Bureau had named the case *Mississippi Burning.*

Horse folded the paper and sat next to his beloved. Thinking. Thinking about his conversation with David D'Arnauld almost a week ago. A conversation about his hopes for a better country by the time the twins grew up.

He shook his head.

This civil rights thing, he thought, has a long way to go.

Acknowledgement

Many thanks to my son, Sam George, for being the extra pair of eyes on the manuscript of this novel. His cogent comments, notations and suggestions are much appreciated. Absent his efforts, this novel would be much diminished.

If you enjoyed this book, the author would be most appreciative if you would take the time to write a review. Independent authors lack the resources of the big publishing houses. We rely on readers to promote our books by writing and posting reviews and by recommending our books to friends. Please locate the book on Amazon. Near the bottom of the page, just above the "More about the Author" section, there is a grey button that reads, "Write a customer review." Please click on that button and leave your thoughts about the book.

Also, leaving the same review on *Goodreads* would be greatly appreciated.

Gary J. George
Cherry Valley, California

Made in the USA
San Bernardino, CA
25 April 2020